T0059046

On Far Malayan Shores

Tara Haigh

On Far Malayan Shores

Translated by Jozef van der Voort

This is a work of fiction. Names, characters, organizations, places, events, and incidents are either products of the author's imagination or are used fictitiously. Any resemblance to actual persons, living or dead, or actual events is purely coincidental.

Text copyright © 2017 by Tara Haigh
Translation copyright © 2019 by Jozef van der Voort
All rights reserved.

No part of this book may be reproduced, or stored in a retrieval system, or transmitted in any form or by any means, electronic, mechanical, photocopying, recording, or otherwise, without express written permission of the publisher.

Previously published as *Das weiße Blut der Erde* by Tinte & Feder, Amazon Media E.U. S.à.r.l. in Luxembourg in 2017. Translated from German by Jozef van der Voort. First published in English by Lake Union Publishing in collaboration with Amazon Crossing in 2019.

Published by Lake Union Publishing, in collaboration with Amazon Crossing, Seattle

www.apub.com

Amazon, the Amazon logo, Lake Union Publishing and Amazon Crossing are trademarks of Amazon.com, Inc., or its affiliates.

ISBN-13: 9781542019736
ISBN-10: 1542019737

Cover design by Charlotte Abrams-Simpson

Printed in the United States of America

First edition

On Far Malayan Shores

Strait of Malacca, 21 May 1877

In a few hours, we will reach the Indian Ocean. A long journey lies ahead of us. If it weren't for my beloved diary, I don't know how I would pass the time after the end of my shift. I can't understand why I am the only sailor on board who sets his recollections down in writing instead of washing them away with rum. After all, one learns a great deal when travelling – especially in the port cities, even when stopping only briefly to take on fresh victuals. Naturally, my habits make me the object of laughter and ridicule – a gruff, manly sing-song disgorged from throats well-oiled with cheap rotgut. The voices emanating from the crew quarters below deck ring as loudly as in a church, and even drown out the whip-cracks of the waves against the ship's wooden hull. Since we left Singapore, the sea has been so rough that it makes one dizzy to write by the flickering light of a paraffin lamp, and I am finding it hard to hold my pen steady. I can only hope I will still be able to decipher my shaky hand in years to come.

'Maybe he's writing love letters,' growls Mate Johansson. 'A girl in every port,' roars another. Laughter breaks out once more. Small wonder, since until this morning they believed me to be steadfast in my constancy. I can hardly hold it against them, in light of yesterday's events. Even Captain von Stetten let slip a similar remark – although

only as a joke, as he understands the true situation and knows that I would never betray my wife.

If only I hadn't joined the others on shore yesterday and dozed off in that harbourfront alehouse! Yet one needs to feel solid ground beneath one's feet from time to time; to find some space and surround oneself with fresh faces. English beer is far too strong. A curse on Singapore!

Those heartrending cries still echo in my ears. The ship's enormous hull must have muffled them on the landward side, and anyway, the crew were still loading her up until deep into the night. Did that mean I was the only one who heard that voice? Fate apparently singled me out to follow those cries, leading me to that shadowy creature. They say that everything in life happens for a reason.

He must have believed that he could simply steal away from the scene – yet the moon was too bright, and at that hour there wouldn't normally be any carriages left at the harbour, so he should have expected to attract some curious glances. Perhaps he didn't care. A man travelling in such an elegant coach must wield a great deal of influence, and I expect he has nothing and nobody to fear around these parts – aside from the misfortune that ultimately befell him. I still shudder to recall his piercing eyes. They looked the part on such a heartless human being. He was the devil incarnate. And I struck a pact with him, just so I could bring an end to that wretched wailing . . .

CHAPTER 1

Hamburg, 1898

Ordinarily, Ella was happy to undertake the forty-minute walk to work from her home on leafy Harvestehuder Weg – especially when she had the early morning shift. The fresh air did her good, and the stiff breeze that so often blew through Hamburg could put a spring in even the weariest step. But when the weather was very bad, walking was out of the question – and today, the rain was lashing down in buckets. Mother had telephoned for a cab immediately after breakfast. That came with rather awkward consequences, since a twenty-one-year-old daughter of a humble sailor and a schoolteacher who could afford to be driven to work in a carriage represented an object of curiosity to onlookers, to put it mildly. This morning, to avoid further inflaming the smouldering resentment of the doctors – and especially the attendants – Ella once again instructed the driver not to drop her off in front of the main entrance to the Neues Allgemeines Krankenhaus – the New General Hospital. As a rule, she dismounted on the other side of the road or down one of the side streets as Father had advised her to do after one of Ella's colleagues had recently been unable to resist asking her how she could afford a carriage ride from the two hundred marks that a young female hospital attendant earned each month.

'I can't really afford it, but I would have arrived late otherwise.' This was not an excuse that Ella could use very often, of course. Other excuses had followed, until the constant need to come up with a new story on the way to work every time it rained had become a source of distress to her. Rumours were already circulating among the doctors about her place of residence, as well as the fact that her family had a telephone. It was unheard of for people of humble origins to live in an exclusive quarter on the banks of the Alster, surrounded by wealthy businesspeople and industrialists. That was a privilege not even the hospital directors could afford. Once again, it was her father who had advised her to say that her family was living with relatives in an apartment building. Nobody had made any further enquiries since then, thank heavens.

The fifteen-minute cab ride along the Alster and across the city wasn't long enough to come to a decision. Should she continue to exercise discretion and be soaked to the skin? Or should she risk being dropped off directly in front of the entrance to the hospital?

The portico of the enormous red-brick building was already in view. Through the rain-spattered window, Ella could just about make out one of the other attendants entering the building. She was a little early today – most of her colleagues usually arrived later. She decided to take a chance and revise her previous instructions to the coachman.

'Please stop here, by the entrance,' she called to him.

He slowed down.

Ella instantly regretted her decision, for at that precise moment, a woman approached holding an umbrella that was whipping back and forth in the wind. At this time in the morning, she was sure to be a colleague. Unfortunately, everybody knew everybody else at the hospital, even though there were 160 nurses working here across several separate pavilions. Ella hoped the attendant would be too busy trying to hold her umbrella up against the wind to even notice the carriage, or to examine the person getting out of it.

She had already counted out her money before she dismounted, and after handing it to the coachman, she lowered her umbrella to conceal her face and danced around the puddles that lay between her and the steps leading up to the entrance. With any luck, her colleague would already be inside – but it was not to be. She had just mounted the top step and was within reach of the door handle, when two spindly legs clad in woollen stockings and sturdy brown men's shoes came into view beneath her umbrella. Ella exhaled. She knew only one attendant who dressed so practically yet unflatteringly.

'Good morning, Ella.' The greeting came from the familiar voice of her colleague Mathilde – the longest-serving attendant, who had worked here since the pavilion opened nine years ago. She knew about Ella's family situation, and was as quiet as a grave. Mathilde was in her mid-thirties, had a very agreeable temperament, and always wore a smile on her lips. One might even say she was a friend – although right now, she more closely resembled a drowned rat. The poor thing was soaked to the skin and was looking wistfully at the departing carriage.

'I wish I had your luck,' she added, but with a benevolent smile that Ella answered with a sigh and an innocent shrug.

'Let's go inside,' Mathilde urged, understandably enough, although they had by now found shelter from the rain under the portico.

Mathilde would no doubt want to chat before their shift started. She knew everybody, and was always well informed about both doctors and patients alike. Right now, however, they needed to hurry, for the night-shift attendants would want to clock off on time.

5

'Are you going to the Baltic coast again this summer?' asked Mathilde on the way down to the changing rooms in the basement, with their countless lockers.

'I've already put my name down on the list,' answered Ella, reflecting that scarcely anyone would choose to forgo a vacation funded by the hospital managers, given their meagre wages. 'What about you?' Ella asked.

'The hospital directors have encouraged those of us who haven't yet signed up to miss out on the trip this year, in return for extra pay. We're understaffed. They intend to compensate us if we stay here and work, and I could do with a little extra money right now.'

'Then they should hire more staff,' said Ella indignantly.

'People like you don't grow on trees. English nurses don't speak a word of German, and the Swiss ones prefer to stay at home. They can earn a good deal more there.' Mathilde's explanations cut straight to the heart of the matter.

'I've heard that the hospital will start training its own nurses from next year. We'll have more workers then,' remarked Ella.

'Not before time. Germany leads the world in so many different ways – I mean, we're lucky that we've even been able to get health insurance for the last few years, for example – but when it comes to nursing . . . At any rate, if it weren't for the cholera outbreak six years ago then nothing would have changed. We had to learn some difficult lessons before we managed to beat the disease. It's hard to imagine now. At the end of next year, we'll be entering a new century,' said Mathilde fervently as she took her uniform out of her locker and draped it over a chair. Then she fell silent and looked over at Ella somewhat wistfully.

'How often I've envied you your time in London,' said Mathilde.

Ella nodded sympathetically, although her training over there had by no means been easy. But that was a sacrifice one made willingly, since St Thomas's Hospital was considered one of the best training establishments in the world, and Ella was also able to perfect her schoolgirl English while she was there.

'By the way, I've finished that book you lent me,' added Mathilde, once she had removed her outdoor shoes.

Ella wondered which book Mathilde was talking about, since she had lent her quite a few. She looked quizzically at her colleague.

'You know – Florence Nightingale, *Notes on Nursing*. Though it wasn't an easy read, what with my English. To think what that woman set in motion, all by herself. It's extremely impressive,' gushed Mathilde.

'If it weren't for Nightingale, there still wouldn't be any trained nurses to this day,' Ella agreed.

'I'm quite certain that your Miss Nightingale knows more than any of the doctors here,' Mathilde speculated.

'You may be right there.' Ella grinned.

'I still think you would have made an excellent doctor,' remarked Mathilde – not for the first time.

'But then I would have had to study in Switzerland. I preferred to go to St Thomas's.' As if to emphasise her point, Ella pulled on her nurse's cap. She wore her hair coiled into a heavy bun that tugged painfully at her scalp – one of the few things she couldn't stand about her profession. Women doctors didn't have to wear caps. But at least the attendants' uniforms were comfortable, and they were free to tie their aprons as loose or tight as they liked.

'They've already started calling you the herb witch, at any rate,' said Mathilde mischievously as she fastened her own cap on with hairpins.

'If only Gutenberg knew that I took it as a compliment – though if anything, he should really have called me an apothecary. It just goes to show how little he knows about the healing arts.'

'But how would he know about them? He was only trained to carve people up and stitch them back together again.' Mathilde shrugged.

'There are plenty of books he could read,' answered Ella as she examined herself in the small mirror inside the locker, adjusted her uniform, and tucked an unruly lock of brown hair underneath her cap.

'Believe you me, in his view, Hahnemann is a heretic who should have been put on a bonfire,' said Mathilde, who – like Ella – had made a careful study of Hahnemann's teachings on homoeopathy. This shared knowledge was one of the cornerstones of their friendship.

'We'll end up there ourselves one of these days,' answered Ella with a smile – although her apprehension about getting into trouble was not entirely unjustified. Still, it was so much more important to be able to look into the eyes of a grateful patient who had been restored to perfect health with the help of a little 'witchcraft', as Gutenberg would call it. That alone made all the risks worthwhile.

In fact, Ella had to admit that she rather enjoyed being a medical lone wolf. For one thing, she was convinced that she was doing the patients good; yet there was also a certain frisson involved. After all, what she was doing was against the rules. Even in England, it was deemed inappropriate for nurses to treat patients under their own initiative – and for attendants, it was completely out of the question. But Mathilde paid no heed to the rules either, and when they were both on duty there was little reason to fear discovery, as one of them would watch to make sure nobody caught them in the act while the other added their homoeopathic medicines to the patients' drinks. That was impossible in the patients' areas, for obvious reasons. The only remaining option was the attendants' room. Today it was Mathilde's turn to keep look-out. Of course, it would look strange for an attendant to stand rooted to the spot in front of the nurses' station and continuously scan her surroundings, but thankfully, there was a noticeboard hanging there that displayed the shift rosters. Examining these was a daily task on the ward. If anybody came by, all she had to do was clear her throat loudly, make an innocent remark such as, 'I see you're on holiday next week,' or point out that the roster had been changed due to illness.

There was no need for any of those measures today. It took Ella no more than a minute to fill the glass jugs with the homoeopathic agent calendula, which she diluted in alcohol and water so that nobody would notice it. That was standard procedure on the surgical ward – or rather, *their* standard procedure – as calendula helped wounds to heal. The success of the treatment was ironically a source of significant pride to senior attendant Gertrude. It was she who earned all the praise, since of course the doctors had noticed on their daily rounds that wounds healed unusually quickly on this ward. 'Thanks to good care,' was the official line. All in all, everybody benefitted from the new approach, and today once again, Ella and Mathilde successfully managed to supply the patients recovering from surgery in the first wards with medication along with their daily water ration – in other words, they encouraged them to drink before they tended their wounds and changed their bandages. A completely normal working day – or so it seemed, right up until Gertrude stormed determinedly into the patients' area. To judge by her expression, she wasn't best pleased.

'Good morning, Miss Kaltenbach. Doctor Gutenberg would like to speak with you on an urgent matter.'

'What about?' asked Ella.

'I'm afraid I can't tell you that. But the doctor does seem a little irritable, if I may say so.' Gertrude seemed to relish every word. She couldn't stand the fact that she had less knowledge and training than Ella, and that unlike her, she couldn't officially call herself a nurse. They had been rivals from the very beginning.

This must be about the trip to the Baltic coast. Perhaps he wanted to persuade her to stay behind, like Mathilde. Ella decided to put that idea firmly out of the good doctor's mind.

◆ ◆ ◆

Although he wasn't the director of the hospital, Ella knew that Gutenberg was just as influential – but also just as inflexible, and not only because of the white coat he wore buttoned all the way up to his chin. In his mid-fifties with a beard he kept neatly trimmed at all times and an upright posture, Gutenberg radiated a natural authority. As the head of surgery, he was responsible for nearly half of the hospital's thirteen hundred beds. Surgery was one of the two main departments alongside internal medicine, with its epidemic ward. Gutenberg also oversaw a small special department for patients with eye disorders. One word from him, and the thirty or so doctors in the hospital would snap to attention – to say nothing of the humble service staff and attendants. All the same, for Ella to miss her well-earned holiday was out of the question – so she knocked resolutely on his door and immediately stepped into his office, without waiting to be asked.

'Ah, Miss Kaltenbach . . .' Gutenberg studied her pensively for a moment, and she felt uncertain. Perhaps she should have waited for him to call her in after all?

'Please, sit down.' He beckoned her to a chair.

'You wanted to speak with me?' Ella feigned ignorance.

Gutenberg nodded, but said nothing as he continued to scrutinise her.

Ella merely shot him an enquiring look in return.

'I'm sure you remember Otto Krüger, don't you?' he asked, evidently trying to appear nonchalant.

Ella instantly felt hot. Of course she remembered him – she had admitted him and set up a file for him. One thing was already clear: this wasn't about the trip to the Baltic. Ella knew exactly why her stomach was starting to flutter.

'He was a patient here,' she said.

'Correct . . . so he was . . . In fact, Doctor Röttgers was due to operate on him today,' explained Gutenberg.

Ella could guess what had happened, and immediately felt guilty. As cocky as she had been on entering Gutenberg's office, she now felt very small. Not because of the accusations for which Gutenberg was laying the ground with his skilful managerial rhetoric, but because she had obviously been caught in the act. The extent of his knowledge was still unclear, but Ella could gauge it from his self-satisfied smirk.

'Krüger has cancelled his operation. Does that surprise you?'

Ella gave an innocent shrug. She couldn't exactly admit to her boss that she had treated Krüger homoeopathically – at least, not until it was completely clear how much Gutenberg knew.

'Krüger confronted Röttgers, called him a bungler, and suggested that he give up his trade, as he put it.'

'What happened?'

'Krüger's ganglion has miraculously vanished,' explained Gutenberg.

Ella suddenly grew even hotter. Exposed. Caught out. Any minute now, Gutenberg was sure to turn his attention to just how the rock-hard, pea-sized lump between Krüger's ring and middle fingers had been resorbed. Strictly speaking, it had only been an experiment, since Hahnemann himself had never administered more than one homoeopathic agent at a time. But some of his students had already deviated from this rule, as Ella had discovered in England, and so it had been worth a try to give Krüger both ruta and silicea at the same time. Hahnemann's notes and subsequent research had both shown that these two agents could positively influence swellings of all kinds, especially inflammations.

'Well . . . What do you have to say?' Clearly, Gutenberg had already noticed the cogs whirring in her brain.

'But that's wonderful news.' Ella decided to keep playing the innocent. It wasn't easy, though, and her voice had already lost some of its spark.

'Of course it is. But what is less wonderful, Miss Kaltenbach, is the reason behind this development.' Gutenberg's expression grew serious.

How on earth had he got wind of this? Krüger had solemnly sworn not to tell anybody. He was a violinist and had been petrified that a surgical intervention would destroy the dexterity in his finger. Röttgers himself had made him aware of the risks. 'It could even be left completely immobile,' he had warned. It was easy to see why Krüger hadn't wanted to go under the knife. That was why Ella had promised him she would look for alternatives. And when patients were already familiar with homoeopathy, that was like pushing at an open door.

'I see you have nothing more to add, Miss Kaltenbach,' Gutenberg prompted, with a stern expression.

He followed that with a triumphant smile, which confused Ella. It gave her the impression that Gutenberg already knew everything. He didn't keep her in suspense for much longer.

'I wasn't in the least surprised to hear about it, although I was aided by circumstance. You've already made a name for yourself among the internists with your potions. As for Krüger . . . Well, his wife and mine both go to the same hairdresser, and it's a very talkative environment, as you know.'

Now that it had finally come out, Ella's anxiety dissipated. Did he really intend to hold it against her that she had saved a patient from undergoing surgery? That would be absurd.

'You have violated the rules and you know very well that you have exceeded your professional boundaries, irrespective of the fact that your training in London means you are doubtless more capable than can generally be expected of an attendant.'

Ella nodded, but without a trace of submissiveness.

'Really, I ought to fire you on the spot.'

She realised that the threat was an empty one.

'Ought to?' she asked.

Gutenberg shook his head in disbelief and smiled once again.

'Röttgers told Krüger that faith moves mountains. You should count yourself lucky that he only came to me with this, and not the hospital director.'

'Do you share Röttgers' opinion?' Ella wanted to know.

Gutenberg gave a start. The question evidently took him by surprise.

'This form of treatment involves administering small doses of certain substances – some of which are toxic, although there is no suggestion of that in this particular case. Silicic acid is not toxic, and nor is rue in its herbal form,' he said.

That showed Krüger's wife must have mentioned the specific agents – but also that Gutenberg was familiar with Hahnemann's writings.

'That's right – and in any case, the substances in question are diluted to the point that they are chemically no longer detectable. Although, when administered in higher concentrations to healthy patients, those same agents cause roughly the same symptoms as the disease that they cure when diluted homoeopathically for treatment purposes,' explained Ella.

'And so you decided that a little mixing would restore Krüger's health.'

There could no longer be any doubt that Gutenberg had made a thorough study of the subject. He understood the principle of potentisation.

'Did you use alcohol or distilled water?' Gutenberg enquired.

'Alcohol, and then I added it to his drinking water,' Ella confessed.

'Isn't it marvellous how effectively the human body can heal itself, given just a little extra stimulation? Well, I suppose Hahnemann did train in Leipzig. If only he had continued his research here instead of moving to Paris.'

What on earth did Gutenberg want from her? The conversation did not seem to be moving towards her immediate dismissal, at any rate.

'You do realise that the most appropriate course of action in this case would be to punish you?' His face took on a serious expression.

'No, not in the least. Why should anyone be punished for having cured somebody?' Ella replied confidently. But then she relented. 'Of course, the rules. I know . . .'

'Next year, this hospital will finally begin to train its own nurses, in accordance with the high standards applied in England. As part of that programme, you will assume responsibility for teaching our students the basic principles of homoeopathy. By the way, what do you give your patients on your current ward?' asked Gutenberg.

Now it was she who struggled to suppress a smile. But how had he got wind of this too? Yet another blind coincidence? She resolved to find out.

'I take it one of our patients also goes to the same hairdresser as your wife?' she asked.

Gutenberg laughed. 'I've simply noticed that people seem to recover more quickly under your care. I managed to put two and two together. Next week, I would like you to provide me with a rough training schedule, along with the topics you wish to cover. I can use that to persuade my colleagues. So, what do you say?'

Ella could scarcely believe that Gutenberg of all people was on her side – a surgeon who wielded his scalpel with conviction.

'I know it hasn't all been scientifically proven yet, but I've read Hahnemann's work. I expect you to say yes.'

Ella nodded unhesitatingly. At that moment, it felt as though a long-nurtured dream was coming to fruition. No more playing hide-and-seek; instead, she could be recognised for what she knew – could use all her hard-won experience to help people. That was exactly why she had once aspired to become a doctor.

◆ ◆ ◆

There were certain days when the weather seemed to match one's mood. The sky cleared at around three o'clock, just in time for the end of Ella's shift, and the clouds made way for the sun. She relished her walk home, especially the final section along the Alster. The endless grey of the morning had vanished, and she found herself surrounded by a vibrant springtime vista that seemed even more colourful than usual – no doubt thanks to Gutenberg's earlier proposal. Ella was burning to tell her parents the good news, and Rudolf too, of course – a sophisticated man who paid tribute to her as a nurse, or a 'healthcare pioneer', as he had recently called her. He had given notice that he would be coming over for tea that afternoon – though, in fact, it was Mother who had invited him.

'You must come and pay us another visit. Perhaps for a cup of tea? My goodness, the last time must have been with your father, when you were just a little boy,' she had said to him during the anniversary celebrations at the dockyard the previous week.

'I can still remember your superb pastries,' he had answered charmingly. Mother's baking must certainly have made a lasting impression on him. She knew as well as Ella did that Rudolf was making advances towards her daughter, and she obviously felt he was a suitable candidate. What mother wouldn't dream of marrying off her only daughter to an aristocrat? That was what people called matchmaking. But she might just as well have saved herself the trouble, for Rudolf was very handsome, and blessed with superb manners and witty repartee. A man of his rank could have any girl he wanted, and he moved in the highest circles. Ella had only made his acquaintance thanks to the happy coincidence that Rudolf's recently deceased uncle – a distinguished naval captain – had been a friend of her father's. Rudolf had accepted the invitation to the dockyard in his uncle's stead in order to honour his memory. And after all, flirting with an attractive bachelor whose uncle had been a friend of the family was a perfectly harmless activity.

Despite their lower social standing, thankfully Ella's family didn't live in the sort of run-down tenement that Rudolf von Stetten would presumably never have set foot in. Their apartment block on Harvestehuder Weg was perfectly respectable. It was an imposing three-storey building facing directly onto a boulevard where one could go for a stroll on a Sunday and encounter the city's wealthiest residents. Ella's family belonged here, even though they weren't rich. She knew very well why nobody called her family's social status into question: they dressed appropriately for their surroundings and didn't draw attention to themselves. Besides which, nobody knew that Father could only afford their apartment thanks to a substantial lifelong annuity paid by his brother, who had emigrated to America and made his fortune. The official story was that her father had inherited a considerable sum. Fortunately, talking about money in these circles was generally frowned upon. People preferred to maintain their privacy, exchanging at most a few words about the day's events, or the weather. Apart from the fact that it was a pleasant part of town, the contacts they made here had greatly influenced their decision to live in the area. If it weren't for their neighbour, who was involved in the steel trade and had influential family connections in England, it would never have occurred to Ella to complete her training in London; nor would she ever have been taken on at St Thomas's.

'Good afternoon, Miss Kaltenbach. Isn't it wonderful weather?' Mrs Rottman, the wife of a wealthy banker, was coming out of the house next door. She seemed to confirm Ella's reflections on her neighbourhood.

'Indeed,' she replied with a pleasant smile after returning the woman's greeting.

The building Ella was walking towards looked particularly splendid in the light of the afternoon sun. The Roman-style columns and friezes that protruded from between the ground-floor windows and reached all the way up to the rounded arches of the balconies on the upper floors were bathed in a golden glow and thrown into stark relief by the long shadows. The elegant coach in front of the building lent the scene a touch of extra glamour, since it must belong to Rudolf. This seemed to be a perfect day.

Ella had hoped she would have time to get changed, although there was nothing wrong with the clothes she was wearing. All the same, she paused to examine her reflection in the glass pane of the door to her apartment and smooth down a few stray locks of hair. Working the early shift could leave dark circles under one's eyes, but not today.

Her mother seemingly had the ears of a bat. She appeared at the door before Ella could even dig her key out of her bag. And how she had spruced herself up! Anyone would think that the Kaiser himself was paying a visit.

'He finished his business sooner than anticipated, so he arrived a little early,' her mother whispered in an almost reverential tone.

Ella didn't even have time to remove her coat before her mother seized it and hung it up in the wardrobe. She clearly had no time to lose.

Ella could already hear Rudolf's voice from the living room – though she felt sure that Mother would have referred to it as 'the parlour' in his presence.

'My uncle told me a good deal about your travels together. Life on the high seas must certainly be a very rich and varied experience,' Ella heard their guest say.

'Certainly, but you shouldn't believe everything you hear. There's always a little sailor's yarn woven in,' her father replied, and Rudolf laughed. Before they could continue, Ella entered the room. Her smile of greeting came straight from her heart, which beat even faster than it had on their first encounter during the reception at the dockyard. Rudolf's fetching grin wrought its usual effect.

'Ella.' He made no secret of his pleasure at seeing her again. The gleam in his eyes made her feel like she was falling under his spell. If any other man were to look at her the way Rudolf did, she would be offended.

'I hope I haven't come at an inconvenient time, but I was in the area, and I had already spent half an hour wandering the neighbourhood to pass the time,' Rudolf explained.

'On the contrary, I'm very glad to see you,' Ella answered, and even though this was the expected response in a social situation, she meant every word.

'Do sit down, Ella.' Mother had already drawn up a seating plan, as expected. Naturally enough, she gestured towards the empty spot by the window – next to Rudolf.

'Another cup of tea?' she asked him.

'Yes, please.'

Ella was tickled not only by her mother's behaviour, as she poured tea for Rudolf like a parlour maid, but also her appearance. She normally paid little heed to her unruly grey hair, but in his presence, she had subdued her mane under a hairband and dolled herself up like a peacock. As a fundamentally elegant woman, it suited her. By contrast, however, Father's suit and waistcoat made him look like a dressed-up sailor, whose face and hands were marked by a rough existence on the high seas. A permanently reddened nose – the sign of excessive rum consumption – rounded off the picture. The only thing that matched his elegant outfit was the lavishly carved gold-rimmed pipe, which he puffed with evident relish.

For his part, Rudolf was wearing an obviously tailor-made grey suit that did full justice to his good looks and charismatic demeanour. His burgundy neckerchief suited his dark hair, and overall, he looked every bit the immaculately dressed gentleman.

'You look so radiant today, one might think you were trying to outdo the sun,' said Rudolf, who had clearly noticed that her pleasure at seeing him was genuine. It would be unbecoming for a young lady to admit to such a thing, but since today had furnished her with another reason to be happy, she decided to tell them about her new opportunity at the hospital straight away. She felt sure that Rudolf would be interested, and her parents were guaranteed to be.

'Well, I've had some good news. I am to instruct the new nurses in the principles of homoeopathy.'

Father nodded appreciatively, while Mother raised her eyebrows in astonishment. Rudolf was the only one who spoke – probably because her mother wanted to let him go first.

'My warmest congratulations. You are more than living up to your role as a pioneer,' he said admiringly.

'Indeed – that's our Ella. Whatever she does, she does it properly,' remarked her father.

'Anything else would be a waste of time,' retorted Ella archly.

'You take the words out of my mouth, Miss Ella. By the way, my uncle always used to say the same thing about you, my dear Heiner,' he continued, turning to Ella's parents. 'Such attitudes are likely passed down through the generations.' Although he grinned as he spoke and doubtlessly intended it as a compliment, her parents exchanged troubled glances. It was no secret that Ella was adopted, but it wasn't a matter one discussed over tea.

'It's time for your medicine, Heiner,' declared Mother abruptly, changing the subject – though it was also a convenient excuse to leave her daughter alone with Rudolf.

Father stood up, grumbling. As far as he was concerned, he didn't need any medication for his weak heart.

'Please excuse us,' he announced to the company before following Mother, who was already at the door.

'I hope your father's illness isn't serious,' said Rudolf sympathetically once her mother had closed the door.

'It's his heart. He really ought to stop smoking his pipe.'

'My father was just as stubborn. He drank too much whisky. I suppose we all have our little vices,' he ruminated.

'And what's yours?' asked Ella directly, to Rudolf's surprise.

'I love life,' he answered.

'Is that a vice?'

'Perhaps, if one doesn't get enough of it,' he mused. His smile vanished. He looked her directly in the eye and grew pensive.

'I suppose you're wondering what vices I might have,' speculated Ella.

'No, not at all. To be perfectly honest, I admire you wholeheartedly for forging new paths and doing something that you believe in.'

'Don't you do what you believe in?' she enquired.

'Sometimes, when life doesn't get in the way with all its temptations.'

'I wouldn't have any time for that,' said Ella. That was the price one paid for following a profession out of passion, and in Rudolf's presence, it felt unexpectedly high.

'By the way, I have two free tickets to the opera. The conductor is a family friend,' he said.

'What are they performing?'

'*Don Giovanni.*' Rudolf's tone conveyed both awe and excitement.

'Isn't that a rather dark opera?' asked Ella. One of her colleagues had mentioned it during their break that morning.

'Darkness is part of life too. It usually makes things more interesting.' Rudolf spoke with complete conviction, which made his invitation even more appealing. Strangely enough, the prospect of experiencing something dark at Rudolf's side felt just as thrilling as her covert operations with Mathilde at the hospital.

'All right then. When would we go?' she enquired.

'Tonight, provided you have no other plans.'

'It's rather short notice, but . . .' Ella wondered why she was being so coy – after all, she loved to be spontaneous. Evidently, so did Rudolf. That was something they had in common, and a pinch of darkness on such an otherwise glorious day could surely do no harm.

CHAPTER 2

The last time Ella had been to the opera was in London – one of the rare entertainments she had found time for on her few days off from the hospital. It had been a matinee, which didn't have as strict a dress code as an evening performance. Even so, attending an opera in the West End along with five colleagues felt very different from doing so in the company of a man whom one was not averse to. She had had just two hours to smarten herself up and put on her favourite perfume. Ella thanked the Lord that she had bought a second evening gown last year.

'What do you need so many dresses for?' Mother had protested during their shopping trip to one of Hamburg's biggest department stores, but Ella had already worn her old one to the anniversary reception at the dockyard and to be seen wearing the same gown twice in such quick succession would have been more than just embarrassing, since Rudolf would doubtlessly have inferred that she couldn't afford a second. Ella was thrilled at the prospect of debuting her new dress this evening – especially by the side of a true gentleman in dapper white tie who smelled so alluringly of aftershave.

When he arrived to pick her up, Rudolf looked stunning. His hair was combed back, throwing his striking features into relief, and a white scarf, which contrasted perfectly with the tone of his skin, was around his neck. Naturally, he had given Ella his hand to help her into the coach, showering her with compliments as he did so. Ordinarily, the words 'You look enchanting' were the sort of hackneyed cliché one might hear on the street when showing off a new dress for the first time – but from his lips, they sounded positively impassioned. In fact, Ella had more than once seen passion in his eyes during the short ride to the opera house on Dammtorstraße, since he had spent more time looking at her than at the road.

It came as no surprise that Rudolf knew more or less everything there was to know about the building, for his father had built up one of the best-known property firms in Hamburg. Rudolf had presumably taken it over after his death. Ella had meant to ask him about it, but she had found it far more interesting to listen to his stories instead. She had only ever known the opera house with its current classical façade – its magnificent columns and ostentatious portico – since these features had been added to the otherwise plain building shortly before her birth.

The prestigious venue could hold around two and a half thousand spectators, and its superb acoustics were apparent from the opening notes of the performance. The entire evening had radiated glamour, and it had been bliss to sit in one of the boxes with Rudolf, drawing envious glances from jealous women whose companions more closely resembled barrels that had been squeezed into tailcoats.

Rudolf had offered to translate key passages of the Italian libretto for her, but Ella had declined. She much preferred to concentrate on Mozart's music and the performances onstage – though she wasn't always able to, for she could practically feel Rudolf's gaze on her skin. Every now and then, their eyes would meet and briefly linger on each other. Sometimes she would smile bashfully when he caught her looking, and sometimes he would do the same. Of course, she had encountered plenty of men before whom she found attractive – that was inevitable in a profession where one had to deal with people. Yet Rudolf appeared to be a very special specimen of manhood indeed. How was it possible for her to feel the proximity of another person who was sitting half an arm's length away from her as clearly as if he was touching her? The knowledge that he was by her side made her tingle with pleasure. Little by little, the rush of colours and the voices of the tenors and sopranos whirled her senses into a beguiling blur that made it impossible to pay attention to the events on the stage. And in addition to the assault on her senses, the heat in the box also played its part in sending her blood into a tumult, so that Ella caught herself wondering how it might feel if he were to touch her hand. Barely ten minutes later, after they had exchanged another brief glance, she began to imagine what it would be like if he kissed her.

Ella was grateful when the curtain fell and the interval bell rang. It gave her a few moments to compose herself. When Rudolf extended his hand to help her to her feet, he held her fingers for a moment, and looked at her again with the same shy smile in his eyes. The situation urgently called for a little cooling off.

'I hope I haven't overwhelmed you with all this heavy fare,' he said when they reached the foyer and joined the crowds pouring out of the boxes.

'Not in the least,' replied Ella, although not entirely truthfully. Normally she would have dug out her father's guide to the opera from their library at home and prepared for the show a few days in advance, as this was always helpful when one didn't speak Italian.

Her answer was evidently unconvincing, for Rudolf gave a sceptical look. 'We could buy a programme,' he suggested promptly.

A man of around Rudolf's age – no less attractive, and of gentlemanly appearance – had apparently overheard their brief conversation and decided to intervene.

'Don Giovanni is a nobleman; a lover and a seducer; a murderer and a *bon vivant*. He places his boundless desires above all else – he loves passion, the temptations of life,' he held forth. 'The opera could almost have been written for you,' he added, looking at Rudolf. The two men laughed and greeted each other with friendly claps on the back.

'Aren't you going to introduce me to this delightful young lady?' the walking theatre programme in white tie urged his counterpart.

'This is Hubert Petersen. We've known each other since we were at school,' pronounced Rudolf.

'Ella Kaltenbach.' Ella took the initiative and extended her hand, which Hubert duly mimed kissing. That was apparently the custom in these circles, and Ella relished it, as it suited these elegant surroundings.

'You are a lucky man,' said Hubert to Rudolf. Ella could well imagine what he meant by that – as could Rudolf, since those shy dimples had reappeared on his face.

'As for me – I'm here on my own, poor wretch that I am. But what is it they say? Lucky at cards, unlucky in love,' continued Hubert with a grin, pretending to languish under his ills.

'Do you play cards?' asked Ella casually.

'It's one of my passions. What with all my many sins, I expect I'll go the same way as Don Giovanni. The ground will open up and swallow me. *Questo è il fin di chi fa mal, e de' perfidi la morte alla vita è sempre ugual.* Such is the end of the evildoer: the death of a sinner always reflects his life,' quoted Hubert with an appropriate sense of theatricality.

'Most impressive. You seem to know the opera by heart,' said Ella.

'Only the final scene. It used to be left out of most performances in the past,' said Hubert.

'Probably because it's so horrifying,' mused Ella.

'Then again, perhaps people nowadays have simply fallen for the illusion that good always triumphs over evil,' Rudolf conjectured.

'Do you really believe that evil wins out in real life?' asked Ella in surprise.

'It sometimes seems that way to me, but I am happy to be contradicted by the final scene of the opera. In the end, all of us simply want to do the right thing – but that is certainly the harder path to follow,' answered Rudolf with a grin.

Hubert exchanged a glance with his friend and Rudolf merely shrugged.

Ella concluded that men seemed to have a very different view of the world to women. Father also liked to talk about the ills of life, and often painted a gloomy picture. How nice it was that the finale would be performed on this occasion after all.

◆ ◆ ◆

It had been a glorious evening! A breathtakingly opulent operatic performance – despite the ending, which really had been frightening. Poor Don Giovanni, swallowed up forever by the underworld. Ella was still tickled by the way Rudolf had completely lost himself in the performance during the finale, and had watched with wide eyes that had been trained solely on the events on stage, for once. But as soon as the curtain fell, he directed his applause more at her.

'Splendid! Bravo!' Rudolf joined in with the enthusiastic cries of their fellow spectators, as did Ella, but his radiant smile shone directly at his companion.

'The night is still young. We should round it off with a little drink,' Hubert had suggested. He had been waiting for them by the exit from their box.

'What do you say, Ella?' asked Rudolf.

Ella was unsure, since she knew that she faced a tiring day tomorrow. It was already late, and she always tried to avoid starting an early shift on little sleep.

Hubert seemed to misinterpret her hesitation.

'We should honour Don Giovanni's spirit – drink life to the lees and put our fortune to the test! How about the casino?' he asked.

Rudolf clearly possessed enough tact to see that Ella was not particularly keen on the idea.

'Another time, perhaps,' he said quickly, before double-checking with Ella for form's sake. 'Unless you would like to?'

'I think I would prefer to go for a stroll,' she proposed, hoping that Hubert would take that as a sign that he should visit the casino on his own, if it was so important to him.

He took the hint. 'You wouldn't win anything anyway, you lucky devil. As for me, I can play for high stakes, what with my proverbial ill luck in love,' said Hubert, before bidding her farewell with a discreet kiss on the hand.

Ella was relieved. The night was mild, and the memories of the opera were so wonderful, the last thing she wanted was to taint them with a visit to the local gambling hall.

They wandered down an almost deserted road lined with stately buildings, encountering only the occasional passer-by.

'Hubert is rather an odd fellow.' Ella was keen to see Rudolf's response to her statement – you could tell a lot about a person from their friends.

'Yes, he is. He's very inspiring, in his way, but he can sometimes be too much, even for me,' Rudolf admitted. Ella would have found any other answer disappointing.

'What does he do for a living?' she enquired.

'He's heir to a fortune, as far as I know.'

Ella considered for a moment what she should say in reply. A good-for-nothing, in other words, who whiled away his days. Yet she decided not to offend Rudolf – after all, Hubert was his childhood friend.

'I expect you don't think very much of people like him,' Rudolf continued.

'I prefer not to judge people when I don't know them well enough,' answered Ella diplomatically.

'What would you do if you had so much money that you didn't need to work for a living?' he asked.

'Probably the same as I do now. Otherwise I would feel like I did nothing of any use in life.'

'So you're following your calling?' asked Rudolf.

Ella nodded.

'Most admirable.'

'I suppose you haven't found your calling yet?' Ella probed.

'Unfortunately not. I simply follow my nose – and my heart.' He stressed the final word, looking directly into her eyes as he did so. There could no longer be any doubt that he held strong feelings for her. This wasn't just idle talk, and the absence of any smile this time offered additional proof.

Rudolf offered her his arm.

'Please, allow me to escort you back to the coach,' he said.

Ella hung onto his elbow, and as they walked, they looked just like the other couples who were also strolling along the pavement. It was amazing how comfortable it felt to have him by her side and to walk in step with him. Yet neither of them spoke: no words were necessary right now. Ella didn't find the silence uncomfortable – on the contrary, it allowed her to lose herself in her own thoughts, which centred on one question: had she fallen for Rudolf? The answer came sooner than anticipated: yes – head over heels. Could he read her thoughts? She looked at him, and he smiled winsomely back at her.

Alas, his coach came into view all too soon. She could have wandered through the night with him for an eternity.

'Here we are.' Rudolf got down from the coach and offered Ella his hand to escort her to the door of her parental home.

For a moment, they simply looked at each other. It was wonderful to be able to hold another person's gaze, she reflected.

'May I hope that we might see each other again soon? Perhaps for a picnic or a trip to the coast?' he asked.

'As far away as that?' she countered teasingly.

'I do believe I would travel to the ends of the earth with you,' he answered.

Ella laughed.

'I'm perfectly serious.' He too was grinning, of course, but the earnestness of his intentions couldn't be doubted.

'Perhaps the day after tomorrow. I have no objections to a picnic.'

'What about tomorrow? I don't mean to be forward, but I find it hard to keep my eagerness for your company in check,' said Rudolf.

There could be only one reply to such a charming request.

'It would be my pleasure. Shall we say three o'clock?' suggested Ella.

Rudolf beamed and seized her hand to kiss it – but not entirely out of politeness this time, for his lips brushed against her skin. She hoped he wouldn't notice that her entire body had begun to shake. The trembling continued as he climbed into the coach, smiled at her once more, and drove off.

As she locked the door, it struck Ella as odd that the lights were still on. Didn't her parents normally go to bed early? Perhaps they were curious to hear what their daughter had to say about her evening at the opera. She could certainly believe that of her mother. At any rate, Ella didn't think they could be worried about her getting home safely, given that she had been accompanied by Rudolf. As such, she began to consider how to frame her account of the evening – but her thoughts were interrupted when her mother suddenly appeared in front of her, ashen-faced and with tears in her eyes. Ella's pulse quickened. She had never seen her so highly wrought before.

'Your father . . . He . . .' Mother couldn't say the words.

'What's happened?' asked Ella.

Her mother drew a deep breath before she went on. 'He won't survive the night. A stroke, completely out of the blue over dinner. The doctor came . . . He can't do anything more for him.' She slumped feebly against the wall.

Ella felt as though her heart would stop at any moment. Then it began to race. If only she hadn't gone to the opera! Unable to move, she stared at her mother, who was valiantly wiping the tears from her eyes.

'He can't speak . . . All he can do is move his left hand,' she whispered.

Ella's legs threatened to give out. Her knees began to tremble.

Mother held out her hand, and Ella clasped hold of it.

She felt the need to take her mother in her arms, and went to do so, but Mother shook her head.

'Go to him,' she said.

The door was open. Why was he lying there in the gloom? They had an electric light! Had Mother lit candles for her father as he lay on his deathbed? Ella's eyes grew moist.

Her father must have heard her come in. He moved his left hand, which was lying beside a notepad and pencil, and emitted a guttural noise. Evidently he could no longer turn his head towards her.

Ella went to him and sat down on the bed to take his hand. It felt cold. His grip was weak, but she knew he could tell she was there for him. A gentle, barely perceptible smile passed over his lips, yet tears welled up in his eyes at the same time.

'Father,' Ella whispered, unable to say anything more. He presumably already knew what was happening to him. She wanted to give him the same hopeful words of consolation she often gave to her seriously ill patients – to tell him that he would be back on his feet soon enough – but here, they caught in her throat. She didn't know what to say to him, or how to give him strength.

His hand groped for the pencil that lay next to the notebook. Straight away, Ella placed it into his hand.

Father tried to speak once again. She thought he was trying to say her name, but all that came out was an incomprehensible moan.

With laborious effort, he scribbled something on the pad, which Ella deciphered as 'Forgive me'. What in heaven's name did she need to forgive him for?

'Father, what do you mean?' she asked.

More tears ran down his cheeks.

Falteringly, he began to write again. It clearly cost him great effort to put pencil to paper using his unpractised left hand. He strung the individual letters together in a line.

ORPHANAGEKARLLIES

'What does that mean, Father?'

Desperate now, he tried to speak, but the sounds that came out were scarcely audible.

What did his brother Karl have to do with his desire for for-giveness or the orphanage? Was he trying to tell her that Karl was her father? She needed certainty.

'Uncle Karl? Is he my father?' asked Ella.

It looked as though Father was trying to move his head, but he could neither nod nor answer in the negative. Instead, he kept writing.

ALWAYSLOVEDYOU

Why was he evading her question, even in his death throes?

'Is Karl my father?' demanded Ella with mounting despera-tion. His chest was rising and falling at ever shorter intervals and she sensed that he was drawing his final breaths. Her eyes filled with tears.

Her mother, who had been standing frozen by the door all this time, now came up to them and sat down on the other side of the bed.

'Heiner . . . It's all right,' she whispered to him. She ran her hand gently over his brow, but the gesture failed to calm him.

'Please tell me,' Ella implored.

Her father's hand gripped the pencil so tightly that Ella thought he would snap it in half. Sweat glistened on his forehead; his eyes flew wide open. He seemed to be struggling to reach a decision. Then he lowered the pencil once more and scrawled further letters on the page.

RICHARD

He was pressing down so hard now that the tip of the pencil broke off, but not before he had managed to write an F. He tried des-perately to speak the person's name, but he couldn't. Instead, he produced a noise that sounded like the howl of a wounded animal. His body reared up violently, then went limp as he exhaled his final breath and the pencil rolled out of his hand onto the notepad.

Mother burst into tears and threw herself desperately over her husband's lifeless body.

Ella gazed into his eyes, trying to fathom why he had asked her to forgive him. They were fixed blankly on the ceiling and there was nothing she could do but close them. She hoped he would find peace, whatever the reason he felt he needed forgiveness.

◆ ◆ ◆

Hours later, Ella still couldn't believe that her father was dead. She was so used to seeing him lying on his back like that whenever he took a nap, that to her he just looked like he was sleeping peacefully.

Mother had been inconsolable. Ella had feared that she would suffer a nervous collapse over his deathbed. Why did he have to leave them both so prematurely? Her mother had seen it coming, believing that any seaman who was confined to dry land would inevitably expire before long. Ever since he'd suffered his first heart attack at sea, he had only been able to work in the harbour office. That probably felt like imprisonment to a sailor. Ella could vividly remember their countless strolls along the waterfront, where he would look longingly at the departing sailboats and steamers. His fund of tales about his many voyages and adventures in foreign lands had been inexhaustible. Only one story – perhaps the most important one, since it concerned his daughter – had been left untold. And now it was too late.

It was not until they had called the family doctor – who assured them that her father would be taken to the morgue early the following morning – that his passing began to feel more real.

Mother was now sitting at the kitchen table like a statue, staring silently at a cup of hot milk that she had made herself in the hope of catching a few hours' sleep on the living room sofa.

Ella was in no mood for silence. She had always been aware that her parents had adopted her, so her mother must know about the background to that. Who, if not she, could explain what her father had been trying to say? There was no need for Ella to ask out loud. All she needed to do was to sit beside her mother and place the scribbled pages from Father's notepad in front of her on the table.

'We didn't find you in the orphanage, as we always told you,' she began in a broken voice.

Nothing made sense to Ella any more. Why in God's name had her parents lied to her like this?

'So where *do* I come from?' asked Ella, once she had composed herself somewhat.

Mother still lacked the courage to look her directly in the eye. 'He brought you back from one of his voyages to the South Pacific.'

'The South Pacific? Mother, what are you talking about?'

'Strictly speaking, you must have been born in Singapore,' continued Mother. She now sought to meet Ella's gaze, at least.

Ella feverishly wondered how a seaman could bring a child home with him. A child wasn't a souvenir!

'Do I come from the orphanage there?' she asked.

'No . . . You know the stories one hears about sailors. One of the mates had a dalliance with a woman in Singapore. She must have been a Dutchwoman or an Englishwoman, as otherwise your skin would be a different colour. She urged him to shoulder his responsibilities, and he did. But he wanted his child to grow up at home, and under better circumstances. The mother must have agreed, since your father's friend brought the child on board. The captain had no objections . . . But the mate – I think his name was

34

Johansson – he came down with malaria and died at sea. Somebody had to look after the child.'

'And Father . . . ?' Ella could hardly believe what her mother had just told her.

'You know I can't have any children of my own.'

'How old was I then?' asked Ella.

'No more than a few days. You were a baby.'

'A newborn baby aboard a ship?' The story grew stranger by the minute.

'They brought goats on board to provide you with fresh milk. Your father told me you were everybody's darling. The star of the ship. Back in Europe they found nursemaids for you whenever they stopped in a port.' A smile passed over Mother's face. Her father must have told this story particularly vividly.

Yet Ella was not in a cheerful mood. 'But what kind of a woman gives away her own child?'

Her mother shrugged.

'And how were you able to adopt me in the first place?'

'You know that your father was friends with Rudolf's uncle. Well, the two of them came up with a story together. Heiner told everyone that he was your natural father – that you were the child of a Dutchwoman of ill repute who had died of yellow fever. Von Stetten's word and influence were enough to get hold of the necessary papers.'

'And why did you come up with the story about the orphanage?' asked Ella.

'People talk. We could hardly shout it from the rooftops that your father had been unfaithful to me with a whore, and that you were the result of that connection.' That at least seemed plausible to Ella. Nonetheless, she had the feeling that her life had vanished overnight – that she had become a stranger to herself. And there were still so many unanswered questions.

'Why did Father mention Uncle Karl?'

Mother was at a loss.

'I can't make sense of that myself either,' she admitted.

'Mother, what does it all mean? Uncle Karl, something about lies, and when I asked him if Karl was my father, he wrote down Richard. None of it fits the story he told you. Was this Richard he mentioned at the end my real father?' Ella found it hard to believe that her mother hadn't given this any thought. She was presumably so shaken by Father's death that she had overlooked this significant detail. Now, she reached for the paper and stared at it with a mounting sense of unease.

'It looks as though he didn't tell me the whole truth.' Mother was obviously racking her brains. 'The mate's name was Johansson. Nobody ever mentioned a Richard. If this Richard was your real father, Heiner surely wouldn't have told me that you were Johansson's daughter,' she added.

That made sense to Ella. Her father would have had no reason to pretend that she wasn't this Richard's daughter, since it made no difference whether her real father was a Richard or a Johansson. But this realisation didn't get her any further.

'And what does all this have to do with Uncle Karl?' asked Ella.

'He's been dead for over twenty years. He must have died shortly after you were born. At any rate, we started receiving the lifetime annuity after his death,' pondered Mother out loud.

'Are you sure those two things happened at the same time?'

Her mother seemed to disappear into her thoughts. She furrowed her brow and played with her teacup.

'We didn't hear from Karl for many years, but your father visited him twice. They wrote letters to each other, but . . . the last letters we received came two or three years before he died,' Mother recollected.

'They must have been very close, though,' speculated Ella.

'It seems odd to me too, now that I think about it . . . All these years and I never gave it a thought,' began Mother.

'What do you mean?' Ella probed.

'Heiner never showed me the documents. But the annuity was definitely paid, as we would never have been able to afford this apartment otherwise.'

'Do you know where Father keeps all his important paperwork?'

'Yes, in his desk and in the living room cabinet,' she answered.

'We should look for it,' Ella remarked. One thing was clear: there was something about her father's story that didn't make sense.

◆ ◆ ◆

Ella couldn't bring herself to watch while her father was wrapped in a linen sack and taken away at an ungodly hour of the morning. Shortly before the arrival of Fischer, the family doctor, she had planted a farewell kiss on his forehead and told him that she would forgive him, no matter what truths eventually came to light.

For her part, Mother accompanied Doctor Fischer out of the apartment, along with the two men from the morgue. Where she found the strength was a mystery to Ella. They were both exhausted, having spent half the night engaged in wild speculation until Mother had finally nodded off. They had resolved to immediately start searching through Father's papers for documents relating to the now mysterious lifetime annuity; yet it felt disrespectful to do so in his presence, even though he was nothing more than a lifeless shell.

Unlike her mother, Ella hadn't managed to sleep at all, and had called the hospital first thing to take the day off. Work was out of the question today. Coping with her father's death would be difficult enough as it was. And then there were all the unanswered questions. Despite her lack of sleep, they kept Ella awake even now, and simultaneously prevented her from giving in to the tears that constantly welled up in her eyes.

Her mother seemed to feel much the same, although she looked considerably more composed than she had just a few hours ago. Ella had thought she would go back to bed, but she did just the opposite.

'Let's start looking for his bank documents now,' she said resolutely.

While Ella was plagued by questions about her identity, her mother was presumably consumed by the thought that her husband had pulled the wool over her eyes. If Ella had been in her mother's position, she too would probably have accepted Father's explanations without delving any deeper. A woman who couldn't bear children naturally wouldn't ask questions when she was suddenly presented with a child to raise as her own. Besides, Mother had always trusted Father's word.

Her father's filing system left nothing to be desired. All the paperwork relating to their home and finances and all their banking affairs was stored in his desk, as expected. The only useful items were statements from the Reichsbank showing the monthly payments. Yet the amounts listed were in pounds sterling, which brought in around a thousand marks per month, depending on the exchange rate. A small fortune.

'Why British pounds?' her mother wondered.

'Have you never seen these statements before?' Ella asked.

'No. Why would I? Your father always took care of the finances.' Ella could see that she regretted that now.

Ella had expected the annuity to be paid in dollars. But there was a further detail that left them both even more baffled. The handwritten statements gave no clue to the name of the person making the transfers – they listed only a number and the name of a bank. The money came from the Hongkong and Shanghai Banking

Corporation. One thing was clear though: the monthly payments certainly didn't come from Uncle Karl.

In the end, there was only one way to get an answer.

'I expect the bank will be able to provide me with details.' Her mother must have read Ella's mind.

'I'll come with you,' said Ella, who was now burning to know who was transferring these enormous sums every month.

'No . . . You should rest, Ella, or look for his diaries. He always kept a diary at sea. They must be in the cabinet.' There was no end to the revelations about her father. Until this day, Ella had had no idea that he kept a diary. Her desire to accompany her mother to the bank vanished, along with her sense of leaden fatigue. Perhaps the diaries would hold information about what happened back then. In any case, they offered the perfect opportunity to become reacquainted with her father.

CHAPTER 3

Ella was surprised that it had never occurred to her before to venture a peek inside her father's cabinet. A sense of basic respect had always prevented her from sniffing around in other people's private possessions, so doing so now left an unpleasant taste in her mouth, even though her father was dead. Yet her burning curiosity overcame her good upbringing and even the pain caused by the loss of her father, which had been submerged under so many questions . . . Now, as she searched for answers by reading through his account of his life, it felt as though he were still alive. As she leafed through the pages of a diary she had selected at random from the box in front of the sofa, Ella could almost hear his voice – as if he were sitting opposite her and telling her a story about the boundless freedom of the high seas. The powerful illusion didn't last long, however, as just a few sentences from his diary were all it took to bring the sense of loss flooding painfully back and her eyes filled with tears. Reading his words called up so many memories of him; of the incidents he would tell them about after every voyage and the souvenirs he brought back from all over the world – perhaps a hand-carved elephant from Morocco, or a bottle of fragrant oil purchased during a stop on the Suez Canal.

Ella wiped away her tears. The paralysing melancholy that had fallen over her gave way to curiosity once more.

She looked at the box of diaries and pulled out the next one, hoping that he had arranged them in chronological order. He must have begun writing down his experiences as a young man, for the first entry dated back to 1868. He would have been twenty-six years old back then. Mother had told her that he had joined the crew of a sailboat for the first time aged just eighteen. Hadn't they met each other the year before he started to keep his diary? Ella read the opening lines and, as expected, they mentioned her mother. He could see a glittering future ahead of him, and had decided to capture the wonderful moments he spent with her in writing so he could relive them over the long weeks he would spend at sea. Did her mother know about this? Ella decided she would show her these passages.

The next four books could safely be skipped, as on flicking through the first diary Ella could see that it covered a period of three years. It looked like he hadn't recorded every single day, but only the events that had struck him as significant. She reflected that she would probably have done the same. As a seaman, he more than likely wouldn't have had time to write every day. Anyway, the year 1877 was what she was looking for: the year of her birth. It seemed she hadn't reached far enough along the box, since the book that lay open in her hands dated only from 1875. Perhaps it would also include the following years, like the other diaries? But to her disappointment, she saw that it ended in October 1876. The final entry discussed a long voyage to the South Pacific. Ella scanned through the text. The plan was for the ship to bring rubber back to Germany, as well as a cargo of tin and spices that would be loaded up during a stop in India. Right now, however, she was far more interested in what happened in 1877 in Singapore. Surely the next diary would tell her – and yet the narrative resumed in May 1878. The intervening period must have taken up an entire diary on its own. Had Father filed it out of sequence?

Ella's hopes soon evaporated, as the remaining diaries were all arranged in the box in chronological order. There could be no doubt that this particular diary was missing. Perhaps the sensitivity of its contents had led him to store it elsewhere? Ella stood up and peered into the cabinet, but it was otherwise empty. She and her mother had already gone through every drawer in her father's desk, and there wasn't a diary to be found. He must have had a good reason for keeping the entries from the year of her birth secret. Ella rummaged through the box again, thinking that it might have fallen underneath the others by accident. A vain hope. What on earth had he had to hide? After all, adopting the child of a deceased seaman was nothing to be ashamed of. Or perhaps it was the circumstances that he had wanted to conceal. Perhaps she really was his daughter, and the story about the mate was as untrue as the official version. Perhaps he had wanted to spare Mother the distress of knowing that Ella really was the child of one of his lovers. In other words, perhaps the story that he had supposedly invented was really the truth. But Ella had no time to pursue these thoughts. Just then, the lock on the front door flew open. Mother must be back from the bank.

She entered the room with slumped shoulders. Ella didn't even have to ask what had happened.

'They can't give me any information because they don't know anything themselves,' she declared.

'But these are exceptional circumstances. Couldn't the bank make any inquiries?' wondered Ella out loud.

'That's exactly what I said to the staff there, but it seems the whole purpose of a numbered account is that the owner should remain anonymous,' her mother explained.

Ella felt the last spark of energy drain from her body.

Yet her mother looked less defeated than might be expected.

'I've known Clausen for many years now. He made an exception for me,' she hinted.

'So he gave you the name after all?'

'No, but at least we now know where the money comes from.'

'I thought it came from Hong Kong,' said Ella with surprise.

'No. It comes from Penang. Clausen sent a telegram. The Hongkong bank has an office there.'

'Penang? Where is that?' Ella wanted to know.

'In Farther India. Penang is a British Crown colony. At least, that's what your father told me,' her mother recalled.

'Isn't that near Singapore?' asked Ella.

'Yes, that occurred to me too. There must be some connection between your birthplace and those payments,' she observed. She sighed helplessly and sank into the armchair, without taking off her coat.

'Why would somebody from Penang make monthly payments for the child of a German sailor who died of malaria on his way home? And all the while, your father tells us tall tales about Uncle Karl.' Her mother said exactly what Ella was thinking.

'What if it's this Richard F?' she suggested.

'But who is he, exactly? The whole thing makes no sense,' said Mother, sounding resigned. 'What about you? Did you find anything useful in his diaries?' she continued.

Ella shook her head.

'I fear your father will take this secret with him to his grave,' Mother sighed.

Ella reflected for a moment that the identity of her real parents was ultimately of little importance. She had grown up believing she was an orphan. Did it make much difference whether she came from the orphanage, or whether she was the product of a sailor's dalliance in a foreign port? Until now, no – yet because her father had obviously made such a secret of the matter and hadn't even told his wife the whole truth, suddenly Ella could think of nothing else. And then there were these mysterious payments, which must be connected to her birth since they had begun at the same time. The mystery of her origins now weighed her down more than even her grief, but Mother was probably right. Under the circumstances, they wouldn't ever find an answer.

◆ ◆ ◆

Ella woke suddenly and was unsurprised to see that her mother was still asleep, though she had drifted off in the living room armchair as she still couldn't bring herself to lie down in the bedroom they had shared – on her husband's deathbed. Ella had managed to shut her eyes for a few hours too, in the end, and it must be around midday by now.

The box containing her father's diaries was still standing in front of her. It was pointless to keep rummaging through it. Ella closed the lid and placed it straight back in the cabinet. Her stomach rumbled loudly. She considered making a little breakfast for her mother too, but decided it would be better to let her rest.

Now that she felt slightly refreshed after eating two pieces of bread with jam and drinking a cup of strong coffee, the stream of thoughts and questions that she had kept at bay while she ate came flooding back once more. They were joined by a mounting unease as she glanced at the clock in the living room. It was already half past two, and Ella had agreed to meet Rudolf at three o'clock. Cancelling was impossible – even if he also had a telephone and Mother was sure to know his number – for waking her up was out of the question. Besides, Rudolf would already be on his way to collect her. She would have to give him the sad news in person. Rudolf knew her father; his uncle had been his best friend. Decency dictated that she would have to tell him about his death sooner or later – but did it really have to be today? And was it seemly to meet with a suitor on the very next day after such a tragic bereavement? It was not; and yet all such thoughts were washed away by the hope that Rudolf might know something about Father's past that would shed light on her origins. It was very possible that his uncle might have mentioned something to his family, even if many years had passed since then. That glimmer of hope was enough for Ella to hurriedly change her clothes and leave a note for her mother on the kitchen table. Rudolf was a friend of the family too, which further justified her decision.

To avoid Rudolf ringing the bell and waking Mother up, Ella decided to wait for him on the street. You could set your watch by the man. The wheels of his coach rolled up to the front door at three o'clock on the dot. Rudolf beamed, and the sun shone down from an immaculate blue sky as though nothing had happened. Yet Ella couldn't quite manage to hide her despondency, which didn't escape Rudolf's notice. He gave her a disconcerted look before dismounting and walking up to her.

'Miss Kaltenbach. Have I come at a bad time?' His voice was filled with concern.

Ella forced herself to smile.

'To see you looking gloomy on such a glorious day! I expect you've had a tiring shift at the hospital,' he conjectured.

She decided to make it brief. 'Father died last night.'

Rudolf stood thunderstruck before her, unable to make a sound.

'It happened while we were at the opera. He had a stroke,' said Ella.

Rudolf took a few moments to digest this news. 'I'm very sorry to hear it. Please accept my deepest sympathies. Under the circumstances . . . I'm sure you'd prefer to be alone . . .' he stammered.

'No . . . Some fresh air will do me good – though I don't want to burden you with my gloomy thoughts.'

'There can be no question of you being a burden. You're quite right, it will do you good,' he said, and proffered his arm. She accepted it gladly, although his presence had lost all its power of attraction at that moment.

The news of her father's death must truly have been burdensome to him, or at least touched him deeply, for no other words were spoken during the short ride to the nearby park. Ella was thankful for that, as it allowed her to distract herself by concentrating on the vivid sights offered by the coach journey – the passers-by and the verdant scenery – and to remind herself that life went on as usual.

They continued in silence until they reached a patch of woodland known as the Sierich Grove, where Rudolf helped her down from the coach.

'It makes a pleasant walk. I've heard that they plan to make a civic park here one day,' said Rudolf, taking in his surroundings.

'What an excellent idea,' answered Ella, who was grateful for his efforts to lead her thoughts onto other subjects, even if they didn't remain there for long. The local flora was beautiful; the trees and meadows simply magnificent – yet everything seemed to fade into insignificance at present as her mind was occupied with one thought only: she simply had to find out whether Rudolf knew anything about the circumstances of her adoption, or if his family had ever discussed the matter. Fortunately, Rudolf broached the subject himself. He was evidently empathetic enough to interpret her sorrowful expression.

'I can readily understand how difficult things must be for you right now. It was the same for me when my father passed away last year, and just a few weeks ago I lost my uncle too. I tried to impress upon myself that all things come to an end, including our

46

lives. That's why we should live them to the fullest, while there is still time,' he said. The sentiment was no doubt correct, but not especially comforting at present.

'Father's death . . . It isn't the whole story,' Ella began, after they had walked on a few paces. She knew that Rudolf would be surprised.

'I don't know if you are aware, but my parents adopted me when I was an infant. Father made a sort of confession on his deathbed, about the background to my adoption.' Ella mentioned only the official version of her origins, since she supposed that Captain von Stetten wouldn't have told the 'truth' to anybody in his family. There was a chance that Rudolf might know about the alleged adoption of Mate Johansson's child, but he certainly wouldn't know that her father had passed himself off as the natural parent of a child he had fathered with a whore, as stated on her falsified papers – though Ella now had to assume that neither version corresponded to the truth.

'Did he tell you who your father is?' asked Rudolf, putting two and two together. His surprise was written all over his face.

'No, he didn't. There was no time for that. All I know is that he lied to us. He always told us that we received a lifetime annuity from his late brother in America – but in fact, the payments came from Penang, and they started in the year of my birth. And then he wrote something about a Richard F on a notepad. He died with the pencil in his hand. Beyond that, he could tell us nothing more.'

Ella was unsurprised to see Rudolf's eyes widen.

'So this Richard could be your father?' he speculated.

'If only I knew . . . Why would this man have snatched me from my mother and given me away? Though perhaps all he did was send us the money,' Ella pondered.

'But why *should* this man send your family money? It almost seems as though somebody were paying alimony.' Rudolf stopped for a moment and thought carefully. 'But that can't be it. Because if that was the case, your adoptive mother would not only have to be your real mother, but she would also have to have been married and to have conceived you in Farther India,' he continued. His brow furrowed. 'On the other hand, the start date of the payments does suggest that they have something to do with your birth. You could be illegitimate – the product of an affair.' Rudolf's reasoning was perfectly logical.

'This mysterious Richard – my real father? In that case, he would have to be an Englishman or a Dutchman, wouldn't he?'

'Is that so important to you?' asked Rudolf.

'Strictly speaking, no – but ever since I learned of these inconsistencies concerning my adoption . . . I can hardly think of anything else,' admitted Ella.

'You really want to know who your true father is?' asked Rudolf frankly.

'I would love to, yes! Although it would change absolutely nothing about my life . . .' Only now did Ella fully acknowledge the fact.

'The sums came from Penang, you say? That's an island off the coast of the Malay Peninsula, to the south of Siam . . . It's in British hands . . . Perhaps there's another explanation for the payments. When did your uncle pass away? Wasn't he called Karl?' Rudolf pondered.

'He died about a year before we started receiving the annuity,' said Ella.

'It's certainly odd that it took so long for the payments to start. And no, I think we can also safely assume that the money wouldn't have been diverted through Penang, for whatever reason.' It was reassuring to know that Rudolf shared her opinion, and that they would no longer have to scratch their heads over annuity payments from Uncle Karl.

'What would you do in my position?' asked Ella.

'Much like you, I would be interested to know who had been paying my family an annuity for so many years . . . and to be perfectly honest, if this Richard *is* your real father, that interests me all the more!'

'I had hoped to find clues in my father's diary, but the entries from my birth year have disappeared. He must have destroyed them, or hidden them.'

Rudolf grew thoughtful and gazed into the distance. 'Where would I hide something like that?' he wondered out loud.

'We haven't searched very thoroughly yet. Perhaps they're tucked behind a cabinet, or under a loose tile or floorboard.'

'It's possible . . . Supposing you knew his name: would you really undertake the arduous voyage to Farther India?' asked Rudolf.

Ella nodded without hesitation – taking even herself by surprise, since strictly speaking, she had already forged other plans. Her presence was needed at the hospital to train the new nurses.

'I know that the question is absurd, really, since I can't necessarily imagine that your uncle would ever have mentioned any delicate matters relating to my father in family circles, but . . .' Ella hinted.

'You mean to ask whether my family ever discussed your adoption?'

Ella was relieved that he understood what she was getting at.

'The topic did come up . . .' He seemed to sink into deep thought once more. 'Every now and then. But I would need some time to reflect on the matter. Speaking for myself, all I know is that you were adopted.'

Rudolf looked as though he genuinely planned to give it some careful thought, as it was plain to see that the subject was playing on his mind. Nonetheless, it would be a minor miracle if he could remember anything that would help her.

♦ ♦ ♦

Two hours in the fresh air had certainly done her good, as had her conversation with Rudolf, who seemed to possess more qualities than she had realised. To his good looks and exquisite manners, she could now add sensitivity and an obliging nature. When they had said their goodbyes on the street in front of Ella's building, he had promised to look through his father's personal effects for any clue as to her origins. It was touching to see how worried he was about her. He had even offered to send over a servant to help her mother manage the household. He couldn't imagine that she was capable of any such work at present, and his assessment was accurate. Her mother had only woken up at around half past six that evening in a desolate state, and remained so even after drinking a cup of extra-strong fresh coffee that Ella had brewed for her as soon as she woke up. Ordinarily, Mother would have mentioned Ella's meeting with Rudolf, but she made no comment.

'I'm not hungry.' That was her only reply when Ella had asked whether she should bring her something to eat in the living room. She had shuffled into the kitchen like a frail old woman and slumped down feebly once more at the kitchen table, where she now sat as if she had been turned to stone.

Ella poured her another cup of coffee. But she refused to touch it.

'Please drink something, at least,' Ella urged her, sitting down beside her. Her mother seemed to have aged years over the last few hours.

She obeyed reluctantly, her hand trembling as she lifted the cup to her lips.

'Don't you want even a little bite to eat?'

She shook her head.

'Giving up on yourself won't bring Father back,' Ella pointed out with concern.

'I know that, and his death is bad enough as it is . . . I just don't know what to believe any more,' she finally answered.

'Father will have had his reasons. Perhaps his story is true and there's a logical explanation for why Uncle Karl's money was paid from Penang. Maybe this bank has offices in America too, and everything about the annuity will make sense.' At that moment, Ella realised that she was only saying these things to console her mother. She didn't believe it herself, even though it could plausibly turn out to be the truth.

'He lied to us . . . I dearly wish I knew why,' her mother said. Ella felt the same.

'I wonder why I didn't grow suspicious much earlier. A lifetime annuity from his brother? One only pays into an annuity contract when one has a family. Karl didn't have anyone. So why would he make provisions for your father and for us? None of it makes any sense! But I can only blame myself for that. A sort of blindness descends when one suddenly receives the means to live well.'

There was no time for further reflections, for the doorbell suddenly rang. They never normally had visitors in the early evening.

'It might be the doctor. Papers to sign . . .' her mother conjectured, but she was proven wrong.

Ella was astonished to find Rudolf standing at the door.

'Please forgive me for intruding. I wouldn't normally have ventured to call without notifying you in advance, under the circumstances, but I simply couldn't stop thinking about the matter of your adoption . . .' he began agitatedly.

'Is there news? Have you discovered something?' asked Ella urgently. She immediately invited him inside.

'Who is it?' her mother called from down the corridor.

'Would you prefer to discuss this in confidence, or . . . ?' he began cautiously.

'No. Mother must hear everything. She wants to know what happened back then too. It's Rudolf,' she shouted towards the kitchen in answer to her mother. 'I hope it's nothing bad?' Ella sought reassurance.

'Not in the least.' Rudolf took off his coat and handed it to Ella. 'My deepest sympathies,' he said on entering the kitchen and spotting her mother.

She nodded gratefully and offered him one of the empty chairs.

'I've told Rudolf about the inconsistencies relating to the adoption,' Ella explained.

'Please sit down,' her mother urged him.

Rudolf did as she asked, and Ella likewise found a seat at the kitchen table.

'I spent the rest of the afternoon wondering how we might shed light on the matter. My father is dead. I'm sure he must have heard something back then, but what use is that to us? None at all . . . After all, I can't ask him any questions about it now. The same goes for my uncle. What a pity . . . He was close friends with Heiner, and the captain of the ship to boot. But then it occurred to me that my mother got on very well with my uncle. She loved listening to tales of the high seas.'

'Clara?' asked Mother.

'I decided to ask her.'

'But your mother suffers from forgetfulness, doesn't she?' remarked Mother.

'That's true, but strangely enough, she can still clearly remember things that happened many years ago,' said Rudolf.

Ella caught herself picking at her fingernails out of sheer anxiety.

'What did she say?' she asked bluntly.

'I think it's best if I try to use her own words as far as possible.'

Rudolf took a deep breath before going on. 'It seems that your dear father mentioned a completely heartless human being – the devil incarnate . . . This person must have been very influential.'

Ella's breath caught. What was Rudolf talking about?

He seemed aware of the import of his revelations, and so proceeded carefully. 'She said that Heiner was given money to take the child,' he said.

'You mean, somebody paid the annuity to my father in return for adopting me?' Ella could scarcely believe what she was hearing.

'That would be my interpretation,' said Rudolf.

'Did Clara know his name? Did she mention a Richard?'

Rudolf shook his head.

'Did she tell you anything else?' asked Ella.

'He must have owned a plantation. That was apparently what Heiner thought anyway, since plantation owners in the British Crown colonies have grown extremely wealthy.'

Ella struggled to maintain her composure.

'I've done a little research. Penang is primarily a trading outpost. Most of the plantations are located in Malacca, on the Malay Peninsula. Mainly in the south, in a region called Johore, which is also under British control – although there are plenty of Dutchmen living there too. They were the previous administrators.' Rudolf looked pensive, then continued: 'Considering that there can't be more than a hundred rich families in Malacca who own plantations – perhaps two hundred at most – and there can't be all that many whose surname begins with an F . . .'

'You mean, it might be possible to find my real father?' asked Ella.

'I think so.'

Ella's mother had remained silent throughout this exchange, her face blank. The scale of the lie that her husband had told her throughout his life was difficult to grasp.

'He must be very wealthy,' added Rudolf.

'Ought we really to call him to account, after all these years? He's been sending us money for so long, after all,' interjected Mother.

Ella felt the same. The financial aspect, which Rudolf had quite rightly brought up, held no interest for her whatsoever – yet the question of who this man was began to rage within her like a wild-fire. And there was another question that came with that too – one that Ella had already given some thought to, but which gained new force in light of these revelations.

'How could a mother do that? Give away her own child?' she burst out. The thought was a painful one, and only stoked the fire even further.

'It's difficult for me to say this, but in such circles, it wasn't unusual to enlist the services of women of easy virtue . . .' Rudolf tailed off.

Ella could imagine what he was hinting at, given Father's lie about Mate Johansson. The possibility had been raised before, but it now weighed on her even more heavily.

'Do you really think I could find out?' asked Ella once more.

'If you could enquire locally then I'm certain of it,' opined Rudolf.

At that, Mother looked over at her. One didn't have to be a mind reader to see what she was thinking. The question came soon enough: 'Surely you don't want to travel to Malacca?' she asked, her eyes bulging.

Ella shrugged non-committally, although her desire to do so had only been born at that very moment.

'What about your plans? At the hospital?' Mother went on. Her words felt like a bucket of cold water, but though they poured directly onto the raging fire of Ella's curiosity, they didn't quite manage to extinguish it.

'And then for a woman to travel alone to a foreign country and ask questions that some people there might find uncomfortable? My child, it's far too dangerous.' Ella was unable to argue with that, at any rate.

'I would be happy to accompany your daughter – provided that she would want me to,' said Rudolf, turning to Ella.

Mother shot him an accusatory look, while Ella offered a grateful one. All the same, the thought of hunting down the devil, as Father had apparently referred to him in Clara's presence, seemed almost absurd at that moment. Yet even that thought wasn't enough to quench the flames of her curiosity.

◆　◆　◆

Ella had hoped she would find deliverance in sleep, and that her head would be clear again by the following morning, but the exact opposite had been the case. She had been plagued by nightmare after nightmare: Father sobbing incessantly as he begged her for forgiveness; a horned creature with cloven feet that prowled through the rainforest by night and loomed over her cradle; somebody counting money into Father's hand. Even her walk to the hospital failed to refresh her. It was inadvisable to make any decisions in this condition – but she did so anyway, partly for her mother's sake.

At breakfast, her mother had begun to torment herself again with questions. On the one hand, she didn't exactly seem thrilled that her daughter was considering journeying to Malacca; yet on the other, Ella was sure that her mother would never find peace or get over her husband's death until she found out what had happened all those years ago. After all, one could only forgive somebody when one knew what had really happened. Although Ella had resolved to confront the truth so that she could learn who she really was and where she came from, each step she took towards the hospital seemed to call everything into question once more. Would it not be better to leave the past undisturbed?

It came as no surprise to Ella that Gutenberg agreed to see her straight away. He probably assumed she wanted to talk to him about the training programme for the new nurses, and so his face fell when she outlined her intentions, her travel plans and the reasons for her decision.

'A glittering future lies ahead of you. You're putting all that at risk! And yet, to be quite honest, I would probably do exactly the same thing if I were you,' he told her.

It seemed as though Gutenberg was positively encouraging her to undertake the journey – yet his next words told her how wrong she was.

'In the end, it boils down to a choice between the past and the future. Rationally speaking, one should always look ahead,' he continued.

'But how can I look to the future when I feel I have become a different person overnight? When the solid ground on which I have built my life has suddenly started to shake?' Ella almost stuttered as she endeavoured to communicate her feelings to her employer.

Gutenberg nodded sympathetically.

'The new training programme won't start until the new year.' Ella tried to make her extended absence palatable to him, but she failed.

'We need to begin recruiting a long way in advance, developing training plans, looking for suitable staff. That won't be done overnight,' he told her unequivocally.

'It would only be a few weeks,' Ella tried to persuade him.

'And how should I explain it to your colleagues? Quite apart from the fact that the hospital directors won't be prepared to grant you such a long unpaid leave of absence. We're short on staff, so we would have to find a replacement for you straight away.'

Now it was Ella's turn to nod thoughtfully. It seemed that she was not only obstructing her own professional prospects, but also putting her very employment at the hospital at risk.

'Röttgers will be delighted, at any rate,' said Gutenberg. That much was clear to Ella too.

'Are you sure you don't want to take some more time to think it over?' Gutenberg's appeal was an urgent one.

Mathilde, whom Ella had told about her plans immediately before her meeting with Gutenberg, had taken the same view. 'Just don't rush into anything. I'm sure it will all look very different in the morning.' Mathilde's words were meant well, but Ella didn't agree.

Should she be tormented by nightmares for yet another night? Should she spend the rest of her life grappling with questions for which she would never find an answer? What would a few more days of uncertainty do to change all that? Ella plucked up her courage.

'I will go to Malacca,' she declared in a surprisingly steady voice.

Gutenberg took a deep breath as he reconciled himself to her decision.

'I wish you the very best of luck and a safe journey,' he finally answered sincerely. Here too, Gutenberg's words chimed with those of Mathilde, whom Ella bumped into straight after the meeting. Mathilde's warm hug gave Ella strength, though it also held the pang of a farewell. Before her lay the ward on which she had worked; here were the patients that she so loved tending to. This was where she could have trained a new generation of nurses. Ella closed her eyes to shut out everything beyond Mathilde's arms around her.

'Look after yourself, Ella,' whispered Mathilde.

'I won't be travelling alone,' said Ella, once Mathilde had released her from her heartfelt embrace.

'Are you going with your mother?' she asked.

'No, with Rudolf.' Mathilde's expression immediately lifted. She had listened to Ella's rapturous description of him on the day after the anniversary celebration at the docks.

'Well then, in that case nothing can go wrong,' her friend grinned.

From her lips to God's ears!

CHAPTER 4

Ella had postponed her travel preparations until after Father's funeral, and not just for Mother's sake. She had felt the need to bid him farewell. She owed that much to him, as well as to his friends, who had congregated in large numbers at the cemetery this morning. Mother hadn't shed a single tear. That alone spoke volumes. His betrayal of her – and ultimately of his daughter too – removed any misgivings Ella had felt about going to the harbour with Rudolf that very afternoon to book their tickets for the big voyage. The steamers didn't depart every day, and waiting any longer was out of the question.

Ella stood rooted to the spot in front of the colourful poster for the Imperial German postal service's steamship line, which advertised the company's fortnightly East Asian service. It inspired yearning and excitement for a journey to places that she only knew about from hearsay – and, of course, from her father's stories. Ella's heart beat faster, and for once not because of Rudolf, who had accompanied her to the harbourfront office of the North German Lloyd Shipping Company early that afternoon so they could buy their tickets. Looking at that poster was enough to send you into a dream world. It depicted an imperial steamship travelling along an unmistakably Asian coastline against an apricot-pink horizon. The thick jungle that awaited her there was no more than a vague grey silhouette on the poster, but there was a kind of canoe floating near the shore full of people from all the ports that the steamship line called at. A woman in a kimono represented Nagasaki, while a man swathed in billowing red fabric and wearing a flat hat must be from China – the North German Lloyd called at Hong Kong and Shanghai. There was also another figure on board with a turban on his head, presumably to represent the region around the Suez Canal.

'They say that Malays generally wear very little clothing,' remarked Rudolf, who must have thought the same thing as Ella when he saw the fourth occupant of the canoe – a short, dark-skinned man who wore only a red garment that resembled a loincloth.

'I've heard that it's very hot out there. Too much clothing might be a disadvantage in those regions,' mused Ella.

Rudolf laughed.

'That's one way of looking at it . . . Although perhaps it's more a sign of a primitive culture,' he answered.

'I expect you'll change your mind once we have to cope with the heat in all our finery. Though as a man, you can at least take off your jacket without looking completely uncivilised,' said Ella.

'On the contrary – women have the advantage there. You can wear light and airy summer dresses, while all we have is short trousers.'

'Like little boys wear?' laughed Ella, immediately picturing Rudolf in shorts.

'Other countries, other customs. Even the British Army wear shorts, judging by a photograph I saw recently. With pith helmets on their heads too. It isn't an outfit that commands respect, I have to admit. Not to mention all the pests it leaves you exposed to.'

'Pests?' asked Ella.

'Mosquitoes. I've been told that they practically eat people alive. And let's not forget the tigers and cannibals,' he added with a grin. It evidently amused him to see Ella's eyes grow wider and wider.

'You know how to put a lady in the mood for a voyage,' retorted Ella promptly, and Rudolf laughed again. It felt so good to have a few moments' distraction from recent events – to feel alive again, and to look to the future without despair. Rudolf seemed to sense this.

'I'm happy to see you smile again, Ella,' he said with visible satisfaction.

Ella realised that this was the first time he hadn't called her 'Miss Kaltenbach'. Given all they had experienced together and the journey that lay ahead of them, anything else would have been absurd.

'We should book our tickets, Rudolf,' said Ella, emphasising his name in a way that he could only interpret as a sign of approval.

He gave her his hand to escort her into the harbour office. It almost felt like he was asking her to dance.

'There really are tigers in Malacca, though,' he said.

'I'm sure they won't eat me,' answered Ella, before seeking further reassurance. 'What about the cannibals?'

'They live on the neighbouring islands out in the Pacific. But I think German flesh would be too tough for them anyway,' explained Rudolf as they reached the counter. The adjacent desk was selling tickets to the New World – to America. There was a long queue. It seemed that nobody wanted to travel to Asia.

'The *Danzig* departs tomorrow morning, I believe?' Rudolf asked the booking clerk – a stocky young man who wore a blue jacket over a white shirt, just like his colleague. It came as no surprise to Ella that Rudolf had already researched the various travel options. A businessman like him surely wouldn't leave anything to chance. She felt very glad that he was accompanying her.

'Indeed, at half past ten,' confirmed the man behind the counter.

'Are there any cabins available in second class?' asked Rudolf.

'I'm sorry – I'm afraid there are only twenty-three second-class cabins. Let me take a look,' said the clerk, who began leafing through a list on the counter in front of him. 'Yes, they're all booked up. We still have five spots in third class, but then you would have to share your cabin with other passengers. As for first class . . . Only three cabins have been booked so far. There are still sixteen left.'

'Third class is out of the question,' Ella intervened, as she knew from her father how uncomfortable the conditions would be – indeed, 'uncomfortable' was an understatement.

'The *Danzig* has a good third class. The cabins are clean, and the catering is decent,' responded the clerk. He might well be right. Father had always sailed on tall ships, and never on a modern steamer.

'The first-class tickets must cost around eight hundred marks?' The way Rudolf phrased it made it sound like a question.

'Between eight hundred and thirty and one thousand and sixty, to be precise,' the clerk clarified. That was a considerable sum. As a schoolteacher, Mother earned eight hundred marks in a month.

Rudolf raised his eyebrows, although he could certainly afford it. He reached into his jacket for his wallet, clearly intending to pay for both of their tickets, but Ella forestalled him.

'We'll take two cabins in first class. I presume I can settle the bill with a cheque?' she asked. She had agreed with her mother just that morning that they would pay for the tickets. After all, Rudolf was only travelling for her sake, and he would be neglecting his business for many weeks as a result.

'Certainly,' answered the booking clerk.

'Out of the question. I'm the one paying for the tickets.'

Ella had known Rudolf would say that. 'Please don't make things awkward for me, Rudolf. You're already doing me a huge service by coming with me on this trip.'

He was clearly unhappy about this. Ella could see him struggling with himself. She already had her chequebook in her hand and was reaching for the pen that the clerk held out to her.

'That comes to one thousand, six hundred and sixty marks,' he said.

'Ella . . .' began Rudolf once more.

'I won't argue with you. Mother insists on it too.'

As she wrote out the cheque, Ella quickly glanced over at Rudolf. He was shaking his head, but he seemed to have admitted defeat, since he remained silent until she had handed her cheque and passport over to the clerk.

'The champagne on board is on me, then.' Although he spoke with a wry smile and a theatrical gesture, Rudolf obviously wanted to preserve his honour.

Ella was relieved to see he had recovered his humour. How would she get through the long journey if not at his side? Thirty-six days on the high seas, if Mother's estimate could be believed. But at least she no longer had to travel as an unaccompanied woman.

'I'm the one who should be thanking you. But I have no objections to the odd glass of champagne, given a suitable occasion,' Ella replied warmly.

◆ ◆ ◆

As she packed her bags the following morning, Ella couldn't recall ever having experienced such emotional turmoil. Her mood shifted every fifteen minutes according to whatever thoughts happened to be drifting through her mind. On buying the two tickets, her excitement about the voyage had grown. After all, she was about to undertake a journey in first class together with a man who was making advances towards her. Yet all that pleasurable anticipation had disappeared by the time Rudolf brought her home. Her father's death now overshadowed all other emotions – seemed to stifle them at birth. But those feelings in turn vanished when her mother once again gave voice to the bewildering tangle of questions about her husband's secrets. At least she had finally come to approve of her daughter's voyage – although presumably only because Rudolf would be going with her.

With all these thoughts gnawing away at her, it wasn't surprising that it took her so long to pack two suitcases and a trunk, even with her mother's help. The only easy part had been the night before, when she had picked out the reading material she wanted to take with her. There were still so many books about all kinds of new treatments that she intended to read on the voyage. After all, she would have to keep herself busy for four weeks while she travelled halfway around the world and crossed four major bodies of water.

When the time came, to her surprise her mother made their farewell surprisingly short and painless.

'Look after yourself, my child,' she said at the door as she helped Ella carry the two suitcases out to the coach, which Rudolf had already fetched from his home.

Her mother looked on bravely, but remained silent as Rudolf rolled up his sleeves and helped lift the bags onto the coach. All that remained was one final embrace. There was no need for Mother to say anything more; Ella could see in her eyes that she missed her already.

'Have a safe journey, and write to me as soon as you can,' she called after the departing coach. She kept waving until they turned onto the main road that led to the harbour.

Rudolf was silent, which Ella was grateful for, as during the journey her emotional carousel had whirred into action once more.

'You've brought more luggage than I have,' declared Rudolf abruptly after a while, just to break the silence. He had only one normal-sized and one small suitcase with him. Ella's bags were significantly bigger and heavier, as he couldn't have helped but notice while loading up the coach.

'The books alone take up so much space,' explained Ella.

By the time they reached the harbour, however, she realised that with Rudolf present, her plans to study might not be viable. His effusive chatter about the foreign lands they would see was infectious, and he had extensive plans to explore unfamiliar cultures – all of which ensured that her excitement once again gained the upper hand, for now.

'The *Danzig* will be sure to stop in Spain or Portugal. We can take a look around when it does. Lisbon is meant to be very interesting, and so are the Greek islands. Delightful and idyllic, I've been told.'

'Will we even be allowed to leave the steamer? The *Danzig* isn't just a passenger ship after all,' Ella pointed out.

'Yes, that's true, but it's a very luxurious vessel. We'll benefit from the fact that it's relatively small. The crew will have to stop more often to take on coal, which means more opportunities to go ashore,' reasoned Rudolf.

'Small? On the high seas?' Ella could recall her father's stories all too well. 'Small' meant having to pray every day that they wouldn't encounter a heavy swell.

'If we were sailing around the Cape of Good Hope, there would be cause for concern – however, the North Sea and the Mediterranean are relatively calm at this time of year. There's no need to worry.' Those words were anything but reassuring, coming from the lips of a landlubber. The Mediterranean in particular could be treacherous, not to mention the strong winds of the Indian Ocean. As the daughter of a seaman, she was well aware of all this.

Yet Ella forgot her concerns once the coach reached the end of the landing stage where the *Danzig* was moored. 'Small' was a relative word. Ella guessed that the steamer was over six hundred feet long, and at least sixty feet wide. 'Imposing' was a more accurate description, and with four funnels, Ella assumed that the engine would be powerful enough to cope with even rough seas – a triple-expansion steam engine that could achieve speeds of up to thirteen knots. Rudolf had apparently done a lot of research.

The landing stage was a busy place, with a few dozen passengers bustling around the foot of the lowered gangplank. Their clothing made it possible to guess who was booked into first, second and third class. Even from a distance, there were two carriages that didn't look as though they were for public hire, and a remarkably well-dressed coachman opened the door of one of them to reveal a smartly dressed man who would no doubt be joining them in first class. The coachman unloaded five suitcases, while the passenger – who was in his mid-forties and had a thick beard and round belly – smoothed down his blond hair, which the wind had whipped into disarray.

The second-class passengers were just as easy to spot. The men wore suits, and there were two women wearing tailored dresses and fashionable hats. However, the majority of the passengers gradually filtering onto the ship looked like the people Ella knew from Hamburg's tenements: men in simple jackets and woollen trousers, which neither fit properly nor matched each other in colour. After all, what worker could afford to buy a tailored suit? The few women were clad in the plain white dresses typical of the working classes. Some of them also wore aprons and headscarves. Their leather cases looked worn, and a few of them only carried wicker baskets – presumably because they couldn't afford to buy suitcases made of decent leather. They would be travelling below deck, in cabins that they would have to share with other people. Ella immediately felt guilty. As a mere hospital attendant, she really ought to be putting up with similarly humble conditions herself. The question of why this wasn't the case began to gnaw at her once more.

'Look at all the luggage the people are bringing with them,' marvelled Rudolf, interrupting Ella's thoughts.

Whatever it was, the crew carried it aboard – all of them young men in white sailors' uniforms. They took charge of Rudolf and Ella's cases too, once Ella had shown them their tickets. It was time to bid farewell to Hamburg – to her old home, but also to her professional dreams. That was a bitter pill. Yet her excitement at the journey outweighed the resulting melancholy. Ella was also glad that her mother had decided not to accompany them to the harbour. Wherever she looked, she saw floods of tears; the passionate embraces of fathers clinging to their children or saying farewell to their wives. She was deeply touched at the sight. Her own mother had pulled herself together valiantly that morning and managed not to cry, though it perhaps wasn't surprising, considering how many tears she had shed the night before, that she had none left when the time came to say goodbye the following day – especially when the parting wouldn't be forever.

The ship's horn sounded and a visible sense of unease instantly took hold of the passengers, and of Ella too.

'Mr and Mrs von Stetten?' asked the sailor on the steps leading up to the access hatch. That had a nice ring to it, but Ella corrected him. They evidently looked like a married couple to other people.

'Oh . . . I beg your pardon,' came the prompt apology once the sailor had read the second ticket.

Rudolf laughed it off and ostentatiously extended his arm to escort her up the stairs.

Ella remained silent for a moment and considered turning round to take one last look at her home – but then dismissed the thought. It would only make the parting more painful, and would not be in the true spirit of her journey. After all, she wasn't emigrating to America, and one didn't stop to look back when boarding a train either.

Rudolf, being a true gentleman, offered the bigger cabin to the lady – although strictly speaking, 'cabin' was an understatement. 'Elegant apartment' would have been a more accurate description, and not just because Ella had never sat in such comfortable chairs before. There were fine fabrics as far as the eye could see, from the curtains to the upholstery. The floral patterns matched the deep-pile carpet and the fine porcelain platter laden with fresh fruit. Even the washbasin was adorned with flowers – an arrangement of amaryllis and roses with ornamental grasses, whose sweet scent filled the cabin. It would be easy to get used to all this, although the obsequious 'Certainly, madam' from the cabin boy might take a little longer. Being addressed like that made Ella feel completely out of place.

She had just decided to test out the bed when she felt a fierce rumble emanating from the heart of the ship and the floor began to vibrate gently. The captain must have given the order to set sail.

Immediately, there was a knock at the cabin door. Ella called for Rudolf to come in. He had already told her that he wanted to be on deck with her when the ship left port.

'Aren't the cabins splendid? But we need to hurry. We can toast the start of our great expedition in the bar afterwards.' Rudolf's high spirits were unwavering, and he invited her to take his arm. Ella did so as soon as they left the cabin.

Just then, the door of the neighbouring cabin opened and out came the well-fed man whom she had noticed on the pier. He smiled at them winningly.

'Well, we're off. All hands on deck!' he called without ceremony, and Ella instantly warmed to him. Old money didn't talk like that – in other words, he couldn't be an aristocrat or a person of rank. He must be a prosperous businessman, and a friendly one at that. Already, he was extending his hand in greeting.

'Otto Ludwig,' he said by way of introduction.

'Ella Kaltenbach.' She shook his hand. Then it was her companion's turn: 'Rudolf von Stetten.'

Otto looked confused. Like the sailor earlier, he must have been expecting them to share a surname.

'My fiancée,' added Rudolf.

Ella did her best to conceal her surprise. At any rate, Rudolf's bold approach had an immediate effect. Otto's face relaxed noticeably.

'What a lovely couple,' he answered, as he made his way towards the steps leading to the upper deck. It sounded as though he had said it to himself, although in the knowledge that they could both hear him.

'Are we engaged now?' asked Ella with a grin.

'No, but now nobody will ask any stupid questions. We'll be taken more seriously as a couple, and none of the sailors or officers will pursue you either.' It would have been foolish to argue.

'What if somebody asks to see my engagement ring?'

Rudolf nodded thoughtfully, since Ella's objection likewise admitted no argument.

'I'm afraid that problem may not be so easy to solve at short notice. Perhaps at the first stop? There'll be a jewellery shop in every city.'

'But what will we do until then? Hide in your cabin? I suppose I could wear gloves.' Ella enjoyed goading Rudolf, as he knew that she wasn't being serious.

'I would prefer the first option.' Ella forgave Rudolf his immoral proposal, as he clearly had his tongue firmly in his cheek.

'We aren't quite married yet, my dear Rudolf,' she retorted archly.

'All right then, gloves it is. How unromantic,' he replied, feigning a hangdog expression.

'As it happens, you're in luck – I happen to have a ring with me that is big enough to serve as an engagement ring for a first-class passenger. Nobody will know that the diamond is really just paste,' Ella clarified.

'How I would love to give you a real diamond ring.' Rudolf smiled.

Ella was relieved that the ship's horn sounded just then, and another passenger hurried out of one of the rearmost cabins. She merely gave a broad smile by way of response.

Even after over a week at sea, Ella still hadn't tired of going on deck just before dinner to take a short stroll and gaze out at the horizon. Around that time, most of the first-class passengers were still in their cabins smartening themselves up – one of the disadvantages of believing oneself to be a member of the upper classes. Ella had only two evening dresses, which made the decision easy for her.

The passengers in second and third class didn't need to worry about that sort of thing. They much preferred to stroll casually along the deck, or sit in the wicker chairs and enjoy the remaining warmth of the day. Rudolf would also join them, and usually fell asleep whenever he did so. Shortly after sunset, a soothing twilight would descend over the sea and there was no better backdrop for allowing one's thoughts to roam freely. The half-light receded into the distance, giving a feeling of peace and serenity. Father had often spoken of this. Ella was beginning to fall in love with the sea, just like her father had.

Here on deck, she could think of him – feel close to him – without having to brood over the turmoil of the days before her departure or feel his loss as painfully as she had until very recently. Did time really heal all wounds so quickly? At any rate, Ella wondered what had happened to the last few days. She still hadn't read a single one of her books. Time seemed to slip through your fingers here, not least thanks to the ship's catering, which served six meals each day – three large, and three small. Yet there was more to it than simply stuffing one's face. One fell into conversation, made introductions, talked about everything under the sun. Because every passenger had a different reason for undertaking the long journey and a different destination, the topics for discussion seemed inexhaustible. In the end, she spent most of her time at sociable gatherings in the dining hall or the tea room or, in the evening, playing chess and nine men's morris and listening to the ship's band – an ensemble of three talented sailors. On two occasions, Rudolf had even persuaded her to join in the morning gymnastics classes on deck, which had been surprisingly varied. Distraction also came in the form of occasional views of the countries and coastlines they passed – though only the white chalk cliffs of Dover in the English Channel had impressed Ella, as the *Danzig* had sailed close enough to them for the passengers to admire them in all their glory. The greater distances to the Dutch, French, Spanish and Portuguese coasts made it impossible to experience them in as intense a manner. The land masses lying in the mist appeared taller, flatter or greener by intervals, but were often nothing more than a diffuse grey line.

Yet it wasn't just the daily routine that rendered her plans for self-improvement impossible. Long sea voyages evidently sent all good intentions out of the window – including Ella's plans to read her medical books. She simply couldn't summon the necessary motivation. She couldn't even rouse herself to write a letter to her mother, which she had intended to send the next time they stopped at a port – let alone record her recollections of the journey, or take advantage of the extensive on-board library to learn about the countries and cultures that the ship was steaming towards. She managed to read only rarely – usually just before she fell asleep under the dim light of her bedside lamp. Ella's explanation for it was the endless vista of the sea, which changed constantly according to the weather, and practically chained her to the railings. Likewise, the rhythmic rolling of the ship's hull over the waves seemed to gradually lull her to sleep, lifting all pressures from her mind. The monotonous rumble from the engine room and the salty sea air also played their part. Soon enough, she grew accustomed to idleness and was inclined to postpone all plans until the following day – after all, the journey was long enough.

'I'll be as round as a pufferfish by the time we get to Malacca,' sighed Rudolf, who had suddenly appeared beside her at the railing. He seemed to have got used to the on-board routines too, and you could already plan your day around him: when he woke up from his nap, that meant it was time for dinner. Ella was also worried that she would soon be unable to fit into her dresses, but there was scarcely anyone on board who could resist the delicious fare. Just like every evening, the waiter presented her with a menu printed especially on board the *Danzig*, complete with ornamental lettering, and here too, there was no shortage of variety: chicken soup with rice, almond-crusted fish, beef fillet – which was called 'chateaubriand' in elevated circles – mixed vegetables, beef tongue in red wine sauce, roast turkey, mixed salad. And for dessert: strawberries, vanilla pudding with hot raspberries, croquembouche with ice cream, fruit, small French pastries, and coffee.

'With so many wonderful things to eat, it's hard to know where to start,' Ella confessed once they had sat down at their usual table in first class.

Their surroundings also reflected the price they had paid for their journey. The furniture was made from elegant tropical woods, two chandeliers hung from the ceiling and the table was adorned with the finest porcelain. To avoid having to resist the temptations on the menu, Ella persuaded herself that choosing between all these delicious dishes must take up at least as much energy as the gymnastics class, even if it were only mental energy. Or perhaps the sea air simply increased her appetite?

'They really know how to pamper a person here,' remarked Otto, her cabin neighbour, who clearly hadn't been one to pass up a good meal even before the voyage, judging by the way his belly strained against his black tailcoat. He had sought out their company from the very first evening. Otto Ludwig was indeed a businessman, and was one of the few passengers who would be accompanying them all the way to Malacca. Apparently, the only other people who would be disembarking in Penang were third-class passengers – seamen who would be taking up duty aboard another steamship in the imperial fleet. Besides, Otto was certainly far warmer and wittier than the dreary civil servants from second class who were on their way to China, and who had also sought out their company from time to time.

'That gentleman seems a little intrusive to me,' Rudolf had discreetly whispered to her in a private moment on the first evening; however, he had quickly dismissed his initial reservations when he learned that Otto did business with both the Malays and the British. He traded in rubber, buying it at source, and seemed to know everyone who was anyone in Malacca, which had made Rudolf warm to him. Ella hoped he would be able to help them in the search for her real father, but she hadn't come up with a credible pretext to ask him for assistance. Telling him the truth would have given the impression that she was trying to hunt down a wealthy parent. That was Rudolf's view, anyway, and Ella couldn't dismiss it out of hand. But all in good time. There was no shortage of conversation topics when Otto was around, anyway. Today, they had an obvious subject to discuss, since the heavy swell coming in from the Atlantic had caused many passengers to excuse themselves from the evening dinner. Peering over the partition of their private area, they could see that the large dining hall was half empty.

'There's nothing worse than seasickness,' Rudolf asserted confidently, since he had once crossed the English Channel in rough seas.

'People make the mistake of eating too little. The best thing to do is to eat rich, fatty foods, and ideally keep to the middle of the ship.' Otto, who had already made several journeys to Malacca, surprised even Ella with his theory. 'Earlier, on the old steamships, I would always get seasick. But that wasn't due to the swell; rather, it was the unfortunate mixture of kitchen smells, engine exhaust fumes and stuffy cabins. On this ship, everything is in perfect order. One of the most comfortable voyages money can buy,' he continued. Otto clearly enjoyed his role as a worldly businessman, and doubtless possessed an impressive fund of general knowledge.

'That might only be true of the first-class cabins – though the Lloyd certainly commands a high price for those,' objected Rudolf.

'I think the price is perfectly fair. A steamship like this one consumes around six hundred and fifty tons of coal per day. By my estimation, that amounts to a daily sum of about fifteen hundred marks – not to mention the cost of the crew.'

'You're evidently a very good businessman. The likes of us pay little thought to such things,' said Rudolf admiringly – yet he shot Otto an irritated, almost arrogant look, which surely didn't escape him.

'Oh, nonsense – I just know how to do basic arithmetic,' said Otto with a dismissive wave. 'Though I know I can be a little small-minded at times. I'm sure you don't need to know about the price of coal in the property business,' he went on light-heartedly. Rudolf had already mentioned that he worked in that field when they had introduced themselves on the first evening.

Ella couldn't escape the impression that Rudolf felt inferior to Otto, and that he deeply admired him. It was the way he smiled sheepishly at such moments and always changed the subject whenever business topics came up.

'Well, I think I'll have the chateaubriand.' Rudolf was doing it again.

'You can tell that there's blue blood in those veins,' joked Otto. 'For me, it's just a very good piece of beef.'

Otto too seemed to admire Rudolf – the gentleman whose social rank he would never achieve, despite all his hard work and his self-made fortune. Their dialogue couldn't have illustrated Ella's thoughts about her travel companions any more clearly. Rudolf tried to conceal certain insecurities behind his aristocratic manners, with the intention of making Otto feel subconsciously inferior – but Otto wasn't so easily rattled.

'What are the prices like in Hamburg at the moment? I'm thinking of buying something. An apartment, around six hundred and fifty square feet. One in a good location.'

'Exorbitant,' answered Rudolf curtly. He looked for the waiter and beckoned him over.

'What sort of price are we talking about? Sixty thousand?' Otto probed further.

'Somewhere in that region, yes,' Rudolf responded tersely again.

'We should definitely do some business, then. I'm sure you have an office in Hamburg.'

'Certainly,' replied Rudolf, no less laconically than before. Ella could make no sense of it. What good property agent would so obviously rebuff a wealthy customer like Otto? Of course, it was perfectly possible that Rudolf was used to a different style of client, and that Otto didn't seem good enough, what with his simple manners and his humble background. What did she know about Rudolf's commercial affairs, anyway?

'Would anybody like an aperitif?' Ella noticed how grateful Rudolf was at the waiter's arrival, and she hoped there would be no further discussion of business matters. It seemed to be a topic that Rudolf strongly preferred not to talk about over dinner. He didn't return to the subject, at any rate. Ella couldn't blame him, though she wondered why Otto looked at the other man so pensively. His expression brightened up once more after the aperitif, however, and his invigorating smile returned. The evening was saved.

CHAPTER 5

You didn't need to be clairvoyant to predict that Rudolf and Otto's friendly mealtime relations would cool off after the previous evening. The first sign of it came when Otto failed to appear at breakfast as usual – and he certainly wasn't ill, since Ella had spotted him taking his morning stroll on deck. It was a pity that the otherwise harmonious mood on board had hit a sour note today of all days, for the *Danzig* was now steaming towards Lisbon. They were finally within view of land again, and it was a sight for sore eyes. The Portuguese coast was blessed with sandy beaches and an extraordinary amount of greenery. Lisbon itself was situated in a bay on the northern bank of a river, which widened into a sort of inland sea before narrowing again as it joined the Atlantic. The city was spread along the river's shores.

Ella had learned that nearly one hundred and fifty years earlier an earthquake of enormous proportions and an accompanying tidal wave had reduced Lisbon to rubble, costing thousands of lives. Only a few buildings had survived the tremor. Her father had once told her about the Belém Tower, which every ship entering the harbour had to sail past, just as they were now doing on this glorious morning. The square, white tower loomed before them, around one hundred feet tall and capped with four turrets. The remains of a fortifying wall could be seen underneath it too. Father had also told her that there must once have been a second tower opposite it, and that the Portuguese had used the two buildings to bring enemy ships into a crossfire. That tower had suffered the same fate as the rest of the city during the earthquake. It came as no surprise to see that none of the buildings now drifting into view were dilapidated or in need of renovation, and that the city's brightly coloured, multi-storey houses looked so magnificently modern.

Lisbon was a young city that seemed to grow from the river up into the hills. Ella was keen to explore and hoped that the *Danzig* would stop in the port for at least a few hours, so she asked the waiter, who confirmed that that would be the case. Five whole hours to look around. That would be particularly worthwhile in a city whose bustling centre was so easily accessible on foot.

'What do you say to a stroll through town? Perhaps we can buy a few souvenirs?' she suggested to Rudolf, who – like Ella and all the other passengers – was standing at the railing admiring the handsome buildings, squares and boulevards. The streets looked as though they had been plotted with a ruler and seemed more spacious and less confined than in cities that had grown gradually over the centuries.

Surprisingly, Rudolf seemed to need a moment to mull over her proposal.

'The local racecourse is meant to be terrific. The Portuguese are mad for horseracing,' he replied – and to Ella's amazement, even Otto (who must have unobtrusively joined them and overheard their conversation) agreed with him.

'Indeed – *O Americano*,' he trilled, drawing a bewildered look from Rudolf and Ella.

'What do the Americans have to do with it?' asked Ella.

'The racecourse. That's its name,' explained Otto.

Because Otto seemed to share his obvious enthusiasm, Rudolf refrained from retorting with his usual aristocratic bearing. All the same, Ella could see that Otto's inexhaustible general knowledge remained a thorn in Rudolf's side.

'We could take a carriage. We'll see more of the city that way, and it'll be more comfortable too.' Rudolf's arguments were persuasive.

Nonetheless, Ella pulled a sceptical face, as she wasn't especially keen on horseracing.

'Is there even a race on today?' she asked in the hope of persuading them both that there would be no point in visiting an empty racecourse.

'Yes, our waiter is going too. He heard it from the captain.'

Ella realised she had made a tactical error.

'Well, if we have to.' Her reluctant agreement was nonetheless accepted with enthusiasm. Yet Ella didn't regret her decision, for the racecourse lay on the edge of the city, which meant she was given a full tour. On foot, she probably wouldn't have seen anything beyond the few buildings in the port, or perhaps she would just have made it as far as the Praça do Comércio – which Otto, in his capacity as self-appointed tour guide, described as a shining architectural example of how the Marquês de Pombal had rebuilt the Lower Town of Lisbon after the 1755 earthquake. Ella had to admit that it felt good to cross this spacious square in a stately carriage and admire the buildings with their beautiful arcades. They also passed the newly opened railway station, known as the Rossio. Ella had never seen such unusual, horseshoe-shaped entrance portals before, though the bell tower in the middle of the station façade made it look more like a government building. Otto even knew that it was a terminus station, and that it had been completed only two years ago. Rudolf's face grew longer and longer in response to Otto's extensive general knowledge.

'It's a good thing that the library on the *Danzig* is so well stocked,' said Otto, who had evidently noticed Rudolf's expression and pulled a small book out of his jacket pocket.

The racecourse proved more worthwhile than Ella had expected, not because of the horses or the building, which looked fairly new, but rather because the crowds in attendance were so interesting. Stylish women promenaded up and down in tailored dresses, and those who considered themselves particularly elegant also carried parasols. It was more exciting than any Parisian fashion show. From among the mass of people on the turf, Ella heard voices speaking English, German, Dutch and, naturally, Portuguese, and it was no different on the grandstand. Once they reached the stands, however, the tedious part of the proceedings began – although that was apparently a view held only by Ella. Rudolf and Otto had acquired betting slips and placed their wagers, albeit after only a cursory inspection of the horses and a quick glance at the odds.

'In my experience, it's usually the second favourite who wins it,' Rudolf declared.

For once, Otto had no experience and nothing to add, so he acquiesced to Rudolf's enthusiasm and placed a bet on the same horse. That evidently boosted Rudolf's ego. A ceasefire was thus declared between the two great rivals, though it lasted only until Rudolf's theory was proven false. The first race was won by the favourite, while the second went to the horse in third rank.

'Ach, never mind. At least we had the pleasure of watching and sharing in the excitement.' So Otto brushed off his substantial loss of one hundred and fifty marks, which he had paid in at the counter just like Rudolf. All the same, his face had a slightly red tinge to it. Rudolf, by contrast, had gone elegantly pale, as was becoming for a blue-blooded gentleman.

Ella refrained from passing comment.

'There must be a lavatory around here somewhere.' Otto withdrew, presumably partly to avoid any further discussion of their not inconsiderable loss.

'I think I'd like to take a look at the stables. Would you care to join me?' asked Rudolf. He must have known that the question was purely rhetorical, since he had asked her the same thing shortly before the races, and she had declined. He seemed to need a little time alone to compose himself after his disastrous bet.

'I'd rather stay here and look at the people,' she answered truthfully. Rudolf nodded, and just a few moments later, he had been swallowed up by the crowd on the steps. What was there left for her to do beyond watch the next race? In the final analysis, men all seemed to share a certain compulsion to gamble. At any rate, spending time with her 'fiancé' was anything but boring. But could she really agree to marry such a man? Ella wasn't sure. The question now preoccupied her far more than the elaborate hats of the women around her, which she would have liked to inspect more closely. What had happened over the last few days to the fluttery sensation that she usually experienced by Rudolf's side? The waves must have lulled it to sleep, just like everything else. Every now and then it reappeared – especially when he flashed her his rakish smile, or let her take his arm – but it was no longer as strong. Yes, she liked him, despite his obvious weaknesses and affectations. And she couldn't thank him enough for coming with her on this journey. Ella decided to dismiss the thought and focus on the elegant ladies' hats once more.

◆ ◆ ◆

They had agreed to meet at the carriage no later than half past four so that they could make it back to the ship on time. Ella was already there, but alone and kicking her heels. As far as she could recall, Rudolf always carried his watch with him, hanging from a gold chain and tucked inside his waistcoat pocket. She had noticed Otto holding a pocket watch too. On top of that, there was a clock mounted on the grandstand that was impossible to miss. It gave the time as twenty-five to five – yet there was still no sign of the others. Ella scanned the crowds on the grandstand and by the exits. They definitely weren't there. Should she go down to the stables after all? Had something happened to Rudolf? Horses were unpredictable, and Rudolf could be reckless. What if he'd unwittingly approached a stallion and made personal acquaintance with its hooves? All kinds of scenarios presented themselves to Ella – yet none of them accounted for Otto's absence.

Ella's state of uncertainty came to an abrupt end, however, and her worst fears seemed to have been realised, for Rudolf was staggering towards her, holding a handkerchief to his brow. Thankfully Otto was by his side.

She hurried over to meet them.

'In the name of God, Rudolf, whatever has happened? You're bleeding! Let me take a look.'

Rudolf lifted the handkerchief from the wound.

Ella could see at a glance that he had suffered an abrasion, which needed to be cleaned urgently.

'We need some fresh water.'

'Already taken care of. We went to the washrooms,' remarked Otto, who was remarkably calm under the circumstances.

'Those damned gypsies!' Rudolf cursed, pressing the cloth back down over his forehead. It was clearly painful, as his face contracted into a grimace.

'Gypsies?' asked Ella.

'I went to the stables and they attacked me there. Three young men. All of them obviously troublemakers. If you can't tell from the rags they wear then you can smell it on them. They stole my wallet.'

'You can count yourself lucky that it wasn't any worse. Their sort often carry knives,' said Otto.

Rudolf nodded stoically, conceding the point.

'At least my papers are all still on the ship. But what should I do now? All my money is gone,' said Rudolf.

'You had all your cash with you?' asked Otto.

'Should I have left it on board for somebody to steal it from me there? You hear of that happening to people all the time,' Rudolf tried to justify himself.

'But not on the *Danzig*,' objected Otto.

Even now, the two of them couldn't stop chipping away at each other. Ella resolved to put an end to it, and put her arm around Rudolf. Her proximity and her consoling gesture would surely do him good.

He visibly relaxed at her touch.

'I'm glad that you escaped with just a fright,' she said.

'If only it were just a fright,' lamented Rudolf, wincing with pain once again.

'Men are all such milksops. It's a harmless graze. You'll be right as rain in a few days. It won't even leave a scar. Besides, I have enough money for both of us.' Ella did her best to cheer him up.

Rudolf nodded hesitantly and gave her a grateful look, but Otto seemed irritated by her remark.

'We should hurry. I don't expect they'll wait forever, not even for first-class passengers,' Otto pointed out.

Ella found it strange that Otto showed so little sympathy. He certainly wouldn't talk that way if he had been the one robbed. Ella expected to hear further barbed remarks from Otto on the way to the carriage but surprisingly he refrained, and simply eyed Rudolf thoughtfully instead. Was she imagining it, or did Rudolf return his pensive look when their eyes met for a long moment by the carriage?

Ella was still amused at how pathetic men could be. She found it entertaining to see Rudolf stand in front of the mirror every morning to monitor how his graze – for it was no more than that – was healing. She had seen similar behaviour at the hospital. Men always believed themselves to be terminally ill. Rudolf's injury was barely worth mentioning, and would have healed on its own even without the salve they got from the on-board pharmacy. Mommsen, the ship's doctor, had also made light of Rudolf's hypochondria.

'I fear we'll have to keep you here in the infirmary,' he had jokingly threatened. By now, Rudolf had recovered his sense of humour too – and in the meantime, absolutely everybody on board had heard about the robbery. He seemed to enjoy recounting the tale, which grew more dramatic with each telling – he should start writing adventure stories. But it went down well with their fellow passengers, and provided Rudolf with the attention he apparently needed. Ella found it all rather amusing, for she could tell her own heroic stories about all kinds of injuries from her day-to-day work, and yet during her pre-dinner strolls every evening, she would still be approached by anxious women asking how her fiancé was bearing up. Otto too had just appeared on deck and was wandering in her direction, so she expected to hear a similar enquiry now – but none was forthcoming. He nodded politely in greeting and joined her at the railing.

'Beautiful, isn't it?' he said, looking out at the sea in front of them. He didn't say so much as a word about the fact he hadn't joined them at dinner for the last three nights. Ella had seen him in the company of two civil servants on one evening, an English spice merchant on another, and on a further occasion he hadn't appeared at all. The reason was obvious: he and Rudolf were avoiding each other. Was he here to talk to her about it? If so, it seemed he needed to approach the subject indirectly.

'You're a nurse, aren't you?' he finally began.

'Yes, I am. Why?'

Otto seemed to be struggling with himself, but in the end, he turned away from the sea and looked straight at her.

'Did Rudolf tell you that he was struck with a blunt object?' he asked in a serious tone.

Ella could make no sense of this, and paused to consider whether she had noticed this detail in Rudolf's version of the story.

'No . . . he only told me that he was attacked.' Now that she thought about it, Ella found that strange. After all, he had described everything else to her in the liveliest detail.

'Perhaps one of the men punched him. Gypsies sometimes wear large rings.' As soon as she said it, Ella realised that although that was possible, it was unlikely, as the wound would have looked different. It was too large to have been caused by a fist.

Otto gave her a correspondingly doubtful look.

'Why do you ask?' Ella enquired.

'I've spoken to various people; nobody saw any gypsies. The area was closed off, and the stables are located on the premises. How would they have even got inside?' continued Otto.

'I hope you don't mean to imply that Rudolf . . .' Ella began indignantly.

'I'm not implying anything, but I can tell you what I saw,' he interrupted.

Ella grew hot. Why in the world would Rudolf invent such a story? No normal person would do that.

'The lavatory was on the way to the stables, so I thought it would be interesting to have a peek at them. They were certainly interesting. But what was much more interesting was the fact that Rudolf clearly injured his head on one of the beams in there.'

'What?' Ella was unable to say anything more. She realised that Otto would have no reason to invent his story either, unless his goal was to discredit Rudolf.

'But why would he tell everybody about the gypsies?' pondered Ella.

'I don't want to make any accusations, so I leave it up to you to draw the right conclusions,' answered Otto.

Off the top of her head, Ella could think of only one explanation. A person who struck their head so hard against the beam of a stable must be very clumsy indeed.

'I'm sure Rudolf would have been very embarrassed to have had such a silly accident,' she reasoned.

'Certainly . . . Very silly indeed, since he didn't hurt his head on one of the cross-beams; rather, he struck it against a beam that held up two upright posts attached to the wall.'

Ella feverishly considered how he might have injured his head against a wall like that.

'Did you see it happen?'

'He stood in front of it and scraped his head against it. His face was twisted in pain,' said Otto.

Ella struggled to make sense of that at first, and endeavoured to come up with an explanation.

'Perhaps you just didn't see the gypsies. They might have pushed him against the wall . . . during a scuffle.'

'Possibly,' said Otto, more to himself. He didn't seem entirely convinced.

'You don't like him, do you?' asked Ella frankly.

'I like you,' he answered, before taking a deep breath. 'You know, throughout my whole life, I've always been able to rely on my gut instincts. There's something fishy about this story. I simply wanted to ask you to – just . . .' Otto groped for words, and found them after another deep sigh: 'Just be careful.'

'I'm sure I don't know why,' said Ella automatically, in Rudolf's defence.

'You're obviously wealthy, otherwise you couldn't afford a first-class ticket,' Otto replied.

'What do you mean by that?' Ella didn't like the turn this conversation was taking. 'Rudolf moves in the best circles and is a family friend,' she stated.

Otto remained silent.

'I mean no offence, Miss Ella. I wish you a pleasant evening,' he said, before turning away from her and continuing his stroll.

'Careful?' murmured Ella to herself. Why in the world did she need to be 'careful'?

What with all the new impressions she had been bombarded with over the last few weeks, Ella had finally brought herself to set them down in writing – partly in a letter to her mother, and partly as entries in a diary, although she didn't keep it as diligently as her father had kept his. Following their last stop in Colombo to take on coal, they had only four more days at sea before they arrived in Penang. Ever since they had reached the Indian Ocean, the days had grown so hot that the upper deck was now festooned with white linen canopies. Ella sat in their shade, feeling the cool sea breeze blow across her face, and leafed back to the beginning of her diary. Now that they were so close to their destination, it felt good to take stock of the journey.

The first entry had been written on the evening of their excursion into Lisbon. In hindsight, she was amazed at how agitated she had initially been following the events of that day. That was the advantage of a diary – you could look back on supposedly distressing events and laugh at them. Ella could clearly remember how she had wanted to confront Rudolf with Otto's suspicions in order to gain peace of mind. Yet instead, she had casually asked him exactly how he had sustained his wound, since Otto had noticed blood on one of the beams in the stable. It had been exactly as she had assumed. Ella read the underlined sentence in her diary: *The gypsies pushed Rudolf against the wall of the stable during the scuffle.* That had settled the matter – although Rudolf had plainly been surprised to learn that Otto had seen him in the stables.

All along the North African coast from Gibraltar, past Malta, to Egypt, Otto and Rudolf hadn't exchanged a single word beyond polite greetings whenever they happened to cross paths on board. Yet curiously, their ill feeling had lifted when they went ashore at the Egyptian trading post of Port Said.

Every day at sunset, a bewitching display of colour is reflected on the surface of the sea – and after that, in the evening, the sight of the moon casting its pale light on the waters is a balm for the soul.

Ella smiled as she read this entry. It was impossible to bear anyone any rancour in such surroundings. During their trip ashore in the land of the pharaohs, Rudolf had even submitted to Otto's description of how Bedouins lived in a village to the south of the port without puffing up like a peacock.

Ella read on, and was once again amazed at the thirty-five thousand marks that the *Danzig* had paid to enter the Suez Canal. The passage had taken eighteen hours, but it had been worth it. Flamingos, egrets and pelicans had all put in an appearance.

The lakes behind the dams were simply magical. A colourful ribbon lined their sparsely vegetated shores, with the desert beyond shimmering in gold.

Ella sighed at the memory of this natural spectacle, and the sound woke up Rudolf, who had been dozing in a lounger alongside her all the while. He stretched and looked at her sleepily.

'Your diary . . . I should write a diary too. What are you reading about right now?' he asked.

'Suez, and the journey past the mountains of the Sinai Peninsula. Do you remember those blazing colours – everything bathed in light, and those gleaming bluish shadows?'

Rudolf closed his eyes and nodded, relaxing at the memory.

'I can also vividly recall that blazing heat,' he added.

Ella had to agree. There had been no cooling sea breezes in that region. Over the Red Sea, the air was still, and the columns of smoke from the funnels on the *Danzig* had risen almost vertically into the sky. Some of the crew had been forced to stop working, and no wonder, for down in the engine room, the temperatures had easily reached around sixty degrees centigrade. Four of the work-ers had been taken ill with circulatory collapse, a condition that resulted in convulsions. Ella had helped the ship's doctor tend to the men, though all that had really been needed was to bring them on deck so they could rest and breathe in the fresh sea air. Cold compresses had also helped them recover.

'Do you remember the flying fish too?' asked Ella, although she knew what Rudolf would recall most vividly in that context. He nodded and smiled at her.

'Nobody at home will believe it. A fish leaping in a huge arc and landing directly in the chef's cabin,' he said. 'I also remember the lights in the sea on our second night on the Indian Ocean.' So Rudolf had decided to bring that up after all.

Ella could recall it too. Rudolf was referring to the pulsating colours of the sea – a magnificent spectacle that had revealed itself to them one cloudless night. Thousands upon thousands of jellyfish had risen from the depths like spirits, only to sink back down again, and the sea had genuinely begun to glow as a result. A luminous carpet drifting past them. Dolphins had accompanied their vessel in droves almost daily at that time. It was one of the most thrilling sights the ocean had to offer. On that evening, they had grown close to each other. Closer than ever before.

Why didn't I kiss him? it said in her diary. *I wanted to so badly when we were at home.* Even now, Ella was unable to answer that question, though she had vowed to herself that she would carry that beautiful moment in her heart for the rest of her life. It was hard to imagine a more romantic evening: dinner on deck under a starlit sky; a glass of red wine; reminiscences about the voyage so far; loving glances; his hand on hers; the same flutter she had experienced during their first encounters in Hamburg; and then the magical moment – the glowing lights in the sea, beneath a twinkling firmament. He had looked deeply, silently into her eyes, and she had seen that he desired her. She could see the same yearning in his eyes again now. Once again, she wondered why she couldn't give in to her own desire to kiss him. She had so often imagined how it would feel to kiss a man. His lips must be rougher than her own – would explore hers ardently. His kiss would surely heighten the fluttering sensation in her belly – would strengthen her desire to yield to him – yet once again, her mounting passion dissipated without a clear reason. Ella fended off his amorous looks with a kindly smile, which he accepted without pulling a face. Why couldn't she give way to her feelings and accept that she was growing closer to him – to her 'fiancé', who had played that part so impeccably? Ella didn't know.

Rudolf reached for her hand and, despite everything, she enjoyed the sense of closeness that came with it – though she also felt guilty for rejecting him during all these weeks at sea. She gave up searching for the reason, and all but forced herself to continue reading her diary. He would understand. She flicked forwards to their excursion into Colombo, where the *Danzig* had had to stop once again to take on coal. There had been plenty of time to explore the city, and they had been especially keen to visit Mount Lavinia and Victoria Park. The first of these was an exquisite spa hotel situated in front of a picturesque cliff face immediately overlooking the sea, and was run by a German landlord. How lovely their day in Victoria Park had been too – a landscaped garden full of beautiful trees, lakes and ornamental plants.

Rudolf's gaze lingered on her once more. It unsettled her. Had her behaviour towards him cooled lately because she didn't entirely trust him? It felt dishonourable to always answer him with a kindly smile, which he could only interpret as a promise that she would one day yield to him. The thought of that caused her smile to freeze over. Rudolf noticed, broke off eye contact and looked back up at the sky, where heavy monsoon clouds hung in the distance.

'It's been a wonderful voyage,' declared Ella out of pure embarrassment. What a meaningless phrase.

Rudolf ignored her. That he didn't pressure her was to his credit.

Yet Ella still felt like a traitor – to Rudolf, to his concern for her, and to herself. The soporific sea waves brought forth a certain lethargy, and over the course of the voyage, they must have lulled to sleep the attraction she had previously felt towards him. Perhaps her feelings would change once more when they reached their destination and found themselves on dry land – yet Ella was shocked to find that in her current mood, she couldn't even bring herself to hope that they would.

CHAPTER 6

As soon as the *Danzig* arrived in George Town harbour, Ella realised just how invaluable the English language skills she had acquired in London would be. Like the Malay Peninsula itself, the island of Penang was in British hands – an Imperial Crown colony. They had had eight hours to explore George Town, and only Rudolf had been identified as a foreigner by the local British residents, thanks to his unmistakable German accent. Ella wasn't surprised that the United Kingdom had snatched up this island to the south of Siam, for Penang seemed to be one big botanical garden. George Town itself was full of impressive villas boasting magnificent grounds, while the native stilt houses were scattered from the tropical green hills all the way down to the sea. Between these dwellings burst forth luxuriant palms, thickets of bamboo, banana plants, vines, tropical ferns, breadfruit trees, and a whole host of other colourful flora that Ella didn't recognise. The most impressive of these was a tree that must have been at least fifty feet tall, and consisted of a single trunk from which extended a fan of branches tipped with small palm leaves. Otto knew its name, of course – Ravenala, or the 'traveller's palm'.

The first few hours on shore had been exhausting, and they were all glad to be back on board. It was just as hot there, but substantially less humid, for there was always a breeze in the harbour.

'It feels as though somebody is constantly slapping me in the face with a hot, wet towel.' Rudolf summed up how they all felt.

It seemed to grow hotter by the hour on board as they made their way south. According to Otto, there were pirates operating in the Strait of Malacca, but they didn't encounter any, thank heavens. They probably preferred to target small sailboats, and would never attack a steel colossus like the *Danzig*. That was Rudolf's theory, and Ella found it both plausible and reassuring.

The temperature didn't drop even at night, as the *Danzig* finally entered the port of Singapore and moored at the Borneo Wharf, the landing stage belonging to the North German Lloyd. The harbour was gigantic, and lay behind a handful of small islands from which the lights of countless stilt houses cast a golden glow on the now ink-black sea. As far as Ella could tell, every single passenger was on deck to admire the view and to catch a first glimpse of Singapore.

But it wasn't just the chaos of the brightly lit port that nipped all romantic stirrings in the bud. Now that they had reached their destination, the many questions that had gnawed at Ella before her departure returned to the fore, and were suddenly joined by new ones. Had Father known this Richard for a while already? Where exactly had this mysterious man handed her over to his care? Was her real mother a whore, or was there another reason why her natural parents had given her away? On top of that, she needed to get used to the idea that the country now spread out before her was really her homeland.

Even before their luggage was unloaded, Otto had offered to help them with anything they needed. For his part, he would remain in Singapore to meet with local businesspeople. It went without saying that they would disembark together.

'I can recommend a hotel to you – unless you wish to continue your journey today? I'll be staying there myself.' Otto's offer had convinced even Rudolf to follow suit.

Standing with all that luggage on a foreign dock in the midst of the hustle and bustle of the port left Ella feeling rather forlorn. It was all so alien, and the new sights and sounds overwhelmed her. In addition to that, the mix of ethnicities and cultures made her mind swirl as the realisation dawned that she was the foreigner here. Around her, people of all nationalities and races flooded the docks – mostly, she guessed, these were Chinese, Malays and Indians. There was a lively jumble of dock workers, fruit sellers with their wheeled stands, and passengers, who either poured towards the jetties where smaller boats were moored or simply stood around and watched the goings-on in the port while they waited for their ships to depart. Ella was so busy trying to process all these different impressions that she didn't even manage to cast a final look back at the *Danzig* to bid it farewell, as she had planned to do.

'We should take a rickshaw.' Otto was now in command, but neither Ella nor Rudolf knew what he meant by that statement.

'A what?' asked Rudolf.

Otto pointed to a handful of miniature two-wheeled carriages at the side of the road, though not one of them had a horse harnessed to it. Instead, they rested on two wooden beams that lay on the floor. Ella thought she could see some Malayan 'coachmen' standing in front of them.

'A Japanese invention. They're quick, manoeuvrable and ideal for short distances,' explained Otto; yet only after the muscular Malays had loaded their bags onto four rickshaws – they needed that many due to the sheer volume of Otto's luggage – and gestured for them to board did Ella realise that the vehicles would be drawn not by horses but by humans.

Otto spoke to the men in their own language – Ella understood only the words 'Beach Road' – and then they were off, at considerable speed. She had grown weary after just a few steps in this humidity, but the men pulling these rickshaws seemed completely untroubled by the heat.

'Where are we going, anyway?' Ella called ahead to where Otto was seated.

'To Raffles. A small but very fine hotel,' Otto answered, shouting over the background noise of the street and what sounded like the chatter of a thousand voices.

After a journey of just a few minutes past seafront stilt houses and a handful of villas on the landward side of the road, Raffles came into view. It lay in an idyllic spot, directly overlooking an inlet of the sea. The regal-looking driveway was lined with palm trees and had a stately air, while the three-storey whitewashed building with its arcades on the ground floor gave the impression that it had been built fairly recently. Its location and its sea views were beyond compare.

'It isn't the cheapest hotel around here, but that improves your chances of getting a room. I've already booked mine by telegram,' explained Otto once they had arrived at the entrance and had their luggage unloaded by the white-uniformed staff. At that moment, Ella decided it was high time to tell Otto the real reason she was here. He seemed to know everyone and anyone, so he might be able to provide them with some useful contacts to speed up their search for the sinister Richard F. A farewell drink, suggested by Otto, presented the ideal opportunity. Ella was surprised at how quickly the essentials were told. She only had time to take two sips of her drink, which a waiter had served to them as they sat on their rattan chairs, surrounded by palm trees.

'The matter seems clear enough to me. This Richard is presumably your real father, who wanted to get rid of his illegitimate child . . . Unless his wife had an affair and he wanted revenge; but I consider that unlikely, since as far as I'm aware, the former scenario is nothing unusual in this part of the world. He must be an

Englishman or a Dutchman. And however complicated or sensitive the circumstances that led him to do it, anyone capable of such a course of action must be a monster.' Otto's summary spoke to Ella's heart, and once again raised the question of whether she even wanted to track down such a 'monster' in the first place.

'I still need to know who he is,' she nonetheless replied, for her curiosity outweighed both her moral sensibilities and the accompanying fear. 'For that very reason,' she added, since Otto fixed her with a pensive look.

'We have to assume that he's rich, and owns a plantation . . .' Otto was lost in thought for a moment.

'But which plantation? What do people grow here in the south?' asked Rudolf.

'If he's wealthy, we can discount everything other than palm oil or rubber. There's plenty of money to be made here with tin too, but you won't find that on a plantation. Besides, the profitable tin mines are all in the north of Malacca. In any case, I would start by looking for people who cultivate rubber trees locally,' Otto advised.

'What makes you rule out palm oil?' Ella enquired.

'Because the big rubber plantations are here in the south. There are admittedly a few small palm oil plantations around these parts too, but they aren't as big or as profitable as those elsewhere,' he explained.

'I'm not sure I follow you entirely. Why do you think it was somebody from the south?' Rudolf put Ella's thoughts into words.

'Your journey began as an infant at the port of Singapore. Firstly, the large monthly payments prove that he's a wealthy man, so we need only consider large and lucrative plantations. Secondly, we need to look at plantations in the south of Malacca, most likely between Singapore and Johore, since I can't imagine that anybody would take a newborn baby on a journey of several days across Malacca purely to give the child away in Singapore. He could easily have done it in

Penang, or in Trengganu on the east coast. So the plantation can't be too far away from the port here.'

'Most impressive. You would have made an excellent detective,' said Rudolf admiringly, without a trace of irony.

'I'll ask my trade contacts first thing tomorrow. The rubber buyers know almost every supplier there is, and I can't think there would be all that many families with surnames beginning with F who cultivate rubber in the south. If you like, I can also recommend a very nice boarding house in Johore. You'll get to the plantations quicker from there.'

'I don't know how to thank you,' said Ella from the bottom of her heart.

'If I'm entirely honest, I'd be just as interested to know about my own origins,' said Otto, speaking more to himself as he gazed through the palm trees out to sea.

Otto's encouragement washed Ella's final nagging doubts into the ocean. Yet the prospect that she might soon come face-to-face with her natural father was still a source of fear. What sane person would be determined to make acquaintance with the devil?

◆ ◆ ◆

Although Ella couldn't recall ever having slept in such a comfortable bed, and despite the luxuriousness of her room, she had only managed to get a few hours' sleep – and not just because of the heat, which even an electric fan mounted on the ceiling failed to dispel. Ironically, she could have enjoyed a long lie-in, since Otto could hardly be expected to return from the city with news that morning. There would even have been enough time for a leisurely breakfast with Rudolf, if he weren't still asleep. Ella therefore decided to postpone breakfast and walk down to the beach for a short stroll, so that she could digest her initial impressions of

Singapore and take in some new ones. The air was pleasantly cool in the morning; the heat of the sun was already making itself felt, but the air was free of its usual stuffy humidity. Small canoes floated along the shore past Raffles, reminding Ella of the poster she had seen by the office of the North German Lloyd. Malayan men really did wear nothing more than knee-length strips of fabric wrapped around their hips, while the 'skirts' worn by humble fishermen were even shorter. Two of the seamen smiled warmly and waved to her as they drifted past. They were young men and they outright stared at her – yet their gaze was not importunate; rather, she felt it was more the fact that the sight of a white woman must still seem rather exotic to them, despite their colonial rulers having lived in the region for many years. Ella took this encounter to be a warm welcome, and it strengthened her resolve to press on with her search for an unknown person in a completely foreign land. Yet for that, she needed Otto's help. It wouldn't do any good to present her case to the local police. After all, what evidence did she have beyond the confession of a dead man and a few bank statements?

Returning to the hotel, Ella decided to drink a cup of coffee on the terrace, and she selected a shady spot to sit. An Indian servant in a white uniform appeared instantly. At the next table, two Chinese men wearing resplendent outfits and with bare heads were sitting opposite a man in a white tropical jacket. They were drinking tea, and one of them held some documents in his hand. Businesspeople, no doubt. One never saw such exotic-looking figures in Hamburg, nor did anyone ever conduct their business in the open air – let alone in such a sweet-smelling ambience. Singapore seemed to be one big bottle of perfume, from both the blossom of countless plants and the tempting culinary aromas that had already begun drifting towards her from the many portable food stands. It was an intoxicating combination, and she had hardly seen anything of Farther India yet. Ella wished that the reason for her visit could be different. The heart-pounding unease she had felt on the previous day re-emerged suddenly when she spotted Otto. He had returned much sooner than anticipated and she had only just finished her coffee and eaten a pastry.

'Good morning, Miss Ella.' Otto's cheerful mood and broad smile couldn't be solely attributable to the beautiful morning, but surely had something to do with the document case he was carrying.

'Good morning, my dear Otto. I didn't expect to see you back before lunch,' Ella admitted. 'Did you manage to find anything out?'

Otto nodded cheerfully and sat down beside her.

'As I suspected, it was a good idea to visit the suppliers,' he said, opening the leather case in front of her. A handwritten list and a map immediately sprang into view.

'I don't want to build your hopes up too much, as I've been told that a few plantation owners have sold up, and some of them went back home to Europe. There were epidemics and harvest failures that forced them to give up their land. I can only provide you with the names of the plantation owners who still live here.'

'How many are there?' asked Ella.

Otto set the list out on the rattan table so she could read it.

'There are eleven rubber plantations with owners who have a surname beginning with F, and who my contacts tell me have at least one family member or worker named Richard. They're all Dutch or English.'

Ella examined the list: Ffresen, Fokkes, Ffeerinck, Fökkink, Fleerkatte. Those must be the Dutch names. Otto had written them down in a numbered list along with their addresses. Underneath them were some unmistakably English names: Francis, Forney, Foster, Fuller, Frye, Fowler. To her considerable surprise, the list went on. There must have been a dozen other names on it.

'Those are all the names beginning with F that belong to other nationalities, or to natives with smaller plantations. I've added them for good measure, in case the names at the top of the list prove fruitless,' explained Otto in answer to Ella's enquiring look.

'Do the numbers match the marks on the map?' she asked.

'That was the trickier part; however, a British friend of mine who has lived here for many years helped me with that. He had his foreman with him. I wouldn't have been able to sketch out the locations without his considerable local knowledge,' said Otto.

That explained the circles on the map, then.

'They're very far apart.' Ella foresaw weeks of wandering through the jungle with Rudolf.

'It will take you a while, but you can visit most of the plantations on a circular route starting from Johore. There's plenty of accommodation for travellers in this region. Or you could travel out and back to each of them in turn. That would take a day per trip.' Otto did his best to raise Ella's spirits.

'Thank you . . . I don't know how I can ever repay you,' she said.

'By looking after yourself, and by getting in touch with me whenever you need help. In a few days I'll be in Johore, staying at a boarding house that I would like to recommend to you most warmly. It's run by a Chinese woman named Lee – a very charming lady. I've written the address on the back of the list,' he explained, before standing up.

'Do stay for a cup of coffee or tea,' said Ella, and not just out of politeness. She had to admit that she had grown used to Otto's company, despite the tensions between him and Rudolf. And she would miss the interesting conversations they had had on board too.

'I've already had my tea, and I have a lot of appointments ahead of me. Besides, I won't be far away,' was Otto's friendly but firm answer.

All the same, Ella watched sadly as he disappeared towards the river.

Surprisingly, Rudolf seemed to genuinely regret having missed Otto. She showed him the map and the lists while he ate his breakfast, and he was full of praise for the man.

'No wonder he's such a successful businessman,' he said – from Rudolf's lips, a true compliment.

Speaking of 'business', German marks didn't get you very far in Malacca. According to the Indian waiter, there were a few shops that accepted alternative currencies, but only if you were prepared to incur substantial exchange costs. He therefore advised them to change their money into the local currency – ideally before the banks closed at twelve.

'We should base ourselves in Johore and visit the plantations from there,' said Rudolf unexpectedly, on the way to the nearest bank. Ella was surprised, since he didn't seem to have studied Otto's map in particular detail over breakfast.

'Shouldn't we try the plantations in the south first?' asked Ella.

'The distances are all very short, so it wasn't necessarily someone from one of the plantations closest to Singapore.' His argument couldn't easily be dismissed.

'Besides, consider the difficulty of travelling straight across the south of the country. We'll only manage it by travelling outwards from Johore. The roads connecting the plantations are unlikely to be of the best quality, so we should also make sure we hire a roadworthy carriage.' Rudolf was probably right there too. Ella didn't have much experience in reading maps, but it was true that the bigger roads radiated out from the cities towards the interior. That ruled out visiting the plantations marked on the map via a circular tour on unpaved roads.

'First of all, though, I'll try to arrange for some money to be telegraphed out to me,' said Rudolf as the bank building came into view.

'You don't need to do that, Rudolf. You're here on my account,' Ella reminded him.

'I didn't have an opportunity to do it on board . . . I don't mean to offend you, but it goes against my upbringing, and above all my disposition, for a woman to . . .' Rudolf tried to explain himself.

'It's an exceptional situation, and I'm sure it's only right and proper, considering that I have access to the financial resources that my father received for the very same reason we are here,' Ella declared.

Rudolf nodded reluctantly, before accompanying her obediently – and above all, with a more relaxed expression – to the Post Office Savings Bank, which stood in the main post office on Raffles Place, close to the hotel. The bank was housed in an impressive building, with a massive portico held up by columns and capped with two towers. According to the hotel reception, this was the cheapest place to change German marks into the local currency – the silver dollar, known in the region as the ringgit. Ella had feared that the bank would accept only pounds sterling, but they had no problems, although they had to pay an additional charge as their currency was uncommon in these parts.

'It would have been easier for us if your mysterious father had a tin mine,' said Rudolf as they reached the Chinese-owned carriage hire company – a recommendation from the helpful bank employees, and likewise easily accessible on foot.

'What makes you say that?' Ella enquired.

'Travelling by train would be more comfortable, and there would always be a breeze to cool the carriage,' answered Rudolf.

'There's a railway? In Malacca?' asked Ella incredulously.

'There have been railway lines in the north and east for a few years now. I know why too, thanks to Otto. That's where the tin

mines are, and the heavy ore needs to be transported somehow.'
The prospect of having to travel in an unroofed carriage through
the scorching heat, which grew almost unbearable in the afternoon,
was as unappealing to Ella as it was to him.

'They're selling straw hats up ahead.' Ella was glad to have spotted the market stall.

'A pith helmet would suit me better, though,' Rudolf countered
with a grin. He seemed to have recovered his sense of humour. He
also assumed responsibility for haggling with the carriage company,
negotiating a good price for two weeks. A small supplement would
then be payable for every additional day. Ella could live with that.

Everything seemed to be going miraculously smoothly.

Back at Raffles, the bags were quickly loaded and Ella was
told that the journey to Johore was perfectly safe, since they only
had to travel northwards across Singapore along well-paved roads
before making a short ferry crossing to the south coast of Malacca.
If they made haste, they would be able to reach Johore by the early
evening.

Ella reflected on how quickly her lethargy of the last few weeks
on board the *Danzig* had fallen away, despite the heat and the countless new impressions that this foreign and extraordinarily varied
culture was bombarding her with. The sheer rush of colours they
encountered at every corner as they drove their carriage through the
city was simply exhausting. Ella would have liked to take a closer
look at one of the magnificent Chinese temples they passed, with
their curved roof beams that were unheard of back in Germany. The
buildings themselves were generally decked in red and gold, and
from the street you could smell the incense sticks that the worshippers placed on the urns of their forebears – alongside banknotes, as
Ella had discovered during a brief stop at a well immediately in front
of one of the temples. All the same, the hour-long carriage ride to
the north still offered plenty of opportunity to feast her eyes on the

confusion of different cultures that coexisted here – and all in perfect safety, since Rudolf was the one holding the reins. That meant Ella could take in the sights and sounds of the region at her leisure.

As soon as they disembarked from the brief ferry crossing between Singapore and the southern tip of Malacca, all that colourful urban flair abruptly vanished. The houses here were smaller, flatter and humbler – though Ella remembered that Singapore's prestigious stone buildings were found only near the coast and at the harbour. The indigenous dwellings resembled huts or the sort of rustic stables that Ella knew from back home. Their roofs seemed to be thatched with reeds, and their frames were wooden. Yet even these habitations grew sparser as they continued on their way. Although they were at some remove from the coast and a long way from any water, many of the dwellings they encountered were still built on stilts. Wooden ladders led up into the living quarters, which had no exterior walls on the front, and therefore no windows or doors either.

'It's probably how they protect themselves against wild animals, though there's also more ventilation from below that way. After all, it's very humid here, and the monsoon must cause floods from time to time too.' With his background in real estate, Rudolf seemed to be in his element. Tall, pitched roofs and large windows would keep the interior cool, as the heat would rise and could escape through lateral openings underneath the roof. Rudolf must have secretly read all this in the library on board the *Danzig*.

For her part, Ella had eyes only for the carvings on the houses that they passed close enough to admire.

Initially they had been surrounded by thick tropical vegetation that made it impossible to look into the hinterland beyond the edge of the road, but halfway through their journey, the jungle was gradually beginning to clear. There was a fork ahead of them, which prompted Rudolf to stop the carriage and study Otto's map. As he did so, Ella stood up, in hopes of catching a glimpse of Johore in the distance. A handful of houses offered the only hint that they were approaching the town – though Otto had said that it was really more of a village. In the other direction, an even green extended to the horizon. Ella squinted to see better against the light of the setting sun. She felt sure that there was an offshoot of a rubber plantation in front of her, for the trees were far too regularly planted to have sprouted according to Mother Nature's sense of order.

'That way leads straight into town,' said Rudolf, pointing in the direction of the area where Ella had seen a few initial houses scattered across the landscape. She took a look at the map in Rudolf's hand just to make sure.

'The other route looks a little shorter, though,' she pointed out.

'If we travel that way then we'll cross a plantation,' said Rudolf, who didn't seem particularly keen on the idea.

'Indeed, and it's one from Otto's list too,' Ella went on, having spotted one of his markings on the map.

Rudolf looked sceptical – presumably because the alternative route offered a paved road. Yet it really was longer, since it curved around the edge of the rubber groves.

'We could ask somebody about this Richard while we're there,' Ella suggested. She saw no reason to take a detour. Why not kill two birds with one stone?

'At this time?' Rudolf objected.

'There might still be somebody working the fields.' Ella couldn't bear to waste valuable time for the sake of politeness. Besides, the track through the plantation didn't look all that bumpy, although it was narrower than the road that lay ahead of them.

Rudolf gradually seemed to warm to the idea.

'How should we broach the subject? After all, you can hardly ask them directly about your real father, can you?'

Ella was well aware that this wouldn't be a straightforward undertaking.

'He must be around the same age as my father. We need to find out if he was a worker or a plantation owner, and whether or not he's still alive,' she summed up.

'And how do you plan to ask all that?' Rudolf looked flummoxed.

Ella's morning cab rides to the hospital in Hamburg had given her plenty of practice in coming up with plausible excuses, and a few ideas presented themselves already.

'Perhaps somebody called Richard lent me some money in town, or left something lying on a bench,' Ella mused.

'I could pass myself off as a businessman – somebody like Otto. Tell them that the plantation was recommended to me.' Rudolf's grey matter kicked into gear.

'Well then, what are we waiting for?' asked Ella.

'I'm still sure we won't encounter anyone at this time of the afternoon, though,' interjected Rudolf once more.

'Who does the plantation belong to, anyway? After all, it's the first one we've encountered since leaving Singapore, so it's a very likely candidate,' said Ella.

Somewhat hesitantly, Rudolf consulted the numbered list of plantation names. Ella guessed that his reluctance was because he was tired and didn't want to have to tackle the possibly more challenging route through the plantation.

'The Foster plantation,' he finally answered.

'Richard Foster,' said Ella, more to herself. The idea that this man might be her real father sent a shiver down her spine.

'It would be better if we found some lodgings, had a bite to eat and then set off first thing tomorrow morning.' Rudolf was as stubborn as a mule. He wasn't normally so averse to spontaneity.

'Would you do me the favour if I implored you? I won't sleep otherwise,' said Ella. No gentleman could possibly turn down her request, and her plan met with success. Rudolf was unable to cast off his self-appointed role, and gave a sigh of resignation as he put the map back in its bag; but then he reached for the reins more spiritedly and steered the horses towards the Foster plantation.

Ella had never previously considered where rubber came from or how it was produced, though she was familiar with the rubber tree as an ornamental plant. The first thing she noticed on the wide track through the rubber plantation was an intense odour that reminded her of cut flowers, although the scent was a little sweeter than that. Within this shady forest of tall trees crowned with thick oval leaves, the fragrance was most intense in the areas where the rubber was being harvested. Native workers used long knives to cut through the bark of the trees. So much for 'we won't encounter anyone at this time of the afternoon'. Ella withheld an ironic remark, however, as she was fascinated by the sight.

'They scrape the bark away from the trunk, and the tree starts to bleed,' explained Rudolf, who was just as interested as she was.

A white fluid flowed along a channel carved into the trunk before collecting in a small bucket attached to the tree. Dark-skinned young men flitted through the forest, clad only in aprons wrapped around their hips. Most of them were busy pouring the small containers into larger pails, which they tied onto wooden yokes with ropes. They then lifted these onto their shoulders to distribute the weight more evenly and make it easier to carry. The men looked like living sets of greengrocers' scales, struggling to maintain their balance with each step. The workers carried the buckets to a large cart that was drawn not by horses but by water buffalo, which were presumably stronger and better suited to transporting heavy loads.

'Back-breaking work,' remarked Rudolf.

Just then, Ella heard the sound of a rapidly approaching horse. The dull thud of its hooves on the hard forest floor was unmistakable. She turned round and saw a young Malay man riding towards them.

'I hope we're allowed to use this road. It might be private,' speculated Rudolf, who had also noticed the man.

Once the rider reached them, however, their doubts were dispelled by the warm smile with which he greeted them. The young man must have been in his early twenties, and unlike the workers, he was wearing a pair of trousers and a white shirt. His thick, black hair was well-groomed and he was extraordinarily attractive. Only his almond eyes and tanned skin showed him to be Malayan.

'Where are you going?' His English betrayed only the slightest hint of a Malayan accent.

'To Johore,' answered Ella.

He brought his horse into step with their carriage and Ella noticed that he seemed to study her for just a moment too long. Perhaps that was because white women didn't generally wander into this part of the peninsula.

'Around half a mile from here you'll find a fork in the road. Keep left – the path to the right is private,' he explained.

'Thank you,' replied Rudolf curtly. It clearly hadn't escaped his notice that the young man had addressed himself solely to his female companion.

Ella decided to take advantage of his obvious fascination.

'The private road leads to the Fosters' house, I presume?' she asked.

'Yes, why?' answered the rider in surprise.

'My father used to work in the rubber trade. He told us we would need to pass by the Foster plantation in order to get to Johore. If I remember correctly, it belongs to Richard,' she said in a conversational tone.

'You must be mistaken – there isn't a Richard Foster on the plantation,' the man replied.

Ella cast a meaningful glance at Rudolf. That meant they could already cross off one of the possible plantations. Rudolf looked amazed at how quickly she had elicited this information from the young Malay.

At that moment, a shriek rang out through the forest, followed by a confusion of voices in the local language. The rider immediately dug his spurs into his horse and rode up to a group of workers.

She watched in astonishment as two of the workers bound the wrists of a bare-chested young man, threw the rope over a sturdy branch, and hauled him upwards until he could only just stand on the tips of his toes. The lad kept shouting '*tidak*', which meant 'no' in the local language – one of the few words that Ella had retained from the ethnographic guide she had read in the library on board the *Danzig*.

One of the workers fastened the rope to the boughs of the rubber tree. An older, dark-skinned hulk of a man, whom Ella estimated to be in his fifties, emerged from the undergrowth. He looked Indian, and carried a whip in his hand. Ella could imagine what he planned to do with it.

Rudolf immediately slowed the carriage. He looked every bit as stunned as Ella.

'Rough customs,' he said in dismay.

Just then, the Indian seemed to notice them for the first time. His hostile glare spoke volumes. Evidently he expected them to leave immediately.

Once again, Ella heard a desperate '*tidak*' from the captive's lips, followed by a torrent of words she didn't understand. Even at a distance, it was clear that the man's entire body was trembling with fear. The Indian lifted his whip to cast the first stroke, but then the rider shouted something to him as he reached the scene of the action. He dismounted from his horse and entered into a discussion with the giant.

Although Ella couldn't understand a word, she could tell from his tone of voice that the young Malay was doing his best to win the Indian over.

Ella fervently hoped that the worker would be released. Perhaps it would help if they remained where they were and refused to drive on until the lad was free again. The presence of unknown observers might encourage them to leave him alone – but there, Ella was mistaken.

The Indian handed the whip to the young Malay and immediately took up position in front of the captive. He called something to him. Ella thought that the captive would once again beg for mercy – but he remained silent. Instead, he closed his eyes and clenched his jaw in expectation of his punishment.

The first stroke of the whip cracked against the man's back, leaving a red mark on his skin. Before the second blow, the rider turned to face them, as if he thought it wrong that they should watch this abhorrent spectacle. Ella couldn't believe that this pleasant young man was capable of such brutality; it just didn't conform to his warm demeanour and the winning smile he had flashed at them earlier.

The second blow of the whip came down on the captive's skin, and he gave a suppressed cry.

'Rudolf, we can't let this happen.' Ella was on the point of leaping down from the carriage to confront the torturer.

The third stroke of the whip left its mark.

Rudolf was the first to dismount, and he marched up to where the workers were assembled. 'Stop that!' he called to them.

The young Malay paused instantly, though he looked not at Rudolf but at her. Ella thought she could see in his eyes that whipping the worker sat uneasily with him.

'Go on your way,' the Indian ordered, turning to face Rudolf.

Ella couldn't bear to remain where she was any longer. She too dismounted and hurried over. She simply couldn't allow such a barbaric act. The only question was whether she or Rudolf could do anything to stop it.

'What did that man do to make you treat him like this?' Rudolf demanded of the Indian. Ella marvelled at his courage.

'What business is it of yours?' came the scornful reply.

'In the name of humanity, I ask you to let this man go.' Rudolf's voice was firm, earning the respect of the young Malay, at least. He lowered the hand holding the whip.

'Keep going,' the Indian commanded.

'Stop, or I will take the matter up with the owner of this plantation,' Rudolf threatened.

To Rudolf's obvious chagrin, the Indian merely laughed. It seemed the Fosters didn't care how their plantation workers were treated.

'I deserve it.' Astonishingly this interjection came in clearly intelligible English from the lips of the captive, of all people. He turned to face them, and his eyes seemed to beseech them to depart. With good reason too, for the Indian had by now drawn a machete from his horse's saddle and was holding it threateningly towards Rudolf.

'Please, go on your way.' The young Malay also urged them to leave – almost implored them. 'Everything is as it should be.'

The Indian – presumably the foreman of the plantation – made it unmistakably clear that he was not to be trifled with. His machete sliced through a branch as if it were paper. He fixed his eyes grimly on Rudolf as he wielded his blade.

'Rudolf, let's go.' Ella hoped he would listen to her.

'The lady has more sense than you. Go now.' This was presumably the Indian's final warning before he resorted to violence. Yet what had really moved Ella to give up on her rescue attempt was the imploring gaze of the young rider.

'Please, Rudolf,' she urged him, before anything worse happened.

Rudolf nodded reluctantly.

It almost seemed to Ella that the rider and his victim both breathed a sigh of relief. What a bizarre situation. Ella turned away and walked with Rudolf back to the carriage. Once they had reached it and Rudolf had helped her aboard, she turned back once more.

The workers were standing rooted to the spot. Nobody moved. Everybody seemed to be waiting for her and Rudolf to finally drive away. They did so with heavy hearts, and behind them, another whip crack echoed through the forest, followed by a shriek.

CHAPTER 7

Although Ella remained shocked to the core, not another word was spoken about the incident in the rubber forest for the rest of their half-hour journey to Johore, which proved to be bigger than Otto had described it. As they travelled from the edge of the town to the centre – the Colonial District – the stilt houses gradually disappeared, and even gave way to a few stone buildings, whereas Ella had been expecting a handful of huts. Nonetheless, the place was minute compared to Singapore. According to Otto's map, the boarding house he recommended with the rather uninviting name of The Dragon's Breath was close to the sultan's palace, and a peek through the palace gates as they passed revealed a huge, imposing building standing on a slight elevation and surrounded by land-scaped gardens. An unusually wide tower adorned the centre of the façade, which was made of light-coloured stone. With such a residence, it was easy to imagine how powerful and wealthy the sultans must once have been, and how they had controlled the fate of the country for centuries.

Now, however, the British were in charge, though Ella knew from her many conversations with Otto on board the *Danzig* that the old rulers still exerted influence over their sultanate and officially cooperated with their colonisers. They allegedly did so in order to hold together the melting pot of different cultures that existed here – but in Otto's view, that was just a flimsy excuse that allowed the British to snap up Malacca's valuable resources in return for preserving the sultan's status and wealth. Be that as it may, there was no shortage of ethnic or cultural diversity here either. An Indian temple standing right beside a Catholic church – the Church of the Immaculate Conception, according to the map – provided the best possible illustration of that. Nor did they have to wait long for their first Chinese temple. Ella had already spotted its red masonry.

The boarding house itself was also Chinese-owned, and The Dragon's Breath turned out to be tastefully decorated and was in no way as terrifying as its name suggested. They were greeted by an atrium decked in colourful tiles with an ornamental fountain at the centre, whose soothing plash could be heard from every room, since they all had windows that opened onto the courtyard. Ella could already detect the scent of incense emanating from the central room on the ground floor – presumably the reception – which was occupied by an older Chinese lady. That must be Lee, whom Otto had mentioned.

The name 'Otto Ludwig' instantly rewarded them with a beaming smile and two particularly lovely rooms. Ella would have gladly gone straight to bed, but now it was Rudolf who insisted that they plan out the rest of their search that very evening.

Before their food had even been served in the restaurant next door, he had laid out the map on the table and compared it to Otto's list of names.

'We can already cross one name off the list,' Ella remarked.

Rudolf seemed lost in thought.

'The Fosters, no? There isn't anyone called Richard on the plantation,' Ella prompted. He finally nodded and crossed out the word 'Foster' with a pencil.

'We should start in the south and work our way north,' he said, pointing at the relevant marks on the map.

'What do you think? How many will we manage per day?' asked Ella.

'No more than two. But it depends on the condition of the roads. And as for the plantations further north . . . In all likelihood, I think we'll have to find lodgings on the way.' Rudolf's assessment seemed realistic to Ella, judging by the roads they had travelled on so far.

'Perhaps we'll be lucky and the families will know each other,' mused Ella.

Rudolf's sceptical expression suggested just how likely he thought that was.

'We'll be on the road for at least two weeks, then,' Ella concluded.

'Unless we split up. I can travel more quickly on horseback than the two of us can by carriage. It must be possible to hire a horse here somewhere. You take the plantations to the west, and I'll try the ones in the north that are further away. What do you think?'

Ella took a closer look at the map.

'The roads here in the west look to be well paved. It'll only be a few minutes' drive – half an hour at most. I could even arrange for somebody to drive me. I'm sure it won't cost the earth.'

Rudolf nodded.

'I'm excited to see which of us finds your real father first. We should drink to that,' he declared as he saw the waiter approaching with their wine and two glasses.

'I worry that I'm just chasing a phantom,' Ella murmured.

'No, I don't think that's true,' answered Rudolf – surely just to lift her spirits. He seemed so convinced they would find this sinister Richard that Ella was utterly baffled by his confidence.

◆ ◆ ◆

The next morning, Rudolf had made Ella promise that she would hire somebody to drive her to the Ffresens' plantation. For his part, Rudolf would head north to investigate a Dutch plantation and a British one, as agreed the previous evening. It would be much quicker to get there on horseback, and he could manage two or even three plantations in a day that way. Ella wasn't an accomplished rider, but she also didn't feel like making small talk with a hired coachman. Nor could she find a driver at such short notice; that was a service offered only by big hotels, and it needed to be booked in advance. According to the owner of the boarding house, however, the route was safe, even for a woman. Ella therefore plucked up her courage and set out on her own. By all accounts, it was impossible to miss the Ffresens' plantation. There would be a sign pointing out where to turn off the road towards it. The only problem was that signs tended to become overgrown fairly quickly in these parts. Nonetheless, Ella managed to find it after just under an hour on the road.

Unlike the plantation she had passed through yesterday with Rudolf, there was grass growing between the trees here. She reasoned this was because the plantation was closer to the sea, and was therefore supplied with more moisture, although it also meant the air was much muggier here.

The main road was well paved and the house belonging to the Dutch owners already in view. Although she caught the attention of the workers, nobody asked any questions. As she trundled the last few yards up to the main house, Ella considered what reason she should give for her visit – but she had no time to come up with a suitable pretext.

'Richard! We have a visitor!' called an excited voice from somewhere in the house. It was a young voice, and belonged to a woman who couldn't be more than thirty years old, to judge from her appearance as she stepped out from the shadow of the veranda. A man of around the same age with red hair and a stubbly beard emerged from the barn opposite. Ella might as well have turned her carriage around right then and there, for the Dutchman was clearly too young to be her father – yet it was too late for that.

'You must be Elizabeth,' the young woman surmised as Ella brought the carriage to a halt in front of the house. For a moment, Ella considered saying yes, but that would inevitably lead to complications. Once again, her improvisational skills came to the fore.

'My name is Ella Kaltenbach. I was looking for Richard,' she announced. Ella could read people well, and she was sure that a little humour would help this young Dutch couple to accept her fabricated pretext for her search.

'My husband?' laughed the young woman, as Ella had expected. Likewise, Richard himself, who had by now reached the carriage, clearly took it as a joke and laughed out loud.

'We're always happy when people come to visit. It happens so rarely. Will you have a cup of tea with us? I've just made some,' said the woman, who introduced herself as Mila.

'Yes, please – but only if you tell me who Elizabeth is,' answered Ella.

'She's the new lady at the mission. They're collecting money, and I thought that you . . .' said Mila.

'I owe you an explanation too,' Ella began as the young woman beckoned her up to the veranda with a welcoming gesture.

'You certainly do!' said her husband, clearly tickled.

'My father passed away recently. He had a few debts, and one of the bills was made out to a Richard, whose surname began with an F. My mother spilled some water on it and we couldn't read the rest of the name. All I know is that he has a rubber plantation here in the south, and that he must be in his mid-fifties.'

117

'Darling, why don't you tell her that I'm in my mid-fifties?' joked the Dutchman. His wife laughed.

'We could make good use of somebody who wants to settle a few debts,' he went on.

'Ach, it looks like both of us are out of luck. But do stay for a cup of tea,' said Mila, as she poured a cup each for Ella and her husband.

'How long have you been living out here?' asked Ella.

'Since we were children, but we've only been running the plantation for seven years now. Seven years of bad luck! We took it over from my father,' said Mila.

'And you? How long have you been out here?' enquired Richard.

'Since yesterday,' answered Ella truthfully.

'How do you like Malacca?' Mila seemed genuinely interested, so Ella was only too happy to make small talk.

'It's very hot, but so colourful in every respect. The people are very friendly too. They smile so much.'

Mila nodded, and she too smiled.

'Not all that glitters is gold, though. I sometimes get the impression that civilisation hasn't quite taken full root here yet,' said Richard.

'Indeed. The local customs are rather harsh – if not outright medieval. Just yesterday I saw a worker being whipped on a plantation. He was so young . . .' Ella recounted.

'On a plantation?' asked Mila in surprise.

Ella nodded.

'That's unusual . . . Where did you see that?' Mila probed.

Ella preferred not to name the plantation directly – after all, it was nearby, and Ella assumed that the rubber farmers in the south would all know each other.

'In the very far south.'

'Not the Fosters' place?' asked Richard promptly.

Ella shrugged. A new arrival could hardly be expected to know her way around.

'That wouldn't surprise me,' said Mila.

'Why not?' Ella's curiosity was piqued.

'One hears all sorts of things about that farm. Many of the natives talk of strict discipline,' Mila explained.

'It's said that there's a curse on the property,' said Richard.

'A curse?' Ella gaped.

'Idle talk among the natives. Especially the workers from Sumatra. They see nothing but ghosts everywhere,' declared Mila.

'Idle talk is inevitable when somebody withdraws from the public eye and hardly ever appears in town. Ever since he died . . . Wait a minute . . . Didn't you say you were looking for a Richard? Marjory's husband. Your father always used to talk about him. He was called Richard, wasn't he, Mila?'

Mila nodded.

Ella instantly grew hot. To think that they had already crossed that very plantation off the list!

'When did he die?' Ella enquired.

'That must be twenty years ago now. When I was still a boy. It's a pity my father is no longer with us. He would have known the exact date,' said Richard after a moment's thought.

'Did he have any children?' asked Ella, her heart pounding.

'One ravishingly beautiful daughter. Her name is Heather. She must be nearly forty now. By all accounts, she used to be very vivacious. Father even danced with her once, at the harvest festival in Johore. Mother never let him forget it and would tease him about it all the time – that's why I remember it so clearly. I think she was jealous . . . but since then . . . we only saw Heather two or three times in town after that, I think,' recalled Mila, lost in thought.

'Yes, it's truly odd,' said Richard.

'Who runs the farm now?'

'Marjory, his wife.'

'Perhaps I should get in touch with her at the earliest opportunity,' mused Ella.

'I'm afraid you won't have any luck there. She rarely receives any visitors – not even the people from the mission.'

'That's how they are, the English. Splendid isolation.' Richard grinned.

Although there was no reason whatsoever to assume that the late Richard might be her real father, Ella couldn't let go of the name Foster.

'Did your father know this Richard well?' she asked.

'He didn't have a good word to say about him. It's all so long ago now, but my father always thought he was avaricious. He tried to buy our plantation on a few occasions . . .'

'Enough of that talk. One shouldn't speak ill of the dead,' Mila reprimanded her husband.

'Well, you've already seen what happens on his plantation, even all these years after his death,' Richard hinted nonetheless.

Ella nodded pensively. It seemed that Richard Foster had had a wicked streak. Hadn't Father spoken of the devil? Ella fervently hoped that she wasn't a blood relation of these Fosters.

In the end, Ella spent a very enjoyable afternoon with the young Dutch couple as they wanted to know all about life in old Europe, their parents' homeland, and she was happy to oblige. Their hospitality would remain in her memory for a long time to come. Yet on the way back to Johore, she found her thoughts once again circling uneasily around the Foster plantation. She tried to convince herself that her interest was due to the unpleasant incident she had witnessed and the fact that it was clearly an unhappy place. But she had to acknowledge that perhaps it was the talk of a curse on the plantation that made it seem more interesting than it really was. Ella forced herself to be reasonable, knowing very well that every visit she paid to any of the plantations on Otto's list would leave her feeling agitated. Each of them doubtless had its own story – some interesting detail that would make her imagination run riot. By pure coincidence, the Foster plantation was the first they had visited – though admittedly, its geographical proximity made it a more likely candidate to reveal something about her origins.

Yet Ella's unease refused to lift. There had to be more to it than that. Although she knew neither Marjory nor Heather Foster, she couldn't stop thinking about them. The daughter of the house was said to be very beautiful. Heather might be Ella's half-sister – perhaps even her sister – although strictly speaking, that would depend on the precise circumstances behind the events of the past and she couldn't grasp the implications of that idea. Ella cracked the whip to urge her horse on faster. She wanted to get back to her lodgings as quickly as possible to discuss what she had learned that day with Rudolf. He had promised that whatever happened, he would be back by dusk, and Ella guessed that sunset was less than an hour away.

In the end, she had no trouble getting back to the board-ing house before dark, but the same apparently couldn't be said for Rudolf, for when she pulled up in her carriage, his horse was nowhere to be seen.

Ella decided to tend to her own horse first, and led it up to a public trough intended for everybody to use. An elderly Malay woman was selling hay there.

Although Lee had already assured her that morning that Johore was a safe place, her sense of unease grew as the evening fell. The trough also attracted a horde of mosquitoes, as did the manure around it, and the effort of unharnessing her horse made her an easy target. Ella's face was drenched in sweat from the humid air and she waved and flapped her arms like a dervish, much to the amusement of three dark-skinned men who were standing across the road by a grocery shop. They obviously meant no harm, but Ella was still glad when her horse finally lifted its head from the trough and obediently allowed itself to be led back to the boarding house.

Just to make sure, she asked Lee if Rudolf had appeared and left a message for her. He hadn't, so she decided to sit in a wicker chair in the courtyard and wait for him – but after a short while, the feeling that all was not well became almost unbearable. She tried to convince herself that nothing would have happened to him; she had seen for herself how rough the roads could be in this part of the world, and distances were hard to gauge. He must still be on his way. Or perhaps he had also been met with hospitality elsewhere, and had used the time to make further enquiries.

After another hour spent pacing up and down like a caged animal, Rudolf still hadn't appeared, but Ella's stomach was beginning to growl.

Lee knew where she could find something to eat at this time.

'My brother runs a restaurant at the back of the building, but I think he'll be closing soon. There are a few stands on the big square at the end of the road, though. They're open at night too,' explained Lee.

'Please could you let Mr von Stetten know where I am when he arrives?' Ella could count on Lee to tell him. All the same, she wondered whether it would be better to wait, since it was now the middle of the night. Yet there were bright lights burning on the square at the end of the road, and even at this distance she could see there were plenty of people around. That removed any doubts she had about leaving her lodgings after dark. Besides, Rudolf would probably be back before long.

Ella was glad she had forced herself to join the crowds, but she couldn't help but feel a little uncomfortable, for it was clear at first glance that she was not just the only woman, but also the only European sitting at the tables in front of the small row of food stands. After studying the menu, Ella was relieved when two European-looking men sat down at a neighbouring table. Going by their pith helmets and white uniforms, they had to be British.

'I'll have the chicken curry.' Ella gave her order to a young Malay woman and then turned round to take a closer look at her surroundings.

A few stone buildings with their lights still on made her feel like she was back in civilisation, but that impression was soon undermined by the people's table manners. An Indian couple was sitting at the next table, and both of them were eating with their hands from palm leaves, which served as a sort of dish. They mixed the curry with the rice and kneaded it into small balls before eating it, leaving their hands and fingernails stained yellow. Other countries, other customs. Ella hoped she would be given a plate, as she had ordered from the same stand as the Indians. Some of the guests were squatting by a low wall that encircled a tall tree – mainly young men who were only having a drink. Still others were standing around in conversation. Ella then had to do a double take when she saw two lads approaching her holding hands. At first, she thought they must be a father with his adult son, but she had to dismiss that idea when they strolled into the light cast by the paraffin lamp mounted on the first stall. It seemed to be normal here for young men to walk around hand in hand. Nobody else took any notice. Ella watched the two of them in fascination as they examined the menu on the food stall and stepped fully into the light. Then she gave a start. There could be no doubt about it – she knew these men. The more athletic of the two was the rider they had met on the way through the Foster plantation, and the other was certainly the young worker whom he had flogged. And now they were walking hand in hand through town? Ella stared at the two of them as if hypnotised.

'Your lemonade,' Ella heard a voice say beside her. The young Malay woman was serving her drink.

Ella turned back to the young men and was shocked to see that they clearly recognised her too, and were now staring back at her. Then they began to talk – evidently about her. She had the impression they were debating something. A smile appeared on the rider's face, and the other gave a resigned shrug and nodded. This couldn't be happening! They started to walk towards her. Ella's breath caught. What did they want from her?

'*Selamat petang*,' they declared promptly when they reached her. By now she was familiar enough with the term to know it translated roughly as 'Good evening'.

Ella cautiously returned the greeting. She could sense the young rider's embarrassment. His companion was staring outright at the floor, as if he were ashamed of himself.

'I wasn't sure it was you,' said the man who had virtually jumped at the chance to whip his friend.

'Indeed,' Ella answered curtly. Although she found this meeting profoundly uncomfortable and she instantly pictured him before her with the whip in his hand, she decided to talk with him. After all, he worked for the Fosters.

'Ella Kaltenbach. And what's your name?' To take the initiative in this way and introduce herself first was a bold move – one that was considered unbecoming for a fine lady back in Hamburg. But she wasn't at home, and the ends justified the means in this case.

'Amar,' he answered, surprisingly bashfully, before pointing to his companion. 'And this is Mohan,' he added.

Ella examined them both as they stood somewhat nervously in front of her. She had already detected some curious glances from the British at the neighbouring table. Judging by their surprised expressions, they evidently considered it unusual for an unaccompanied European woman to converse with two Malayan men, and they were watching warily as a result.

'How is your back?' Ella asked Mohan.

'It'll be better in a couple of days,' he murmured, looking at the edge of the table. He still didn't dare meet her eye.

'Is everything all right, madam?' one of the British onlookers interrupted. He seemed genuinely concerned for her. Evidently the region wasn't so safe for women travelling alone after all.

Ella nodded at him and smiled, to his visible relief.

'There's plenty of room at the table. I'm sure you'd like something to eat too, wouldn't you?' Ella asked.

Amar and Mohan exchanged glances and then both nodded. It seemed that the situation took some getting used to for them too. The waiting staff and two other guests also looked up when the men sat down with Ella.

'I think we owe you an explanation,' said Amar.

Ella took a closer look at him. His black hair and brown eyes seemed to gleam under the paraffin lamp. Once again, she wondered how she could have misjudged him so badly. It was hard to believe that a man with such a gentle face was capable of flogging somebody.

'I borrowed a cart. We have so many, and I thought nobody would notice,' began the younger of the two.

'He brought it back, but somebody caught him,' Amar clarified.

'But that's no reason to whip anybody! Or is that the custom in your country?' asked Ella indignantly.

'No,' answered Amar, sighing deeply.

'But it is on the farm?' Ella hinted.

Amar nodded. 'It isn't right,' he added.

'So why did you flog him?' Ella demanded.

'Because Raj would have beaten me otherwise,' Mohan explained.

'You mean that bloodthirsty Indian giant?' Ella wanted to be sure she had the right man.

'Raj isn't bloodthirsty, but the Fosters have instructed him to punish things like that very harshly. Besides, Mohan is one of my workers. I'm responsible for him,' explained Amar.

It was slowly dawning on Ella why Amar had persuaded the Indian to let him take over Mohan's punishment.

'I know how to use a whip – how to hit somebody without hurting him very much,' said Amar in self-justification.

'Do they teach you that at school here?' asked Ella pointedly.

'No, I learned it on a cattle farm. Buffalo need to hear the crack of a whip from time to time, as they won't move otherwise,' said Amar, who had by now lost his initial reserve at the unfamiliar situation and was even smiling.

'So why do you work for the Foster plantation?' Ella couldn't figure the man out.

'They pay well, and this was the first incident of its kind,' he said. His companion nodded. He clearly felt it incumbent upon him to confirm what Amar said.

'I've only been on the plantation for a few months. The Fosters recently hired a lot of Malay workers who don't speak English, so they needed somebody who can speak both languages,' Amar continued. It sounded like an excuse.

'Your English is truly superb, from what I can judge as a German. Did you learn it on the cattle farm too?' asked Ella with a smile.

'I learned it at school. Thanks to our occupiers,' he answered, with a sidelong glance at their British neighbours. He didn't seem to hold them in high regard.

'Are you and your companion in the rubber trade too?' Amar asked.

'No . . . We're just travellers. Why do you ask?' Ella replied.

'I saw your companion this morning. He was riding along the road where we met yesterday,' said Amar.

Ella was startled. That was impossible. Rudolf had wanted to visit the plantations in the north.

'Are you sure?' she demanded.

Amar nodded.

Despite her best efforts, all the composure Ella had mustered so far immediately vanished. Her unease was impossible to conceal.

'Is everything all right? I hope I haven't said anything wrong . . .' Amar seemed to sense the agitation his remark had caused.

'He . . . Rudolf . . . I've been waiting for him since dusk. He was travelling alone, and . . . he still hasn't returned.'

Amar and Mohan exchanged glances.

'If you like, we could look for him,' Amar offered without hesitation.

'But where would you look? He might be anywhere.' Why on earth had Rudolf changed his plans?

'If he isn't back by daybreak then I will look for him,' Amar insisted.

'You don't have to. I'm sure he'll turn up . . .' Ella tried to sound optimistic.

'There are snakes around here, and the ways are treacherous. A branch on the road would be easy to miss, or his horse might take fright.' Amar's explanations weren't exactly reassuring.

'You aren't giving me much hope . . .'

'It's happened to me too in the past. But somebody always comes along. There's no need to worry.' His words were well intentioned, but just then they were far from consoling.

'Your chicken curry.' The waitress served it on a plate and with cutlery. Although it smelled delicious, she had lost her appetite. The idea that Rudolf might be lost in the jungle or lying helplessly on the side of the road made her stomach close up. Ella fished a few ringgits from her leather purse and placed them on the table.

'Don't you want it?' asked Amar.

Ella shook her head. 'If you like curry then please help yourself,' said Ella.

Amar ignored the food. He was visibly concerned at her agitation.

'I have a few biscuits in my room. He might already be waiting for me.'

Amar nodded sympathetically.

'If I hear anything . . . where can I leave a message for you?' he asked.

'I'm staying in the Chinese boarding house at the other end of the street,' she said, and stood up to leave.

Amar nodded.

Ella fervently hoped that Amar wouldn't hear anything about Rudolf's whereabouts, since whatever the truth turned out to be, she felt certain it wouldn't be good news.

◆ ◆ ◆

With every hour that passed, the hope that Rudolf would return to their lodgings that night dwindled further. After two more hours of pacing up and down the courtyard, Ella had given up waiting up for him there. Anybody who walked past the entrance and glanced inside would have wondered what she was doing there in the middle of the night. Yet she found no rest in her room either. More and more questions began to present themselves: about the Fosters, about Rudolf's presence on their property that day, and about Amar too – and not just how such a mild-mannered person knew how to wield a whip. He had been sitting on the steps of the house across the road for hours now. That meant Ella had two reasons for constantly going to the window overlooking the street: to keep watch for Rudolf, and to check whether Amar was still waiting there. Why was he doing that? To protect her? To launch a search for Rudolf if he didn't reappear by dawn? At any rate, there was no question of getting any sleep tonight. The oppressive humidity and an armada of mosquitoes played their part in that. There was nothing worse than lying motionless on the bed, staring at the ceiling, and finding no relief in sleep. For the fifth time, she got up and went to the window. Amar was sitting resolutely on the steps – as if he had taken root there.

After another hour of restlessness, Ella found it harder and harder to raise herself from the bed at all. Her body was tired, but her incessant thoughts stopped her mind from switching off. She had expected Amar to have fallen asleep by now, but he was still sitting upright in the same spot. From time to time, she saw his eyes gleam under the streetlight as he looked up at her window.

It must be five or half five in the morning by now and the sky was starting to brighten in the east. Ella gave up any further attempts to get some rest, and instead reached for her diary to write down at least a short summary of the last few hours. It felt good to unburden her soul in this way.

The next time she looked outside, the day was already dawning. Amar was still there. It was already so bright that he must be able to see her at the window. Was she imagining it, or did he smile up at her? She decided to write that down in her diary too, but there was no time. At first, she had assigned no special importance to the sound of an approaching carriage, since Rudolf was travelling on horseback. But then somebody drove into the courtyard of the boarding house. Ella hurried over to the other window that overlooked the atrium. Two uniformed policemen were standing by the fountain talking to Lee, who must have already returned for the early shift. She pointed up to Ella's window, looking deathly pale. Barely three minutes later came a knock at the door. Ella's heart began to race. She could put two and two together. Something must have happened to Rudolf.

When she opened the door, a middle-aged Malayan police officer with speckled grey hair stood in her doorway. His expression grave, he introduced himself as Officer Puteri.

'Miss Kaltenbach?' he asked, and Ella nodded.

'Has something happened to Rudolf? An accident? I've been up all night waiting for him,' she said.

'He was found by some farmers by the side of the road this morning. They couldn't do anything for him,' he explained, with great sympathy.

Ella grew dizzy and clung to the doorframe. It took her a moment to regain the faculty of speech.

'Did he fall?' asked Ella.

'We don't know, but there don't appear to be any external injuries. It was probably the heat. His heart may have given out, or perhaps he was bitten by a snake. We won't know for certain until the coroner completes his investigation.'

'Where did they find him?' Ella demanded.

'Around a mile outside Johore,' said the younger of the two officers.

'I'm very sorry . . . If there is anything we can do for you . . . The police station is in the town centre.' Puteri looked at her thoughtfully for a moment. 'Were you close to him?' he asked.

'He's a family friend, and he accompanied me on the journey here,' Ella answered. The fact that he had passed himself off as her fiancé on board and that she would have given anything to kiss him a few weeks ago was of no concern to the local police.

Puteri appeared satisfied with her response. 'You can collect his personal effects tomorrow,' he said.

Ella nodded.

'My deepest condolences,' said the younger policeman before he too turned to leave.

Lee was standing rooted to the spot in the corridor. Ella could see in her face that she was deeply affected by the news.

'I need to rest now,' murmured Ella in a choked voice.

Lee nodded understandingly and followed the policemen downstairs.

Ella closed the door behind her. For a moment she was unable to move. All the same, she felt drawn to the window to check whether Amar was still sitting there. He was. Ella opened it and revealed herself to him.

Amar looked up at her. The two policemen had just left the building and were climbing into their carriage.

Ella simply shook her head in response to Amar's questioning look.

She thought she could see sympathy in his eyes – he looked sad, and his shoulders sagged; there was nothing more for him to do. Amar stood, looked up at her once more, and then disappeared from view in just a few steps. Ella hoped that he would get some rest now.

She closed the window and finding she could no longer hold herself upright, collapsed exhausted onto the bed in the hope of recovering her strength with some sleep.

CHAPTER 8

Ella still felt utterly exhausted when she woke up, even though she must have slept until around midday, judging by the position of the sun. For a moment, she tried to convince herself that it had all been a dream. Rudolf was sure to be sitting in his room next door, and he would tell her all about his journey of the previous day over breakfast.

But he wouldn't. Rudolf was dead. Why should she even get out of bed? Should she carry on without him? Searching for a phantom, and exposing herself to all sorts of dangers? Was it even worth it? Ella seriously considered travelling back to Hamburg. Would anything in her life really change if she found out who her real parents were? Surprisingly enough, that last thought was what gave her the strength to get up, and a few gulps of water from the jug on the locker seemed to reinvigorate her spirits. Give up? No. Out of the question. Ella decided to freshen herself up, put on some clean clothes, have a quick breakfast and then go to the police station. Perhaps there would be some new information about how he had died. Besides, he apparently had some personal effects on him that needed collecting. She supposed these would be just his passport and his pocket watch, as well as the copy of Otto's map that he had drawn up yesterday morning.

Around an hour later, that same map was lying on the wooden counter of the austere police station, which was decorated only by two framed paintings of the sultan's family. The younger of the two policemen who had brought her the terrible news during the early hours of that morning was reaching into a linen bag for a second time. Ella was unsurprised to see Rudolf's passport and watch emerge – however, she could see that there was something else still inside the bag. The young policeman rummaged for it and then placed it on the counter. It was Rudolf's wallet.

Ella froze. Hadn't that been stolen from him in Lisbon?

'Could you confirm receipt?' asked the policeman, placing a document on the counter that listed the items.

Ella was unable to respond. Instead, she picked up the wallet and leafed through the banknotes she found folded inside it. There had to be at least three hundred marks in there.

'Is everything in order?' the policeman enquired.

'Certainly . . .' answered Ella, lost in thought, though that was far from the truth – and things grew even more puzzling when a receipt from the Lisbon bureau de change fell into her hands. Ella couldn't believe her eyes. Rudolf had exchanged one thousand marks. The betting slips tucked behind the receipt amounted to roughly the same amount in Portuguese réis. He had gambled away a small fortune.

'Mr von Stetten will be examined tomorrow. We still can't say what caused his death,' explained the policeman once Ella had finally looked up from the wallet.

She nodded mechanically. The cause of death was certainly of interest to her, but right now, she was far keener to know why Rudolf had lied to her.

She signed the document without really looking.

'Can I do anything else for you?' asked the policeman.

Ella shook her head – but then something occurred to her. She unfolded the map on the counter.

'Could you tell me exactly where he was found?' she asked.

The young man didn't need long to think about it. He pointed at a spot along the road that she had already travelled down with Rudolf. It was the route through the Foster plantation that led back to Johore.

'Are you sure?'

'Yes. I was there myself,' he confirmed.

'Did you interview any of the workers on the plantation there?' she enquired.

'A few of them saw him in the afternoon. He was riding back to Johore.'

'So he was on his way back . . .' said Ella, her brow furrowed.

'That's what the witness statements suggest, but of course, he could well have been travelling in the other direction just before he died. We don't know the exact time of his death.'

'Thank you for your help.' There was nothing more to say, but plenty of food for thought.

◆　◆　◆

Rudolf's brazen lie about the gypsies had almost entirely extinguished Ella's grief for her 'fiancé' by the time she got back to her room in the boarding house. It was now perfectly clear why Rudolf had claimed that he had been robbed. He had gambled away the majority of his travel budget and had only three hundred marks left. Taken together, his loss on the horses and the alleged robbery both pointed to an obvious answer: he had obviously intended for her to finance the entire journey. Ella would have been happy to do so – after all, she had paid for their tickets too – but this flagrant betrayal weighed heavily on her. Otto had tried to warn her. Her conversation with him on board immediately after their trip to the racecourse now echoed in her mind. Did Rudolf have any more secrets up his sleeve? She would probably never find out – though at that same moment, it occurred to her that she should take a look through his luggage.

Ella no longer had any qualms about opening Rudolf's suitcases, which Lee had already placed in her room. Inside the larger suitcase, she found his clothing – which was familiar enough to her – as well as some toiletries in a cloth bag, and three pairs of shoes in a separate bag. There was nothing else of interest. The main compartment of the smaller case contained more shoes and underwear, but it also had a sewn-up side panel and two other, smaller compartments. These held two books of travel writing and a quantity of newspaper cuttings. Ella removed the entire bundle of papers and spread them out on the bed. Rudolf had prepared for this journey more thoroughly than she realised. One article was about rubber cultivation in the south, and described the wealth of the local plantation owners. There was also a map of Malacca.

Ella couldn't believe her eyes. The map was in colour and looked newer than Otto's – but the most striking thing about it was that the route from Singapore to the Foster plantation had been marked out. Ella picked up the map and stood in the light by the window. There was no doubt about it: Rudolf had sketched out this route and this route alone. Why on earth had he singled out this particular plantation? What facts had he been withholding from her? He must have learned much more from his mother than he had let on – or perhaps even from his uncle, when he was still alive. Clearly, he had told Ella and her mother only half the truth in Hamburg. There could be no other explanation for why he would mark the Foster plantation on his map.

There was no time to ponder the matter further, for when she placed the map to one side and casually looked out onto the street, she saw Amar. He was sitting in exactly the same place as the previous night. Her mind raced. Amar might be able to find out who had seen Rudolf at the plantation. Perhaps one of the workers would know what he'd been doing there. It was worth a try. At any rate, there was no way to avoid going downstairs now, since Amar had already spotted her and was waving up at her. His presence alone spoke volumes. There was no doubt that he wanted to see her.

A warm smile could provide so much hope and consolation when it came from the heart. Ella sensed that Amar felt deeply for her loss. His eyes were sad, and as they looked into hers, he seemed to be trying to gauge how she was feeling. Was that why he remained silent for so long? In any case, it was Ella who spoke first.

'You waited here all night.' Her voice was filled with gratitude and appreciation.

'I was worried about you.'

'About me?' she asked in surprise.

'You might have gone to look for him yourself,' he explained.

'Do you already know . . . ?' Ella began to ask, to check whether he had interpreted the police visit correctly.

He nodded mutely.

'I've found a map in one of his suitcases. According to the markings, he was trying to get to the Foster plantation,' she said.

'He was visiting the Fosters? But why?' asked Amar.

Ella debated whether she could fully trust him. Was it really any of his business to know whom she was searching for and why she was really here? She looked directly into his eyes once more, and felt sure that he wouldn't reveal her secret. He would hardly have sat outside her window all night if he meant her any harm. Besides, he was the only person she knew who also knew the Fosters.

'I'm searching for my real father,' confessed Ella.

'Here in Malacca?' Amar could scarcely believe it.

'All I know is that his name is Richard, and that his surname begins with an F. He might be Richard Foster. Rudolf must have known that, or at least suspected it.'

'Nobody has ever spoken of him at the plantation. I didn't know that Mrs Foster's husband was called Richard,' said Amar thoughtfully.

'That's unusual, don't you think?' Ella observed.

Amar nodded thoughtfully.

She sat down beside him on the wide ledge. 'Do you know anything about the other members of the family?'

'Mrs Foster manages the farm, together with Raj.'

'Is that the Indian I saw?'

'Yes. He's spent half his life working on the plantation. Raj is her right-hand man.'

'And clearly a very harsh one . . .' Ella recalled.

'I can't say anything bad about him,' replied Amar.

'And the daughter? I believe her name is Heather?'

'I've barely even seen her. They say she's very shy, and that she almost never goes out. I've never spotted her in town.'

'How old is she?' asked Ella.

'I don't know. It's hard to say. The one time I saw her close up, she looked like a young woman. Her skin is as white as snow and she's very beautiful. Like a princess,' he gushed.

'She seems to keep herself hidden away like one too,' answered Ella.

Amar had to grin at that, but then he looked at her for a moment.

'You have her eyes,' he declared.

Ella was struck by that remark, for it suggested that this woman might actually be a blood relative. Then again, how often was it said of people that they resembled somebody or other? She had heard comments like that all the time at the hospital, and never taken it as a sign of a genuine family relationship. For that reason, she tried to take his comment in good humour.

'The eyes of a princess. I'll take that as a compliment.'

Amar smiled again, but he didn't stop looking at her.

'You really could be sisters . . . It's the way you move too, and your curly hair . . .' he went on.

Ella's heart raced. Was she already so close to her goal?

'Perhaps all young European women just look the same to you,' she said, trying to avoid losing herself completely in speculation.

'You should see her for yourself.' Amar seemed enthusiastic about the idea.

'And how should I arrange that? You've just told me that she almost never leaves the plantation.'

'The Fosters have a guest house. They occasionally hold parties there for the British residents in the region, and sometimes people stay the night. When I started working for the Fosters, a young Dutchwoman stayed there for a while too. That was when I saw Miss Foster for the first time. The two of them were talking, and had gone for a stroll in the garden.'

'Perhaps she was a friend of the family?'

'No, she was only passing through. Mrs Foster made her acquaintance in town.'

'How do you know all this?'

'I was the one who drove Mrs Foster into Johore to buy supplies,' said Amar.

'And she simply invited the young woman to stay with them?'

'On the way back, I heard her say she was an artist. Her name was Esther and she played the violin. You could sometimes hear her playing all the way from the fields. When we heard it, we would stop working and listen.'

'Was that why Marjory invited her to stay?' Ella found that hard to believe.

'No, she did so because of her daughter. "You'll be good for Heather" – those were her exact words,' explained Amar.

'So should I pass myself off as an artist and wait until Marjory comes back into town for supplies?'

Amar laughed heartily.

'Esther only stayed for a few weeks. She must be back in Holland by now. But she might have met you . . . during her travels . . . and perhaps she told you all about her wonderful stay with the Fosters . . . And now that you're travelling through too, perhaps you're curious to see what it was like for yourself . . .'

Now it was Ella who had to laugh. This Amar seemed to share her talent for improvisation – like her, he certainly wasn't at a loss for plausible pretexts. Yet there was a catch.

'The thing is, I can't play any instruments, only a little piano,' she had to admit.

'Can you sing?' he asked.

'Even the parrots in the jungle can sing better than I can,' Ella confessed.

'How about painting?' suggested Amar.

'I can paint tolerably well. I used to draw with charcoal as a child. Portraits, studies of plants . . .'

'So you *are* an artist after all,' declared Amar.

'But I can't pass myself off as a Dutchwoman.'

'Nobody will hear the difference. Your accent sounds similar to hers,' Amar assured her.

'And where will I find a sketchbook and charcoal to draw with?'

'Two streets down from here.'

Ella thought it was a crazy idea. Yet she saw no other way at present to find out who her family was. She felt that it could be the Fosters, although the notion that she might be the daughter of the late Richard Foster made her uncomfortable.

'I think I'll need to practise a little first.'

'I'd be happy to serve as a model,' said Amar. His smile was gorgeous. Maybe she really should try to sketch it.

◆ ◆ ◆

Ella could hardly believe that she had agreed to Amar's mad idea, and she had to admit that she had done so not just because of her desire to meet her presumed half-sister, but because Amar had ignited a blaze of curiosity within her. Yet she couldn't quite pin down exactly what she was so curious about. Was it the plantation, which was ruled with an iron fist by its matriarch? Was it the princess, who locked herself away in a golden cage? Perhaps Marjory Foster was even her mother – that couldn't be ruled out altogether. Whatever the reason, this place seemed to exert a powerful force of attraction that she could no longer resist.

Ella had deliberately taken the longer route to the plantation to avoid travelling past the place where Rudolf's body had been found. Before she set out, she had briefly considered stopping there to say a quiet prayer for him – but given his shabby behaviour and flagrant betrayal, she had dismissed the idea. Amar had offered to accompany her, but that would have been far too dangerous. Raj might have seen them together, and as the matriarch's right-hand man, he would have told Marjory about it before long. To make her look more plausible, Amar had provided her with a second-hand easel. Ella felt like a thief planning to steal a valuable painting from a museum – though in this case, the painting was a secret that she hoped to elicit from the Fosters. The thought of that lifted her spirits, for the nearer she drew to the Fosters' house, the more absurd her plan to pass herself off as an artist began to appear.

This time, Ella was relieved to meet with only a few curious looks from the workers as she drove through the plantation. She would probably have lost her nerve if she had seen Raj. Shortly before she turned off onto the road leading to the Fosters' estate, Ella stopped the carriage and asked herself for a final time if she really wanted to take all this upon herself. The answer was a resounding yes. And after just a few minutes' drive, she came upon a view that not only piqued her curiosity even further, but was also extraordinarily beautiful. The plantation's rubber trees extended to the foot of a gentle hill, up the side of which wound a driveway leading to a house that truly deserved to be called 'stately'. Two palm groves surrounded a white three-storey mansion, which had two bay windows and a balcony the size of a veranda on the first floor. There must be countless rooms inside it; indeed, the house certainly seemed far too big for the two people that apparently inhabited it.

As soon as she reached the hill, Ella caught sight of an expansive, well-kept garden that ran all the way to the other end of the rubber plantation. In it stood a smaller house that looked like a pavilion, embedded in a sea of flowers. If Ella wasn't mistaken, those were oleander bushes entwined around the building in countless different colours. There was clearly a gifted gardener at work here, for when Ella dismounted from her carriage to take a closer look, she noticed that the flowers were even arranged by hue. The red blossoms grew tallest, reaching almost up to the roof of the pavilion, and were joined on one side by pink flowers that gave way to a deep purple – while on the other side, the colour seemed to fade to a shade of apricot before losing itself altogether in a cascade of white blossom. It didn't take her long to identify the gardener: an older woman wielding a set of pruning shears, who Ella guessed to be in her sixties. She had her hair in a bun and wore a black dress with padded hips that looked slightly old-fashioned, and which was certainly far too warm for the local climate. At any rate, it didn't look like the outfit of a maidservant. At that moment, Ella realised that she could lay to rest one of the many questions that had been tormenting her, assuming that her investigations had led her to the right plantation. If this woman was Marjory Foster, it seemed unlikely she could be Ella's real mother. She was probably too old for that.

Ella wondered whether she ought to approach her, but the woman made the decision for her, for she looked up, placed her shears in a bucket and walked towards her. This had to be Marjory, and she didn't look especially pleased, even at this distance. That much was clear from her rapid pace.

'Who are you?' she called to Ella in a harsh tone. Ella nearly lost her nerve, but Amar had warned her in advance.

'I'm a friend of Esther's,' she called back. She hoped it would work.

At any rate, Marjory must have heard her. After a moment of surprise, her brisk march slowed to a stroll, and Ella now saw curiosity instead of disapproval in her eyes.

'My name is Ella van Veen,' she announced, as Marjory reached her and examined her from head to toe.

'You must be Marjory Foster,' she added.

Marjory nodded.

'So you know Esther? How is she?' she asked. Ella had to think quickly, for she didn't even know where Esther was living at that moment.

'We met while travelling, and she said such wonderful things about this place. I'm an artist passing through the area, and Esther's descriptions really captured my imagination.' Ella prayed that that would fend off any further enquiries from Marjory.

'She enjoyed her time here, then,' said Marjory. As she spoke, a complacent smile crept over the corners of her mouth, which had hitherto been locked in an angry pout. It was a miracle that she could still move her lips, considering how grimly pursed they had been until now.

'It's so beautiful here.' Ella spoke with conviction – a simple glance at the house, the garden and the pavilion sufficed for that. 'I would dearly love to draw your pavilion. I've never seen such beautiful oleander bushes,' Ella gushed further.

'And you say you're an artist.' Marjory looked at her approvingly. Amar's plan seemed to be working.

'That's overstating it somewhat. But I enjoy drawing.'

'I do admire people with artistic gifts. Alas, God didn't grace me with such talents,' declared Marjory rather soberly.

'But surely anybody who can cultivate such beautiful flowers and arrange them so perfectly is a god-gifted artist, no?' said Ella, and she meant it, although she hoped her remark wouldn't be interpreted as an attempt at flattery. From her watchful blue eyes, she could tell that Marjory was an intelligent woman.

A noise from the house made Ella look up. Someone was moving by the window. She thought she saw a female outline behind the curtains.

Marjory followed Ella's gaze, but said nothing. She seemed to be lost in thought for a moment.

Ella was sure that Heather was interested in the new arrival, but the fact that she didn't show herself at the window proved Amar right. She appeared to be rather timid.

'I'm sure you have a long journey behind you. How would you like a cup of tea?'

The tone of Marjory's voice had grown so mild that Ella could scarcely believe it of her, and she was only too happy to accept the offer.

To describe the furnishings inside the house as elegant and stylish would be an almighty understatement. Ella had seen the interiors of a few mansions in Germany while visiting her patients, but the Foster residence far exceeded all of those. That was down to the finely woven oriental rugs on the floor in the hallway and the drawing room, and the chandeliers in a style she had never seen before, with beautifully cut teardrop-shaped crystals. The furniture was made from tropical wood and polished to a mirror-like shine. The scent of flowers hung in the air, and on the wall of the entrance hall there were two breathtakingly beautiful paintings that clearly depicted an English landscape. Ella couldn't tear her eyes away from them.

'England, our old home. We used to spend many weekends in the southwest, on Dartmoor. Sometimes I miss those green meadows, the heaths and the moors,' explained Marjory, who stopped at Ella's side and admired the paintings with every bit as much interest and admiration.

'Jaya,' Marjory called into the house.

A young Indian girl came rushing in, as if from nowhere.

'Make us some tea please, and tell Heather that we have a visitor,' Marjory instructed her.

The young woman – who was dressed in a maid's black uniform with a white apron and cap – nodded and disappeared through a doorway behind the stairs.

'Esther was a most charming young lady. Are you from Holland too?' asked Marjory, while gesturing for Ella to follow her into the drawing room.

'I come from Rotterdam,' said Ella. She tried to roll the 'R' slightly, although there was no way that an Englishwoman would be able to tell the difference between a German and a Dutch accent in English. Another lie. Ella felt extremely uncomfortable, yet she had blurted it out without really knowing why she had chosen Rotterdam, of all places. She would just have to keep up the pretence now.

The drawing room was downright regal in character. The light olive fabric of the upholstery was framed by extravagantly carved white wood and stood in attractive contrast to the enormous oriental rugs, which depicted hunting scenes. The two chandeliers on the ceiling were even bigger than those in the entrance hall. The Fosters truly seemed to have a weakness for art, for there was no shortage of paintings. Even the gold-trimmed grandfather clock next to the entrance displayed such exquisite craftsmanship that it must have been worth a small fortune, and there were flamboyant marble statues standing on painted ledges too. Yet Ella's favourite item was a sofa that had one seat facing forwards and the other in the opposite direction, so that two people could sit together and converse without having to turn their heads. Marjory seemed particularly attached to this piece too.

'A souvenir from France – they call it a *tête-à-tête*. Heather and I like to take our afternoon tea there,' explained Marjory.

Ella continued to survey the room, but then froze. Above the sofa hung a portrait of a couple. The woman looked like a youthful Marjory, and Ella could guess who the man must be: Richard, her presumptive father. His gaze was extraordinarily chilling. He looked stern and careworn, with a bony, consumptive face. Ella felt herself grow nauseous. Could somebody like that really be her father? She found it impossible to believe that she might share anything with him; nor did she want to. If even a painting of him could be so repellent – and one showing him as a young man, at that – then what kind of person must he have become later in life?

Marjory had clearly noticed Ella's eyes resting on the painting, but she said nothing. Out of the corner of her eye, Ella thought she saw Marjory adjusting the sofa cushions in embarrassment. Perhaps she didn't mention the painting because she didn't like the portrait herself. That would be understandable. But in that case, why was it still hanging there? She could easily have taken it down.

'Please, have a seat. The tea will be here soon enough. You must try the biscuits too. Our cook used to work in England, and she does a most tolerable job, for an Indian,' said Marjory, before sitting down at a circular table inlaid with mosaics.

Ella had scarcely made herself comfortable before she heard steps outside the door. Jaya entered and placed a silver tray on the table, laden with a teapot, three cups and a plate of biscuits – all made of the finest bone china – before pouring the tea.

'Thank you, Jaya. That will be all,' said Marjory.

Ella felt as though she was sitting before a queen. It was clear that she had her household and her staff fully under control – even down to minor details, such as the tray, which had been polished so diligently that it virtually sparkled.

'Would you like some milk? Oh, excuse me, I shouldn't even ask. We English are probably the only people in the world mad enough to pour milk in our tea,' laughed Marjory.

'Oh no, I'd love some. I lived for a time in England and I learned to appreciate your habits.'

'In England, you say? What did you do there?' Marjory asked.

Ella cursed her loose tongue. Then again, it couldn't do any harm to talk about her profession. There were plenty of artists who had to do conventional work when they couldn't live off their art alone. Ella decided to risk it.

'I trained as a nurse there.'

Marjory nodded approvingly. 'A practical profession is worth its weight in gold. Was it your work that brought you to Malacca?' The questions were becoming increasingly probing, but she managed to come up with a suitable excuse, thank goodness.

'I'm interested in traditional Indian and Chinese medicine,' answered Ella truthfully.

'Well, you can find both here, and save yourself two arduous journeys to India and China. A clever decision,' Marjory replied. Then she looked up impatiently.

'What's keeping Heather?' she asked, and called for Jaya. This time, the maid didn't appear quite so quickly. Marjory rose to her feet, ready to reissue her order to fetch Heather from upstairs.

'Perhaps she's tired. If you would allow me to draw your beautiful garden once we've finished our tea, then maybe I can stay for a while yet,' said Ella. That appeased Marjory, and she relaxed once more.

'I'm excited to see your work,' she said, and took a sip of tea, looking at Ella the whole time.

Ella was now in need of a plausible explanation for why she intended to capture the glorious colours of Marjory's garden only in black-and-white charcoal – and whether the results would be at all passable remained to be seen.

◆ ◆ ◆

She could still feel Marjory's eyes on the back of her neck as she set up her small easel beneath the shade of a palm tree on the lawn in front of the oleander house – so called because the magnificent blossoms concealed the bulk of the building when you stood directly in front of it. The fragrance was beguiling. Perhaps it would calm her nerves at the prospect of trying to draw a picture that didn't resemble the work of a child. Yet as soon as Ella picked up her charcoal, her confidence grew. It felt so familiar, and reminded her of a time when she used to take great pleasure in drawing.

'You would have made a wonderful artist,' her art teacher always used to say to her at school.

Ella clung to the memory, and reflected that it was actually rather original to draw a house like this in black and white.

When she examined them more closely, the bushes seemed to take on a life of their own. If she looked beyond the colour and concentrated more on the fresh shoots and the shapes of the buds, she might be able to draw something that forced the viewer to see the house with new eyes.

Encouraged, Ella put her charcoal to the paper. The outline of the circular building quickly took shape. How extravagant the façade was, with its classical ornamentation. She managed to capture it in an interesting way on her sketchpad, and exhaled in relief. Next up, the branches, which shot upward like tentacles. They almost looked a little threatening, and yet they had a dreamlike quality – somewhat like an enchanted palace that you might see in an illustrated book of fairy tales.

Ella heard steps approaching, and her muscles clenched, as she expected it would be Marjory. But why didn't the steps come any closer? She turned round.

Amar hadn't exaggerated. The woman standing in the shade of the small palm grove truly was as beautiful as a princess. Her face was flawless and her skin as white as porcelain – no doubt because she barely left the house.

'I'm Heather,' Marjory's daughter said by way of greeting.

Was this beautiful woman really almost forty years old, as the Dutch couple had told her? She looked significantly younger, although that might be thanks to her immaculate, pale complexion. At that age, Ella was amazed that Heather was still so shy that she preferred to converse from a distance.

'I'm very pleased to meet you,' Ella called back to her, though it felt like a trivial thing to say. As she spoke, she reflected that Heather doubtless had good reasons for her behaviour. Perhaps she had poor circulation, or other health problems that made it impossible for her to come any nearer. That might be why she was steadying herself against the trunk of a palm tree. She seemed to have difficulty breathing too. Ella felt the best thing to do would be to approach her and greet her from close up.

After just a few steps, she sensed that Heather was already starting to feel better. Now that she was out of the sun, Ella could make out her face more clearly. There could be no doubt that she had her eyes and her high cheekbones – and even the way she smiled was recognisable to Ella. It was like looking into a mirror. Heather really must be her half-sister. Besides this, though, there was something else that made her feel this way: Heather exuded a special kind of warmth that Ella had very rarely encountered among strangers, beyond the occasional particularly endearing patient. There was a sense of unspoken connection there, just like with her own family. That was how Heather's presence felt to her: familiar.

'I'm sure your picture will turn out wonderfully,' said Heather, though she didn't spare it a glance. How could she even tell from that distance?

'It isn't finished yet, but you can take a look at it now if you like,' Ella offered.

At that, Heather's captivating smile vanished as quickly as it had appeared. Ella had the impression that she was actively avoiding looking at the easel in front of the oleander house. Her drawing couldn't be as bad as all that, surely.

'Please show it to me once it's finished. I'm sure the house will look very different to how I know it,' said Heather distractedly, before casting a fleeting look towards the easel. 'It's good to see things in a different light,' she continued.

'I'm trying to capture what makes the house so beautiful beyond those glorious colours.'

Heather abruptly changed the subject.

'My mother tells me you used to live in England, and that you are a nurse,' she said, her endearing smile returning as she looked into Ella's eyes, her expression kind.

Ella nodded. 'I had a wonderful time there.'

'You probably know England better than I do. I only remember it from my childhood,' Heather declared. 'You simply have to tell me all about what you got up to there,' she added.

'I'm afraid that would take much longer than an afternoon.'

'An afternoon? But you must stay! At least for dinner. Ideally for a few days. There are so many beautiful things to see here, and then you can tell me all about England, no? Please say you will?'

Just a few minutes earlier, Ella would have accepted the offer without hesitation – but now she wondered whether Marjory might not uncover the truth with all her questions. Yet being close to Heather made it worth the risk, even if Ella couldn't explain her odd behaviour.

'All right. I'd be delighted,' she said.

'I'll let Mother know, and the staff too.' Heather beamed – but all the same, Ella sensed that she was in a hurry to get back to the house.

◆ ◆ ◆

To Ella's overwhelming relief, her charcoal drawing of the guest house had turned out well. Although lacking colour, it gave the sprawling, creeping vines a life of their own. They seemed to be grasping at the house, but protecting it too. Her drawing was romantic and yet gloomy at the same time. It really did remind her of a haunted castle from a fairy tale. Ella had worked on her sketch all afternoon, but neither Marjory nor Heather had appeared again – only Jaya, who had supplied her with cold, freshly squeezed mango juice and lingered for a quick chat. Her parents were from Bombay. After her mother's death, her father had emigrated with her to Malacca and was now working in a rubber factory. Another Indian – an older woman named Devi – also worked here part-time in the kitchen. She had come here with her family from England years ago, and had brought her knowledge of English cuisine with her. Jaya had a gentle, kindly nature, and Ella reflected that a woman like her surely wouldn't survive here long if she were treated badly. It seemed that the Fosters' house was subject to different laws to their plantation.

Later, when Jaya called her in for dinner, they managed to exchange a few more brief words.

'Do you know why Heather never goes out?' Ella couldn't resist asking the question, but did her best to pose it casually.

Jaya didn't seem to know, though, and merely shrugged.

'Heather only dared to come out as far as the palm trees earlier. It's odd.'

'She avoids the oleander house.' Jaya seemed certain of that, at least.

'But why?' Ella pressed her.

Once again, the only answer was a shrug. There was no point asking any further questions, as Jaya was in a hurry to get back to the main house and help out in the kitchen.

It was Jaya too who brought them their dinner in the drawing room.

'I hope you like English cuisine,' said Marjory, as Jaya served up a steak and kidney pie to follow the superb chicken soup starter. Ella already knew the dish from her time in England. Delicious, but an acquired taste for Germans.

'A culinary adventure for those who aren't already familiar with it,' remarked Ella diplomatically.

Heather laughed. Inside the house, she seemed transformed – unconstrained and at ease.

'Devi always uses two teaspoons of Worcestershire sauce instead of one. That makes it more flavoursome,' said Marjory.

That very sauce was what made the dish taste so odd to the German palate. All the same, it was perfectly edible and Ella helped herself to a large slice.

'And what do you think of the local cuisine?' asked Heather.

Ella was glad that the conversation had kept to such trivial topics so far – thanks in part to her knowledge of the English national character. One could talk to the British about the weather for hours and that subject alone had taken them from the sherry aperitif right through to the chicken soup.

'I have to confess that I haven't tried a single Malayan dish yet,' admitted Ella.

'Best to avoid them. They'll only upset your stomach. Why on earth do they make everything so spicy?' Marjory pondered. That too was typical for the British. They preferred plain dishes, ideally with steamed or boiled vegetables. In that sense, Marjory was a laudable exception, with her two teaspoons of Worcestershire sauce.

'To stop it from going off. Most people living in hot climates like Farther India have no way to refrigerate their food. Meat keeps for longer when it's spiced and dried. The local cooking methods all make perfect sense,' Heather explained to her mother.

'Typical Heather. She loves this country, and always tries to defend it. You'd be forgiven for thinking she was a native,' said Marjory wryly.

'My skin would need to be a few shades darker for that,' answered Heather.

'Oh, don't you worry. You're my fine English lady, and it becomes you perfectly,' said Marjory warmly, with the shining eyes of a mother who obviously loved her child a great deal – a love that Heather seemed to reciprocate wholeheartedly.

'I must say I'm rather looking forward to the dessert. It's treacle tart,' announced Marjory cheerfully.

'I'm afraid I won't be able to stay for it. I don't want to travel back in the dark,' said Ella.

'Nonsense. Of course you'll stay here. You're our guest. Jaya will prepare the oleander house straight after dinner and I'll send somebody to collect your bags.' From Marjory's lips, it sounded like an order. It was exactly what Ella had wanted to hear.

'But Ella could sleep in the house. We have plenty of rooms,' objected Heather.

'I think Ella will be more comfortable out there. That's where all our guests stay. Besides, Edward is coming tomorrow. What if he wants to stay here? If he does, Ella will be able to retire undisturbed.'

Ella thought she could guess why Heather looked so disappointed. If she stayed in the house, they wouldn't be separated by half the garden, and they could sit down and get to know each other better. Ella sensed that Heather longed to spend time with her just as much as she herself yearned to be near Heather. All the same, the depth of sadness that now welled up in Heather's eyes was astonishing.

'I very much appreciate your generous offer,' Ella said. Just then, the treacle tart arrived – but even that couldn't lift Heather's spirits.

CHAPTER 9

Ella was gently woken by the first rays of the sun filtering through the cascading flowers. The light had a warm glow, tinted as it was by the red petals of the oleander blossom. It was an extraordinarily beautiful place. Her bedchamber was spacious, with gleaming polished floorboards, and a wardrobe and dresser made from exotic woods and decorated with elaborate carvings. Best of all was her bed. Ella was lying quite literally in a cornucopia of flowers, her blanket and pillow embroidered with floral patterns – each a work of art in its own right. The guest house also had a generous parlour, which was no less tastefully decorated than the drawing room in the main house. Ella had made herself comfortable in one of the chairs there the night before as she wrote in her diary.

It was time to get up. She was looking forward to making use of the elegant marble bathroom, the lavender soap, and of course the breakfast that Jaya had said she would leave inside the doorway at seven that morning. She had kept her promise. Fresh juice, pastries, English marmalade, butter and tea were all waiting for her underneath a fine mesh cover – presumably to keep the mosquitoes at bay. Over breakfast, Ella wondered how she should start her day. Perhaps she could persuade Heather to come with her into town? It would surely be good for her. Right now, however, Ella much preferred to enjoy the view over the neighbouring rubber fields from her small terrace. It was still very early in the morning, so she decided to take a short stroll over to the plantation.

Just a few moments later, it felt as though she had plunged into a completely different world. It was unnaturally quiet and Ella could distinctly hear every single step she took over the dried leaves and the hard floor. Soon enough, the forest swallowed her up altogether. It was doubtless very easy to get lost among the endless rubber trees, which must originally have been planted in even rows. A little further on, she came across a line of trees that were undergoing tapping. White fluid trickled down the etched-out runnels into containers hanging at the end of each incision and Ella was fascinated to see that a tree could bleed from its wounds, just like a human. She ran her hand over the trunk of a tree that had had some of its bark removed. It was still perfectly smooth, and she was curious to know how the rubber would feel too. The fluid was viscous and cool to the touch, sticking instantly to her fingers. A few rows further down, she saw the first workers entering the forest, carrying large buckets and fanning out among the rubber plants.

'What are you doing here?' came a voice from behind.

Ella jumped and turned round. In front of her stood the Indian giant, holding a sickle-shaped knife in his hand. Her heart almost stopped. Now Marjory would be sure to find out that she had already been seen on the plantation with a companion.

Raj stared at her without saying a word. It seemed to Ella as though he were trying to gauge her thoughts. His eyes were piercing, and she was afraid that he might try to skin her, just like the trees.

'I'm a guest of the Fosters,' she explained, trying to keep her voice steady.

Raj was clearly surprised to hear that. Only now did he seem to notice that her fingers were coated with the white fluid.

'The trees look as though they're bleeding,' said Ella, more out of embarrassment.

'The white blood of the earth. They say that it heals afflicted souls,' he answered, without looking away.

The man was speaking in riddles. The best course of action was to explain to him that she needed to get back to the house, since Heather would already be waiting for her. It was unwise to trifle with a knife-wielding man who had his workers flogged.

But then he hefted his blade, slicing the sharp, sickle-shaped knife into one of the trees. He ran it in a spiral down the bark before peeling the trunk like a piece of fruit. Instantly, a few light patches appeared and the white fluid welled up. He too ran his hand over the trunk, just as Ella had done.

'Where is your companion? Mrs Foster didn't mention him,' he asked abruptly.

Ella wondered whether it wouldn't be safer to go straight back to town.

'He's dead. Most likely an accident,' she answered frankly.

Raj's face turned to stone. Ella felt certain that this was the first he had heard of it.

'He was here . . . on his own . . .' he said thoughtfully.

'Did you see him?'

'This place brings bad luck to strangers. It's cursed,' he said, without responding to her question. As he spoke, he gazed mysteriously at the treetops, as if the reason lay hidden up there.

'I don't believe in curses.' Although it cost her some effort, Ella's staunchness seemed to impress the man. The corners of his mouth curved upward into a mysterious smile – yet his face froze abruptly when the sound of an approaching carriage filtered towards them. Through the rows of trees, they could see that it was heading towards the house. The Fosters evidently had visitors.

Raj looked alarmed and sprang into action, running towards the edge of the forest.

Ella followed him and recognised the two Malayan police officers who had brought her the news of Rudolf's demise.

'The police . . . So it begins . . .' he murmured to himself cryptically.

'What do you mean?' asked Ella, now perplexed.

'Will they mention your name? What do you think?'

Ella felt burningly hot, and not because Raj hadn't answered her question. It was possible that the two policemen might discuss Rudolf's female companion with the Fosters.

Raj couldn't help but notice her unease. 'It was I who fetched your luggage from the boarding house,' he said.

Ella's heart almost stopped. So he knew that she wasn't a Dutchwoman – that she was the German Ella Kaltenbach.

'If anybody asks me about you . . . then I'll tell them I haven't seen you with him,' he offered, to Ella's astonishment.

'Why would you do that for me?' she asked.

Raj turned to her and looked her straight in the eye.

'Destiny is unalterable. Misfortune befalls all who try to oppose it.' He looked back over at the Fosters' house, where the two policemen were just then being shown inside.

◆ ◆ ◆

Ella didn't dare to go back to the guest house until the policemen's carriage had been swallowed up once more by the rubber forest. There was nobody to be seen at the main house. Should she let a little more time pass? But what was the point in hiding away uselessly inside the guest house, waiting for Marjory to come out and ask her why she hadn't said anything about her companion's demise? Ella decided to put an end to the agonising uncertainty, and walked over to the house to wish everybody a good morning and ask Heather whether she would like to go for a stroll or a drive into town.

Jaya opened the door in a state of considerable agitation.

'The police were here. A German man died near our planta-tion. I overheard the conversation,' she whispered after inviting Ella inside. 'Mrs Foster is waiting for you most impatiently,' Jaya went on.

For a moment, Ella considered turning back; Marjory clearly had a bone to pick with her. But she took a deep breath and entered the drawing room, where the older woman met her with a beam-ing smile.

'Good morning, Ella. You seem to be a very late riser,' she said, walking up to her.

Ella instantly felt a weight fall from her heart – but then Marjory's expression grew serious once more. Was she about to get to the point? She was.

'I don't know if you're aware, but the police were here just now. It seems that a German man died close to the plantation.'

'Yes, I saw the policemen from the guest house,' said Ella.

'Well, I would greatly appreciate it if you would refrain from mentioning this to anybody. We are expecting a guest this evening, and . . . people talk . . .'

Ella nodded, but decided to sound Marjory out.

'What did the police want? The man was German, you say?'

For a moment Marjory seemed to debate whether she could confide in Ella. 'The man visited the house the day before yesterday and introduced himself as a rubber merchant. I told him that we've already appointed our buyers, and he left again. The ideas these Germans have . . . We sell to British customers, and that's the way it should be.'

Ella nodded thoughtfully. None of it made any sense. Rudolf knew that this was where her presumptive father lived, so why hadn't he mentioned it to Marjory? Perhaps she was keeping that quiet, since it was of no concern to an outsider.

'Oh my child, look at you! You're all aflutter. Why don't you have a glass of gin to steady your spirits? I needed one too after the gentlemen had left,' said Marjory.

Ella really wasn't in the mood for drinking gin, but she accepted all the same. It was clear that Rudolf's visit to the Fosters couldn't have had anything to do with his death, for Marjory wouldn't have discussed it so openly otherwise. Her request for discretion on the matter was perfectly understandable.

Marjory handed Ella a glass of gin and ice. She had poured herself a second helping too.

'To the reinvigorating effect of good old Gordon's.'

Ella raised her glass.

'That's what we like to see. The day promises to be a lively one if we're indulging in alcohol at this time in the morning.' It was Heather's voice. She was standing in the doorway with an amused smile. 'What shall we do today, Ella? Or would you rather go back to your charcoals? I know – I should show you some lovely spots to inspire you.' Heather was full of enthusiasm and good humour.

'Wonderful,' said Ella.

'I just need to get changed first. My shoes are completely unsuitable for the rainforest,' said Heather, before disappearing towards the stairs.

Marjory sighed and took a sip of her gin. 'It's obvious Heather likes you. She rarely goes out, so it looks as though your company is doing her some good.' As she spoke, Marjory laid her hand on Ella's arm. Her smile was warm and maternal.

Ella decided to use the opportunity to ask about Heather's odd behaviour.

'Is she afraid of going out on her own?' she asked.

'She has always been very shy, even as a child,' explained Marjory.

'Is it possible that she's afraid of the guest house? I had that impression yesterday . . .' Ella suggested carefully.

'Oh, come now, don't get carried away. You're reading far too much into things,' answered Marjory. Her smile had lost all its warmth and looked false. One thing was clear: the guest house was evidently a taboo subject among the Fosters. Yet Ella was burning to find out what the matter was with Heather.

◆　◆　◆

For all that Heather apparently never left the house, she proved to be a surprisingly adroit rider. The Fosters had their own stables for horses used on the plantation. Heather had advised Ella not to use her carriage horse, since those animals were unused to being ridden and tended to be skittish. Ella's horse therefore remained at the Fosters', where it was lovingly tended to by an Indian stable boy. Instead, they had ridden out on a pair of Bajau ponies. The breed had apparently been introduced by Chinese traders, and they were noble animals with narrow heads, high withers and a long, fine mane. They were also only around twelve hands high, so Ella was happy with Heather's suggestion. She wouldn't have felt entirely at ease on one of the big, sturdy horses used by the workers.

It was fun to ride out on these agile yet elegant animals. Heather sat astride Marjory's Bajau, which was a little more stubborn and headstrong – 'Just like Mother,' Heather had conceded with a wink while they were saddling their animals – while Ella's pony responded sensitively to the slightest touch of the spurs or the reins. The ponies were as meek as lambs and virtually unflappable, making them an ideal choice, for after just fifteen minutes' ride across the plantation and along a narrow trail through tropical vegetation, the path grew steeper. Heather's incessant questions eased off at this point, as even she was forced to pay attention to the route – sections of which had fairly steep drops off to one side. Ella had been telling her about her work back at the hospital, including her unorthodox additional treatments. Surprisingly enough, Heather was very open-minded about naturopathic medicine, although she had never heard of Hahnemann. The Indians on the farm had already cured her mother of a few ailments with their Ayurvedic techniques.

Ella was amazed at the surprisingly close rapport she shared with Heather. She simply had to be her older half-sister – there could be no other explanation for why they felt so at ease with each other, laughing together and dispensing with the usual formalities that strangers typically addressed each other with.

'Your sunhat has slipped,' Heather remarked when they had nearly reached the top of the hill.

'My skin has already got used to the sun, but you're quite right. At this rate, I'll be mistaken for a local before long,' said Ella. After her lengthy sea voyage and the many days she had spent sunbathing on deck, she could no longer pass herself off as a fine young lady with the fair, translucent complexion of a princess.

'People here always stare at me like I'm a wonder of the world,' said Heather.

'Well, you're as white as snow. I'm sure somebody with dark skin would feel exactly the same way in Rotterdam. But personally speaking, I like the Malayan complexion. People look healthier somehow with so much colour in their faces – especially the men . . . ' Ella gushed.

'I see they've made a more favourable impression on you than the men back home,' remarked Heather wryly.

'The average Dutchman isn't nearly as fit and athletic, in any case,' Ella declared. She had almost blurted out 'German man', and had nearly mentioned Hamburg instead of Rotterdam earlier, which would instantly have called her identity into question.

'That explains why so many English ladies take native lovers. The better choice, no doubt,' said Heather.

They were now riding side by side, and Ella noticed that Heather was lost in thought.

'Why? Aren't there any handsome Englishmen available? Is there nobody you've taken a fancy to?' asked Ella innocently.

'Englishmen?' answered Heather, making a scornful noise.

'Haven't you found the right man yet?' Ella enquired. They had been chatting like good friends so far. Why shouldn't she be able to ask her this question?

Heather seemed to have lost her humour. She looked sad, but forced herself to smile and answered: 'The right man can turn out to be the wrong one too.'

The happy, carefree mood they had enjoyed during the ride so far seemed to vanish into the depths of the valley that now opened up before them. Ella decided not to ask any more questions. Like Heather, she gazed out over the rainforest, which extended into the distance, meeting the sea just before the horizon. The shrieks of parrots rang through the jungle and the spray from a waterfall churned the surface of a river into an incessant roar, while monkey calls and the twittering of exotic birds added their weight to the cacophony. From their vantage point, the result was an almost hypnotic wall of noise. It was an appropriate moment for silence, though not an uncomfortable one. All the same, Ella hoped that Heather would recover her cheerful disposition on the way home.

Later that day, as she sat on the small terrace in front of the guest house and reflected on the afternoon, Ella came to the conclusion that Heather must be a little temperamental. She couldn't believe that it was solely because she'd been disappointed in love, though her response to that topic had been fairly unambiguous. She seemed to be carrying another weight on her shoulders too. Why else would she have such an aversion to this beautiful guest house? It was all very strange. In any case, Heather's dislike of male company showed itself once more over their early dinner, when Marjory reminded them both that a family friend would be coming to visit – a certain Edward Compton, who was the local British governor. At that, the relaxed atmosphere of their lavish meal – which they had seasoned with recollections from the day's excursion into the jungle – quickly disappeared. Heather made no secret of her reluctance to spend the evening with him.

'We need to stay on his good side.' Marjory attempted to lay down the law after growing tired of Heather's sorrowful expression, but she failed.

'But he has absolutely nothing to do with the rubber trade,' she objected.

'They safeguard our lives, though, and our business. What do you think would happen around these parts if the British Army weren't here? We would have to leave the country. The military presence ensures law and order,' Marjory went on. She drained her glass of brandy as if to emphasise her words.

'Law and order? Mother, they're here for exactly the same reason as in every other colony – it's all about rubber and tin.' Heather's retort took Ella by surprise.

'Malacca only became a Crown colony very recently, and it still has the character of the Straits Settlements – as you very well know,' explained Marjory with a disapproving look at her daughter.

'Straits Settlements?' Ella ventured hesitantly.

'Unlike the Portuguese, we Brits didn't march in to conquer the region with military might. Your own countrymen in the Netherlands made an agreement with the local sultan, and Penang was then acquired legally by the British Crown over one hundred years ago.' Marjory appeared to be a full-blown British royalist.

Ella nodded submissively – after all, she was officially a Dutchwoman and had to pretend to be well-informed.

'Don't listen to her, Ella. All that talk of the Straits Settlements is just splitting hairs. We took possession of this country through entirely underhand means,' said Heather rather pointedly. She clearly wanted to pick a fight with her mother.

'Heather is misrepresenting the facts. There are treaties with the local sultans. Trade treaties. Most of the *bumiputras* are happy that we're here – there haven't been any tribal wars since our arrival. The country lives in peace, and business is flourishing,' Marjory explained to Ella. She had apparently decided not to discuss the topic with Heather any further.

'You sound like Father.' Heather clearly took a different view.

To Ella, Heather's remark seemed almost childishly petulant – yet to her great surprise, it hit home, as Marjory took it visibly to heart. She fell silent, firing only a disapproving look at Heather, before pouring herself another glass of brandy.

'I expect that right now, every country in Europe is searching for a place in the sun somewhere,' said Ella in a conciliatory tone. Marjory responded with a grateful smile.

Heather likewise nodded and shrugged – presumably a conciliatory gesture too.

The palpable tension in the room slowly dissipated once Marjory topped up their drinks and the alcohol began to soothe their spirits, diverting them towards more trivial topics. They discussed horses, and of course the weather – especially the unusually dry conditions for this time of year. Yet Heather still didn't seem quite at ease, for the closer the hour of Compton's visit drew, the more often she looked at the clock on the wall. Ella thought she saw Heather literally flinch when she heard the distinguished guest arrive. She too could hear the sound of his coach approaching the house.

'Perhaps it would be better if I retired to bed,' Ella suggested. What business was it of hers what the British discussed among themselves?

'Out of the question.' Marjory insisted that she stay.

Heather shot her an almost imploring look.

Barely two minutes elapsed before Jaya opened the door and announced 'Governor Compton' in such a reverential tone, one might think that a royal visitor was entering the house – and indeed, this Edward Compton did have a certain regal air. A powerfully built, smartly dressed man in uniform stood before her, with neatly trimmed hair and a moustache. He cut a rather good-looking figure, all told.

'Marjory,' he cried, as she virtually fell into his arms. 'Heather,' he said next, with no less enthusiasm, though she gave nothing more than a polite smile in return. But he paid her no heed, for his gaze had already fallen on their guest. Two rows of pearly white teeth and a glittering pair of eyes flashed at Ella.

'Our visitor from the Netherlands – Ella van Veen.' Marjory presented her much as a market trader would present some fresh vegetables, and soon enough, she found herself face-to-face with the governor.

'*Enchanté.*' The royal visitor had courtly manners. He would doubtless have got on well with Rudolf.

'Why don't we make ourselves comfortable?' Marjory suggested – though really it was an order, which even Heather obeyed. She avoided the sofa, instead choosing an armchair positioned as far away as possible from Compton, who sat down next to Marjory.

'I hope you like it here in Malacca,' Compton opened the conversation. How could Ella have responded other than in the affirmative?

'I love the intoxicating floral diversity one finds here,' she said.

'With your arrival, Malacca is certainly richer by one particularly enchanting flower.' Compton's remark was charming and flattering, and a man in his position could no doubt afford to hand out compliments of this kind.

Ella received it with a modest smile and looked over to where Heather was sitting. She was wearing a contemptuous smirk and looked like a wax figure. Ella realised that Heather couldn't stand this Compton, and she had presumably known him for a long time. But then Ella noticed his restless eyes wandering down to her décolletage, and she began to favour maintaining a certain distance too.

'What news is there, Edward? How is the railway coming along?' Marjory was evidently interposing herself to prevent any further flirting.

Compton instantly adopted a serious expression, making him seem more like a businessman.

'We're hardly making any progress at all in the north. The bridge over the Perak River might be finished by the end of the century, if we're lucky,' he went on.

'Three years to build a bridge?' exclaimed Marjory in surprise.

'We don't have enough good workers, and above all biddable ones. The Chinese were hardworking, but lately they prefer to trade. The Indians would rather work in the factories, and as for the Malays . . . they don't understand the meaning of the word "work", damn them. They're like little children; no use whatsoever. It's as though they've just been vomited out of the jungle.' Edward's tone was so contemptuous that Ella lifted an eyebrow in consternation.

'I probably haven't spent enough time in the country yet, but I've had the good fortune to have encountered nothing but warm, intelligent and thoroughly refined people so far.' Ella enjoyed his reaction to her comment. He was obviously unused to being contradicted by a woman.

'Perhaps here in civilisation – but believe me, the *Orang Asli* are good for nothing at all.' By that, he meant the indigenous Malays who still lived in the rainforest, as Ella knew from her reading on the boat.

'But with such a superb governor in charge, I'm sure the industriousness of the local population will be quite the equal of any Liverpool docker in just a few years,' declared Heather abruptly.

Compton seemed to deliberately ignore her sarcasm, so Ella decided to lend Heather some support.

'Clearly, the Netherlands fell lamentably short in educating the local workforce. We didn't even get them to adopt a single variety of Dutch cheese,' said Ella with a sigh.

How Compton laughed at that.

Marjory laughed too, presumably just to oblige him. Heather smirked, but for different reasons altogether.

Ella had expected Compton to at least show some irritation, but the governor's self-confidence was apparently unshakeable. Indeed, her words seemed to have the opposite effect. She had the impression that his gaze was no longer merely lascivious, but even somewhat besotted. When his eyes met hers, they betrayed his infatuation. He seemed to view her as a sporting challenge, and for a long moment he stared at her in silence, with a fascinated smile.

'Mary Bridgewater always has plenty of cheese, at any rate,' he said to Marjory, who was wiping tears from her eyes.

'Is she Dutch?' asked Ella.

'I'm afraid she'll only be able to offer you a selection of the finest English cheeses – provided we can persuade you to join us at her annual garden party,' said Edward.

'I'm sure Ella will be delighted to attend,' said Marjory.

Ella shot a questioning look at Heather.

'Mary is the most amiable English lady I know – apart from Mother, of course,' said Heather, to Marjory's visible satisfaction – and Compton's too.

Since a second meeting with Compton now seemed inevitable, Ella decided to refrain from making any other satirical comments. After all, she was a guest at the Fosters' house, and she had already had her fun.

CHAPTER 10

Enduring Edward Compton's company for over an hour and a half cost Ella a superhuman effort. Self-congratulation bled into dazzling national pride and endless panegyrics on civilisation – specifically British civilisation, of course. Ella had wanted to point out that Berlin was actually on the verge of surpassing London in cultural terms, but she had bitten her tongue – partly out of politeness and respect for Marjory, but also to avoid raising any suspicions about her supposed Dutch origins. When Heather had finally grown exhausted from fulfilling her obligations towards her mother and had withdrawn to her room, Ella had seized the opportunity to follow suit. The encounter with Compton and her day out with Heather were both worthy of an entry in her diary, but Ella could no longer summon the energy to write. Instead, she enjoyed the cooler air on her terrace now that the temperature had dropped. What a shame Heather couldn't join her here. Ella and her half-sister could have made themselves very comfortable with the help of the tea and biscuits that Jaya had brought her.

Yet the night was still young, and so Ella began to consider taking advantage of the quiet evening hours to write a letter to her mother telling her of the voyage – and of more recent events too, of course. Just as she stood up to fetch a pen and paper, she flinched in shock as a shadow emerged from the pitch-black forest of the plantation. Ella stepped out of the light of the paraffin lamp to help her eyes grow accustomed to the dark. Somebody was heading directly towards her, and had deliberately chosen a route that avoided the main house. She briefly debated retreating inside and locking the door, but then she recognised him: Amar.

Her paralysing terror lifted instantly as he reached the terrace.

'Amar?' Ella was unable to hide her surprise, or her joy.

'I wanted to see how you were getting on,' he explained, and then glanced at the Fosters' house. The lights were on downstairs, so Marjory must still be up.

'I shouldn't be here,' said Amar.

Ella quickly extinguished her lamp.

'Nobody can see you now.'

Amar exhaled and his expression visibly relaxed.

'I have some tea, if you like.'

Amar demurred.

'The chairs are very comfortable,' said Ella. At that, Amar finally overcame his reserve.

'Did you find what you were looking for?' he asked as Ella poured him a cup of tea.

'It certainly feels that way. Heather *must* be my half-sister,' she answered truthfully.

'Does she sense it too?'

'Hard to say.' Ella hadn't even considered the question. 'She's strange . . . and yet it feels like we're already good friends.'

'And how are you getting on with Mrs Foster?'

Ella hadn't really thought about that, and she did so as she took a sip from her teacup.

'It's peculiar. Sometimes she's very kind and thoughtful, and other times she can be standoffish and dismissive . . .' she said, almost to herself.

'It sounds like you've got the measure of her.'

Ella had to grin at that.

'I was afraid you would be staying in the main house with the Fosters, and that I wouldn't be able to visit you without attracting attention.'

'That's what Heather wanted. She doesn't seem to like this guest house very much.'

'People say it's cursed,' said Amar.

'Raj told me the same thing. But I like it here.'

Amar laughed, and then regarded her for a moment. Unlike Compton, Amar's eyes rested on her face, not her décolletage. He was caring, affectionate and warm, and Ella felt no discomfort as she held his gaze.

'I actually had plans to ride into town tonight for the puppet show, but I needed to know whether you were all right,' said Amar.

'A puppet show? Isn't that for children?'

He gave another refreshingly unaffected laugh. 'A shadow play from Sumatra. It's like a theatre performance. The puppeteers tell stories from their homeland – ancient legends,' Amar explained.

'I would love to see that,' said Ella.

'They're only here for one night.'

'I could drive us into town.' Ella was amazed at herself. It was a crazy idea, but what could she do here other than write a letter that would spend weeks in the post anyway? Yet if she was honest, she knew that her reasoning was spurious. Being close to Amar not only felt good, but also gave her a pleasant thrill – a sensation that only intensified when he beamed with joy.

'Won't people notice if we take the carriage?' he asked astutely.

'I can also ride tolerably well,' said Ella.

'Too dangerous. It's dark, and the road through the plantation is uneven,' he replied.

'If only I had wings.'

'I have a sturdy horse that can carry us both. He's as fast as the wind and could follow the route blindfolded.'

Ella would have turned down the invitation had it come from Compton. But more than anything else, it was the way Amar said it that led her to believe he had only good intentions, and no lewd ulterior motives. Perhaps it was naïve to trust a man she barely knew, but Ella felt she was a good judge of character; it was a skill she had acquired over many years of working as a nurse. As soon as she made her decision, she set all other thoughts to one side and simply looked forward to the shadow play.

◆ ◆ ◆

There was something quite magical about riding through the night in this part of the world. A glass of champagne couldn't have provided a more effervescent thrill. Yet it wasn't the eerie dance of flickering light and shadow cast over the plantation by the moon that left her body trembling; rather, it was the opportunity to nestle against Amar's back – to feel him closer than ever before. He was muscular; Ella could sense that just as clearly as she felt the thud of his heart through her hand. It seemed to beat in time with her own.

She was sorry that the ride was so brief, but also excited about what she was about to see. The show was obviously about to start, for among the rapt audience, only two young Malays took notice of them and began to whisper to each other. They evidently found it strange to see a Malayan man attending a theatre performance in the company of a European woman. Yet all other eyes were already fixed on the stage.

'Those two probably think you've kidnapped me,' remarked Ella.

'But that's exactly what I've done,' declared Amar with a mischievous glint in his eye.

Ella hopped off the back of the horse and landed on the dusty ground. 'I'm sure they'll ask me in the morning where on earth I've been,' she said, as she skipped out of the dust cloud and tried to brush the dirt from her clothes.

Amar laughed, then dismounted and fastened his horse to a fence alongside several others. To judge by the number of stalls around them, he must have brought her to the market square. She could see the back of the sultan's palace from here, which meant that Lee's boarding house must be behind it.

There were around a hundred spectators, all of whom had already taken their seats – although 'seats' wasn't quite the right word, for the people were sitting on woven mats scattered across the ground. The audience looked up at a raised stage with a white curtain hanging from a horizontal beam. The set-up reminded Ella of a *Punch and Judy* show.

Ella and Amar approached the side of the stage, where she could see a table with holes in the top that held the puppets. They looked as though they had been impaled on wooden skewers, and their arms dangled lifelessly at their sides.

'How are the puppets controlled?' asked Ella.

'The puppeteer – the *dalang* – stands underneath the stage. Do you see those thin sticks attached to the limbs? They're used to move the arms, and sometimes the head too,' Amar explained. He seemed to be just as fascinated by the grotesque, grimacing faces as Ella was. A few of them had round heads and looked very comical. There were even animal puppets too.

Ella followed Amar to a spot fairly close to the side of the stage, and barely a minute later a light came on. Now anybody who stood behind the curtain or moved anything behind it would cast a shadow on it.

A fine tinkling of miniature bells began, followed by the voice of a narrator. Naturally, she couldn't understand a word, but she had Amar to help with that – though right then, his whispering in her ear and the delicate tickling of his breath against her cheek was far more interesting to Ella than the plot he was broadly outlining for her.

'Princess Candra has fallen in love with the crown prince of Jenggala. She is the incarnation of the goddess of love, and he is the avatar of the god of love. The story is about the flames of passion,' he breathed. Ella looked him in the eye, and he gave a shy smile. She felt so overwhelmed that she couldn't return it, and simply savoured being so close to him.

'After many adventures, they find their way to each other in the end and have a child, whom they call Raja Putra,' he whispered.

How beautifully the torchlight glittered in his eyes. Don't look away! But he did, and Ella followed his gaze back to the illuminated screen, across which birds were flapping – or rather, their black outlines. The puppeteer worked the rods so skilfully that the shadows could easily be mistaken for living creatures. A puppet resembling a young girl pranced on from the left, stopping by a flower. That had to be the princess. She caressed the blossom with her delicate hands. Although the staging lacked colour and the figure could only be identified by its silhouette, it still seemed real. The music and the narrator's sonorous voice had a hypnotic effect, drawing the audience into this golden, glittering world – and by Amar's side, Ella was only too happy to succumb.

The market square remained crowded after the performance, and although Ella had already dined with the Fosters, the smell of grilled meat wafting towards her nose was irresistible. Now was the perfect opportunity to become acquainted with the local cuisine, and why not eat from a palm leaf too? It was a totally novel experience to knead slices of crispy grilled chicken, seasoned with spicy curry sauce, into balls before devouring them with pleasure – a feast for the senses that she certainly wouldn't forget any time soon. All the same, Ella wondered how she would ever manage to get the yellow stains off her fingers.

'Use only your right hand,' Amar had instructed her when she had tried to tackle her curry with both hands. She now understood why: the left hand was reserved for more intimate uses in the lavatory, and was therefore considered unclean. But that wasn't all she learned from Amar that night. Ella had noticed that she was the only person who sat with her back against one of the posts holding up the stage, with her legs outstretched – a posture that revealed the soles of her shoes to other people. That was considered rude, and a gesture of contempt, so she was now sitting properly in accordance with local etiquette – or rather kneeling, with her feet tucked beneath her and her palm leaf resting on her lap. Admittedly, it took a while to get used to sitting like this while eating; but everybody was doing it, and without slouching either. It seemed that one developed the necessary abdominal strength over time. Amar had, at any rate – he was sitting upright, but he looked relaxed, and his white linen shirt was partly unbuttoned, allowing Ella to peek beneath the fabric. He also had beautiful hands, which showed scarcely any signs of manual labour in the fields. Although they were powerful and much larger than her own, he handled his food far more adroitly than Ella could.

After they had eaten, he helped her to her feet and led her over to a musician on the other side of the square. There they found a stand selling rice wine, which Ella much preferred to any English brandy or sherry. It washed away the spicy flavours of the curry, and left her feeling pleasantly exhilarated. Or was it the exotic sounds that made her feel so intoxicated?

'What a beautiful song.' Ella was enchanted by the voice of a young man playing a kind of bulbous guitar, which was decorated around the middle with multicoloured inlays. Its tones were flatter than the guitars she knew, but it seemed able to produce a much wider range of notes.

'What instrument is that?' she asked.

'It's called a gambus,' Amar explained.

'It must be very difficult to play,' mused Ella, admiring the skill of the musician who was able to coax such extraordinarily delicate sounds from its strings.

'Not in the least. We learn it at school.'

'You play it too, then?' she asked.

Amar nodded, and made eye contact with the gambus player. He spoke to him in the local language, and before Ella knew it, he was holding the instrument. By this point, he had attracted the attention of around a dozen onlookers. Amar closed his eyes, his hands gliding over the strings as though he had done nothing but play the instrument his whole life long, and then he began to sing. The song seemed to be a well-known one, judging by the delight on the faces of the spectators – especially the women. Amar's voice was a little higher than she had expected, and soulful, with a note of melancholy. While his eyes were closed, Ella had the opportunity to study him without the fear that he might catch her looking at him the way a woman looks at a man whom she finds deeply attractive; from his glossy hair, even features and prominent chin to his full lips. Her eyes lingered on the latter, and she caught herself wondering how it would feel if he kissed her – how he would taste. His heartfelt song stole her senses away. If only he would never stop! But her wish wasn't granted, for the final notes rang out on the gambus and Amar opened his eyes once more.

Ella didn't stop gazing at him. The way he looked back at her set her body ablaze. She could feel herself getting lost in his eyes. They communicated a desire to be near to her, without embarrassment or shame. Then he smiled a relaxed smile that was a simple expression of how happy he was just then. The world around them seemed to fall away. The formerly distinct voices in the background merged into a vague sing-song, and the outlines of the people she had seen so clearly only moments before coalesced into a colourful blur, with Amar glowing like a beacon at its heart.

'Did you like it?' he asked.

Ella was unable to reply. She gave a gentle smile – but just then, the sound of loud, aggressive voices brutally shattered her reverie. They seemed to be coming from the other side of the square, from one of the houses overlooking the market. The shrieks of a man's voice pierced the babble and hubbub around them and the crowd abruptly fell silent. A door flew open and a young man ran out of the house, followed by two British soldiers, whom Ella recognised from their uniforms and pith helmets.

'Stop!' one of the soldiers shouted at the young man. Only now did Ella recognise him. It was Mohan, the young worker from the Foster plantation.

Amar stood up and pushed his way through the crowd. Three other young men had leapt to their feet too.

'Mohan!' he called.

A warning shot rang out, but still Mohan refused to stop. Then came the crack of a second shot, just as Mohan was turning a corner to escape down a side street. He hit the ground like a felled tree, but Ella could see he was still moving. The paralysing shock that had overwhelmed her fell away. She scrambled to her feet and broke into a run.

By now, the first of the men had confronted the soldiers, hurling insults at them, and Ella saw Amar join them at the front of the crowd as she made her way towards the injured man.

'Stand aside!' yelled one of the soldiers.

'Let us through!' bellowed the other, but the human wall refused to move, allowing only Ella to pass.

She reached the victim, and saw at a glance that the bullet had hit him in the leg. The wound was bleeding heavily, and the young man's face was twisted in agony.

The soldiers fired a warning shot in the air.

Ella flinched. Although her whole body was now trembling in fear, she needed to tend to the injured man. A piece of her skirt served as a makeshift tourniquet, which she used to stop the bleeding by tying it tightly around his leg just above the wound.

Two young women hurried over to help – a Malay woman and an Indian.

'Fetch some cloth for a bandage. Hurry,' Ella instructed them.

They disappeared towards the neighbouring houses.

The first cracks had appeared in the human wall in front of the soldiers.

'Out of the way!' one of the officers shouted.

After a third warning shot, nobody dared to oppose the soldiers any longer. Women pulled their husbands back, and children wept and wailed.

One of the British soldiers grabbed Ella's shoulder from behind and spun her round roughly. Only then did he seem to realise that the woman standing protectively in front of the injured man was a European.

'Who are you?' he asked brusquely.

'I could ask you the same question! Are British soldiers murderers now?' retorted Ella, with the courage of pure desperation. 'What has this man even done?'

'He's a rebel. We found weapons in his home,' he explained, though in a less imperious tone than before.

'Whether rebel or otherwise, he needs to be taken to hospital or he'll die. The bullet has severed his femoral artery.'

The soldier briefly bent down to examine Mohan.

'Are you a doctor?' he asked her.

'I'm a nurse. St Thomas's Hospital, London.' Ella knew that the hospital was famous in Britain – the most prestigious in England. It worked. The officer nodded with respect.

'Will you go with him?' he asked.

Before Ella could answer, Amar appeared. He stood behind the officer and shook his head, as if to say: 'Don't do it.' Ella ignored him.

'Of course I'll go with him.'

'I need to take down your details. Do you have any identification?' the officer demanded.

'No, not with me.'

'With the greatest respect for your courage, madam . . . your name!' he demanded impatiently.

'Ella van Veen.'

'Are you Dutch?' he asked, and Ella nodded.

Two Malayan men were hurrying towards them with a stretcher. Ella could see a wagon drawing near too.

'Can we take the man to hospital now?' asked Ella urgently.

The officer thought for a moment, then nodded.

She helped the two attendants lift Mohan onto the stretcher.

'I'll meet you at the hospital,' Amar whispered to her.

'Make room there!' shouted the officer, before forcing Amar and two other men back onto the market square.

Three women appeared at once with clean cloth for Ella to bandage the wound.

One of the Malayan helpers gave Ella his hand to help her up onto the seat of the wagon, but she refused and climbed into the back to stay close to the victim. Mohan's eyes were filled with gratitude, and despite the pain he must be suffering, he managed to smile at her.

'Don't be afraid. You're going to live,' she told him, smiling back at him encouragingly.

She saw the same gratitude in Amar's eyes when she took a final look back at the market square just before the wagon departed. As well as the dust and the curry sauce, her blouse was now spattered with Mohan's blood. Perhaps she ought never to wash it again, as a souvenir of the most extraordinary night of her life.

It was only now, though, that Ella fully realised the danger she had put herself in. The British probably wouldn't normally let a native off so leniently, and they could easily have fired at her too. It seemed that the colonial occupiers were quick to reach for their guns – especially if it meant an opportunity to shoot at the *Orang Asli*. Edward Compton's contemptuous words rang in her ears. A man with such inhuman views could well pass them on to his subordinates, and that might even mean she would be in trouble for having helped a 'criminal' – yet no true nurse would have behaved any differently, whatever the danger. There would doubtless be anger towards the British too, and she could already sense it among the attendants who took charge of the wounded young man and rushed him into the two-storey, palm-fronted local hospital. Ella didn't understand the first two vehement curses that she heard, but the third was clear enough, as she heard the word 'British'.

'They bring nothing but misery, the English,' remarked another nurse when Ella briefly summarised what had happened. An Indian doctor, who Ella guessed was in his mid-fifties, joined them.

'He hasn't lost too much blood, but the bullet is still inside his leg. The wound must be cleaned, and then a herbal poultice placed on top,' she instructed the staff, as though she were the doctor on duty. It would have been absurd to observe the usual hierarchy, given the situation, and the staff knew that too.

'Don't worry. Our clinic might not look like a hospital in your homeland, but we'll take good care of him,' explained the doctor in a friendly manner while the attendants lifted Mohan onto a wheeled bed.

'Do you have any rock rose tea?' she asked.

The doctor looked as though he had never heard of it.

'Myrrh resin tea?' Ella hoped this description would be more familiar to him.

He gave a start, and paused for a moment at the door. 'Are you a doctor?'

'No, but I'm a nurse and I've studied naturopathic medicine. In England.'

'Why rock rose?' he asked.

'It's antibacterial, and it combats infections. You can also use it externally to clean the wound,' she explained.

'Do they teach that in your homeland? Where do you come from? Germany?' he enquired.

Ella automatically answered in the negative. She had to stick to the same story she had told everybody else.

'I'm from the Netherlands,' she replied.

The doctor took note of her words. 'I'll be sure to try that out. You should come back again tomorrow, or whenever you have time – or are you just passing through?' the doctor asked.

'No, I think I'll be here for a while yet,' said Ella spontaneously.

'Doctor Bagus,' he said, extending his hand.

'Sister Ella.'

'Pleased to meet you,' came the reply.

One of the sisters called to him from inside the hospital.

'I'm looking forward to hearing what you have to tell us about the state of medicine in your home country,' he said, before hurrying indoors.

Ella was surprised. The doctors here seemed to be much more open-minded than in Germany. Perhaps it was because they hadn't distanced themselves as much from the traditional healing arts that had been handed down to them – and then of course there was the presence of Indian medicine in the region, which recognised only two categories: surgeons and Ayurvedic doctors, who were responsible for everything else.

'Miss Kaltenbach,' she heard Amar cry in the distance. Ella wondered why he had only just arrived. A wagon transporting a severely injured patient surely ought to have been much slower than his horse. Perhaps he hadn't been able to get away any quicker, what with all the confusion at the market.

'How is he?' he asked when he reached her.

'He'll be in good hands here,' said Ella with such conviction that Amar sighed in relief.

'Jump on,' he urged.

'Don't you want to see Mohan?' she asked in surprise. She thought the two of them were friends.

'The British will question you if you stay here,' he explained, and held out his hand to help her onto his horse.

Ella didn't hesitate. Being questioned sounded dangerous. Compton might find out what had happened – and whatever he knew, Marjory would know too before long.

Although it was quiet in front of the hospital and there were no British officers in sight, Amar dug his spurs into his horse's flanks and rode off as if the devil himself were in pursuit.

Ella had thought that Amar would take her straight back to the Fosters' house, but instead, after a short while, he stopped at a clearing that bordered a small lake hidden inside the jungle. Fed by a waterfall and bathed in a pale glow from the nearly full moon, it lay just a stone's throw from the centre of town. Even so, Amar told her that the lake was only ever frequented by locals and never by the British.

He soon revealed the reason why they had stopped here. 'I think I owe you an explanation, and it's possible that your absence tonight has already been noticed. If that's the case, I won't be able to talk to you undisturbed.'

It had already occurred to Ella that Jaya would probably have returned to collect the tea things – or that Marjory might even have gone out to check on her guest herself.

'The officer told me that Mohan is a rebel and that they found weapons in his house, but I thought he was a simple plantation worker,' Ella said as the two of them made the short walk down to the shore of the lake.

Amar was plainly struggling with himself. Only once they had reached the water's edge did he begin to speak. 'The officers are telling the truth.'

'A rebel? But what does that mean?'

'Resistance against the British occupation.' The emphasis Amar placed on that final word made it clear that he wasn't particularly fond of the British either.

'Taking up arms against the English?' Ella could scarcely believe what she was hearing.

'They're exploiting our country – they have done for many years now, all under the pretext of trade and treaties.' Amar's voice was filled at once with both resignation and rage.

'And what about your nobles, the sultans? Shouldn't they be taking action?' Ella wondered.

'They were the ones who signed the treaties with the British in the first place! They've sold our country. First the Portuguese, then the Dutch, and now the English.'

'Does that mean that you're also . . . ?' She didn't dare to finish the question.

Amar nodded.

'But there must be another way.' As soon as she had said it, Ella realised that she couldn't come up with any better alternatives.

'They don't take us seriously – they think of us as beasts. If we're lucky, we might find work on a plantation or a job in the factories. But that isn't the life we want, and the raw materials – tin, rubber – they belong to us, and not to the colonial occupiers,' Amar explained, his voice seething with fury.

How could she argue with that? 'But what's the use of taking up arms and rising against them? The British will certainly outnumber you, and even if you manage to kill them all, more ships will arrive with even more soldiers, and then you'll be at war.'

Amar took her words to heart, and shrugged helplessly.

'I don't know what I would do in a situation like that either, but in any case, I abhor violence,' said Ella.

'The guns . . . They're just for our own protection,' he explained.
'Protection?'

'Why do you think so many plantations are British owned? They always want more land, and they threaten the small farmers who don't want to give up their property. They scare them, say they'll burn their plantations down if they don't sell up. We want to protect ourselves. How can we do that without weapons?'

'By not letting them intimidate you. By not showing any fear in front of them,' asserted Ella with conviction.

Amar paused for thought once more, gazing out for a while at the pale grey of the lake, before turning back to face her.

'You are a very brave and clever woman,' he said. In his eyes, she saw respect mingled with surprise – but once again, she also felt that sense of connection; a warmth that could sweep all troubling thoughts aside in the blink of an eye. If only this incident hadn't ruined their wonderful evening and brought such a brutal end to her daydreams. Under any other circumstances, this beautiful place would have elevated her burgeoning feelings for this man. 'Not now; not here,' Ella thought to herself, but she still felt an urge to kiss him. Why couldn't they look away from each other?

'We should go back . . .' she said eventually, not because she was afraid that her absence might be discovered, or because she missed the oleander house; rather, it was the fear of giving in to her feelings for a rebel – one who was sincere, who had confided in her. For that very reason, she felt more drawn to him than ever before.

◆　◆　◆

Ella peered through the open door of her bedchamber at the grandfather clock in the small parlour, which she could see from her bed. It was already half past eight in the morning. The excitement of the previous evening had taken its toll, for it had been well after midnight by the time Amar brought her back to the plantation – unnoticed, since he knew routes on which they would be guaranteed not to meet another soul. All the same, the edge of the forest was an exposed spot, so their farewell had been brief.

'Look after yourself.' His words still echoed in her ears. She could have said the same to him, for the British would very likely find out about the connection between him and Mohan. Ella fervently hoped that nothing would happen to him. Yet she too had drifted into dangerous waters, and not just because she had helped Mohan and confronted the officer. Jaya must have collected the tea things last night and no doubt would have tried to ask the house guest if she needed anything else. That meant Jaya at least must have realised Ella had slipped out. Then again, who would Jaya tell? Reassuring herself with that last thought, Ella got out of bed. She still felt as heavy as a bag of lead, but if she stayed in her room any longer, she would be forced to explain herself, since she had retired early yesterday, just like Heather. All the same, she placed her cheek on the pillow one last time, closed her eyes, and recalled the wonderful moments of the night before – the look in Amar's eyes, and that moment by the lake when she had yearned for him to kiss her. Her daydreams came to an abrupt end with a knock at the door, however. It was probably Jaya with her breakfast. She was evidently under the impression that Ella had already completed her morning ablutions and was dressed for the day.

'I'm still getting ready. Could you leave the tray on the table outside?' Ella called loudly enough for Jaya to hear. She had come a little later today, which suggested she was aware of Ella's absence the night before. When somebody went to bed late, it made no sense to bring them breakfast first thing in the morning.

Ella heard the rattle of porcelain and breathed a sigh of relief that it really had just been Jaya.

Now that she was fully awake, she could no longer daydream about the romantic atmosphere of the night before; instead she began to wonder how it was even possible that her heart had begun to burn for Amar so quickly. Just a few weeks before, Rudolf had ignited a fire of almost equal intensity. How had it been with him? The question tormented Ella as she washed herself in the bathroom. 'Different' was her immediate answer, but that didn't satisfy her in the least. After all, she had thought she was in love with Rudolf too, and her heart hadn't beaten any slower in his presence. Ella paused and looked at her reflection in the mirror. No – with Amar, it was more than just butterflies in her stomach. It was the sense of familiarity and intimacy – the urge to touch him, to yield to him.

With Rudolf, that feeling had been purely erotic in nature – an illusion born of primal urges – but with Amar, it originated more in a desire to be closer to him. Ella was shocked at this realisation, for Amar not only came from a completely different culture, but was also embroiled in the resistance against the British. Yet those facts did nothing to dampen her feelings for him. 'It's his openness,' she said to herself. That was a major difference between him and that fraudster whom she had been so taken in by . . . And there was something else too, which she mulled over as she ran her brush through her hair: the honest feelings of a straightforward man who eschewed convention, and to whom all shallow repartee was foreign. That was the diametrical opposite of Rudolf's world, with its hierarchies and intricacies. Amar quite simply wasn't the kind of man who felt he had to play certain roles in order to impress women. That was what it boiled down to.

Resolving her dilemma in this way felt more invigorating to Ella than even the heartiest breakfast, though she still sat down to enjoy the food that had been left for her on the terrace. The peace didn't last for long, however, for a carriage was approaching the house. It was audible even at this distance. Ella assumed that the British would be looking for her, and a lump of toast caught in her throat. To her great relief, however, she saw that it was the Fosters' coach. Barely a minute later, it stopped in front of the house and Raj helped Marjory down. They must have driven into town to go shopping, for the back of the coach was laden with bags and boxes, which Raj carried into the main building. As he did so, Marjory cast a glance over at the oleander house and waved. Ella had been expecting that. Part of the terrace was visible from the main house – the section that caught the sun in the morning. If only she had taken a seat in the shade, where she couldn't be seen! There was nothing for it but to return her greeting. Ella hoped that Marjory would have to go inside first to help put the shopping away, but to no avail; Marjory walked directly towards her. Ella just had time to swallow her toast and wash it down with a gulp of tea.

'Good morning, Ella. I hope you slept well,' Marjory said.

'It's simply wonderful here. It must be the scent of the oleander – one falls into a deep sleep that couldn't be more restorative,' Ella gushed.

Marjory gave a knowing nod and cast her eyes pensively over the oleander bushes.

'Do you have any tea left? I could do with some refreshment. My mouth is quite parched from all the dust on the way into town.'

Ella made an inviting gesture, and she sat down in the wicker chair opposite her while Ella poured her some tea.

'It seems that the town is no longer a safe place,' Marjory began.

Ella shot her a questioning look.

'Last night there was a fracas at the market. I heard it from Edward. By the way, he asked about you,' said Marjory.

From her tone, Ella could tell she wasn't just making small talk and her hand began to tremble involuntarily. It cost her some effort to pass the teacup without spilling anything. Marjory's watchful eyes took note of everything and Ella tried to downplay her growing nervousness with a winsome smile.

'He told me that one of our workers was injured. It appears that the man is an insurrectionist – they found some guns in his possession,' Marjory went on.

Ella felt sure that Compton would also have mentioned the European woman who tended to the 'insurrectionist' and stood up to his subordinates.

The way Marjory was looking at her felt familiar – there was something maternal about it that reminded Ella of the way her mother looked at her when she knew she had done something wrong. She felt cornered. What should she do? Deny all knowledge and risk being exposed? She would lose Marjory's trust if that happened. Ella decided to go on the offensive, just as she had always done with her own mother in the hope of avoiding punishment.

'I saw it all for myself last night. A most regrettable incident that ruined a perfectly pleasant evening for everybody there,' she said.

'Really? You were in town?' Marjory looked surprised.

'For the shadow play . . . My boarding house recommends it to all visitors, and I have to say, it was breathtakingly beautiful,' Ella enthused, entirely truthfully. At the same time, she thanked heaven once again that she was so adept at finding plausible excuses.

'A young European woman is supposed to have tended to our worker,' Marjory hinted. It wasn't a question. She knew full well that the woman she spoke of was sitting opposite her. Another reason for Ella not to regret having put her cards on the table.

'I was the one who treated him. The man would have bled to death if I hadn't,' she admitted openly, and with a nurse's inner conviction that couldn't be denied.

Marjory raised her eyebrows in surprise. 'In that case, I owe you my thanks. From what Raj tells me, he is a hard worker – leaving aside his questionable inclinations,' said Marjory.

'Do you really believe that this man is an insurrectionist?' Ella asked the question to sound Marjory out – to see whether she suspected Ella of any political motives, or of having sided with the local population. That wasn't implausible, given that her conduct had bordered on rudeness during Compton's visit.

'Why else would he be stockpiling firearms? Malays don't go hunting – not with guns, at any rate,' said Marjory.

Ella nodded to show interest.

'As much as I would like to keep him on once he has recovered – particularly because he is a good worker – I am obliged to let him go. Even we plantation owners can't afford to get on the wrong side of the authorities.'

So a British landowner apparently had no choice in how she dealt with the matter – but Ella could see through Marjory's words, and she refrained from commenting.

'It's very much to your credit that you saved a man's life – but these days, when one fraternises excessively with the locals or cares too much about them, one can very easily fall into disrepute,' Marjory added in an unmistakable tone.

'My interest in politics has always been small. People are all that matter to me, and to be perfectly honest with you, I can't approve of British soldiers shooting at young Malay men.' Ella too made herself unmistakably clear.

Marjory nodded respectfully, despite her differing views. What needed to be said had now been said. She emptied her teacup and stood up.

'I'm sure Heather will be waiting for you most impatiently. I'm truly delighted that you're both getting along so well.' With these words, Marjory suddenly seemed a different woman.

Ella sensed that her joy was unfeigned and she acknowledged the compliment with a warm smile. She too was happy at the prospect of doing something with Heather, though she would have much preferred to spend the day with Amar. Yet that would evidently be much trickier now, given Marjory's attitude and the many eyes and ears that carried all news to her.

CHAPTER 11

Although they hadn't explicitly discussed it the evening before, Ella knew that Heather would once again have come up with plenty of plans for the day. Going to bed early seemed to have done her good, for Ella hadn't expected to find Heather in such an upbeat mood after Compton's visit last night. Her high spirits were infectious, and helped Ella shake off the tensions from the morning.

'Let's ride to the coast.' Heather's wish was Ella's command. Anything, so long as they could spend time together.

'That will certainly do you good.' Marjory's remark had cemented their plans, and it went without saying that Heather had already instructed the stable boy to saddle their ponies.

The ride this time was significantly less taxing than their excursion into the hilly hinterland, and much shorter too. Ella knew part of the route already, for they were riding south towards Singapore. They were aiming for a road just a couple of miles outside the town, which branched off towards a beach Heather had occasionally visited as a child with her parents to strengthen her constitution with the salty sea air. Halfway through their journey, Ella was surprised to find that Heather still hadn't asked her about her trip to Johore the night before. Marjory must have told her all about Ella's confession that she had tended to one of her workers – and yet Heather hadn't mentioned it once, instead regaling her with childhood memories and descriptions of the local beaches. By now, however, they were travelling at a leisurely pace along well-paved roads that were easily navigated, and Heather used the opportunity to question her after all.

'Mother told me about last night's events at the market,' she began.

Ella merely nodded.

'Did the soldier really shoot at that man? How did it come to that?'

'They found guns in his home. It seems that he's part of the resistance. Mohan ran away, so they fired a warning shot, but he wouldn't stop,' answered Ella.

'I don't understand how people are capable of things like that . . . of shooting at their fellow human beings.' Heather looked indignant, and Ella was surprised that she was standing up for her worker. 'Perhaps we would behave in exactly the same way if we had foreigners in our country . . . rise up against them, defend ourselves,' Heather mused.

'All the same, Marjory will let him go,' Ella pointed out.

'She has no choice. Besides, she's a royalist through and through and she's convinced we aren't doing the country any harm,' explained Heather.

'She told me to pay no heed to the interests of the native population in future,' said Ella.

'Well-intentioned advice. That really is frowned upon,' Heather confirmed.

'By whom? By you British, or by the Malays?' Ella asked.

Heather merely laughed, to Ella's bafflement.

'Why are you laughing?'

'Did you ride to Johore alone last night, perchance?' The question took Ella completely by surprise.

'Of course not,' Ella replied.

'Did Raj go with you?' Ella could tell from Heather's expression that the question wasn't a serious one.

'No.'

Heather was clearly bursting with curiosity.

'I suppose Marjory has already discussed this with you,' Ella stated.

'She thinks you rode into town on your own.'

'Marjory? But nothing escapes her – she can practically hear the grass growing,' exclaimed Ella in surprise.

'You overestimate her.' Now it was Heather's turn to be mysterious. Ella's curiosity was piqued too.

'Come, tell me,' Ella urged.

'I asked the stable boy this morning. He sleeps in the out-building, in case a fire breaks out or a storm frightens the horses,' Heather explained.

'And? What did he say?' Ella probed.

'He said only one horse went into town.' Heather grinned.

'Well, there you are, then. That tells you I was alone.'

Heather laughed again. The conversation was evidently amusing her more and more.

'Amar's horse was the one missing,' Heather finally revealed.

'So you're spying on me now.' Ella delivered her accusation with a mischievous grin.

'A most attractive man, isn't he?' said Heather.

'You know him, then?' Ella was surprised. Amar had told her that only Raj was allowed onto the Fosters' property, and that he had barely seen Heather at all.

'We met once in the stables,' said Heather.

Ella was astonished at her directness.

'Do you like him?' Heather asked.

Ella saw no reason to lie to her, and nodded.

'You wouldn't be the first woman to fall under the spell of the men around here.'

'I haven't fallen under his spell.' Ella's protest rang hollow even to her own ears – after all, she was already missing him, and had been wondering how he was all day long.

'No man is worth wasting your feelings on,' declared Heather abruptly with a stony expression. She seemed to be drifting back into the same dark mood as before. Ella was familiar enough with Heather's views on the male sex by now, but she had thought that her dismissive attitude applied only to Englishmen.

Heather dug her spurs into her horse's flanks and rode on ahead towards the sea, which now lay before them at the end of the road, enticing them onwards with snow-white sand and shady palm trees.

Ella couldn't make sense of Heather. How was it possible for anybody to have such dramatic mood swings? No sooner had they reached the sea and tethered their horses in the shade of a palm grove than Heather's eyes once again began to sparkle more brightly than the sun. Ella had been expecting her to continue interrogating her about her feelings for Amar, but the subject of men seemed to have been dropped altogether.

'Isn't it glorious here?' she called instead. With that, Heather unselfconsciously began to undress. Ella would never have thought that an Englishwoman would go swimming without a bathing costume – in fact, she hadn't expected to swim in the sea at all. She didn't have her own costume with her, in any case.

Barely a minute later, Heather was in the water, as naked as the day she was born.

'Come now. There's nobody around, and nobody will find us here either,' she whooped over the waves as she dived and splashed.

Ella preferred to verify that for herself, and she cast her eyes over the small cove, which seemed to consist of only three clumps of palm trees. There was just a single path leading here – the one they had come down – and so she decided to trust Heather. She still had to muster her courage before she could strip off entirely, but she eventually managed it and joined Heather in the sea. The water was refreshing, and it was such fun to fling herself into the gentle surf and be pushed back by the crests of the waves. Although she and Heather appeared not to have as much in common as she would expect two sisters to share, they really did seem to be cut from the same cloth when it came to their love of water. They drifted on their backs together like boats, and Ella savoured the feeling of floating and the saltwater splashing against her skin.

'You've gone red,' Ella declared. Heather's skin was unused to the sun.

'On my neck?'

Ella looked more closely, and gave a start. Heather had a crescent-shaped birthmark in exactly the same place as her own. There could no longer be any doubt that they were half-sisters.

'What's the matter? Is it as bad as all that?' asked Heather, placing her hand on the spot.

'No . . . but we should still go back into the shade.'

Heather waded out of the sea and sat down at the foot of a palm tree that had grown into a sort of natural bench, making it an ideal place to sit and rest.

Ella lingered in the water and looked over at her half-sister. Although her growing certainty about that made her happy, and gave her the feeling that her journey had been worthwhile, it came with the bitter realisation that she had also acquired a stepmother who had her workers flogged and who certainly wasn't easy to get along with.

'Come on. We need to dry ourselves off, and we shouldn't get back too late,' Heather called over to her.

Ella suddenly remembered that she had been press-ganged by Compton to accompany the Fosters to the annual garden party thrown by a British woman who lived locally. Family obligations must be met.

◆ ◆ ◆

A formal visit called for thorough preparation – and not just in terms of clothing. Heather's suggestion that they should get back as early as possible had proven wise. Ella was very glad that she had packed a suitable dress, and her blue evening gown – which she had already worn on special occasions during the crossing – was exceptionally elegant. Her curls had grown particularly unruly in the hot climate, but Heather lent her a few hairpins to tame them with. Like Heather, Ella opted to wear her hair up, leaving two strands that wound down her temples and curled playfully around her earrings – likewise borrowed from Heather's jewellery collection.

Marjory's hairstyle was austere compared to Ella's and Heather's, as was her black outfit, while Heather's salmon-pink dress was more understated. She must have put on a corset too, judging by her perfect waist – and to think that she was wearing one in this heat! Even Raj, who had been promoted to an elegant coachman for the evening, was clad in a grey suit that looked very smart on him.

The hour-long coach ride to the north proved entertaining, albeit rather exhausting, as Ella was given a lengthy who's who account of the invited guests. Marjory held forth, with Heather adding titbits here and there. It was impossible to remember the names of all the high-ranking officials, fellow British plantation owners, tin mine operators travelling down from the north, and influential traders. All Ella had taken away from the lesson was that the powerful people who effectively governed the country all congregated at Mary Bridgewater's once a year to celebrate and do business. The only details she had found interesting enough to retain were those concerning Mary Bridgewater herself – though they were limited to vague conjecture, since nobody seemed to know exactly why this sixty-three-year-old woman exerted so much influence throughout Malacca. She didn't come from a noble family, nor did she occupy a particularly high rank.

'There are rumours that Mary is distantly related to the royal family.' Marjory's explanation seemed the most likely to Ella. From all these descriptions, she imagined Mary's house to be more magnificent than it was, and certainly bigger and more impressive than the Fosters' – yet the exact opposite proved to be the case. At first glance, it reminded Ella of the middle-class cottages she had seen in England. It had a masonry foundation and a wattle-and-daub façade with dark beams intersecting patches of white plaster, and was capped by a steep tiled roof lined with dormer windows. There was even a lawn, and if it weren't for the palms dotted throughout the extensive garden, the European plants would have made Ella think that she really was in England. Rose bushes wound their way up the sides of the house – perhaps thanks to the altitude. It was significantly cooler up here than on the plain or by the coast.

'Little England,' exclaimed Ella, as Raj stopped the coach by the entrance to let them out.

'You're right – though Mary's house is the exception to the rule around these parts. If you aren't put off by the thought of a three-day overland journey then you and Heather should travel even further north, to the Cameron Highlands. The climate there is almost the same as at home, except that one can also grow tea,' said Marjory. Then she began to wave almost frantically at a woman of around her own age. That must be the hostess. She was wearing a hat adorned with a floral arrangement that perfectly matched the pattern of her dress. This walking flower shop immediately abandoned two uniformed officers and their female companions and hurried over to Marjory, greeting her and Heather with a warm smile.

'Mary,' trumpeted an overjoyed Marjory as she climbed down from the coach.

'Marjory,' came the no less delighted reply. Then it was Heather's turn. The lady embraced her like her own daughter.

'Let me have a look at you.' Mary had clearly known the Fosters for many years, and appeared to be a close friend of the family.

'We have taken the liberty of inviting a delightful young lady from the Netherlands. She's our guest, and has quickly grown very dear to us.' Ella was almost embarrassed by Marjory's effusiveness, so she decided to introduce herself directly.

'Ella van Veen.'

'Delighted to make your acquaintance. I can still vividly recall the wonderful flowers that grow in your homeland. What wouldn't I give to plant a few tulips here, but I fear they wouldn't thrive in this climate.' Ella sensed that Mary's pleasure at her visit was genuine. Some people simply radiated warm-heartedness and generosity, and Mary Bridgewater was one of them.

'Malacca is blessed with such wonderful floral variety that not even the flower market in Rotterdam can compare,' answered Ella.

'Very true. I fear that's why I've fallen so deeply in love with this little patch of earth,' admitted Mary.

'Mary,' came a voice from the stables, where the arriving guests were leaving their horses to be looked after. Another new arrival, then – and a weighty one at that, judging by both his girth and the many medals dangling from his uniformed chest.

'My guests are calling . . . But we must talk again later. It's rare that one encounters a fellow flower enthusiast, and I want to hear all about the market.' With that, Mary made her excuses, nodded at Heather and Marjory, and departed to greet her guest.

'I think she likes you,' Heather remarked.

Ella was unable to escape the impression that Marjory wasn't pleased with this development. After all, Mary had spent longer talking to Ella than to her supposedly close friend. It seemed that the value of a visitor here was gauged by how much time this mysterious Mary Bridgewater spent conversing with them.

'Let's join the other guests,' suggested Marjory.

The idea wasn't a bad one, but Ella had spotted somebody among the throng of people surrounding the buffet whom she truly wasn't looking forward to seeing again: Edward Compton. She hoped he wouldn't ask her about her night-time intervention at the market in Johore.

Ella had successfully freed both herself and Heather from her mother's invisible reins – Marjory had become engrossed in conversation with a woman around her own age who was also a major landowner, and hadn't noticed Heather absconding with her guest, whom Marjory had intended to show off to the other partygoers. The two of them headed towards the garden, as far away from Compton as possible, and Heather took it upon herself to give Ella a little taste of colonial life.

'Those two own a tin mine in the north, and they're so influential that a railway line is currently being built out to their property,' Heather whispered as they walked towards an English couple around Marjory's age. They must be very wealthy indeed, for there was a young Malayan boy standing beside them holding a parasol over the lady's head to shield her complexion from the sun. How absurd – it was about to set anyway. Imperial power was on full display here, though their hostess seemed to convey the exact opposite of all that in her manner.

'There you are!' There was no mistaking it – that was Edward Compton's voice. Ella couldn't believe her eyes. He was bearing a small plate laden with samples of Mary's legendary English cheese selection, which he had lovingly arranged especially for her.

'We British may not be famous for our cheeses, but you should at least give us a fair chance and try them for yourself,' he said with a charming smile.

Even Heather was unable to suppress a grin. It seemed that Compton could be pleasant after all, though his attempt to flirt with Ella by pursuing her with a plate of cheese was somewhat clumsy.

Ella sampled a slice, and not just out of politeness. 'Indeed! The Cheddar tastes just like in your homeland – perhaps even better,' she declared.

'Are you familiar with England?' he asked in surprise. Marjory obviously hadn't told him everything about her yet, as Ella had assumed.

'I trained as a nurse there, and learned to love the country,' she answered truthfully.

'Then I'm sure you must feel very much at home here,' he concluded.

'Mary's house certainly does remind me of my trips to Oxfordshire. I saw some similar architecture there.'

'You can detect the English influence everywhere in Malacca these days,' Compton replied, while Ella swallowed a second piece of cheese in polite acknowledgement of his kind gesture. She also offered a slice to Heather, who accepted somewhat more reluctantly.

'One wonders whether that is entirely a good thing,' she remarked. After all, the neatly arranged cheeses on the plate couldn't distract from the fact that this was the man who ordered his troops to shoot at young *Orang Asli*. Ella couldn't bring herself to swallow a third slice.

'Schools, roads, trade . . . Malacca has never had it so good,' gushed Compton with such conviction one was almost inclined to believe him.

But Ella knew better. 'Apparently not everybody sees it that way,' she stated.

Compton gave her a knowing smile, which didn't surprise her, since she knew from Marjory that he was aware of her nocturnal escapade.

'Perhaps you've merely gained the wrong impression,' he suggested.

'In all honesty, I don't believe that's the case.' Ella saw no reason to curry favour with Compton.

'If I weren't so impressed with your courage . . . but it was also for Marjory's sake that I spared you from being questioned over the incident at the market.' He had finally come out with it. There was no longer any reason to stand there exchanging meaningless pleasantries. Besides, Ella could see that Heather was already suffering in his presence. She clearly preferred to remain silent, which had the advantage that the remaining slices of cheese were disappearing one by one into her mouth.

'Is it a crime to help an injured man?' Ella asked frankly.

'Not in the least . . . But it's all over and done with now. Let's move on to more pleasant topics. At any rate, I couldn't possibly hold anything against such an enchanting lady.' Coming from a man of his stature, the compliment was a flattering one, and Ella accepted it with a polite smile.

Heather handed the plate to Compton.

'Delicious, quite delicious . . . But cheese makes one so thirsty. Please excuse me while I visit the buffet for a refreshing glass of wine.' With that, she was gone.

Compton seemed glad to have Ella all to himself. She could sense that the other guests – mostly officers – had begun to notice them and were starting to whisper, which made her feel uneasy. They might think she was flirting with him. A patronising glance from a man around Compton's age wearing a pith helmet and shorts was enough to confirm that impression.

'I would love to show you a side of the country that you haven't yet seen. Perhaps you'll change your mind once you've travelled by train through the jungle and crossed bridges over deep gorges. None of that would be there without us.' Compton was proving uncomfortably persistent in his attempts to win her over, both for himself and for his imperial overlords.

'I greatly appreciate your offer, but I'm afraid I've fallen so deeply in love with the local culture and customs that I would prefer not to have my illusions shattered.' Ella hoped her rejection would do minimal damage to his feelings, though she had certainly made herself clear enough.

'Only with the local culture?' came the prompt retort, which took Ella completely by surprise.

'With the people too.' She stuck to her resolve to show no weakness in front of men like this Compton, although she noticed that her pulse had quickened. Perhaps she had been seen with Amar after all. But what if she had? She didn't have to explain herself to anybody – least of all to Compton, governor or not!

Compton took that personally, for his hitherto friendly smile suddenly froze.

'Well, Edward, aren't you going to introduce me to this charming lady?' interrupted the officer in short trousers, who had just joined them.

'Please excuse me, gentlemen. Mary is looking for me.' Ella thanked her lucky stars that she had spotted the hostess at the buffet, and that she wasn't surrounded by guests for once.

'I'm coming!' she called to her audaciously, though Mary hadn't even looked in her direction. It worked. Mary beamed from ear to ear. To Edward and the other officer, it would look as though Mary had beckoned her over, and Mary Bridgewater's wishes seemed to carry as much weight with Compton as with everybody else. At least he would now be spared any further loss of face. He could take the clown in shorts with him on his silly train trip, if he liked.

By now, Ella understood why Mary Bridgewater seemed to pull so many strings around here. Her powers of observation were superb, and she was an impeccable judge of character. She also knew all there was to know about everybody and everything, which made it easier to get people to do her bidding, and Compton appeared to be just another of her willing subjects.

'You mustn't mind Edward – he makes advances towards every pretty young lady who comes his way. He should stop and ask himself why nobody has ever taken him up on his offer.' Mary always seemed to get straight to the point, and had apparently been watching them the whole time.

Ella was so dumbfounded that Mary laughed out loud.

'And then the cheese! How clumsy he was, cutting it up into little pieces like that. He must really have taken a shine to you,' Mary declared.

'Unfortunately, the feeling is not mutual,' Ella pointed out hurriedly.

'That was clear enough,' laughed Mary. 'All the same, you should try not to make your aversion too obvious, as Edward can behave like a sulky child sometimes. Especially in light of your impressive escapade last night . . .'

'You know about that?'

'Everybody knows about it, and most of them admire you for it,' Mary declared. Her eyes flitted towards the governor. 'He's look-ing this way. Give him a smile to placate him.'

Ella did as she was told. Like everybody else, she couldn't help but yield to Mary's natural authority. Compton returned the smile promptly, although Ella was sure it was meant more for Mary.

'Men . . . They really do give us a cross to bear,' Mary reflected as she plucked grapes from the buffet and devoured them with relish. 'Most of the women around here aren't exactly blessed with good fortune on that front. Least of all myself,' said Mary.

'Are you married, or were you?' asked Ella.

'I was! But he had another woman. I saw to it personally that he ended up wading through swamps in India, getting eaten alive by mosquitoes. I hope they finish him off.'

Ella was beginning to understand the extent of her influence. But why did Mary's eyes now linger on Heather? She was standing beside Marjory, but seemed lost in thought and didn't look especially happy.

'Heather seems to have drawn the short straw with men too,' said Ella, hoping that Mary would take the bait. She did.

'Did she tell you that?' asked Mary in surprise.

'No, but I've noticed she's very fearful, and very cautious around men. I even get the impression that she hates them.'

Mary nodded and reflected for a moment. 'Well, it's not such a big secret. Most people knew about it at the time . . .' she began.

Ella was almost bursting with curiosity.

'His name was Jack,' Mary continued.

'An Englishman?' asked Ella.

Mary nodded.

'Heather was involved with an Englishman?' Ella presumed that this Jack was the reason Heather appeared to be so dismissive when it came to romance.

'I think it would be more accurate to say she was passionately in love with him,' said Mary, speaking a little more quietly now.

'Did he have an affair?'

'No . . . As far as I know he was redeployed, and took the opportunity to vanish into thin air, along with all his supposed feelings for Heather,' said Mary.

Ella stared at Heather, who now noticed her looking. To make sure she had understood Mary correctly, she spelled it out: 'He abandoned her?'

'Jack broke her heart,' said Mary, who by now could no longer bring herself to smile in Heather's direction. She used the grapes as a cover to make herself look preoccupied – with her mouth full, she couldn't be talking about other people.

Mary proffered the bowl to Ella, but Ella felt sure they would only catch in her throat. How Heather must have suffered. Yet this only explained her behaviour in part. Her opinions about men made sense now, but not her fearfulness. Why was she so temperamental, so subject to mood swings? What made her stay away from the oleander house? Could such an odious betrayal really destroy a person in that way? Ella resolved to find out, as gently and tactfully as possible.

◆　◆　◆

It would have been a lie to say that the remainder of Mary's party didn't have its sunnier moments. That was mainly because Compton had kept away from her, and because the rest of the guests were all interesting in their own way – be it the businessman from London who manufactured cloth here, the Belgian engineer who (unlike Compton) told exciting stories about the construction of the railway, or the wife of a plantation owner who sponsored local orphans and even gave lessons once a week. That lady in particular shed a different light on the role of the British in the country. Nothing was black and white, though that didn't change the fact that one nation – the United Kingdom – was enriching itself at the expense of another. All the same, on the way home, Ella talked enthusiastically about the party in general and the agreeable people she had met. Surprisingly, her comments fell on deaf ears with Marjory, who was strangely taciturn. Perhaps the evening had been too tiring for a lady of her age. At one point on the journey, she even nodded off to sleep, resting her head against the side of the coach. Only Heather passed occasional comment on Ella's chatter – especially when Ella mentioned her fascination with Mary, who had so confidently forged her own path through a world otherwise dominated by men.

'Do you really believe she's related to the royal family?' asked Ella.

'Nobody knows for certain. But you might say she's the queen of Malacca. Nobody would ever dare to go against her will,' said Heather, speaking in hushed tones to avoid waking up her mother.

'She strikes me as a very warm-hearted person,' declared Ella.

'No wonder you get on with her so well,' said Heather.

Ella received the compliment with great pleasure.

'You have more in common than you think, though.' Heather lowered her voice even further.

Ella gave her a quizzical look.

'It seems she has a taste for native men. She's rumoured to have an Indian lover, and Mother even thinks she's having a secret affair with her gardener.'

'Well then, we don't have anything else in common after all,' answered Ella with a grin. Heather was obviously referring to Amar, but he wasn't a gardener. Still, she took a moment to think of him and hoped she would see him again soon.

'Your eyes tell a different story,' Heather replied.

Ella admitted defeat and shrugged her shoulders, feigning innocence.

Initially, she had resolved to find a quiet moment to talk to Heather about her former love – ideally at a time when Marjory wasn't present. But Marjory had been snoring for a while now, so Ella decided to seize the opportunity, given that they were already talking about matters of the heart.

'These things happen from time to time – generally when one least expects it.'

'The curse of love,' said Heather.

'Was it a curse for you?' Ella was direct, but compassionate.

Heather slowly seemed to realise what she was driving at and glared at her suspiciously by way of reply.

'Mary mentioned . . .' Ella began cautiously.

'She's always sticking her nose into things that are none of her business,' came the combative retort, delivered at normal speaking volume. Ella hoped Marjory wouldn't wake up.

Ella considered backing down – but when would she be able to discuss this with Heather if not now?

'He hurt you very badly, didn't he?'

Heather's expression turned to stone, her eyes narrowing and glittering with fury. Given her reaction, Ella realised that this hadn't been the right moment after all.

'I'm sorry . . . I shouldn't have asked,' she relented.

'Mary Bridgewater is an almighty blabbermouth. You shouldn't believe everything she says, especially when she's talking half-truths.'

Ella had the impression that Heather was speaking in her mother's voice – but she didn't understand what she meant by 'half-truth'.

'Mary Bridgewater,' exclaimed Heather in such an outraged tone that she woke up Marjory, who gathered herself and looked somewhat distractedly at her companions.

'Ah . . . You're talking about dear old Mary . . . Isn't she quite charming?' she said.

Ella sighed in relief that she clearly hadn't heard any of their conversation. She could see that Heather was struggling to compose herself.

'Yes, a most delightful lady,' she trilled in a honeyed voice, but shot a meaningful look at Ella.

CHAPTER 12

Ella woke with a start, drenched in sweat. Although normally soft and tinted by the oleander blossom, the light this morning was so blindingly bright that she had to squint her eyes. She could still vividly recall her nightmare. In it, Heather had been lying naked in Edward Compton's arms by the side of the hidden lake that Amar had shown her. Ella had to sit up in bed before she could shake off the images from her dream. What had possessed her to open her mouth yesterday? It had only served to deepen the riddle of Heather's strange behaviour – and even worse, she had probably incurred Heather's displeasure too. That was the last thing she wanted.

Ella's assumption was proven correct soon after breakfast, which she ate on the terrace as usual. She felt guilty for having offended Heather. There were only two ways to tackle such a delicate situation: she could either steer clear of Heather until her temper had settled, or attempt to restore normal relations straight away. Ella had picked up her easel with the intention of sitting in an obvious place in the garden where Heather could see her – but then she dismissed the idea, for her inner unease was growing by the minute. She kept looking across at the Fosters' house. On a normal day, she would have headed over there by now to wish Heather a good morning and make plans for the day, yet the building showed no signs of life.

To put an end to her growing uncertainty, she decided to walk straight over to the house. Back to normality – or so it seemed to begin with.

'Good morning, Miss van Veen.' Jaya greeted her with a warm smile, just like always, and Ella immediately felt calmer.

'Is Heather up yet?' she asked.

'No, but I can go and check on her if you like,' Jaya offered.

'Oh no, please don't. The party was very tiring yesterday,' Ella demurred, and debated adding that she would come back again in an hour – yet Marjory forced her hand.

'Ella. Come and join me.' Her voice rang out from the drawing room.

Ella peered inside and saw Marjory sitting at her desk by the window. The fact that she hadn't wished her a good morning was a bad sign, but she soon made up for the omission – albeit alarmingly formally – once Ella had stepped inside and joined her.

'Heather is indisposed. She sends her apologies.'

Ella's throat instantly felt tight. Was it really such an unpardonable sin to ask an adult woman about an unhappy love affair? Surely it wasn't the end of the world – and yet it seemed to be for Heather.

To Ella's surprise, however, Marjory made no further mention of Heather's indisposition.

'Nothing but paperwork, all day long,' Marjory sighed. 'Yet the most tiring part of it is making decisions, whether weighty or trivial. Would you like a cup of tea?' she continued.

'No, thank you. I've just had one,' Ella answered. Marjory gestured for her to sit down on the sofa by the desk, and she complied.

'It must be extremely challenging to manage a plantation as big as this one. You have my utmost respect.' Ella hoped the conversation would remain on general topics, but Marjory's obvious nervousness suggested it wouldn't.

'Perhaps you can offer me some advice,' she said, giving Ella a meaningful look.

'What could a nurse possibly advise you on?' Ella asked, puzzled.

'On staffing matters. I am currently facing the difficult decision of whether to dismiss an employee,' explained Marjory with a self-satisfied smile.

'Mohan?' asked Ella. Perhaps Marjory had reconsidered, and he would be able to stay on after all once he had recovered.

'That decision has already been made, thankfully. It's simply impossible for me to employ a rebel here on the plantation.'

From Marjory's expression and the fact that she was discussing all this with her, Ella could draw only one conclusion: she was talking about Amar. How on earth had she found out that he was also involved with the resistance against the British? Asking her that might be taken as a confession of his guilt, however, so Ella merely looked at her questioningly.

'The decision relates to Amar.' Marjory finally came out with it.

Ella had to watch her words very carefully – she mustn't say anything that would implicate Amar, but she couldn't lie either.

'One of your workers,' Ella remarked.

'Indeed . . . and from what Edward has told me, he's often been seen in Mohan's company. The two of them appear to be friends,' said Marjory.

Ella had difficulty hiding her growing anxiety. At least Marjory hadn't mentioned the fact that he had been seen with her too.

'Is that reason enough to dismiss him?' asked Ella.

'I'm not sure. What do you think of him?'

By now, Ella knew Marjory well enough to realise that she knew more than she was letting on. Had Heather told her that she had gone to see the shadow play with Amar? Or even that she had feelings for him?

'I'm afraid I don't know him well enough to be able to form an opinion,' Ella answered cautiously.

'But you rode into town with him, didn't you?'

Ella felt like she was undergoing a police interrogation. There was no point in lying.

'Of course . . . I wanted to see the puppet show, and I didn't want to go into Johore on my own.' She spoke as if it were the most natural thing in the world. Marjory seemed to accept it, for she nodded and visibly relaxed.

'That's the most unfortunate thing about our little world out here – one can't go anywhere without being seen. The officers told Compton, and he relayed the information to me. He believes that Amar is a rebel too.'

'He probably thinks that about every Malay,' Ella couldn't resist adding.

'You may be right there. All the same, please heed my advice and keep your distance from the local population in future – especially Amar. You might bring us all into disrepute otherwise.'

Ella sized Marjory up. If she had known that Ella harboured feelings for Amar, she would have reacted differently – Ella was certain of that. So Heather hadn't betrayed her confidence after all. Yet she couldn't rule out the possibility that the soldiers had seen them together that night and drawn their own conclusions. And if Compton knew that, he certainly wouldn't be pleased at the thought that she preferred to watch the shadow play with a Malayan man over joining him on a train trip, given that she had rejected him at Mary's party.

'So you want to dismiss him because Compton is suspicious of him? Does he have any proof?' asked Ella.

'Even if he did, he certainly wouldn't mention it to me. It's none of our business either. We depend upon the protection of the

Crown,' answered Marjory unequivocally. 'But you could put in a good word for Amar with Edward . . .' she added.

'Me?' asked Ella in surprise.

'Just go to the opera with him, or give him a few kind words . . . We women know well enough how to wrap men like Compton around our little fingers,' answered Marjory with a complacent smile.

'I'm afraid I'm quite the wrong person to flatter a man's wounded vanity, or give him false hope.' Ella likewise made her position unmistakably clear.

Marjory sighed, but then managed to muster up a gentle smile.

'I can completely understand your reservations in this case. Men are a tricky subject, don't you think? Anyway, what do you have planned today? Would you like to do some drawing? Raj is driving into town – he could take you with him.' Marjory was obviously finished with the subject, and she also made it quite plain that Heather wanted to remain alone today. One thing was certain, however: Ella had to warn Amar about Edward Compton.

Ella wanted neither to draw nor to accompany Raj into town on the coach, but she thought it wise to accept Marjory's offer for appearances' sake – after all, if anybody would know where Amar was, it was Raj. Yet asking him directly about Amar was out of the question. It was already bad enough that Heather and Marjory knew about her night-time excursion into town. Once again, however, Ella was able to rely on her gift for improvisation.

'Do you have the day off today, then?' she asked Raj, after he had helped her onto the coach in a surprisingly gentlemanly manner. He was evidently prepared to take her with him – indeed, he seemed to do everything Marjory wanted or suggested.

'No, I'm going shopping for Mrs Foster. It'll take around three hours, and then you can come back with me,' he explained.

'Ah, then I suppose that young man with the whip will be looking after the plantation,' Ella remarked, with an innocent smile.

It took Raj a moment to realise what she was talking about.

'You mean Amar?'

She feigned an innocent shrug, and Raj began to laugh.

Ella was puzzled at that.

'I take it we're talking about the young man who likes to take young ladies out to watch the shadow play,' said Raj with a smirk.

'How do you know about that? Did Mrs Foster . . . ?' she asked frankly, since their cards were already on the table.

'Mrs Foster? Was she there too?'

Ella was baffled by his question.

'I saw you myself. A wonderful performance, don't you agree?' Raj added.

It really did seem impossible to go anywhere in Johore without everybody spying on you.

'He rode into town just now to visit Mohan at the hospital. I can drop you off there, if you like.'

Ella gaped in astonishment. She had completely misjudged the man. His helpful and friendly manner was in complete contrast to his terrifying appearance and brutal punishments.

'I can't make you out at all,' Ella declared.

'What do you mean by that?'

'I had a very different impression of you when we first met.'

'I was just doing my job.'

'With a firm hand,' Ella pointed out.

'Mohan had stolen something . . .'

'I was told that he merely borrowed it,' she clarified.

'His reasons were what mattered. I've known for a long time that he's been working for the resistance, and he's free to do so, but not with equipment from this plantation,' replied Raj placidly.

Ella had no answer to that. But she was surprised at how much the Indian knew. And his proximity to the Fosters meant there was much more he might be able to reveal to her. It was worth a try, at any rate. She allowed a few moments of silence to pass to make her question seem more nonchalant.

'It's a pity that Heather didn't want to come with us. She doesn't get out very often.'

'No, indeed she doesn't.'

'Perhaps that's natural when one spends so many years living on a plantation, so far from town,' mused Ella – although she knew perfectly well that that couldn't be the reason.

'Possibly,' answered Raj.

'There's one thing I don't understand, though . . . She seems to be downright afraid of certain things. The guest house, for example . . .'

Raj gave her a penetrating look, and was clearly debating whether he ought even to reply.

'She's such a cheerful and vivacious person otherwise,' Ella added.

'I expect everybody is afraid of something. In India, we believe it's part of one's karma to overcome those fears,' he said.

His remark made Ella conclude he must be hiding something, for she knew that karma related to an individual's past life. Hindus believed in transmigration of the soul – but what did that have to do with the oleander house?

'Do you mean to say she might have lived here once before?' Ella hoped to draw him out a little further.

'People can be afraid of past events in their current life too,' he said.

'But how can one be afraid of a house?'

'You ask too many questions. Some things answer themselves.' Raj's final remark unambiguously blocked her from asking anything more.

Ella now felt certain that he knew more than he was letting on, but his solidarity with the Fosters seemed to prevent him from revealing anything more. Further enquiries would have been pointless. Something must have happened in this house that Heather was afraid of. At any rate, Ella didn't believe in curses. There were plenty of other things to be afraid of in life – that something might happen to Amar, for example.

Raj had promised not to tell anybody where he had dropped her off, and Ella hoped he would remain true to his word. Although her first meeting with him had given no indication that she could trust him, she did so now. Amar must have a certain degree of faith in Raj too, as he would hardly have shared his intentions with him otherwise. In any case, Amar proved easy to find in this small hospital, not least because the attendants remembered who she was and directed her to a ward on the first floor.

On entering the hospital, Ella could see straight away that the care provided here wasn't particularly advanced, and the clinic seemed short on capacity too, as there were hospital beds in the corridor. From what she could judge as she walked past, the patients lying on them were all natives with minor injuries. The more serious cases were presumably kept on the ward. Although the building was old and in urgent need of a coat of paint, she noticed how clean it was. The odour of disinfectant stung her nostrils, just like at the hospital in Hamburg. But there was one crucial difference: before today, she had never seen a hospital ward under guard. As if somebody with serious injuries could run away. Ella had no intention of being scared off by the British officer who stood stock-still by the entrance, as if he'd been posted in front of Buckingham Palace. She ignored him and reached confidently for the door handle. At that, however, the statue sprang into life.

'Excuse me – just one visitor is allowed at a time, and only if they have a legitimate reason,' he explained.

So Amar was still with Mohan, Ella reflected. 'I would like to check on the patient.'

'I presume you aren't a relative,' said the moustachioed officer, who she guessed to be around thirty years old.

'I was the one who administered first aid,' she explained.

'I'm sorry, but I have to follow the rules.'

She then heard steps in the corridor and recognised Doctor Bagus, who was accompanied by a nurse.

'Doctor Bagus!' Ella left the officer and walked over to the other end of the corridor.

'I didn't expect to see you again so soon,' he cried.

'I wanted to check on the patient, but the guard won't let me through,' Ella told him.

The Indian doctor thought for a moment, before turning to the Malay nurse.

'I'll be right back,' he said. 'You do know that the man is a prisoner, don't you?' he added to Ella.

She nodded.

'The wound has healed up very well, by the way. You played a significant part in that, so I think you deserve to see the patient. Follow me.' He smiled.

Judging by his determined expression, Ella felt certain she would be allowed to see Mohan.

'A colleague from Europe. Her opinion is important to me,' he told the officer, who was clearly racked by an inner conflict.

'I'm not a visitor, strictly speaking,' added Ella.

Eventually, the officer gave a nod.

Doctor Bagus smiled with satisfaction and turned to leave. 'Please come and see me afterwards. Room three on the ground floor,' Bagus instructed her.

Ella nodded and stepped inside.

Two pairs of eyes stared at her incredulously: Amar and Mohan. Ella wasn't sure which of them looked more delighted.

'How did you get in here?' demanded Amar.

'I could ask you the same question!'

'I'm his employer.' Amar said it with a smirk, but Mohan nodded in agreement.

'How are you feeling?'

'The doctor says I'll be able to walk again soon,' said Mohan.

'They're going to lock him up and put him on trial.' Amar's smile had vanished.

'Five to ten years,' said Mohan in a husky voice.

'If the British are even here that long.' Amar's fury was written across his face.

'Marjory wants to dismiss you, and the governor thinks you're involved in the resistance too,' said Ella to Amar.

'He's right, of course, but he can't prove anything,' retorted Amar.

'They probably think I'm a spy too by now – at least, so Marjory warned me,' she added.

Mohan and Amar exchanged a worried glance. But that was where they had to leave it, for visiting hour was over. The door opened again, and the British officer gave them a look that made it clear they should depart.

'You'll be back on your feet soon enough,' said Ella, to at least give the impression that she had examined the patient.

She clasped Mohan's hand to say goodbye.

'Meet me at the market in half an hour,' she whispered to Amar before she left the room. Ella thought it better to walk out ahead of him. She didn't want to give anyone the impression that she sympathised with rebels.

◆ ◆ ◆

Ella had fully expected Doctor Bagus to ask her about her experiences at the hospital in Hamburg, but she had to disappoint him in one key respect: her knowledge of so many areas of naturo-pathic medicine came not from a German education, nor even from her English one – although the medical profession in the United Kingdom was admittedly more open towards these forms of treatment – for she had learned it mainly from textbooks. In any case, physicians in this part of the world appeared to be far less self-important than they were back in Europe. Doctor Bagus's office was too small and plain for any delusions of grandeur – indeed, it featured almost no decoration of any kind. A cabinet filled with various medical instruments, a desk and a treatment table that would have been thrown away long ago in Hamburg formed the extent of his personal domain at the hospital.

'I was surprised at your suggestion because myrrh is well known in India. We call it guggul. In Ayurvedic medicine, it's used to treat obesity, joint pain, skin conditions and inflammation, but I would never have thought that it could also promote wound healing when used externally. At any rate, it doesn't grow in your northerly lati-tudes. Where did you hear about it?'

'Most of the better hospitals in England are run by the Church, and I had the good fortune to work for a doctor, Professor Reading, who had a large collection of remedies and formulations going all the way back to the Middle Ages. In our faith, we believe that the baby Jesus was visited by three kings from the East, bearing gifts of gold, frankincense and myrrh. The professor taught me that in those days, myrrh represented the gift of health, and people ascribed universal healing properties to the plant,' explained Ella.

Doctor Bagus was obviously impressed. 'It seems you have engaged extensively with natural healing techniques,' he surmised.

Ella nodded.

'I would like you to share your knowledge with us. There are so few people around these parts with any training . . .'

'I'm afraid I won't be here long enough for that.'

'What brought you to Johore? Are you on a sightseeing tour?'

Ella decided not to tell him the real reason for her visit, given what she had seen so far of this backwater where gossip travelled as fast as the wind.

'I was curious about the local culture, and I wanted to experience some new things,' she said.

'That's unusual for a young lady, if you'll permit the observation. You have my respect. When we first met, you told me you planned to stay a little while longer. Perhaps you might have enough time to give some instruction to the nurses – by giving a lecture, for example. You could stay on the premises and save yourself the expense of lodgings,' he suggested.

'I'm staying in private accommodation, not far from here.'

'Let me guess – with Mila and Richard. They're the only Dutch people around these parts,' he said with a smile.

'I've had the pleasure of making their acquaintance, but I'm staying with the Fosters.' Ella hoped he wouldn't make any further enquiries, but she was disappointed.

'How is Heather? Is she well?' he asked. Ella gave a start, which Doctor Bagus obviously took to mean that she wasn't – or so she judged from his concerned expression. That could only mean that he knew the family, and was thus aware that Heather had had health problems. Ella decided to seize the opportunity.

'She still suffers from all kinds of fears. Not always, but from time to time,' she said.

'I assume you know Heather well, in that case?'

'She's like a sister to me,' answered Ella truthfully.

'I had hoped that after all these years . . .' Doctor Bagus seemed lost in thought.

'Have you treated her before, then?'

'That must be twenty years ago now. I'd only started work two years before, and the Fosters' English physician had passed away.

I fear Marjory would never have put her faith in an Indian doctor otherwise.'

'I know that you have a duty of confidentiality, but has she always been so timid? I'm asking because I'm worried about her.'

'Well, you're free to draw your own conclusions from my reactions.'

'So she was fearful back then too?'

Doctor Bagus gave a slight nod.

'And she never left the house either?'

No contradiction on his part.

'Did she suffer from something more serious?' Ella demanded.

'Have I told you that we have a special ward here for poisonings of all kinds? Generally speaking, the patients are victims of snake or spider bites, but—'

'Poison? Did she try to take her own life?'

'You know I can't possibly tell you that,' the doctor demurred, but his manner spoke for him.

'Poor Heather . . . If only I knew what she was so afraid of,' said Ella, speaking more to herself.

'We were unable to get to the bottom of that at the time, unfortunately,' he sighed.

Ella's mind began to race. So Heather really had tried to kill herself, and her reasons must have had something to do with that guest house. Why didn't she just move elsewhere?

'When one grows close to another person, one usually persuades them to unburden themselves in the end. I hope you manage it with Heather,' said Doctor Bagus.

'I fear I owe you a favour now,' said Ella.

'It would be a pleasure to me and a blessing for the clinic.'

Ella considered it more of a blessing that she had made the acquaintance of this doctor, although he had raised more questions than he had answered.

◆ ◆ ◆

Now that everybody knew she had been at the shadow play with Amar – including people who she would rather didn't know – Ella found she no longer cared when yet more people began to stare at her in surprise across the main market square. She walked straight up to Amar and sat down beside him under the shade of a palm tree.

'We should go somewhere else,' he said, looking at two mounted British officers who were riding across the square.

'Out of the question,' declared Ella.

Amar grinned in response. 'You would make a good rebel,' he whispered.

'I'm already thought of as one back home – though I was never called upon to take up arms there,' she answered.

Amar's expression suddenly grew serious. 'You should come back and stay in town. Mrs Foster doesn't want any trouble. She'll send you away sooner or later anyway, and if she dismisses me then I won't be able to look after you out there,' he said.

'So you've already taken it upon yourself to look after me?' Ella asked.

He didn't answer in words, but his smile told her the truth.

Ella had a truth to share with him too: 'I can't come back yet.'

'Haven't you already found what you were looking for?'

'Yes and no. I'm certain that Heather is my half-sister, but we haven't discussed it openly yet. Though perhaps I'm wrong, and I'm just chasing a figment of my imagination.'

'What do you hope to gain?' he asked.

'Clarity,' Ella burst out – but that wasn't all. 'I think Heather is ill, and I have a feeling she needs me.'

'She has her mother,' Amar objected.

'That's not the same,' she answered.

Amar seemed lost in thought. 'What if you just talk to Heather about it? Tell her your story?'

'I'm afraid of doing that, and I'm not even sure why. Who knows? Perhaps there really is a curse on this family,' said Ella.

Amar shrugged.

'But it must have something to do with the guest house,' she went on.

'All secrets leave traces,' he said.

'I've looked in all the rooms. There's nothing there.'

'Perhaps not at first glance . . . But there might be something behind the house, or underneath it . . .' he mused.

'You're frightening me. What would be underneath it? A grave, perhaps?'

'There has to be something, if she really is avoiding the place,' said Amar.

'Where can I reach you if you no longer work on the plantation?' she asked.

'I'll leave a message with Lee at the boarding house.'

'And where will you live when Marjory lets you go?' Ella had learned from Raj on the way into Johore that most of the workers lodged in a house close to the plantation.

'I'll find somewhere. My family live on the east coast. But I won't leave you on your own . . . unless you tell me to.'

'Do you really think I would do that?'

He clasped her hand by way of response, and Ella drew strength from it.

CHAPTER 13

Raj had picked Ella up from the hospital, as agreed, and had even asked her how Mohan was. He seemed to sympathise with him, despite his strict principles, which included showing complete solidarity with the Fosters and taking harsh measures against any workers who called the local social order into question. They hadn't discussed Heather any further, but at the end of the trip, Ella took the opportunity to ask Raj about another matter.

'It's strange, you know – I've not been here for very long at all, and yet I feel completely at home in the guest house.' Ella had decided to broach the subject innocuously, intending to frame her question as casually as possible – though she nurtured a burning curiosity about the answer.

'All the Fosters' guests treasure their time there,' said Raj.

'Has it always looked the same?'

'The house? Of course.'

'No, I mean the garden. I have the impression that everything out there is growing wild, apart from the oleander. Nobody seems to be looking after the back of the house either,' said Ella.

'I've already told Mrs Foster she ought to hire a gardener. She only takes care of it when she has time, and she generally only cuts back the oleander on the side you can see from the main house,' said Raj.

'What about inside the guest house? Has it always been so beautifully furnished?'

'There used to be different furniture in there.'

'So it hasn't always been a guest house?' Ella pursued the subject doggedly.

Instead of answering her question, Raj looked at her suspiciously. Then his face softened, and he gave an almost imperceptible smile. 'No.'

'I suppose it's always been a place of relaxation.'

'Indeed,' he answered, as the coach drew up to the stables and the boy took the reins.

Raj dismounted and issued instructions in the local language. Once again, he had managed to leave her biggest questions unanswered. Yet the mysterious smile he gave as he looked over at the oleander house had to mean something. He seemed to be signalling that she was on the right track – that she was asking the right questions. But what use were all these speculations when she couldn't even begin to imagine what the guest house might have to do with Heather's strange behaviour?

◆ ◆ ◆

Under normal circumstances, Heather would have met Ella at the stables so that they could spend the rest of the day together, but she was presumably still inside the house, sulking over the offence Ella had supposedly caused. Nor was Marjory anywhere to be seen. Ella therefore decided to take a closer look at the guest house – and once inside, she began to notice things that she had never paid any attention to before.

First, she stood in the middle of the parlour and examined the décor. It was appropriate for a guest house, since it lacked any of the personal touches that lent such an individual charm to the living quarters in the main house and said so much about the people who lived there. And yet the furniture seemed drawn from a different era. Generally speaking, people tended to fill their guest rooms with sturdier, plainer items than these. There were also too many objects that seemed to serve no purpose at all. A bookshelf with just three books about Malacca, for example, or an empty ledge that one would normally expect to be decorated with figurines, vases or books. Now that she looked more carefully, she could see that the room must once have been very lovingly decorated. Perhaps it had been a hideaway for Heather. Ella reflected that the Fosters would have had more frequent social contact while Richard was still alive, and a house like this one, situated away from the hustle and bustle of the main residence, offered the perfect place to enjoy a little privacy. For her part, Ella would probably have turned it into her own personal domain too if she had been in Heather's shoes. It all made sense – yet that still didn't explain why Heather was so afraid of it.

Ella's search through the rest of the house turned up nothing new: no secret compartments behind the landscape painting in the parlour or the pictures in the hallway; no paraphernalia stowed away in the empty drawers. But while the oleander house offered no further hints as to its former use, perhaps there would be more clues outside it. There was little point in rooting around beneath the overgrown oleander bushes, but the garden behind the house was still accessible. It bordered on a wild jumble of rubber trees that had presumably found their way here from the plantation. Ella spotted a fountain that was no longer in use. Although the plants around it had deteriorated into a partially dried-out thicket, it was clear that this place must once have been a shady, cosy spot where one could linger a while, far from the prying eyes of the main house. Like the water feature, the overgrown stone paving also suggested that this place must once have been in regular use. Ella sat down at the edge of the fountain. Despite all these conjectures, she was still no closer to solving the mystery of Heather's behaviour.

Just as she was about to stand up and go back to the house, her eyes fell on one of the rubber trees. From this distance it looked as though somebody had scratched something into the bark – and not to harvest the rubber. Ella walked up and examined the spot more closely. A vine had wrapped itself around the trunk, but when she pushed it aside, the outline of the carving came into view. It must have been made years ago, for its shape was only faintly visible – but there could be no doubt that it was a heart, along with two letters scratched over it that met at its centre. They were an 'H' and a 'J', or possibly an 'I'. The 'H' was obvious – but the 'J'? Hadn't Mary mentioned a Jack? It slowly dawned on Ella that this must have something to do with Heather's fears. She was afraid of the memory of a love affair that had broken down. Ella reflected that she herself would probably also avoid places that reminded her of painful circumstances. This matched up with Doctor Bagus's hints at the hospital too. It really must have been an unhappy love affair many years ago that had turned Heather into what she was now. There was no other explanation.

◆ ◆ ◆

All afternoon, Ella had agonised over whether to talk to Heather directly about her strange behaviour – yet no sooner had she reached the conclusion that she should than she decided it might be wiser to wait a few days. Then again, what use would that be? And was it really so wrong for her to talk to Heather about her failed love affair? She wasn't the only woman ever to be abandoned by a man. Ella could remember all too well the stories she had heard from colleagues who had had similar experiences. Looking back, they had always responded in one of two ways. Some women denounced men for evermore, dismissing them as mangy curs who were only ever after one thing, while others blamed themselves and virtually dissolved into self-pity. Ella was aware how painful a broken heart could be from the countless tears shed by her colleagues, and she knew it was possible that a woman might attempt to take her own life because of a man – yet for that to happen, their relationship would have had to be particularly close, and the disappointment correspondingly extreme. In the end, however, there was one thought that prompted Ella to pluck up her courage and head over to the main house. It had done all her colleagues good to confide in somebody and unburden themselves of all the pain they had been nursing in private. Why should Heather be any different?

Ella met Jaya at the door, and was relieved to hear that Marjory had gone to bed.

'Miss Foster is in her room,' said Jaya. 'Should I let her know that you're here?'

'Is that necessary?' Ella asked, for she was afraid that Heather would refuse to see her.

'Unannounced visits aren't the done thing in this house,' Jaya objected, visibly discomfited by Ella's idea.

'I'll answer for it,' Ella assured her.

It took Jaya a moment to bring herself to let Ella through to Heather unannounced.

'The second-to-last room at the end of the corridor,' she finally said.

Although Ella told herself that she was just paying Heather a visit, and that there was nothing objectionable about that, she still felt as though she was breaking into the Fosters' house as she climbed the stairs. She made her way stealthily so as not to wake Marjory from her afternoon nap, and on reaching the first floor, she quickly scanned the corridor for signs of her presence. Thankfully, she saw only two statues – though they still gave her a fright, for they were life-sized and she briefly mistook one of them for Marjory. Ella's heart was pounding by now, and her footsteps were clearly audible, despite the carpet running down the hall. The floorboards beneath it creaked and groaned and she felt increasingly tense with every step she took towards Heather's room – but once she reached her door, she gathered herself and knocked.

'Heather. It's me. Are you busy?'

Silence from behind the door. Perhaps Jaya was mistaken and Heather wasn't in her room after all. Ella knocked again, hoping she wouldn't wake Marjory.

'Ella?' came a voice from inside.

'Should I go?' asked Ella.

Steps approached the door. Heather opened it and seemed to be debating whether to invite her inside.

'Are you feeling better?' Ella enquired.

Heather nodded, and then threw the door open to let her in after all.

Ella was on the verge of asking why she had been indisposed – but since Heather was probably aware that she already knew the reason, she held her tongue and examined Heather's room instead: wall-to-wall apricot-coloured upholstery, with a matching carpet and a four-poster bed draped in mosquito netting.

'What a delightful room,' said Ella.

'It's cooler on this side of the house. The heat is more bearable here,' answered Heather.

'Do you embroider?' A half-finished piece of needlework had caught Ella's eye. Heather was working on a blanket on which the initial outline of some oleander blossom could already be seen.

She nodded and seemed to relax somewhat.

As she looked into Heather's eyes, Ella thought she could detect sparks of the joie de vivre that she knew and loved her for.

'This one is already finished,' said Heather, pulling out an embroidered shawl. It must have taken her days to complete, and the oleander blooms were simply ravishing.

'You love those flowers, don't you?'

Heather nodded.

'I suppose that's why there's so much oleander around the guest house,' said Ella.

'No – it was Mother's idea to plant that,' said Heather.

'Did you ever live there?' Ella thought her question was harmless enough to avoid plunging Heather into a depressive mood, but she was mistaken, for Heather's smile instantly vanished. She nodded, but avoided Ella's eyes, preferring to stare at the embroidery and run her hands over it.

'I can embroider something for you too, if you like,' Heather announced abruptly.

Ella didn't reply to her offer. She was tired of this cat-and-mouse game, even though she could tell that remembering the past would cause Heather pain. If only she could let that pain out, for once.

'I wish I had a little house like that for myself. The garden behind it must have been very beautiful. I decided to sit in the shade there today and listen to the birdsong. Were there once lilies in the fountain?'

By now, Heather's hands were moving almost mechanically over the cloth. She stiffened.

'What's the matter, Heather?'

She didn't respond.

There was no point in beating about the bush any longer. After all, it was for Heather's own good. 'Heather. I saw the heart carved into the tree trunk.'

Heather began to tremble and she grew pale.

Ella regretted broaching the subject like this, but it was too late. 'Was his name Jack?'

Heather's fingers dug into the shawl and her breath quickened. Why didn't she speak?

'Is that the reason why you're so unhappy? Did he leave you? Spurn your love?'

Heather began to whimper. Ella could see her eyes filling with tears.

'But it's happened to so many other women too.'

Heather stiffened even more. Then she suddenly whirled round to face Ella. Her eyes glittered with rage, as though she had been possessed by a demon. 'That's not the reason!' she snarled.

Ella was so shocked at her furious reaction that she stumbled back a couple of steps.

Heather's hands were now gripping the shawl so hard that Ella could see the muscles on her forearms.

'Go away!' Heather demanded.

'Tell me. Please. Tell me. You'll feel better, believe me.'

Heather was trembling like a leaf in the wind. Tears trickled down her cheeks. 'Why won't you stop asking questions? I love spending time with you, but you never stop.'

'I want to help you, Heather.' Ella refused to give in, though it pierced her heart to see Heather in such a desperate state.

'Why do you keep hurting me like this? Why can't you leave me in peace?' she whimpered.

'Whatever happened back then, I'll understand. Just tell me, please.'

Ella sensed that Heather was battling inwardly with herself. Her body looked like a puppet dangling from strings, but then she stiffened once more and her eyes grew cold.

'Get out!' she screamed like a fury.

Ella was so shocked that for a moment she was unable to move, let alone speak – not even to apologise.

The door flew open. Ella didn't need to turn round to know that Marjory must have heard them.

'Mother, tell her to leave.' Heather had become a little girl, with tears rolling down her cheeks.

Marjory was instantly at her side, ready to take her child in her arms and console her. Only now did Heather let go of the embroidered shawl, wrapping herself around her mother and sobbing unrestrainedly against her shoulder.

At that moment, Ella fervently wished she had left Heather alone. Seeing her suffer made her ache to the very depths of her soul.

'I would be grateful if you would find yourself some alternative lodgings,' Marjory hissed in a cutting voice.

'Heather. Do you really want me to go?'

She didn't reply, burying her face in her mother's shoulder.

'Raj will drive you back into town, and if I might give you one final piece of advice: keep your nose out of British affairs in future.' Marjory's threat was underlined by her determined expression.

Ella turned on her heels and ran out of the room; Heather's sobs rang out after her, and almost broke her heart.

◆ ◆ ◆

Ella was so shaken that she had trouble concentrating on packing her bags. She had to be quick, for Raj was already waiting with the coach in front of the oleander house. Shortly after she had been thrown out, Ella had seen Jaya running towards the stables. It seemed that Marjory couldn't get rid of her soon enough. Ella hoped that Jaya wouldn't get into any trouble or lose her job over the unannounced visit. The fact that she hadn't come to bid her farewell implied that she had at least been given a stern telling-off. She had probably been too afraid to say goodbye too – or perhaps Marjory had forbidden her from doing so.

Yet much as it pained Ella to have caused Heather so much anguish, she was at least relieved to realise that she didn't belong here after all. The hatred Marjory bore for her was indelible. It was better not to be around such people. But what about Heather? Shouldn't she try to fight for their friendship, once this had all died down? Yet what was the use? Marjory's influence over her was too great. It was probably she who bound Heather to herself, chained her up in the house, instead of encouraging her to face her fears and live once more as a free – and above all emotionally healthy – woman.

Heather had behaved like a little girl at Marjory's side. Sometimes she was wilful, like during Compton's visit, and sometimes she could be as cheerful and carefree as a child skipping through a meadow – but whenever she was confronted by her own past, it caused her great pain. That was probably why she withdrew into the supposed idyll of the plantation and avoided all contact with men – to shield her heart from emotion for the rest of her life. Once again, Ella realised that she was standing in front of her suitcase and staring into space. She seemed paralysed by all these thoughts.

'Do you need any help?' came a voice from outside. It was Raj. He was probably wondering why she was taking so long.

Ella had to virtually force herself to put her shoes and the two remaining blouses into her bag. Everything else was already packed. It was time to say goodbye, and yet she found it so hard that yet again she stood indecisively in front of her case. The idea that she might never see Heather again cut her to the marrow. Ella had to admit that she loved her – she felt close to her in a way you only felt with your own family. Tears welled up in her eyes, but she took a deep breath and wiped them away with the sleeve of her blouse, then fastened her second case.

Raj was already knocking on the door.

'I'm ready,' she called to him.

It was obvious that Raj found the situation uncomfortable. Wordlessly, he lifted the bags and walked out to place them in the coach.

'What did you do?' he asked.

'What did she tell you?'

Once again, Raj smiled a faint smile that gave her the impression that he knew more than he let on.

'That sympathisers with the resistance are not welcome at the Fosters' home,' he said.

'That's what she said?' Ella could scarcely believe her ears. On the other hand, she could hardly tell him the truth.

He nodded bashfully, then looked her directly in the eye. 'I feel sure you've done the right thing.'

'How do you mean?' asked Ella.

'You were in the garden. I saw you.'

'Have you been watching me?'

'When I have a reason to,' he answered, with another almost imperceptible smile.

Ella looked into his eyes and strove to understand who this Raj really was: a brutal overseer, or a friend who was sympathetic to her cause?

'His name was Jack, by the way,' he whispered.

Hot and cold shivers ran down Ella's back. He really did know the truth, and now he was telling her.

'What did he do to her?'

Raj's smile vanished and he merely shook his head.

'But you know what happened. Please tell me.' Ella's desperate appeal seemed to fall on deaf ears.

'There's a time for everything. Your presence here is fate. Nobody can change what has been preordained – but it's not my fate, it's yours,' he explained.

Ella knew from experience that there was no point wasting her breath asking him any more questions.

Raj helped her into the coach and Ella cast a final look back at the Fosters' house. There could be no doubt: somebody was standing at the window on the first floor. Heather seemed to be bidding her farewell, and Ella wondered whether Heather's pain could be greater than her own at that moment.

◆　◆　◆

Often, it's the little things that breathe life back into the darkest hours – and in this case, the restorative was Lee's smile. At first Ella wasn't sure whether it was sincere or not, given the trouble she had brought to her house on her previous stay, but when she looked into the woman's eyes, she could see that Lee's delight was obviously genuine. Ella had briefly told her that her visit to 'her friends' had come to an end, and there were no further questions on the matter. Surprisingly enough, however, there was a letter waiting for her.

'It was delivered yesterday, but I didn't have any time to let you know,' Lee apologised as she handed Ella the envelope.

The stamp on the back resembled a signet, making it clear that this was official correspondence. Ella opened the letter by the reception desk. It was from the police. The results from Rudolf's autopsy had come in, and they had invited her to the station to discuss the matter in person.

'Could you take my bags up to my room?' Ella didn't want to lose any more time.

Lee nodded.

It was quicker to walk the short distance to the police station than to wait for a rickshaw to come along. The sun was already setting, and Ella hoped it would still be open at that hour. On the way, she wondered what might have caused Rudolf's death. Although Malacca's climate certainly had fatal consequences for many visitors with heart conditions, Ella couldn't for one moment imagine that Rudolf had suffered that fate. He had been a young man, full of vitality, and throughout the arduous crossing he hadn't shown any sign of a weak heart – at least, not in any anatomical sense.

Less than ten minutes later, Ella found herself sitting in the back room of the police station, wondering why Officer Puteri was shaking his head in disbelief as he held the pathologist's report in his hands.

'No external injuries, nor any internal ones that could have been caused by a fall. No insect bites, and no signs of weakness in the heart. According to this report, Rudolf von Stetten was a picture of health,' he explained.

'But he must have died of something,' Ella objected.

'The only thing we can be certain of is that he died of a heart attack, and that it was likely accompanied by shortness of breath,' Puteri declared.

'I can assure you that Mr von Stetten was as fit as a fiddle. It's impossible.'

'The pathologist can think of only one explanation. He believes Rudolf might have ingested something poisonous. It wouldn't be the first time this has happened. Foreigners often believe that the local plants are all edible, but many of them aren't.'

'But why would Rudolf have picked something from the side of the road and eaten it?'

'I asked myself the same. And even if he did, the report states that there's no way of proving it. So we're still groping in the dark.'

'Perhaps he had a bad reaction to an ingredient in a meal. There are so many stalls here selling food and drink,' Ella conjectured.

'Out of the question. There's never been a case before of a foreigner eating something toxic in their food. Visitors sometimes suffer from diarrhoea, and there was a case of food poisoning once, caused by spoiled meat – but the doctor would have been able to identify that.'

'But he must have ingested the poison somehow.'

Puteri nodded thoughtfully.

'Did he have any enemies? Any business contacts here in Malacca?' he asked.

'Not that I know of.' Should she tell him the truth about her search for her real father? That would doubtlessly prompt him to pay Marjory and Heather another visit, which would inevitably reveal to them that she was really German, and that she believed Heather to be her half-sister. After being thrown out by the Fosters, Ella was unwilling to let that happen.

'Give it some time. Perhaps something will occur to you,' he said. Evidently he could see that she was struggling with herself.

'All I know is that he was on his way to the Foster plantation,' Ella finally blurted, for she knew that Puteri had already visited the Fosters.

'We've already made inquiries there. He met with Marjory Foster to discuss buying rubber.' Puteri gave a start. 'But didn't you just say that he didn't have any business contacts here in Malacca?'

'He never discussed business with me,' explained Ella.

Puteri accepted her explanation. 'We found his horse too, half-way to Johore. A local boy managed to catch it. There was something about it that raised my suspicion, though.'

Ella gave him a questioning look.

'The saddlebag had a leather case inside it, but the strange thing is that it was empty.'

'You mean somebody might have stolen documents from him?' Ella surmised.

'It's possible.'

'But what kind of documents would they have been? I found nothing in his suitcase beyond personal effects, books and maps,' said Ella.

'Perhaps a permit, or a deed of ownership?'

'Impossible. He would have told me about something like that, or at least hinted at it. We spent a lot of time together on board the ship.'

Puteri gave a somewhat helpless shrug. 'I'm afraid we'll have to close the case. There's nothing more we can do,' he said.

What in God's name could Rudolf have had in his saddlebag? He had been carrying his map in his pocket, along with his wallet. Ella could make no sense of it.

'I presume that Rudolf von Stetten is to be transported back to his home country?' asked Puteri.

'Of course,' answered Ella mechanically, though she hadn't given it the slightest thought – and not just because it would have been pointless to do so before the autopsy results were available. She had drawn a line under her relationship with Rudolf, and whom would she have notified of his death anyway? His mother, Clara, who suffered from dementia? He had no other relatives, and even if there were someone to contact, it would take weeks for a letter to reach them.

'A ship will be leaving for Europe in a few days. We can take care of the formalities for you, if you like. You'll need papers . . .'

'Thank you. I'm very grateful for your help,' she said. As she spoke, Ella wondered whether she shouldn't go straight back to Hamburg too. But if she did, she would probably never see Amar again.

'I hope you have a pleasant stay here in Malacca. Do you plan to remain here a while longer?' he asked as he escorted her to the door.

Ella gave an indecisive shrug, but she knew she wouldn't leave – and not just because of Amar. She couldn't shake off a vague feeling that this wasn't the right time to depart. And hadn't Doctor Bagus just offered her the opportunity to do what she had always dreamed of doing back in Germany?

◆ ◆ ◆

There was even more bad news waiting for her that evening: Marjory had decided to dismiss Amar. He had left a message with Lee to let Ella know. Although his handwritten note included a sketched-out map, and the description of the route to his new home didn't look too complicated, Ella decided to wait at the side of the road for the next available carriage to take her to him. That proved a wise decision, for the journey was longer than she had anticipated and took her outside the town centre. She would have been sure to get lost on the way.

All the houses looked identical in the part of town where he now lived, and there were no house numbers as she was used to back home.

The young Chinese coachman stopped in front of a stilt house, which was simple but looked well maintained, just like the garden surrounding it. It lay in the shade of a thicket of enormous fan palms, set back from a road that was still just about navigable by carriage. There was a horse tied to the veranda, standing next to a manger full of hay.

The trip cost just a few ringgits and Ella debated asking the driver to wait until she was sure that Amar was here, but then dismissed the thought. Who else would the horse in front of the house belong to?

At first, however, it looked as though she was mistaken as he wasn't inside the main room of the house – a large, high-ceilinged space capped by a pointed roof. Ella cast her eyes over the simple yet functional furniture. There was a cooking stove in the middle of the room and an aperture under the roof to let the smoke escape. Cushions on the floor served as a sofa, with a low table to go with them. It took a while for her eyes to grow accustomed to the dim interior, and only then did Ella spot the sleeping area. A small staircase led up to a kind of balcony, and when she stood still, her ears caught the sound of regular breathing, which she followed.

Amar was lying on a raffia mat, his chest rising and falling evenly. He was sound asleep.

Ella sat down beside his bed and simply looked him. His relaxed features radiated a natural warmth – but his hand moved in a surprisingly targeted manner for somebody who was asleep, fumbling for hers and resting on top of it. Then his face suddenly came to life. Was he smiling in his sleep?

'Miss Kaltenbach.' The sound of his voice sent an agreeable shiver down her back. Then he opened his eyes. They didn't look sleepy, and were focused on her face.

'You weren't asleep at all,' Ella protested.

'We *Orang Asli* have ears like bats – especially us rebels. We always need to be on our guard, since the British are hunting us.' Then he laughed.

Ella gave him a shove on the shoulder.

For a moment, Amar looked at her in silence. 'Did you leave the Foster plantation?' he asked in a serious tone.

'I'm no longer welcome there,' she answered.

'Did you talk to Heather?' he enquired.

Ella nodded, and was forced to admit to herself that the hopes she'd had when she arrived in this country had dissolved into thin air.

'I feel sorry for her. She's plagued by events from the past, and I expect I probed too deeply. But the strange thing is I'm glad not to be there any more.'

'You mean, because you've discovered where you come from and it's different to what you dreamed of?' Amar asked.

'That might be it . . . I just wonder why he gave me away. I could have grown up in that house with Heather – I would have been there for her, and she for me.'

'These things happen among my people too,' he said.

'The men sleep with whores and then give their children away?'

Amar sat up and seemed to be trying to recall something.

'In my home village, I was told that there was a woman who almost died during the birth of her first son. Her husband wanted to have another child, and she conceived, but her life hung in the balance once more. The baby needed to be cut out, and the woman was left disfigured. She wanted to kill the child, so her husband gave it to a foster family.'

Ella had heard similar stories at the hospital. Of course, there could be all manner of explanations, but one at least could be ruled out: Marjory couldn't be her natural mother.

'It's not uncommon for the British to produce illegitimate off-spring with the local population. The English orphanages must be full of children like that. Were you ever in an orphanage?' asked Amar.

'No. My father passed me off as his own child, and the story was corroborated by a German captain. False documents were issued. My parents told everyone I was adopted, and they kept the truth from me too. Richard obviously paid an annuity for me – but to this day I don't know why.'

Amar looked surprised. 'But how exactly did it all happen? Why would a British man living in Malacca seek out a German family? He could have left you in the jungle, in front of a church or a temple, or given you to a local orphanage,' he asked, with good reason.

Amar's train of thought raised a new possibility.

'If Richard Foster was my father . . . My adoptive father was a sailor. Perhaps Richard left me at the port in Singapore in the hope that somebody would find me and take me to a local orphanage.'

'But in that case, why would he pay an annuity for you?' asked Amar.

Ella sighed. She had no idea. 'Rudolf . . . He probably knew the truth, although I don't know how,' she said.

Amar shot her a questioning look.

'He knew why I was here. And he'd already marked the Foster plantation on his map before we'd even begun our search.'

'Do you think Rudolf tried to blackmail Marjory over the fact that you're Richard's illegitimate daughter? But how would he have known that? What did you tell him?' asked Amar.

'I thought Rudolf knew only that I was adopted. Though I also told him we received money from Penang for my upkeep.' Ella sighed again. Her thoughts were going around in circles. None of it made any sense.

'The police think Rudolf was poisoned,' she said.

'Marjory is an extremely morally upright person, and anyway, Rudolf was seen on the plantation. She would never take a risk like that,' declared Amar with conviction.

His logic was unarguable, but it didn't bring Ella any clarity over the events of the past.

At times like this, the best thing was to stop wasting words and simply fall into somebody's arms. It felt so good to lean against his shoulder; feel his hand gently caressing her. This sense of closeness to him was almost more enjoyable than the thrill she normally felt at his touch. Simply to be held, when she felt so rudderless – that was exactly what Ella needed right now.

CHAPTER 14

Ella missed the iridescent morning light, the soft glow of the oleander blossom and its fragrance. Instead, a gentle puff of wind circulated from the entrance of the house up to the roof, wafting the scent of jasmine tea to her bunk, which had proven every bit as restful as the bed in the oleander house. All the same, it felt strange to sleep effectively on the floor, with just a woven mat and a kind of mattress that didn't look particularly comfortable at first glance. Ella sat up and looked down at the hearth in the centre of the room. Amar was making tea and slicing fruit, dividing the pieces between two bowls.

'Good morning, Ella. Did you sleep well?'

She was delighted that he had started calling her by her first name. She had insisted upon it. In light of his solicitude and hospitality the night before, 'Miss Kaltenbach' felt inappropriately formal.

She answered the greeting with a smile. Not for a second did she regret having stayed with him – partly because he had assured her that they were safe here, since the British had already searched the house multiple times. After all, it was Mohan's home – an inheritance from his deceased parents. Mohan himself couldn't expect to be a free man again any time soon, and the house stood empty. Amar had told her last night why the young man had become involved in the resistance. Mohan's father had died in a tin mine. Nobody there cared about the safety of the workers, and he hadn't been taken to hospital in time. Mohan's mother was severely ill, and without his father's earnings, there hadn't been any money for medical treatment. Things often took on a very different light once one knew the background.

'Do you Germans eat eggs for breakfast like the British? I don't have any bacon, I'm afraid,' said Amar.

'I would have been surprised if you had!' she answered. Amar was a Muslim, so he didn't eat pork. They had discussed that last night too, while they sat outdoors. He loved to tell her about his homeland and its traditions, including its religions. To this day, the arrival of Islam in Malacca was a thorn in the side of the British. Amar explained that the faith had been introduced five centuries ago by Arabic, Persian and Indian traders, supplanting Buddhism and Hinduism – though the Chinese and the non-Muslim Indians were allowed to continue practising their own religions. Amar's account was borne out by the many Hindu and Buddhist temples Ella had already seen.

'That's what I love about this country. In Europe, there were wars just because the old Christians had different opinions to the new ones.' Amar was already aware of the conflicts between Catholics and Protestants. It was truly amazing how much he knew about Europe.

'So, would you like some bacon? I can get you some. There's a Chinese family living two houses further down,' he called up to the balustrade, where Ella was leaning out and pensively watching him make breakfast.

'No – I'm German, not British. We prefer to eat bread and marmalade for breakfast,' she laughed back.

'I don't have that, and I'm afraid I'm not going into town just to buy some from the British.'

'They won't have any German marmalade anyway – just the English stuff, which is bitter, unlike the German version. I don't know how they can eat it,' Ella grimaced.

'I see, I see. It's going to be difficult to keep you happy.'

She had to laugh. Amar's sense of humour and his caring nature – right down to his attempts to make her the perfect breakfast – were balm for her soul.

'I'm happy with anything,' she said.

'Well then, curry and flatbread for breakfast? And some eggs?'

Ella found that hard to contemplate, but she nodded bravely.

'I couldn't imagine anything better,' she answered wryly.

'All right, come on then . . .'

She didn't need to be told twice and hurried down the wooden steps.

A jug of freshly squeezed mango juice and a flatbread were already standing on the low table. Amar served the eggs with a small helping of chicken curry, but thankfully on normal plates and not on a palm leaf this time.

'I hope everything is to your satisfaction, madam,' he joked, and made an extravagantly humble gesture – nodding with his hands clasped in front of his face, as was the custom among Indian servants.

More than anything, Ella loved that he never stopped trying to make her laugh.

'I'm happy to see you smile again,' he said in a serious tone. Once again, she saw concern and affection in his eyes. A similar moment had passed between them the night before, and they had nearly kissed – but then she had made her excuses and gone upstairs to bed.

'*Why didn't you go through with it?*' she asked herself. Perhaps because he didn't push her – and perhaps because their kiss promised to be all the more wonderful for every minute she waited.

'It's very good, I promise,' he said, apparently interpreting her wandering thoughts as reluctance to try the exotic-looking breakfast.

Eggs with chicken curry, first thing in the morning. She took a bite for his sake, and was relieved to find that she didn't need to lie to him, for it really was very tasty. Amar would have seen through her anyway – and she had the feeling that she could read his thoughts too. He ate listlessly, stopping every now and then to stare into space, frowning slightly. His thoughts were clearly elsewhere.

'Don't you like it?' She might as well have asked him what he was thinking about.

It took Amar a few moments to answer. 'They're going to execute him,' he murmured. He obviously meant Mohan. 'I found out yesterday.' He finally gave voice to what was on his mind. The night before, Ella had also noticed several glum looks on his part, which he had then laughed off – presumably to avoid troubling her.

'But they only found two guns in his house. You said so yourself.'

'They want to make an example of him.' Amar was unable to swallow another bite.

Ella felt the same.

'Can we do anything to stop it? Is there nobody who can stand up to the British?'

Amar shook his head.

'What about the sultan? It's his country after all. His people.' Ella found it hard to believe that the British could really do whatever they wanted.

'He wouldn't dare to oppose them. What do you expect from somebody who sells his own land?'

'But there must be something we can do.' She wasn't prepared to simply accept that Mohan would die.

'There is one possibility,' said Amar mysteriously.

'What's that?'

'Do you really want to help him?' he pressed her.

'Of course.'

'He'll be moved to the jail tomorrow. The prison wagons nearly always take the same route, but sometimes they go a different way, closer to the edge of town. If we manage to arrange for them to go that way instead . . .' he hinted.

'Do you have any way of influencing that? Isn't it up to the British officers?' she asked.

'No. The transportation is organised by the hospital. The wagon is merely accompanied by an officer.'

'And who arranges it?' asked Ella.

'Why do you think I was allowed to see Mohan?' he asked in return.

'He doesn't have any family, and you were the foreman at his work. That was what you told me anyway.'

He shook his head. 'Bagus hates the British, just like the rest of us.'

'Does he belong to the resistance too?' she asked. She was stunned at the thought.

Amar nodded. 'If you want to help us then you could carry a message to him. I'm being watched, and they'll wonder what I'm up to if I go. But you don't have to do it . . . I don't want you to put yourself in any danger.'

Ella knew she would be risking her neck, but she had no intention of sitting back and watching while a young man was put to death, merely to set an example.

'I'll do it,' she said without hesitation.

'You just need to hand him the message. I'll write everything down in a letter and tell him which route the wagon should take. With your help, we can free Mohan. A ship will be waiting for him

246

at the coast to take him to Sumatra, and then on to Siam. He'll be safe there, for now,' explained Amar.

Despite having whole-heartedly volunteered her support, Ella needed to take a deep breath. She had become a member of the rebellion overnight.

◆ ◆ ◆

Ella took Mohan's cart to travel to the hospital. It was very small, and so manoeuvrable that it could be drawn by a single horse – even over the somewhat rough terrain on the way to town.

When she arrived, she was very glad she had a plausible excuse for visiting Doctor Bagus: she stated that she was there to discuss his request for her to instruct the nursing staff, and as a result, she didn't have long to wait outside his office. She whiled away the time in the corridor by watching the hospital staff go about their work. It was striking how often people smiled here compared to back home. Interactions with patients seemed a lot warmer and friendlier. The only thing she didn't like about this hospital was the extremely uncomfortable wooden bench she was sitting on.

The nurse whom Ella had announced herself to must have told Doctor Bagus why she was here, for there could be no other reason why he would greet her with such a radiant smile.

'I'm very happy that you've taken the time to think about my request, though I must admit I wasn't expecting to see you again so soon.' He gestured for her to enter his office.

Ella pondered how best to explain her real objective to him, since in truth, the reason for her visit was a very different one.

'You're quite right – I haven't had time to give any thought to what material would be most suitable for the local nursing staff,' she said.

Doctor Bagus looked surprised, then offered her a seat in front of his desk and sat down himself.

'So what can I do for you?' he asked comfortably.

'Amar sent me. It's about Mohan,' Ella admitted, coming straight to the point. She hoped that he would draw the right conclusions from those two names.

Doctor Bagus looked at her somewhat more warily than she had expected.

'You do know that Mohan faces a serious punishment? A disproportionately severe one, in my view,' he said cautiously, trying to gauge whether he had understood her correctly. His response reassured her that she could trust him.

'I have a message about his transportation to the local jail,' she said, before opening her leather bag and taking out a slip of paper that Amar had given her. Most of its surface was taken up with a drawing.

Doctor Bagus studied it carefully. 'Please tell Amar that I will make the necessary arrangements,' he said.

Ella still couldn't believe that a doctor in his position would involve himself in the resistance against the British.

'Why are you doing this? I don't mean that as an accusation – after all, I wouldn't be here otherwise,' she said.

'Why are *you* doing it? You don't even come from this country.' He grinned.

'Because I think what they want to do to Mohan is unfair. He's a young man, and his motives are perfectly understandable,' explained Ella.

'Is that really the only reason?' enquired Doctor Bagus. He was clearly referring to more personal factors. He had probably guessed that she had feelings for Amar and that was why she was lending him her support, but Ella had other reasons too, so she refused to take the bait.

'I'm sure I haven't gained a full insight into the British regime here yet, but based on my experiences so far, I have a clear conscience regarding my own conduct.' She couldn't explain herself in any more detail without mentioning Compton.

Doctor Bagus nodded thoughtfully before he went on. 'They prefer to see their own doctors because they think their medicine is superior – but it's us they come running to in life-or-death situations. Years ago, when I first started here, a young worker was brought in with serious injuries, but my predecessor had to treat a British woman living locally for a simple laceration first, because she complained. The young man died. He could have been saved.'

There was nothing more to say. Ella nodded sympathetically.

Doctor Bagus slipped the note into his coat pocket. 'All the same, I would be glad to meet with you again under different circumstances.'

'I promise,' said Ella, and hoped that her life would calm down soon, for there was nothing she wanted more than to pass on her knowledge to others.

Before she had decided to help Mohan, meeting Edward Compton in town would have been at most a source of annoyance to Ella – but now, things were very different. Was it her guilty conscience that caused her pulse to quicken automatically when she saw him, and made her want to sneak off as unobtrusively as possible? Or was it her instinct as a newly minted rebel? It was hopeless to try and stay out of his sight, however, for she needed to cross the small square in front of the hospital in order to reach her cart. Her fair complexion and hurried pace made her stand out among the few passers-by, although Compton was just then absorbed in conversation with one of his junior officers. The two men were standing by a grocery shop, and Compton's subordinate was holding a bag in his hand and biting into an apple, leading Ella to conclude that they were currently on a quick lunch break. At any rate, it didn't look as though they were undertaking another raid. Compton would doubtless grow suspicious if he caught her leaving the hospital – but on the other hand, wasn't offence the best defence?

'Edward!' she called across the square, feigning ecstatic delight and forcing him to notice her. He looked suitably startled. She had gained the element of surprise, then. Naturally enough, he abandoned his companion and quickly walked towards the lady whose smile signalled that she was surprisingly well disposed towards him – though in truth, her goodwill was simulated. Not that he would notice that at a distance.

'What brings you into town?' he asked, clearly excited to see her again, but he cast his eyes towards the hospital too. The direction she approached him from made it obvious that she had just left the building. Ella hoped her reply would remove any suspicion that she had been to see Mohan.

'I was visiting Doctor Bagus. It seems he appreciates my knowledge of naturopathic medicine, and I must confess that I am interested in traditional Indian medical practices too.'

'Surely not that quackery they call Ayuvada round these parts?'

'No, I mean Ayurveda. Indian medicine is not so well known back in Europe, unfortunately,' she corrected him, courteously amending his mispronunciation.

'I see . . .'

'I will be instructing the staff in homeopathy. Ultimately, that will be of benefit to everybody in the country,' Ella continued.

'I'm afraid it will be a wasted endeavour,' he declared in his supercilious manner. Before he could launch into another sermon on lazy and intellectually impaired *bumiputras* and *Orang Asli*, Ella decided to cut him off – though she took care not to injure his 'superiority'.

'You mustn't forget that most of the nurses are well schooled, and that hospitals don't employ the sort of uneducated day labourers one finds on the railways,' she explained.

How easy it was to keep coarse-natured men like him in line. Compton even looked impressed.

'You may well be right there.' Did he really just say that, without gritting his teeth? He would probably pay her any compliment in the world as long as she kept on smiling adoringly at him.

'My offer still stands, by the way. You mustn't say no, else you'll miss a journey through a breathtakingly beautiful landscape – though I doubt I'll be able to pay it any attention at all, sitting by your side.' Compton could be persistent. Yet it couldn't do any harm to imply that she would accompany him on his railway journey in future.

'I'm too busy at the moment, but I'm sure you'll be travelling north on plenty of other occasions,' she answered.

'Indeed I will . . . and I'll take you at your word.' Coming from him, it sounded like a threat. 'May I escort you back? Marjory is always pleased to see me on the plantation.'

Ella concluded that he hadn't yet heard about her withdrawal into town.

'Heather is somewhat indisposed so I'm staying here for a few days. The Chinese boarding house behind the palace is simply delightful. You can reach me there at any time,' she said, since Lee had said she would be happy to take messages for her.

'I wish you would come with me tomorrow,' said Compton with deep regret.

'You're leaving tomorrow?' she asked casually. That sort of information could be useful for the attempt to liberate Mohan.

'The British Army has to put right what the locals botch. Part of a bridge has collapsed, and they're incapable of repairing the breach,' said Compton.

'The army is being called out just to rebuild a bridge?'

'Not the entire regiment, of course, but we'll need a couple of dozen men.'

'But who will look after us while you're gone?' Ella asked, playing the part of a vulnerable maiden.

'Don't you worry. You're perfectly safe here in Johore.'

'I'm relieved to hear it.'

'Sir, it's time to go!' called the younger officer.

Thank heavens, Ella thought. Compton couldn't seem to tear himself away from her.

'Lieutenant Bennett manages all my appointments,' Compton sighed, before giving her a deep bow. 'I hope you have a wonderful day,' he bid her farewell.

'The same to you – and I hope your expedition goes well.' Her good wishes were all the more convincing for being sincerely felt.

Ella had resolved to hurry back to Amar as quickly as possible to let him know that she had met with Bagus and completed her mission. Yet because she was currently staying with Amar – though she didn't know for how long – she needed to visit Lee's boarding house first to collect her bags. As she did so, she realised she would no longer need the carriage they had hired in Singapore, since she could use Mohan's cart from now on. Indeed, she had already used it to come into town.

Lee made a suggestion that solved the problem: 'I'll give it to a guest who wants to travel to Singapore tomorrow. He can take it back for you.'

Ella calculated how many more days she would have to pay for and handed Lee the money. It was too much, but Ella insisted that Lee keep the difference in return for her services. There was no more time to lose now, as Amar would be anxiously awaiting her return.

◆ ◆ ◆

By the time she returned from town, Ella knew she would be coming back to a bundle of nerves, and she was right. When she arrived at Mohan's house, she had covertly watched as Amar paced anxiously from palm tree to palm tree. It was as if she had gone to try and assassinate Compton himself. Handing over a message was a trivial matter by comparison, although Mohan's life probably depended on it. She embraced Amar, which calmed him somewhat. Yet his tension only fully left him once they were indoors and she had assured him that everything had gone according to plan, and that Bagus was willing to help them. His unease returned once more when she told him of her meeting with Compton, however.

'So Compton saw you at the hospital?' he asked.

'I flirted with him – just like a weak woman should when she looks up to a big, powerful man like him,' explained Ella with a complacent smile, hoping that a little humour would help Amar relax.

For a moment, she was worried that the juice he was pouring would overflow – but then Amar detected the irony and gave a relieved smile. The fruit juice landed in the cup and not on the table. She had never seen him so tense before. He seemed to be consumed with worry and self-reproach. Yet she was far more worried about him than he was about her.

'Will you be taking part in the ambush tomorrow?' she asked as she sat down on a cushion on the floor.

Amar didn't need to reply – she could read his thoughts.

'What if they arrest you too?'

'They'll need to catch me first. Prison wagons of this kind are usually only accompanied by one officer. There are five of us. What can go wrong?'

'Will you be armed?'

'No. No firearms.'

'And what if something does go wrong?' asked Ella.

He didn't reply. Instead, he sat down beside her and took her in his arms.

She cherished being so close to him, but for that very reason, the gesture only increased her fears on his behalf. He seemed to sense her concern, for he clung to her even more tightly. Why did this feel like a farewell?

'Nothing will happen to me. I promise.' Amar's calmness and his strong arms wrapped around her body made Ella believe it.

Then he began to run his hands down her back, to caress her. A hand crept up to her neck, touching her hair. He pressed his body firmly against hers, and the powerful emotions he aroused in her were more intense now than they had ever been before. What if he didn't come back tomorrow? She would never again experience this closeness – would never again feel his breath, how it tickled her skin and caused her own breathing to quicken in turn, just like her heart. She could see the yearning in his eyes as he turned to face her and ran his fingers through her hair. Ella could sense that he longed for the touch of her lips, just as she did for his. Perhaps for the last time! The thought prompted her to let go and simply allow it all to happen.

His lips felt rough at first, but as they became more urgent and began to explore her own – growing moist, lingering for an eternity – Ella couldn't imagine a more tender caress. Her heart throbbed in her throat, which he kissed too. She dared to return his touch, starting at his face and running her hands down his chest. A blissful moan welled up in his throat. Ella could feel his muscles relax as she ran her fingers along his back.

Then he began to explore her body. No man had ever touched her breasts before, and a hot tremor shot through her belly. He kept looking directly into her eyes, and his gaze made her want to yield to him all the more.

She allowed him to lift her blouse away from her body and caress her, kissing her on the breasts. Then he guided her hand to his hips, where a knot held together the cloth that he wore wrapped around his loins. Ella tugged at it, explored his manhood. The cloth slipped to the floor, as did the skirt that he freed from her body. Ella wanted nothing more than to feel even closer to him, to become one with him, but he didn't stop stroking her.

She felt as though she was burning up, and yet she savoured every second of this sweet torment, as the desire she felt for him deep within her washed over her in waves, each more intense than the last, and she felt herself sinking into a sea of passion.

Then their bodies came together in a harmony of movement, just as Ella had known in her heart that they would. They were no longer two hearts beating against each other; rather, they were as one – a single body, a single soul, floating on an ocean of bliss.

Ella woke up with the first rays of the sun, and lay savouring Amar's presence beside her. At some point in the night, he had snuggled up to her back and thrown his arm over her. He didn't seem to want to let her go, for they were still lying in the same position now. The rhythm of his steady breathing felt like a wordless lullaby, and she felt at peace; she couldn't remember ever having felt so perfectly secure. Until now, she had never wanted for anything, and she would always have described herself as a happy person. Yet being with Amar had taught her differently. You cannot miss what you never had, and just a slight touch on her belly was enough to make her realise now that she had lacked so much. Ella placed her hand on his, as though she wanted to keep hold of him; she wanted to feel like this forever. His touch, his kiss, his proximity seemed to reduce all that she had formerly thought of as happiness to mere contentment. That realisation was confirmed when he stretched and began kissing her from her neck down to her back, and it wasn't long before she felt his desire for her growing once more. She couldn't help but return his kiss, but she knew that this beautiful moment would soon come to an end. He knew it too, for he rolled away from her with a sigh.

'I can't be late,' he whispered to her.

Ella nodded bravely, her concern for him welling up again. 'Promise me you'll look after yourself,' she demanded.

'Everything will be all right – or do you think I want to go to jail? Then I wouldn't be with you any more.' Amar's words were sincere, but they did little to calm her. Freeing Mohan would be a perilous undertaking.

'Take me with you into town. I'll go mad with worry if I stay here.'

Amar nodded and rose to his feet. He stood before her, as naked as the day he was born, and she no longer felt any shame to see him like that. Then he gave her his hand to help her to her feet. White skin brushed against dark, but this time it was Ella's turn to let go of Amar. They didn't have much time, and he needed to keep a clear head.

CHAPTER 15

Wandering aimlessly around Johore in search of distraction may have been better than sitting in the garden of Mohan's house and awaiting Amar's return, but it still wasn't very effective as a means of passing the time. A reason for going into town had quickly presented itself over breakfast, however. Mohan's pantry wasn't particularly well stocked, and they had even run out of salt. Ella had briefly occupied herself by drawing up a shopping list, and getting hold of everything she needed would take her until the afternoon at least, which meant she wouldn't have to spend those hours tormenting herself by worrying whether anything had happened to Amar.

Ella and Amar had parted ways at the edge of the town. The centre lay in roughly the same direction as the hospital, but the rescue attempt would be taking place to the west of Johore. Amar had explained the plan to her that four masked men would lie in wait for the wagon. A fruit seller who was working with them would block the way with a movable fruit stall and cause a distraction, while the others would take advantage of the moment of surprise to overpower the officer and free Mohan. A sailboat would be waiting for Mohan, which would carry him safely to Sumatra. From there, he would be able to make his way to Siam. At least there was one detail that reassured her: Amar wouldn't accompany Mohan all the way to the coast, and would instead try to meet her in town at midday, at around the same time as Mohan would be sailing off to Sumatra. But even so, the minimal information she had was still enough to leave her picturing everything that might go wrong.

Ella had to virtually force herself to go to the grocer's shop and make her purchases. She would have much preferred to head in the other direction – but of course, that would have been foolish. It was important for her to be seen in Johore, and especially to be viewed as a regular resident. If someone shopped at one of the local stores, that meant they typically lived in Johore too, whereas travellers would visit these places at most to purchase some food for their journey or to buy something to drink. Ella's long shopping list alone announced that she wasn't just passing through the area, and she was very glad to have it, because she would have forgotten half of what she needed to buy otherwise. But finally, with the help of the hardworking assistant, she soon had everything a household could possibly need.

'You're new here, aren't you?' The unbridled curiosity of the Chinese shop assistant at least provided a distraction.

'Let me guess. You must have taken over from the Jonkers,' the lively woman surmised. With her long plait and skull cap, she reminded Ella of the Chinese people she had seen in her picture books as a child.

'Lots of Dutch people go back to Europe when they get old. Isn't that strange? They come all this way, and then . . .' The woman shook her head.

'What about you? Do you intend to stay here?' Ella asked.

'Malacca is my home. We've been living in Johore for many generations now,' she said, as if it were the most obvious thing in the world.

'Malacca will be a Chinese colony one day,' the woman went on as she wrapped Ella's fruit in paper.

'I'm sure the British won't let that happen,' Ella answered with a grin.

'They'll be gone one day. Believe me.' The woman seemed certain of that.

'What about the Malayans?'

'They have fewer children and they don't have the same head for business.' The woman's laugh cheered her up. Perhaps she was right too – but for now, the country was under the rule of the British Crown. Ella's thoughts immediately flew back to Amar. How sweet it was to think that she might live in that house with him for evermore! Yet the very sweetness of that thought made the aftertaste all the more bitter. It was half past nine, going by the clock behind the counter. Mohan would be free by ten. What should she do until then? Her shopping was all bagged up and a young Chinese shop porter was helping her to load it onto the cart.

After paying for her goods, Ella decided to visit her former lodgings. She and Amar had agreed to meet there at midday, but perhaps there would be news for her about Rudolf's repatriation. Officer Puteri had promised to take care of everything and to leave her a message. The boarding house was very close by, so barely ten minutes later, Ella was standing by the reception desk with a letter in her hand – but not one from Puteri. She was astonished to see the name 'Otto Ludwig' on the envelope.

'He's staying here for two nights,' Lee explained, obviously delighted to see her regular guest again.

Ella opened the letter as she walked towards the fountain in the courtyard, where she sat down to read it.

Dear Miss Kaltenbach,

*My worst fears that you would be gone by the time
I reached Johore seem to have come true – yet to my
relief, I was told it was still possible to reach you via
the reception desk. I asked about your fiancé too, and
I am still in a state of shock. Lee informed me that*

he passed away. Please accept my deepest condolences – though I still hope to express them to you in person.

My journey is coming to an end, and I have concluded my business successfully, but I cannot depart without speaking to you first. There is something you need to know – a matter that is too delicate to put down in writing. Tonight, there will be a party at the Hamiltons'. Anthony and Victoria are my most trustworthy suppliers, and they are celebrating the fiftieth anniversary of their plantation. They are truly the most delightful people, and they have told me to bring friends with me. I am not sure if I have your permission to consider you a friend, but I would be delighted if you would accept my invitation and join me at the party. The Hamiltons have expressly told me that everybody is welcome, so please feel free to come alone or with a guest. I'm sure we'll find an opportunity to speak privately. I have provided directions to the Hamiltons' plantation overleaf, and I am very much looking forward to seeing you again.

Your most humble servant,
Otto Ludwig

Ella had no time to look at the directions, however, for just then, multiple shots suddenly rang out like whip cracks in the distance. A cold shudder ran down Ella's back. Her hands began to tremble. There could only be one reason why shots were being fired right now. Lee had handed Otto's letter to her just before ten. Something terrible must have happened – she was sure of it.

Amar had expressly asked Ella to wait for him at the boarding house, but that was now impossible. It didn't take much imagination to realise that something must have gone wrong during the rescue attempt. Ella didn't know exactly how the plan had spiralled out of control, but she only needed to hurry after the throng of curious onlookers to find out. The mounted policemen hurrying in the same direction confirmed that she was heading the right way: towards the hospital.

Barely ten minutes later, her worst fears seemed to have been realised. From a distance, Ella could already see a police wagon standing in the middle of the road. A group of policemen were forcing back the crowd of onlookers, giving her a clear view of the street. What she saw there hit her like a hammer blow. In front of her, amid scattered pieces of fruit, lay the lifeless body of a Malay man – that much was obvious from the colour of his skin. Ella fervently hoped it wasn't Amar, yet she remained in agonising suspense until one of the policemen stepped aside, revealing the full length of the body lying on the ground. He was the same height as Amar, but he was wearing different clothes, and when the two policemen stepped back to allow a doctor to approach, she finally caught a glimpse of his face. It wasn't Amar, thank God! One of the policemen held a mask in his hand, which he had presumably just removed from the corpse.

Ella could almost physically feel a weight fall from her shoulders. She ventured a few steps towards the scene, and suddenly realised who must have shot the young man. A British officer stepped out in front of the wagon. He was carrying a gun.

Another few steps. The police were questioning the fruit seller, whom Amar had said was part of the plot, as well as a few passersby who had apparently witnessed the attack. A man standing beside the wagon and tending to the horse was also being interviewed. He must be a coachman from the hospital. Then one of the policemen turned to face in Ella's direction. It was Puteri. She didn't even attempt to turn away or hide behind the others in the crowd. She was the only white woman here, and his eyes were trained directly on her. He smiled at her before exchanging a few words with his colleague. It would have been worse if Compton had spotted her, but this wasn't much better. If only Puteri hadn't looked at her for quite so long, for now the officer also turned towards her. Ella recognised him. It was the young man she had seen with Edward Compton the day before – the lieutenant named Bennett. His eyes lingered on her, and she saw a thoughtful, mistrustful expression descend over his face. It would only arouse more suspicion if she turned and fled, so she decided to join the crowd of onlookers instead. Nobody could hold that against her.

An approaching carriage from the hospital drove up to the crowd, and two young Malay policemen immediately began to urge the people to stand aside and clear the way. Ella recognised some of the staff from the hospital. Like everybody else, she had to take a few steps back to allow the carriage to pass. They must be there to take charge of the body. The policemen also had to cross the road in order to let the carriage through, which allowed her to catch another glimpse of the scene. Something caught her eye next to a wall that was overgrown with grass and vines. Was she imagining it, or was there another mask lying there? One of the five men involved in Mohan's rescue must have lost it – perhaps even Amar. Ella considered whether she could somehow push through the crowd to retrieve it, but all such thoughts soon proved fruitless. One of the policemen suddenly noticed the mask too and picked it up. At that, Bennett sprang into action. The policeman held the mask out to him and Bennett nodded. Ella guessed that he had just identified it and was describing the sequence of events. She prayed that it wasn't Amar who had lost it while making his escape, for that would mean the witnesses might have got a look at his face.

There was nothing more to see here. Ella's eyes met Puteri's again, and she nodded at him, before slipping away from the scene as slowly and unobtrusively as possible – not by conscious decision, but because her fears for Amar's safety had triggered a kind of paralysis in her. It cost her great effort to put one foot in front of the other. What if he had been seen? She couldn't even be certain that there weren't any more dead bodies – she had only seen part of the street after all.

◆ ◆ ◆

After spending a full hour sitting motionless on the edge of the fountain and peering through the entrance of the boarding house at a deserted patch of shade underneath a tree, Ella was almost overcome with joy and relief when the man she was looking for finally appeared. Her first impulse was to leap to her feet, rush over to Amar and fall into his arms, but she quickly suppressed the urge – not through common sense, but out of sheer fury at both him and herself. Why hadn't she talked him out of the rescue? Then her thoughts turned to Mohan, and her rage subsided. In the end, they had done the right thing. But had he managed to get away?

Ella stood up, crossed the road and walked over to Amar. His smile outweighed everything else at that moment.

'There you are,' was all he said – yet his obvious anxiety meant his smile wasn't as radiant as it usually was. 'Come on, let's go,' he suggested, before walking over to the boarding house with her.

Ella fetched the cart from the courtyard. The horse was already harnessed. She was burning to know what had gone wrong with the rescue attempt, but she had to wait until they had left the market. She watched Amar as he looked around to check whether there were any policemen nearby, and she took that as a warning not to ask for any details just yet.

As soon as they reached the road leading to Mohan's house, he began to tell her everything of his own accord.

'Everything was going to plan. Bujang, Suib, Tenuk and I lay in wait for the wagon, and Ahad managed to stop it with his fruit stall. He often wheels his stand down that road, but he had a minor mishap – nothing that would strike anybody as unusual – and the fruit fell on the ground. He took his time picking it up, so the officer grew impatient and dismounted, just as we had hoped. But then some children came past. The officer turned around too soon, and Suib had already broken cover. That put the officer on the alert, and he drew his gun. As the other two ran towards him, he shot at Suib, who fell to the ground and didn't move. Bujang and Tenuk managed to disarm the officer, and I got Mohan out of the wagon. The horses were hidden behind the embankment. Mohan had handcuffs on, so I had to lift him onto his horse, and then I took him to the handover point. Tenuk will take him to the coast.'

'Did anybody see you?' Ella asked.

'No, definitely not. And even if they did, I was wearing my mask.'

A weight instantly fell from Ella's heart – though that meant one of the others had been seen instead.

'There was a mask lying in the undergrowth,' she said.

Amar gave a concerned look and thought for a moment before continuing. 'Bujang must have lost his in the melee, then. Tenuk was still wearing his, I know that for sure.'

'Can anybody link you with the two of them?' Ella's anxiety knew no bounds.

'No. They work on different plantations. Who could have seen them beyond the coachman from the hospital and the army officer? And even if they did – would they know all the workers in the area? They can't question everybody in the region and visit every plantation. It all happened so quickly too. Both of them got away. Besides, they'd need to match the mask to the right face anyway,' said Amar.

'How do you mean?'

'We used traditional wooden masks. They have to fit perfectly. We all tried on each other's, and only one of them fit me. If I'd worn any of the others then I wouldn't have been able to see anything or breathe,' he said.

It took Ella a moment to process his words. 'But now somebody has paid for all this with his life,' she eventually pointed out.

Amar remained silent. He was clearly upset by what had happened.

Ella remembered what the Chinese shop assistant had told her, and her certainty about the future of the British colony in Malacca.

'Maybe it would be better to come to an arrangement with the British, or to offer a different kind of resistance. Otherwise yet more people will die,' she said.

'You mean do nothing?' asked Amar wearily.

'They won't be here forever. There are too many of you for that.'

Amar seemed to be mulling over her words. He didn't speak again, but she sensed his relief when she snuggled up to his side. Although she was leaning against him, Ella could tell that right now, it was he who was drawing strength from her.

Ella had spent a long time debating whether she ought to go to the Hamiltons' party. Amar was understandably preoccupied – with himself, with his grief for Suib, with his fears for Mohan, and especially with the question of whether the cost of resisting the British had been too great. For her own part, however, she often found it useful to occupy herself with something completely different at times like this. There was nothing Amar could do about the situation now. Besides, Otto urgently wanted to see her and speak with her. All the same, when they arrived back at Mohan's house and Ella suggested they go to the party together, Amar objected to the idea – but for entirely different reasons than she had been expecting.

'They'll talk about us.' Amar didn't need to explain what he meant by that. Naturally, Ella's experiences so far had made it clear to her that it would be considered indecorous for a European woman to appear at a party in the company of a Malayan man. Yet for one thing, she wasn't British, but was passing as a Dutchwoman; and for another, Ella had no intention of hiding her feelings for Amar. If she did, people would only talk about them all the more when they inevitably saw them together. The best course of action was to remove all grounds for gossip about a European woman and her secret native lover altogether, as soon as possible. In the end, her argument won Amar over, but only for a few minutes. Then he began to look around rather helplessly and tug at his linen trousers.

'But what should I wear? I can't exactly go to the party in my work clothes.' His objection was a valid one, but a solution was at hand.

'Rudolf's suits ought to fit you.' Amar froze at Ella's suggestion. The thought of wearing a dead man's clothing obviously didn't appeal to him in the slightest.

'Nobody is going to make you a new suit in two hours,' Ella remarked with a smile.

Amar nodded and shrugged. What choice did he have?

◆ ◆ ◆

They didn't have time to fetch Rudolf's bags from the boarding house and bring them back to Mohan's house to make adjustments, and Ella hoped she had gauged Amar's size correctly – but unfortunately she had miscalculated, as they soon discovered when he tried on Rudolf's trousers in one of the unoccupied bedchambers that

Lee had allowed them to use as a changing room. They were the right length, but the waistband was much too big. Otto couldn't help them either. For one thing, Amar would easily have fit twice into a pair of his trousers, and for another, he was already at the party, as Lee had informed them at the reception desk.

'Wait a moment. I have my sewing kit here.' Lee volunteered her help and returned barely five minutes later with her equipment. She looked the other way while Amar removed the trousers.

'I learned this from my mother,' she explained, inserting pins into the waistband.

Meanwhile, Amar tried on the shoes. Fortunately, there was one pair big enough for him to wear without grimacing in pain – yet Ella hadn't stopped to consider that Malayan men generally didn't wear closed shoes due to the high temperatures throughout the year, which meant that Amar's first attempts at walking were very unsteady. Ella had difficulty suppressing her laughter as he wobbled his way across the room, clad in elegant shoes and white linen underwear.

Lee really had managed to take in the waistband in just a few minutes. Amar slipped into the trousers and put on one of Rudolf's white shirts and his jacket, while Lee averted her eyes once more.

'You look like a true English gentleman,' she cried enthusiastically once she turned round and saw him in his full outfit.

Ella had to agree.

Amar's disconcerted expression made it clear that he didn't take 'English gentleman' as a compliment. All the same, he admired his reflection in the mirror – and with good reason, for he looked quite gorgeous. The suit certainly suited him better than it had Rudolf.

Ella hadn't the faintest idea what was in store for them at the Hamiltons', but she hoped their party would be less formal than Mary Bridgewater's had been. The fact that the attendees could bring a guest of their choice suggested as much. All the same, Ella wished that in his letter Otto had named a specific time to meet him. She would have preferred to arrive in his company.

Amar knew the plantation from hearsay. The Hamiltons were Scottish, and were generally considered to be hardworking and kind-hearted people, about whom he had heard only good things. Their plantation was also a good deal smaller than the Fosters', as became clear after just ten minutes' drive when the road through the rubber forest opened out into a clearing, in which stood a two-storey house that seemed rather humble compared to the Fosters' residence. It appeared to be made of wood, and had a barn attached to it. Although it was far from grand, Ella thought it had a certain charm. The large veranda was already packed with guests, and bunting dangled from the roof posts. It almost felt like a children's birthday party. The garden was lit with torches and teeming with guests of all ages, and Ella could tell at a glance that the atmosphere was relaxed and informal. Unlike Mary Bridgewater's party, Chinese guests had been invited too, and there were finely dressed Indians and Malays standing by the buffet, which extended a good fifteen feet into the middle of the garden. The best part was that nobody took any notice of her and Amar. There was no welcome committee, and no obligation to shake anybody's hand.

Another carriage pulled up a few yards behind their own, and a mixed couple got out – a Chinese man with a Malay woman. They too were dressed up to the nines. Compton would certainly have changed his mind about *bumiputras* and *Orang Asli* if he had been here. Even Ella was astonished. It was clear that the non-Europeans here hadn't simply put on a costume for the occasion, as Amar had.

'You won't stand out in the slightest,' Ella remarked. Amar's eyes likewise lingered on the couple next to them, and she could see that he was surprised too. This party was shaping up to be a colourful evening.

All the same, they didn't have long to wait before they attracted their first curious looks. People had begun to notice that there were mixed couples in attendance. Ella expected that the other partygoers would start to whisper among themselves, but they didn't – instead, every guest they encountered greeted them with a friendly nod. The other mixed couple also joined the crowd. Their arrival had been fortuitous, for Amar began to look much more relaxed.

Wasn't it said that 'clothes make the man'? It seemed to be true for Amar, at any rate. Although she would have preferred him to throw his arm around her hips, Ella was delighted to see that he had blossomed into a true gentleman as he held out his arm for her, just as the couple in front of them had done. He was a quick learner.

'I'm looking forward to meeting Otto,' said Amar. Ella had told him about Otto on the way here – his warm-heartedness, and his disagreements with Rudolf too.

Ella was looking out for him, but she couldn't see him anywhere in the dim torchlight. He must be elsewhere.

'We should go straight to the buffet,' she said, speaking from experience. People stood close to the food and drink in order to see and be seen. Besides, the drive had taken them down some dusty roads, and her parched throat was calling out for a glass of wine.

The moment they arrived in the glow of the nearest torches, however, they encountered their first raised eyebrows. As Ella had expected, people began to whisper – but she had the impression that it was purely out of surprise rather than for more negative reasons. There could be no doubt that the partygoers here were very different to Mary Bridgewater's guests.

'There you are, at long last!' called a female voice that Ella recognised.

Of all people, Ella now saw Mary Bridgewater hurrying towards her out of the gloom. She too was surprised to see Ella in the company of Amar, but she recovered quickly and scrutinised him, giving him the smile of a woman who knew how to appreciate a handsome young man.

'Otto told me you were coming . . . but aren't you going to introduce me?' Mary prompted her.

'This is Amar,' said Ella, though she was still amazed to hear that Mary and Otto knew one another. Then again, who didn't Mary know?

'Lovely to meet you,' Mary addressed him. Then she looked at Ella, as if to ascertain whether she really was involved with a Malayan man. Why else would she have taken his arm?

'Isn't Otto here yet?' asked Ella.

'He's inside somewhere, loitering with those tedious, cigar-smoking Scots. I couldn't stand it in there any more. Men. Just give them a few cigars and a bottle of Scotch whisky and they gather like a pack of wolves.'

'Have you known Otto for a long time?' Ella enquired.

'Not at all. He told Victoria and Anthony about you, and when Victoria hears anything, it isn't long before her best friend hears it too.'

Ella finally understood how everybody knew each other. She wasn't in the least surprised to see that Mary felt at ease in these more informal circumstances.

'Admit it. You didn't expect to see me here,' said Mary frankly.

Ella nodded.

'Some meetings are written in the stars. That's what the Indians believe, anyway. Come, I simply must introduce you to the Hamiltons. I'm sure they'll take to you right away. Now, where are they?' Mary scanned the garden, but to no avail.

'Would you ladies like anything to drink?' asked Amar. He could easily be taken for an English aristocrat.

'A gin and tonic, please,' said Mary, delighted with his manners.

'And a glass of wine for you,' Amar suggested. That was easy for him to guess – he'd already noticed that she had bought three bottles of the local rice wine in Johore.

Mary watched in fascination as he disappeared towards the buffet.

'A most attractive man . . . Oh, to be young again. What does he do? Is he a doctor?'

Ella was tickled. Amar seemed to be exactly Mary's type.

'No. He used to work on the Fosters' plantation.'

That evidently took Mary by surprise, but she recovered quickly. 'I admire your courage. I wouldn't have been brave enough for that at your age . . . but then again, things were different back then,' she said. 'How are Marjory and Heather?' she asked next.

'I'm no longer staying with them.'

'Really?' Mary gave Ella a penetrating look – naturally enough, since she had previously offered Ella some discreet hints about Heather's past. It was impossible to get anything past Mary, so Ella gave up trying to think of an excuse.

'I simply couldn't stop thinking about what you told me, and then I found a heart carved into a tree in the garden of the guest house. It had the letters "H" and "J" on it. "J" for Jack. I raised it with Heather, but I shouldn't have. I think she wants me to leave her alone in future.'

Mary was obviously deeply touched.

'And there I was, thinking it might have something to do with the fact you make no secret of your enviable affinity with your charming companion . . .' she said.

'No, that definitely isn't the reason,' Ella assured her.

'I'll talk to Marjory about it, when I get the chance. We can't have Heather locking herself up just because of this damnable Jack . . . She should come here, rejoin the world. Scots make good lovers after all,' remarked Mary with a wink.

'If only I could work out why Heather is so sad,' said Ella.

Mary grew serious for a moment. 'We all have our little secrets. Yourself included, no?' She grinned as she spoke. It didn't sound like a threat, so Ella decided to ask her what she was getting at.

'Secrets?'

'You didn't turn up at Marjory's door by accident, did you?'

Ella grew hot, although she didn't have the impression that Mary was ill-intentioned.

'Come now, there's no need to pull such a long face. My lips are sealed – like a vault. I can tell when I have a good and kind person in front of me. You are just such a person, and I feel certain that you didn't have any base motives.'

'But . . .' Ella objected, determined to explain herself to Mary.

'No buts, now . . . It's time I hauled Otto out of this bandits' den. If we wait much longer, he'll be so drunk that he'll have forgotten why he came here in the first place.'

All the same, Mary waited until Amar had gallantly handed over her drink, and she gave him another lingering stare before turning back towards the house. That was the look of a woman who was reputed to have an Indian lover, Ella smiled to herself.

Otto was presumably rather the worse for wear, since it had been a good quarter of an hour since Mary had vanished through the veranda door. Ella had used the time to exchange a few words with Victoria Hamilton – though that hadn't been easy, for her Scottish accent posed a challenge. At times, it sounded as though she wasn't even speaking English. Ella was unsurprised that Victoria and Mary got along so well. They seemed to be cut from the same cloth, and were anything but starchy and status-conscious. A man like Compton would stand out like a sore thumb here, Ella reflected.

In the end, Mary managed to tear Otto away from the smoking room, and he stood on the veranda waving at them almost frantically.

'Otto has already told me how delighted he will be to see you again. He wouldn't stop talking about your journey from Hamburg,' said Victoria.

Ella thought that he must have left out a few parts of the story – namely, the rift between him and Rudolf.

'Miss Kaltenbach!' he called over to her jubilantly.

Ella froze. She had introduced herself to Mary Bridgewater as a Dutchwoman named van Veen.

Otto now bore down on her so exuberantly that he managed to lift her mood, despite her now highly unfavourable situation.

Mary had also just arrived where they were standing. 'Otto was telling me that he has much to discuss with Miss Kaltenbach,' she declared, with a wink at Ella. So that was what Mary meant by 'little secrets'.

Ella was standing beside Victoria Hamilton and Amar was positioned a few feet away from her, so Otto merely greeted him with a polite nod.

'Indeed. You must tell me everything that's happened to you,' demanded Otto.

'Come, Amar. My bridge club are dying to meet you.' With that, Victoria took Amar's arm, and Ella was unsurprised to see Mary go with them too. It looked as though the two ladies were abducting him, the poor thing. He gave Ella an imploring look, which she answered with a mischievous laugh that drew Otto's attention.

His curious glance prompted her to add Amar to the list of topics she had to discuss with him.

'Well, there's an awful lot I need to tell you,' said Ella, debating where she ought to begin.

Although she was burning to know what Otto had to tell her, he insisted that she bring him up to speed with everything that had happened to her first. Ella had intended to work through the events of the last few days in chronological order, but there was one recent fact – Rudolf's death – that stood out and prevented them from continuing their short stroll through the garden. Otto stood rooted to the spot. 'Poisoned?' The pathologist's opinion gave Otto a good deal of food for thought, so it was understandable when he plucked a glass of whisky from a passing waiter's tray.

'They think he must have eaten something toxic.' Ella repeated what Officer Puteri had said.

Otto drained his glass and stared thoughtfully into the distance for a moment.

'It seems that it's fairly common for travellers to believe that a fruit is edible, and then . . .' she continued.

'What nonsense,' Otto interrupted. 'Since you got here, have you ever thought to pluck some unfamiliar fruit from a shrub?' he asked.

Ella shook her head.

'But then how did the poison get into his body?' Otto wondered out loud.

'There were no insect or spider bites,' she added.

'A robbery, perhaps? I know that the natives used to go hunting with blowpipes filled with minuscule poisoned darts. Just a tiny prick would be enough to kill you in a matter of seconds. Perhaps the pathologist didn't see the mark,' Otto conjectured.

'We can rule out a robbery, as he still had his gold watch on him when he was found,' Ella pointed out.

'Where did it happen?' enquired Otto.

'He was on his way back from the Fosters. They were on the list of names you gave us – but the strange thing is that Rudolf had already marked the plantation on a map of his own. None of it makes any sense. When we arrived in Malacca, we passed through the Foster plantation and we were told there was no one there called Richard Foster. So why would Rudolf still note down the location of that plantation? At first, I thought he was copying each of the marks across one by one as he visited them, to make his own map clearer. The markings on the south part of your map were so dense that you could no longer read some of the names of the roads and villages.'

'I don't think that was it. I think he marked it in advance. Though I couldn't tell you why I think that. It's more of a feeling – but it ties in perfectly with what I've found out about him.'

Ella pricked up her ears, and gave Otto an astonished look.

'I just haven't been able to stop thinking about it. The race-course. He gambled away a lot of money, and then that preposterous story about being robbed in the stables . . .'

'Yes, I've come to exactly the same conclusion myself. I found his betting slip, and can you guess where?'

Otto gave a perplexed shrug.

'In the wallet they supposedly stole from him.'

He nodded knowingly.

'Then I truly didn't misjudge him,' declared Otto.

'Rudolf gambled all his money away and wanted me to pay his way without him losing face.'

'Exactly as I suspected. And on top of that, Rudolf was a swindler and a fraud,' he added.

'What do you mean?' asked Ella in shock. His harsh judgment didn't seem to fit the Rudolf von Stetten she had known.

'I made enquiries among my contacts in Hamburg. My good friend Gustav works for a credit bureau, and I can assure you that Rudolf von Stetten – to put it as bluntly as possible – was completely broke.'

'Rudolf?' Now it was Ella's turn to freeze.

'He took over his father's company when he died, but they hadn't been doing well for at least a year before that. The business model was unprofitable, with a focus on tenanted properties in expensive neighbourhoods. You can imagine how often those come up for sale. The bank refused to honour his cheques, and he was rumoured to be an inveterate gambler too. His visit to the racecourse would seem to bear that out,' Otto explained.

'You mean he gambled away the von Stetten fortune?'

'It seems so . . . though what's far more deplorable is to then seek women out in order to live at their expense,' continued Otto.

'But that can't be. He was a close family friend. He knew we were only able to maintain our comparatively high standard of living thanks to an annuity – which turned out not to be an annuity, but payments sent from Penang. Rudolf didn't know any more than that, so he can't have thought that there was much money to be had from me.'

Otto now fell into deep rumination. His thoughts seemed to be running in circles, just like Ella's.

'There's only one explanation. He must somehow have found out that you are really the daughter of a wealthy Englishman. Everything suddenly makes sense then. He embarked on this journey with you knowing who your real father is, and then he paid a visit to the man's family. But didn't you just say that there is no Richard Foster?'

'Not quite. There *was* a Richard Foster, but he's dead, and I feel certain that he was my father.'

'How can you be so sure?'

'He had a daughter – Heather. She has a birthmark in exactly the same place as I do. I stayed with the Fosters for a few days, passing myself off as a tourist and enjoying their hospitality. During that time I grew close to Heather . . .'

'So he must have confronted the Fosters – perhaps even black-mailed them . . .' Otto conjectured.

'Plausibly.' It began to dawn on Ella that there was a motive for getting Rudolf out of the way.

'It's very possible that these Fosters, or somebody working for them, might have done away with Rudolf.' Otto's conclusions were logical, but she couldn't bring herself to accept his reasoning.

'I can't believe that. Marjory Foster is a hard woman, but also a very upright one, and she loves her daughter more than anything. I don't think she would do something like that. Though supposing you're right and he knew more than I did before we left Germany – how in the world could he have proven that I'm Richard Foster's daughter?'

Otto stopped once more, deep in thought. 'I think I need another whisky,' he remarked. Whatever angle they approached the various motives and circumstances from, this thorny situation refused to make any sense – though there had to be some connection between the Fosters and Rudolf's death.

Ella was relieved to see that the bridge club had released Amar from their clutches and allowed him to join them once more – otherwise, Otto might have managed to persuade Ella to join him for a glass of the strong Scottish spirit. Yet Ella's hopes of seeking solace at Amar's side proved unrealistic when she saw that he was being escorted back by Mary.

'Otto, why don't you have a chat with Amar? He's worked on a plantation for many years now, and I swear I've never met anybody who knows as much about cultivating and harvesting rubber as he does.' Mary's manoeuvre was easy to see through, and her glance at Ella made it clear that she wanted to speak with her in private. Ella could imagine what she wanted to ask her.

Otto and Amar both seemed surprised at Mary's suggestion. Otto in particular didn't seem to know what to make of Amar.

Ella was about to explain that he was her companion, but Mary seemed to feel there was another more pressing matter to discuss, and she took Ella's arm.

'Do you work here in the south?' Otto finally broke the silence, thank heavens.

'I'm just borrowing Ella to give her a taste of my homemade sherry,' said Mary charmingly, before abducting her just as Victoria had done with Amar earlier.

Otto seemed to take the hint, but Amar gave Ella an enquiring look. She nodded at him.

'I can imagine what you want to speak to me about,' said Ella, once they were a few steps away from the two men.

'Oh indeed? What, then?' smiled Mary.

'Perhaps about the fact that the Dutch enjoy sherry just as much as the British?' asked Ella wryly.

Mary laughed out loud. 'I had actually intended to leave that subject alone for the time being – however, I suffer from chronic curiosity. But you don't have to discuss it if you don't want to,' she reassured her.

'It would take a weight off my conscience, as I felt very uncomfortable pretending to be somebody else at your garden party.'

'It is rather unusual, to be sure,' Mary conceded.

Ella pondered what excuse she could offer her, and decided to tell the truth – or at least part of it.

'It was Amar's idea. I have a limited travel budget, and he told me that the Fosters sometimes accept guests. The last one was a Dutchwoman.' So much for the truth, Ella thought.

'Yes, so I heard. She must have been a very charming lady.'

'I've already told you that I lived in England for a year, and I couldn't help but notice a certain amount of animosity towards Germans while I was there,' Ella hinted.

'And so you decided it would be better to pass yourself off as a Dutchwoman.' Mary's conclusion was welcome to Ella, as she could confirm it with a clear conscience.

'What a barmy idea! Then again, it's true that Kaiser Bill isn't exactly well loved by the British. To be perfectly honest, his thirst for power fills me with some alarm too. We Brits worry that one day, he might surpass the political and naval supremacy of the British Empire.'

As on so many other occasions, Ella thanked the Lord that she had managed to avoid falling into a trap, and she hoped that the rest of the conversation would be devoted to global politics. Her conversations with Otto over dinner on the *Danzig* had even taught her to enjoy such subjects – yet she was disappointed, for Mary suddenly chuckled to herself.

'You won't believe what I've been thinking about you all this time,' she began.

Ella had no idea what Mary was getting at, but she instantly felt hot.

'You and Heather. You're so similar that I thought you might be sisters at first,' laughed Mary.

Ella felt nauseous. She drew a deep breath and hoped she could manage to keep the conversation from going off the rails. After all, Mary was friends with Marjory.

'Thankfully, I never met Richard – Marjory's late husband – in person, but there were rumours about him.'

'That he was unfaithful, you mean?' Ella probed.

'At any rate, that would explain why you look so similar to Heather. But my imagination ran away with me. I almost thought . . . Ach, it's absurd . . .' Mary downplayed her suspicions.

'Come now, tell me,' Ella urged, struggling to maintain her composure. She was drenched in sweat.

'The same thing happened in my own family. My brother . . . well, he wasn't exactly faithful either, and one day a young woman appeared at our door. Her mother had told her on her deathbed who her real father was. She didn't introduce herself by her own name either,' explained Mary.

'Remarkable,' Ella squeaked.

'So I thought . . . you know?' Mary hinted.

The subject needed to be changed as quickly as possible. Mary was certain to know a few other things about the Fosters, thank heavens.

'I take it you haven't known Marjory for very long?' asked Ella.

'To be perfectly honest, I've known her for longer than anyone – but even so, we only became friends after Richard died. She was something of a recluse while he was still alive. Her husband must have been a very unpleasant person to live with,' Mary revealed.

Ella could well imagine how Heather must have suffered with a father like that.

'It was only many years after his death that Marjory began to maintain . . . a few important social contacts, let's say. After all, she was running the plantation all by herself, and that's hard to do without being involved in the wider community.'

'And Marjory told you about her husband? Did she suspect him of betraying her?' asked Ella.

'It's interesting that you ask me that. No, to be honest, we've almost never talked about Richard,' Mary admitted.

'But you're her close friend. At least, that's what Marjory implied to me.'

'Certainly. We share the same passion – and please don't draw the wrong conclusion there,' laughed Mary.

Ella realised she was alluding to her native lovers.

'We both love oleander. I'm sure you've seen how magnificently it grows in Marjory's garden.'

'I've never seen such a beautiful house in my life. It's like a fairy tale castle,' Ella admitted.

'The strange thing is that it doesn't seem to flower properly at my house. There's only one small bed in my garden where I can get it to grow at all,' Mary sighed. 'And now for the sherry,' she added, as they reached the veranda. 'Victoria and the rest of the bridge club are already quite addicted to it. People say that my sherry is worse than Chinese opium.' She laughed as she bore down on a decanter standing on a small side table.

Whatever the sherry tasted like, Ella knew she would need more than just a glass of it.

CHAPTER 16

Ella had stayed up late with Amar, wrapped up in endless speculations about the Fosters and Rudolf's death; yet against all expectations, she must have finally fallen asleep from sheer exhaustion. Not even Amar's presence and his consoling words had been able to slow down the whirling carousel that was her mind. In his view, it wasn't worth wasting any more thought on the matter. Some things were best left alone. A worthy suggestion, but one that even he had found hard to put into practice. He had promised her that everything would feel like far less of a burden in the morning, but as the first rays of the sun began to fall upon their bunk, her thoughts all came flooding back – partly because her conversation with Otto had stirred up her emotions, but also because she was preoccupied with her experiences last night as a European woman at Amar's side.

That was another topic that she and Amar had discussed until late in the night. The guests of the amiable and easy-going Hamiltons certainly weren't typical for Malacca, but it had still been heartening to learn that there were people out there who didn't reduce Amar to the status of a mere lover, nor her to that of a woman of loose morals – a tourist in search of adventurous dalliances with native men. Otto had listened to her confession that she and Amar were a couple without blinking an eyelid – though that was probably due in part to his whisky consumption. She had found the admission easier to make after a few glasses of Mary's sherry too. Otto seemed to like Amar and had chatted to him for a long while – about rubber, naturally.

The dawn of the new day did nothing to dispel these thoughts, but that changed when Amar sleepily opened his eyes. His kiss put a stop to the chaos in her mind, at least for now.

'When do you want to leave?' he asked.

'Preferably never,' answered Ella. Not because she would rather spend the entire day lying in Amar's arms, but because she faced an unpleasant duty – one that she had learned of the night before when Otto had accompanied them back to Johore. Lee had handed her Officer Puteri's message straight away. At one o'clock in the afternoon, a ship would leave for Germany, and Rudolf's mortal remains would depart with it. There were papers to be signed, so Ella thought it best to arrive early at the harbour in Johore. From there, the coffin would be taken to Singapore before being loaded onto a steamer for the journey home.

'I'll come with you.'

Ella was hoping Amar would say that, for she felt sure she would find it difficult to say goodbye – especially in light of what Otto had told her the night before.

'Did you love him?'

She had been wondering when Amar would ask her that question, and she saw no reason to hide the truth from him – although it would probably have been better not to discuss the topic over their hastily eaten breakfast.

'I loved him, yes, but I couldn't give free rein to my feelings,' explained Ella.

'How do you mean?' It seemed that Amar really could be jealous sometimes.

'I only realised it on the way to Singapore. Whenever we had an intimate moment, it didn't quite feel right,' she admitted to him.

'Perhaps you could sense that something about him didn't add up.'

282

Amar's point was an obvious one, though she hadn't fully realised it until now.

'And why did you fall in love with him?' Amar's persistence left her feeling flustered.

'He was an eligible bachelor . . . from a good family who were friends with my own. He was good-looking and . . . he pursued me.' At that moment, Ella realised it was his social status that had drawn her to him more than anything else.

Amar nodded thoughtfully.

'I was a humble hospital nurse, and when a gentleman takes an interest . . . Well, I started to daydream . . . and then he was there for us when Father died.' She tried to justify herself.

'I'm just a humble plantation worker. Not a gentleman.' A sad note crept into his voice. Was he trying to suggest he wasn't good enough for her? What nonsense!

'He was a fraud,' Ella pointed out.

Amar really seemed to take it to heart that he was no von Stetten – even though Rudolf had proven to be a swindler.

'But what if a man came along one day who could offer you all that? A man of the world, with plenty of money and . . .'

'Look at me,' Ella demanded, for Amar was currently addressing himself to the slices of mango on his plate. He did as she said.

She said nothing more, and looked him straight in the eye. He returned her gaze, and she could almost feel him reading her thoughts. Surely, he must know how strongly she felt about him.

'I love you,' said Ella, for it felt right to her at that moment, and she needed to say it to him.

Amar's eyes gleamed with emotion.

'Anyway, what about you? The way those bridge players looked at you, I thought they were going to eat you alive . . .'

'I find bridge very boring.' Amar had emerged from his melancholy mood, thank heavens. He grinned at her. 'But that suit yesterday – I won't be making a habit of wearing it, I can tell you that now. I have blisters on my feet too,' he complained.

'That's a pity. You looked like a real man of the world last night.' Ella swallowed a piece of mango. How good it felt to laugh and feel carefree again.

◆ ◆ ◆

The harbour of Johore consisted of just three small landing stages, and very little trade came through it. Large sailboats and steamships never docked here. Officer Puteri had instructed her to meet him at the first jetty, and it didn't take Ella long to find the meeting point, where Puteri was already waiting for her. Rudolf too, inside a wooden coffin that lay on the back of a police wagon.

Amar drove the cart towards the landing stage, where a small sailboat was waiting to transport Rudolf's body to Singapore.

'Stop here,' said Ella.

Amar immediately pulled on the reins and brought the cart to a halt.

'I'll handle this on my own,' she said, as Amar made ready to jump down from the cart too. He nodded, seeming to realise that this was a matter for Ella alone, and that it concerned an earlier chapter in her life. Yet it was also wiser for her not to be seen in the company of a Malayan man. Puteri would almost certainly be investigating Mohan's rescue, and he might link her to the operation.

'Miss Kaltenbach.' Puteri's voice was muted. After all, he was there to deliver the body of a deceased acquaintance of hers.

'Aren't you taking any luggage with you?' he asked, looking towards the cart, which Amar had steered to one side in order to let others access the landing stages.

The question took Ella by surprise. 'I wasn't planning on leaving,' she answered.

Puteri furrowed his brow – presumably because at their last meeting, she hadn't said whether she would stay here or head back to Hamburg. It seemed he had assumed the latter.

'I had understood that you were close to Mr von Stetten. My apologies,' he replied, though she had only told him that Rudolf was her travel companion. Evidently, he hadn't really believed her.

'I'm finding this hard enough as it is,' she said in a reproachful tone. He nodded sympathetically and pulled out a folder containing two sheets printed with text in the local language.

'I would kindly ask you to sign these documents, which confirm that the local police have released the body and that Mr von Stetten can be transported to Hamburg.'

Ella hesitated. 'Strictly speaking, I don't have any legal grounds to do so. I'm not related to him.'

Puteri nodded. 'All that's needed is for somebody who knows him to confirm that the handover has taken place,' he assured her.

Ella signed the papers and handed them back.

'Thank you. If you have any problems at all or if you need help with anything – please, come and see me,' he said. Something else seemed to be weighing on his mind.

'The lost documents – they were never found,' he suddenly announced. Ella was unable to follow.

'The ones from the case we found in his horse's saddlebag. We questioned the workers and paid another visit to the Fosters – after all, he might have left something on their property. Business information, or a quotation. I never asked about that the first time I was there,' he explained.

Ella's stomach lurched. If he had visited the Fosters again then he would almost certainly have mentioned her name.

'I presume your inquiries proved fruitless,' she said.

'I'm afraid so. Mrs Foster seemed unaware that he wasn't here alone. She asked me to pass on her deepest condolences to you, although she doesn't know you personally.'

Ella felt as though an ice-cold hand were gripping her throat. She hoped that Puteri would attribute her pallor to the fact that she was here to bid farewell to her dead companion. *'Although she doesn't know you personally'* – what did Marjory mean by that?

'Thank you.' Ella was unable to say anything more.

Puteri nodded, put the documents away and climbed onto his carriage. Before he departed, he gave her a final encouraging smile, but it missed its mark. Ella tried to calmly consider what he might have told Marjory. He would almost certainly have mentioned that Rudolf had a female companion who was staying at Lee's boarding house. Armed with that information, Marjory could easily draw her own conclusions, since she had arranged for Ella's luggage to be fetched from The Dragon's Breath. Ella felt nauseous. At the same time, she wondered why Marjory had extended her condolences in this way, without letting on that she already knew her. Presumably because she didn't want Puteri to draw a connection between Rudolf and the woman who had lodged in her guest house. It was hard to predict what the consequences of that would be.

Two Malay sailors, whom Ella hadn't noticed until now, were squatting on their haunches in front of the wagon. They looked at her enquiringly, and seemed to be waiting for her to bid farewell to the coffin.

She stood motionless at the back of the wagon. Should she say a prayer? She couldn't think of one. Perhaps she could recite an Our Father? No, not for Rudolf, after he had betrayed her so shamelessly. Why did those two men keep staring at her so expectantly?

Ella decided to give Rudolf a final message to take with him.

'I don't know why you did it, but may the Lord have mercy on your soul,' she whispered. Then she made the sign of the cross – not for religious reasons, but to signal to the two sailors that they could go about their work.

They clearly got the message, stood up and climbed onto the wagon to lift the coffin down. At the end of the pier, the ship waited to accept Rudolf's mortal remains.

Ella turned away and looked up to where Amar was sitting. Puteri presumably hadn't recognised him at that distance, and Amar's cart was also standing beneath a grove of palm trees, which meant his face was scarcely visible from here. Puteri had probably taken him for a coachman whom she had hired to bring her here. To be on the safe side, however, she scanned the road leading up from the harbour to make sure his carriage had gone. He was already making his way back towards town. Just then, Ella's eyes fell upon a second vehicle standing on the side of the road, a little above where it curved down to the port. She couldn't believe her eyes. There was no doubt about it: that was the Fosters' coach.

Amar saw it too and confirmed that it belonged to the Fosters. Ella found herself burning to know what they were doing here.

'She's spying on you.' Amar's theory made sense. Marjory must have learned from Puteri when and where Rudolf would be handed over to Ella. Why did she care? Did Marjory want to find out whether Ella was leaving Malacca? Whatever her reasons, her curiosity appeared to be satisfied, for the coach had now turned around and was heading back up to the main road that led out of town towards the north.

Amar was confident that their light and manoeuvrable cart would be able to catch up with the Fosters' slow, heavy coach. It wasn't a risk-free endeavour, for the track that wound its way back up to the main road had sections that fell away to a sheer drop, which it would be wise to navigate slowly and carefully. Yet Amar seemed not to care. Ella would never have thought that their cart could travel so quickly, though at one point their wheels skidded and they only narrowly avoided the edge of the road.

Ella had the impression that the coach ahead of them was speeding up. There were still two switchbacks between them, but they were already close enough to see that the driver was Raj – who else? As long as the two vehicles were both travelling uphill, the greater their chances were of catching up. And it was working. The gap between them was gradually closing, and by the time the coach rounded the next corner, they were right behind it.

'We need to catch them before they reach the road,' Amar shouted above the din of hooves and wheels clattering on the hard ground. Clouds of dust whirled up and enveloped them. Ella held a cloth in front of her nose, but the dust stung her eyes.

Raj turned to look back at them. He undoubtedly knew now who was behind him, and could see that they were trying to intercept him. They were still on steep ground, so Raj had no way of going any faster. The coach was simply too heavy. Instead, he veered from left to right to prevent them from overtaking. After all, that was the only way they could stop the coach and confront Marjory.

Raj's manoeuvres were unsuccessful. The coach lost its balance, and for a moment, it teetered on two wheels, a hair's breadth from disappearing over the edge. That forced him to straighten up into his original course, giving Amar the opportunity to inch past before the coach reached the turning onto the main road. Then he pulled hard on the reins. Their horse bucked and reared, but the cart came to a stop, rolling diagonally into Raj's path as it did so. Raj had to brake to avoid a collision.

'What's the meaning of this?' he yelled furiously.

Ella dismounted, and Amar followed her.

'I want to speak to Marjory. Right now.' Ella knew she was inside the coach, for if Marjory had sent Raj to the harbour on his own, he would have gone on horseback.

'Drive on. You have no right to stop us,' Raj answered.

Ella felt certain he was putting up a front, and that he was only speaking in such a harsh tone because Marjory was sitting inside the coach. She ignored his demand.

Raj leapt down from the coach box and blocked her path. By now, Amar had reached him too.

'Marjory. I know you're in there. I never took you for a coward,' Ella called out towards the coach.

'Why don't you try and talk some sense into her?' Raj ordered his former foreman.

'She has good reasons,' Amar replied.

'I must insist that you leave,' Raj threatened in an authoritative tone, though Ella could tell he found the situation difficult. He was obviously torn between his duty to serve his mistress and the sympathy towards Ella that he had shown in the past.

'Let us through,' Amar demanded.

Raj grabbed him by the collar of his shirt, but Amar knew how to defend himself, even though Raj was a head taller than him. He freed himself from Raj's grasp and shoved him aside with surprising force. Raj quickly recovered his balance and tried to throw himself bodily onto Amar, but quick as a flash, Amar leapt to one side. Raj's fury fell into thin air, and he just managed to steady himself on a wheel of the coach, which began to wobble.

'Stop!' Marjory's command rang out unmistakably from inside. She climbed out and confronted Ella with a venomous glare.

'You are making a grave mistake, Miss Kaltenbach.' Her threat was emphasised by her icy voice. Even Amar and Raj were now frozen to the spot.

'What did you want at the harbour?' asked Ella bluntly. She wasn't going to let Marjory scare her.

'To make sure that you would disappear from our lives once and for all,' Marjory hissed.

'Why? What have I ever done to you and Heather?' asked Ella.

'You lied to us. Your whole charade. You passed yourself off as a Dutchwoman to inveigle yourself into our confidence.'

Ella couldn't contradict her, nor even offer an excuse.

'You keep poking your nose into matters that are none of your business.'

'What did Rudolf want from you? What did he tell you? You might be able to pull the wool over the eyes of the police, but not over mine. I know why he visited you. Did he ask for money? How much did he want?' Ella felt her rage mounting, and her tone was correspondingly aggressive.

'He talked nothing but rot,' said Marjory coldly.

'And did he have to pay for it with his life? Or did you get somebody else to poison him?' Ella was gaining momentum.

'You should keep your vivid imagination under control and take the next ship back to your homeland. There is nothing left for you here. Otherwise . . . well, there are ways and means . . . And now tell this rebel, under whose spell you have evidently fallen, that he should stop obstructing the way.' Having issued her orders, Marjory turned to climb back into her coach.

'Why are you so afraid of the truth?' Ella called after her.

Marjory froze, but kept her back turned. Ella could see she was inwardly shaken.

'How can you be so heartless? Richard is my father, isn't he? You can't bear the thought of it. Was it you who insisted that he dispose of his illegitimate child? Why are you so afraid?' she went on.

'What do you want? Money?' said Marjory quietly, without turning round.

'I was looking for my family . . . but what I've found disgusts me. Money? Richard has already paid me enough.'

Marjory paused, then turned to face her. She looked as though she had aged by years in mere moments. Never in Ella's life had she seen a face so filled with hate – a hatred that seemed to be eating away at her. Marjory's complexion had assumed the colour of white oleander, and her whole body was trembling.

'Get out of our lives,' she croaked. Then, calling to Raj, she got into the coach.

Raj shot a hopeless look at Ella. He had to follow Marjory's orders and drive on. 'Please clear the way,' he said to Amar, who looked at Ella to confirm whether he should do as Raj asked.

Ella nodded. Amar mounted the cart and drove a few yards forward onto the main road to let the Fosters' coach past. She walked back to their cart and Amar gave her his hand to help her onto it. Was she imagining it, or could Ella hear wailing from inside the carriage?

The Fosters' coach trundled past – but just then, when it was only a few feet away from the road, the door flew open.

Ella's heart nearly stopped. It was Heather. She had a desperate look on her face, and called out to her: 'Ella!'

Heather's voice sounded like the howl of a wounded animal. She called out again, but her voice was already much weaker. A pair of black-sleeved hands clawed at her. Ella saw that Heather was crying, but then her mother pulled her back inside. The door slammed shut as the coach turned onto the main road.

'No!' Heather was still audible, though the coach was rapidly receding into the distance.

Ella sat as if paralysed on the cart. Amar put his arm around her. Heather's desperate cries had been so harrowing that Ella was still trembling.

'You have to try to forget about her. Promise me you'll try,' Amar urged her.

'How can I?' Tears trickled from Ella's eyes. 'She's my half-sister, and you saw for yourself what she has to endure from her mother,' she sobbed.

'Heather is a grown woman,' said Amar calmly.

Ella knew that Amar was right, but Heather's cries still echoed in her ears. How could she ever forget?

◆ ◆ ◆

For the last hour at least, Ella had been lying utterly exhausted in Amar's arms, staring out from the veranda at the palm fronds as they waved in the wind. The noise they made reminded her of surf crashing onto a beach. Despite her serene surroundings, she could find no peace. It felt as though Heather's pain had been passed on to her. Why was Marjory torturing her so? Ella had seen no sign of this behaviour during her stay with the Fosters.

Amar could think of nothing else either. 'It was as though she'd lost her mind. Like you, I can't help but wonder what Marjory is so afraid of,' he brooded.

'Perhaps she's scared of being disgraced . . . She doesn't want people to talk about her, and she feels ashamed that her husband betrayed her – and yet that doesn't make any sense either. There has been gossip about him for a long time already. Mary told me that Richard was known to be unfaithful, but in these circles, people would have turned a blind eye,' Ella reflected.

'He's also been dead for so many years now. Nobody speaks of him any more. When I started working for the Fosters, I didn't even know his name,' said Amar.

'His name really never came up?' Ella asked.

'No, not once.'

'Then I expect she never forgave him, and wanted to erase him from her life. Rudolf must have reminded her about the events of the past and reopened old wounds,' she reasoned – though deep down, she sensed that this explanation was too simple.

'So you really believe that she might have had something to do with Rudolf's death? That she did it out of fear that her past would be brought back to light?' Amar asked.

'Perhaps we should go to the police. Officer Puteri did offer to help me,' Ella suggested.

'But what would that achieve? He wouldn't be able to prove anything. All the coroner said was that there were symptoms that resembled the effects of poison. There's no point in thinking about it any more. Fate will punish her somehow, if she did do it,' said Amar.

Ella knew he was right and pushed all these thoughts to one side – but that soon began to make her head throb. She tried to come to terms with the idea that she might never find out the truth. The only thing she felt certain of was that she had a half-sister – and yet Heather had now slipped irretrievably out of reach.

'This whole voyage . . . Pointless,' Ella sighed defeatedly.

'What will you do now? Will you go back to Hamburg?' asked Amar anxiously, running his hand through her hair.

'Don't be silly. How could I ever go back now?'

Amar smiled in relief and kissed her on the brow.

'Besides, I can work here, and probably achieve more than I ever could among those stubborn doctors in Hamburg.'

'And there I was, thinking you might want to stay because of me.'

'Because of you?' asked Ella with a grin. That earned her a second kiss – this time on the lips. For a moment, it helped her to forget everything. The soft whispering of the palms played its part in that too – but then the calm was shattered by the clattering of carriage wheels and the thud of hooves. They could always hear approaching vehicles from a long way away, but whenever a coach passed the short drive to Mohan's house, the noise normally faded into the distance more quickly than it had appeared. This time, however, the sounds grew louder. There could be no doubt that the carriage was coming directly towards their refuge.

Amar let her go and looked out onto the road. Ella followed his gaze, and couldn't believe her eyes.

A large coach was pulling up to the house with a British soldier sitting on the box. Three more armed soldiers got out, along with Lieutenant Bennett. One didn't need to be a clairvoyant to see that this didn't bode well.

Ella followed Amar outside.

'I'm here to place you under arrest,' announced Bennett, squaring up to Amar.

Amar was every bit as bewildered as Ella. The arrest had to be connected to Mohan's rescue – but nobody had seen Amar there. Was that why he managed to remain so calm?

'What am I accused of?' he asked.

'Being a ringleader in the resistance, rebellion against the British Crown, and abetting the escape of a prisoner of the British Army,' answered Bennett formally.

Ella's heart nearly stopped still.

'I'll have to handcuff you,' said the officer, pulling out a pair of manacles.

Amar offered no resistance.

'Where are you taking him?' asked Ella.

'To the prison in Johore.'

'Who issued the arrest warrant?' she demanded. She was surprised that they were taking him to the local jail when the local police were not involved in the arrest.

'The governor himself.'

So Compton was behind this. Amar gave a contemptuous smile.

'Don't worry. The accusations are absurd. The truth will come out,' Amar tried to reassure her.

Ella reached for his hand. Hopefully not for the last time.

Amar looked straight into her eyes, and then climbed into the coach. His smile was meant to be encouraging, but all the same, Ella was afraid that she would never see him again.

CHAPTER 17

To sit alone in Mohan's house and idly wait for news was out of the question for Ella. She immediately struck out for town to speak with Edward Compton personally. After all, it was he who had ordered the arrest. On the way, however, she wondered whether she ought to talk to Officer Puteri first, since the local police were the ones conducting the investigation into the attack on the prison wagon. Then again, how could Puteri go against the will of the governor? Ella realised she would probably get nowhere with Compton either – even if she offered him her hand in marriage and agreed to ride with him on his beloved railway through the north of the peninsula for the rest of her life. But she might be able to find out what evidence the British had against Amar.

The governor's house was marked on her map, and a quick glance had been enough to tell her that it stood close to the centre of Johore.

From a distance, Ella could already see that the colonial headquarters perfectly suited Compton's lordly pretensions – indeed, the equivalent building in Singapore was presumably a royal palace, for that was the governor's official residence. His abode in Johore was an opulent, two-storey stone building with the Union flag hanging over the entrance, and the gardens behind it were surrounded by an eight-foot iron fence capped with sharp spikes.

She brought the cart to a halt in front of the villa and marched up to its entrance, which was guarded as though Queen Victoria herself were living inside. Yet Ella refused to be cowed.

'I want to see Edward Compton,' she declared to one of the two young soldiers stationed with rifles outside the entrance.

He merely gave her a contemptuous look. 'Do you have an appointment?' he asked.

'No, but the governor and I are very well acquainted,' Ella intimated.

It worked. The other officer disappeared into the building.

She used the time to find her horse something to drink. There was a trough filled with fresh water close to the building, but she kept looking back at the entrance to see if the officer had come back.

He beckoned her sooner than expected, with a gesture that was more peremptory than polite. Ella didn't care – the main thing was that the governor was willing to see her.

Compton left her waiting in his office. Men who liked to show off their power seemed to love playing games like this, and so Ella had plenty of time to examine the décor. The furniture looked like it belonged to a French king, with plenty of gilded wood. An oil painting of Queen Victoria hung on the wall, and there was a crystal chandelier on the ceiling too, of course. Compton evidently fancied himself as an absolute monarch.

'Ah, Miss Kaltenbach,' he crowed, after entering through a side door that led to a meeting room.

They were off to a good start. Marjory's lines of communication were shorter than Ella had expected. Compton was already fully briefed.

'I have been expecting you to visit. Would you like a cup of tea?' he asked, politely gesturing for her to take a seat. He sat down himself, but Ella preferred to remain standing.

'Very kind of you to offer, but no thank you. I'm here because I want to talk to you about a man whom your officers arrested today.'

'I know, I know . . . But shouldn't we state the facts as they really are?' His smug grin was perfectly unbearable.

'Amar,' she replied.

'Your soulmate. Or is he merely a lover?' asked Compton, feigning disinterest. So he knew about that too. That was hardly surprising, for she had been at Mohan's house when Amar was arrested – though Marjory might also have supplied him with that information in the meantime. At any rate, she no longer needed to make any excuses. Not that she would have, on principle.

'The former.' Ella made herself perfectly clear.

'I wouldn't proclaim that too loudly. Of course, as a German, you enjoy a very different status. You are a guest here – but you mustn't overstep the mark. Otherwise you could very easily find yourself accused of being an accomplice.' Compton smiled self-importantly.

'But in that case, Amar would need to have committed a crime, don't you think?'

'We have conclusive evidence . . . And for that matter, I find myself wondering why it was that you were spotted at the scene of the attack on the prison wagon.'

'What do you mean by that?'

'Do you really need to ask?' Compton's arrogant manner was repulsive.

'Half of Johore was there. Everybody who heard the shots, at any rate.' Ella tried to justify herself.

'Perhaps . . . But if I can give you one piece of advice, Miss Kaltenbach: it would be better for you if you left the country. My goodwill is not boundless.' Compton clearly enjoyed threatening her and acting the big man.

'I hope you aren't speaking out of wounded pride. That would be unbecoming for a man of your stature,' Ella retorted. She knew how to deal with puffed-up men like this from her many battles with the demigods in white coats at the hospital. He was no different. 'I also hope that defendants are given a fair trial in the British colonies. Anything else would be sheer barbarism,' she continued.

'But of course. We Brits are known throughout the world for our fairness. It's in our blood,' said Compton so cynically that Ella's revulsion grew even more intense.

'I thank you for your time.' She gave up trying to coax information from him about the reasons behind the arrest. It was enough to know that he allegedly had proof. Besides, the battle lines had now been drawn. 'Good day to you,' she announced, though she privately wished plague and cholera upon him and damned him to hell. With men like him in charge of the country, it was no wonder that the native population rebelled against the Crown.

'And to you,' he replied.

Ella spun on her heels and marched out. She urgently needed to find out what evidence the authorities had against Amar. Until she knew that, there was no point in finding a lawyer to defend him in court.

◆ ◆ ◆

When you had contacts who were willing to offer their help, it made sense to use them; Ella had learned that much during her time at the hospital. Amar was in jail, and the jail was run by the local police force. Hadn't Officer Puteri said that she could turn to him for assistance whenever she needed it? He was also a *bumiputra* – in other words, one of Amar's compatriots. Although politically speaking, the police were under the authority of the governor, Ella could well imagine that they would prefer to get rid of the British sooner rather than later, much like everyone else in the country seemed to.

The police station was just a short cart ride away from Compton's palace, and as she expected, Puteri was willing to make time for her.

The small, plainly decorated side room contained only a cabinet, a table and two chairs, but Ella greatly preferred it to the opulence she had just experienced. That was mainly down to the warm smile with which Puteri welcomed her and gestured for her to take a seat.

'You're here because of the prisoner, Amar – am I right?' he asked bluntly.

'How do you know . . . ?'

Puteri smiled, but without the slightest trace of arrogance. 'I have eyes, Miss Kaltenbach. He brought you to the harbour, didn't he? We policemen never forget a face, and we have certain investigative instincts too.'

'Investigative instincts?' Ella asked. He seemed to already know a great deal about her personal circumstances.

'You're still here in Malacca, and the records state that you were present at Amar's arrest. He also used to work at the Foster plantation . . .' Puteri kept smiling his benevolent smile.

Ella sighed and nodded.

'Don't worry. He's quite well. We're keeping him in a private cell, and we treat our prisoners decently,' he volunteered.

'I am aware of the accusations against Amar, and I will try to find him a good lawyer – but to do that, I need to know what evidence there is against him.'

Puteri's expression darkened. 'I'm afraid that exceeds my authority,' he admitted frankly.

'But it's completely absurd. Amar is a plantation worker. They're accusing him of being the leader of the rebellion.'

'Of course it's absurd, for there is no rebellion. There are only individuals who have the courage to stand up to the British,' said Puteri.

'So why has he been arrested?'

'From our point of view, it boils down to abetting the escape of a prisoner. I believe you know what I'm referring to.' He was doubtless referring to his having spotted her on the scene shortly after the rescue attempt.

'Mohan,' said Ella bluntly.

'It seems they were close, and that friendship is now being held against Amar,' the officer informed her.

'Amar was his foreman. That was why he took care of Mohan when he was in hospital,' Ella explained.

'That isn't the problem, though.'

'What do you mean?' she asked.

'The men who attacked the wagon concealed their faces, but one of them lost his mask. Amar was spotted and identified as one of the culprits.'

Ella couldn't believe her ears. She knew that Amar hadn't lost his mask. This proved Compton was trying to place the blame on him. But she couldn't tell Puteri that without also admitting that she had discussed the rescue with Amar. She would incriminate both Amar and herself if she did that. But there was another way of sowing the seed of doubt in Puteri's mind.

'Who identified him? Not the man driving the prison wagon? Lieutenant Bennett?' she asked.

Puteri nodded.

'Bennett is a close associate of Compton's, and I fear Compton has personal reasons for wanting to cause harm to Amar,' Ella intimated.

Puteri seemed surprised at that. 'What reasons might those be?' he asked.

'English men of his calibre suffer from extreme vanity. He made romantic overtures towards me, but I rebuffed him.'

Puteri raised an eyebrow. He didn't seem to find the motive all that convincing.

'When we met at the harbour, do you remember seeing a large coach standing by the side of the road as you drove back into town?'

He nodded.

'That was Marjory Foster's carriage,' said Ella.

'And what does that have to do with Compton or Amar?'

'I don't believe you are fully aware of my reasons for coming to Malacca,' Ella added.

'I'm listening,' said Puteri, a little confused now.

'I came here with Rudolf to search for my real parents, and I now have reason to believe that Richard Foster was my father. He was very likely the man who paid enormous sums of money to my adoptive family on a monthly basis. Rudolf must have realised the truth before I discovered it myself, and so he visited the Foster plantation. Rudolf was a gambler and needed money, and I fear he blackmailed Marjory. I confronted her over it at the harbour because I believe she had something to do with Rudolf's death. She threatened me, in the same manner as Compton did when I saw him just now. He is a close friend of the Fosters. I would like to appeal to your – what were the words you used just now? Your investigative instincts.'

Puteri's eyes had grown wider and wider as Ella spoke, and by the time she finished, his mouth was slightly agape. It took him a moment to compose himself.

'Those . . . those are serious accusations you're making!'

'Marjory's conduct suggests they are true,' she assured him.

'It's plausible . . . very plausible . . . But how does it alter the fact that Amar was seen at the scene of the attack?' Puteri wondered out loud.

Once again, Ella inwardly lamented not being able to simply tell him that Bennett could only have seen Bujang.

'What will happen to him?' she asked instead.

Puteri hesitated before answering. 'He'll face the firing squad.' He looked at the floor.

Ella struggled to breathe.

'The jurors may take a different view, however. There will be a trial,' he added.

Ella didn't hold out much hope for that, knowing the extent of Compton's influence, and she searched desperately for a solution. She had always been able to rely on her gift for improvisation hitherto and there had to be some way of proving Amar's innocence. Suddenly, she realised the answer was lying right in front of her, inside the open cabinet.

'Is that the mask they found at the scene?' she asked him.

'I really shouldn't have told you that,' said Puteri.

'You should be glad you did.'

The officer looked at her in confusion.

'It's a carved wooden mask, isn't it?'

He nodded.

'May I ask you to try it on?' Ella requested.

Puteri hesitated, but she could tell he was curious to know what she was getting at.

He stood up, walked over to the cabinet and picked up the mask.

'Go on,' Ella urged.

Puteri attempted to put it on – but the attempt proved unsuccessful, for the mask didn't fit. He tried again, but couldn't find a way to see through it and breathe at the same time. He put it to one side and stared at her for a moment, before breaking out in a smile.

'You have the heart of a lioness and a razor-sharp mind,' he grinned. 'I'll make sure Amar tries this mask on too.'

'I'm certain it won't fit. That would prove Bennett submitted a false statement in order to make Amar a scapegoat – and that he did so for base motives and at Compton's behest,' Ella concluded.

'I can't make any public accusations against the governor,' said Puteri.

'Well, the officer could also have been mistaken in the heat of the moment. The sun was low in the sky – it might have dazzled him . . .'

Puteri smiled. He looked at her in admiration, but also seemed relieved that he could help one of his compatriots.

'If I'm right, will he go free?'

He nodded. 'I would even testify to that in court,' he assured her.

'But is the court impartial?' Ella was worried – she knew how much influence the British wielded.

'Amar is a civilian, so he comes under the jurisdiction of the local courts, and we are the ones leading the investigation. If he is proven innocent, the British will have no say in the matter. Not officially, anyway . . .'

'What do you mean by that?' asked Ella.

'Do you think Compton will let him live? You should start planning your escape. You'll have two days to make the necessary arrangements,' he said.

'Two days?'

'Amar's trial is in three days' time. Compton evidently wants to secure a quick conviction.' Puteri toyed pensively with the mask in his hand. 'If it doesn't fit him – yes, a conviction will be out of the question,' he said once more, almost with amusement. He seemed to enjoy the prospect of humiliating Compton in court.

'You'll need to find a lawyer. The public defender here tends to avoid ruffling any feathers,' Puteri advised her.

'Can you recommend anybody?'

'There's a firm at the end of the market. Sulung bin Osman is a good lawyer. Whether he would be willing to take on a case like this, I can't say. But I wish you the best of luck.'

Ella was so touched at his willingness to save Amar's life that she reached for his hand and clasped it in her own – a gesture of gratitude that visibly moved him.

'A man fortunate enough to have a woman like you by his side can't be a bad person. You wouldn't love him otherwise,' he said.

'Thank you.' Ella hoped Puteri would keep his promise.

◆ ◆ ◆

Puteri's fears that no local lawyers would be keen to personally oppose the governor proved accurate. Ella had already received her first rejection. Sulung bin Osman had been happy enough to receive her on Officer Puteri's recommendation, but was currently too busy to represent Amar in court. Although his excuse was plausible at such short notice, Ella had realised as soon as she mentioned the governor's name that bin Osman had no intention of getting his hands dirty. He recommended two other lawyers to her, who both turned her down for the same reasons, but the second firm she visited gave her some useful advice: an international law firm that also represented British and foreign clients would be more likely to take Amar's case because they wouldn't fear any repercussions. They didn't mention any names, however. The only one of her acquaintances who might know which firms were involved in 'big business' – or who would at least be able to find out for her – was Otto.

Ella had waited for him at Lee's boarding house for two full hours in order to tell him everything that had happened. The wait had proven worthwhile.

Just like her, Otto saw a link between Marjory's threat and Amar's arrest, and he made it a priority to help her. He also explained to her why international law firms would have nothing to fear.

'When it comes to the real money, everybody has something to hide. Lawyers have a duty of confidentiality, of course, but nobody would ever dare to oppose a lawyer who knows about matters that border on the edge of legality. Nobody wants any trouble, you see,' he said, before taking a sip of the rice wine he had ordered on Ella's recommendation. They were sitting in the small restaurant close to Lee's boarding house.

'And do you have a particular lawyer in mind?' she asked.

'I'll get in touch with Henry Jones this afternoon. He handles all my contracts, and he has offices in London and Singapore. He also represents everyone who's anyone around here. And he owes me a favour,' Otto answered.

Ella looked at him in surprise.

'I scratch his back, and he scratches mine. His son is in the tin business and wants to get established in the German market,' he explained with a crafty smile.

'And you helped him?'

'Of course. It all greases the wheels – and in your case, it might even save Amar's life,' Otto pointed out.

'Officer Puteri thinks we won't be safe even if Amar is acquitted. He advised me to leave the country.'

'That would be very wise, as long as Compton remains the governor here, at least,' said Otto.

'But how should I go about it?'

He gave a calm smile and placidly sipped his wine. 'You're doubtless already aware that you need to get to politically neutral territory as quickly as possible,' he said.

'I've given that some thought already – but for one thing, the German packet boat doesn't stop at Singapore every day, and for another, I assume that Compton's influence extends as far as Singapore anyway.'

'That's quite correct.'

'So what do you suggest?'

'The east coast, my dear. Plain and simple.'

'What do you mean?' Ella asked.

'German freighters stop at a small fishing port called Mersing to pick up raw materials and food, which they then transport to German New Guinea. You'll be able to get back to Hamburg from there. The northeast corner of the island is not called Kaiser-Wilhelmsland for nothing, you know. You'll be safe once you get there.'

The way Otto put it made it all sound so straightforward. That reassured Ella – but it also raised new questions. 'And how do we get to Mersing?'

'The roads are decent, but there are checkpoints. Compton is a clever man. He knows now that you're German, and that you might come up with the bold idea of striking out for the east coast – but there might be a way to put him off the scent,' said Otto, who seemed to enjoy the prospect of playing a trick on the British.

'By travelling on rougher roads?' Ella reasoned.

'That's part of the answer. You'll certainly need to do that to avoid the checkpoints, anyway. But first, you need to lay a false trail.'

Try as she might, Ella couldn't see what Otto was driving at.

He sensed her confusion. 'The next packet ship back to Germany departs in five days. Book two tickets in your name. That will be the first place Compton's people will look, and he'll assume that you intend to leave Malacca via that route.'

She was dumbfounded. Otto was revealing himself to be a born tactician, and he seemed to play the part with relish.

'I'll draw the routes through the jungle for you on a map. I know the area – I've travelled that way myself several times before, and I know what you need to watch out for. You'll get clean away, you'll see.' Then he raised his glass towards her. Ella hadn't managed to drink a drop yet. What if it was bad luck to toast their success already? Yet Otto's unshakeable confidence overcame her reservations.

◆ ◆ ◆

Ella left the cart close to Mohan's house, for she couldn't afford to waste any valuable time. According to Otto, Henry Jones generally remained in his office in Singapore until the early evening. The cart wouldn't get her there in time, but she could manage it on horseback.

She rode as though the devil himself were pursuing her – and to conjure him up, she had only to think of Compton. Including the ferry, it would be at least another hour until she reached the city centre, where Jones's office was – but she got there in time.

Even from the outside of his office, Ella could see that Henry Jones ran a thriving business. The four-storey building wouldn't have looked out of place in the most prestigious quarters of London or on the banks of the Alster in Hamburg. Compton would have been green with envy, for his 'palace' in Johore looked rather modest in comparison.

'Otto Ludwig sent me.' Otto's name served as a key that unlocked the huge double doors leading to Jones's office. Ella had only a quarter of an hour to wait, which she took as a sign that he would give her a fair hearing – and so it proved, once she had passed on Mr Ludwig's warmest greetings. Jones was a slender man with a thick beard that reached down to his chest, and unlike the other lawyers she had visited, he took the time to listen to her concerns. There could hardly be any case more sensitive than hers, but he only lifted his eyebrows once, and otherwise took notes in silence.

'My dear Miss Kaltenbach, I assume that the defendant is very close to you.' His tone of voice made clear that this was a question, and Ella responded in the affirmative.

'How did you meet Otto?' he asked next. Ella had been expecting further questions about Amar's case.

'On the way over from Hamburg,' she answered.

'A most hardworking fellow, and a great sport,' he said, speaking more to himself. Then he leaned back and studied his notes. 'I presume you have come to me because no other lawyer was willing to take on your case.'

She nodded.

'And yet the facts are so straightforward. If the mask doesn't fit, the court will have to find him innocent . . . But you mentioned the governor . . .' Jones murmured thoughtfully.

'Edward Compton.' Ella pronounced his name with the utmost contempt.

'I know. A rather unpleasant fellow, if you'll permit the observation.'

'Will you venture to take the case?'

Jones smiled. 'Strictly speaking, it's inadvisable to place oneself in opposition to the governor,' he said.

Ella's breath caught.

'However, we have already begun proceedings against a company that he holds shares in. Tin. The big business around here. You wouldn't believe how much people pay for licences,' he said.

'And is the governor responsible for issuing those licences?' she asked cautiously. So Compton was corrupt, on top of everything else.

'He knows that we know about it,' Jones confirmed.

Ella exhaled. The way things looked now, Jones seemed to be untouchable.

'So you'll take the case?' she asked again, for confirmation.

'Did you doubt it for a second?'

She shrugged.

'Am I mistaken, or were you at Mary Bridgewater's party?' enquired Jones.

'Were you there too?' Ella could hardly conceal her surprise.

'Of course. We handle all her affairs. She's a charming lady, and extremely influential.'

Ella wondered why he had brought this up. If he didn't have such an obviously sharp mind, she would have simply taken it as a digression and placed no importance on it.

'You weren't on your own that evening,' he recalled.

'Indeed, I was with the Fosters.'

'They own a plantation near Johore, don't they?'

'Do you know them?' Ella could make no sense of his remarks.

'No, not personally,' Jones admitted.

Ella felt that the conversation was moving in a strange direction.

'The odd thing is that nobody really seems to know the Fosters. That can't always have been the case,' he said.

'That's what Mary told me too. But why does it interest you?' Ella simply had to know.

'May I ask you a personal question?' the lawyer asked.

Ella grew hot. What did Jones want from her?

'When were you born?' he enquired.

'Why do you want to know?' she retorted.

'You don't have to tell me, but I can assure you that I have only the best of intentions. My duty of confidentially prevents me from giving you the reasons, however.'

Ella studied him carefully and decided to trust her judgment. Besides, he had already agreed to defend Amar. 'I was born in 1877,' she answered.

'Were you adopted?'

For a moment, she was literally speechless. 'How did you know that?'

Jones drew a deep breath and seemed to be weighing up how far he could go. 'You are the subject of another mandate of mine – one that I was unable to make any sense of, at first,' he explained.

Ella feverishly wondered why a law firm in Singapore would take an interest in her. But hadn't he just asked her about Mary?

'Mary Bridgewater?' she asked.

'As I say, I am unable to tell you who my client is. However, if your assumption were correct, it is very possible that that might have furnished me with a strong motive to take on your case – even more so than my most satisfactory business dealings with dear Otto,' he concluded with a complacent smile.

Ella refrained from probing any further. Whatever her reasons, Mary must have hired him to gather information about her – though he would never reveal the nature of that information.

'I'll issue the necessary documents today. Don't worry – Compton won't risk his career for the sake of a little wounded pride.'

He stood up and gave her his hand, which Ella shook gratefully.

CHAPTER 18

Straight after her meeting with Jones, Ella managed to book two second-class tickets on the next packet ship leaving for Germany, for the ticket offices in Singapore were open until late at night. A single down payment had secured her two berths. Compton would now assume that they planned to leave the country via that route.

Back in Johore, there was still plenty for Ella to do. She had to inform Amar of the plans she and Otto had cooked up together – and of course, she needed to give him the good news that he would almost certainly be set free. Amar must have been through some long and terrible hours – hours of fear and uncertainty. When he was arrested, there was no way he could have known that Compton would use a false statement from Bennett as evidence against him.

As she made her way to the jail, Ella hoped that Puteri would still be willing to meet her at such a late hour, for none of his colleagues were likely to let her see Amar in his cell. As it proved, she was in luck – nor did she need to explain her reasons for visiting. Puteri reacted with delight when she told him of her meeting with Jones, making it clear to Ella that he must be one of the most influential lawyers in Singapore. All the same, Puteri had been surprised to hear that a firm which hardly ever involved itself in native affairs was willing to defend Amar in court. Ella kept the exact circumstances behind that to herself, as well as the details of Otto's escape plan. It seemed unwise to push the goodwill of a public official too far, since that information would probably have forced Puteri into an insoluble moral dilemma – even though he had been the one who had advised her to leave the country as soon as possible once Amar was acquitted.

Whatever happened behind the walls of the prison was beyond the authority of the British Army. Officially speaking, Puteri was merely conducting an interview, and had allowed an important witness to attend.

'I can't give you more than ten minutes,' he warned once they reached Amar's cell at the end of a dimly lit corridor.

He unlocked the door and gestured for her to step inside.

'I'll wait here. You can speak freely, but don't talk too loudly. I can hear every word out here in the corridor,' he whispered. Puteri's offer not to eavesdrop on them confirmed Ella's impression that he wanted to know as little as possible of what she had to discuss with his prisoner.

It was obvious that Amar had suffered a good deal of inner turmoil since his arrest. Although he smiled when he saw her and instantly stood up to take her in his arms, the light in his eyes was extinguished. The cell was clean and the bunk looked fairly comfortable, but being locked up like an animal in a room with barred windows would leave its mark on anybody. He virtually clung on to her.

'I was so afraid I would never see you again,' he said, and began to kiss and caress her.

'Are you all right?' Unbelievably, it was Amar who posed the question to her, once he had let her go and examined her in the light of the paraffin lamp that hung from the ceiling.

'Don't worry. One of the very best lawyers has agreed to defend you. I spoke to Puteri. The mask . . .'

'I know. They made me try it on, but it didn't fit,' Amar told her. He grinned as he spoke, and Ella took that as a good sign. It seemed to be dawning on him that there was still hope he might escape being sentenced.

'What with everything I'm accused of, I never would have thought that the mask would serve as evidence – nor would I have expected the police to ever think of it . . .' he said.

'But it wasn't the police . . .' Ella hinted.

Amar looked at her in astonishment. 'It was you?'

'I saw it in Puteri's office, and then I remembered what you told me about how the masks were made,' she explained.

Amar shook his head in disbelief and ran his hand gently through her hair. 'Whatever would I do without you?' he said.

His loving gaze spoke volumes, but there was no time to lose herself in his eyes.

'I'm certainly glad we can disprove one of the charges against you,' said Ella.

Amar's optimistic smile remained unbroken. He evidently thought it would all be over once he was acquitted, and that they would be safe after that.

'Officer Puteri thinks Compton won't leave us in peace. We need to get away from here. I've booked tickets on a boat to Hamburg, but only for appearances' sake, to mislead Compton. We need to go to the east coast. There we can board a freighter that will take us to a German colony. It was Otto's idea – he wants to help us. But we'll need to make our way through the jungle. We only have Mohan's cart. I don't know if it can cope with travelling through the bush, and then I have to think about what supplies we'll need on the way . . .' Ella was aware they had only ten minutes. They needed to settle everything as quickly as possible.

By now, Amar was speechless and staring at her incredulously. Ella wasn't surprised at that, for even she could hardly believe what she had accomplished over the last few hours.

'Why don't you say something? Or do you want to stay here?' she asked him.

Amar finally recovered. 'Bujang can help you. He ought to come with us.'

'But isn't he on the run as well? He was the one who lost his mask. Surely somebody must have spotted him at the scene.' Ella lowered her voice even further, even though she trusted Puteri. They were talking about one of the men who had freed Mohan after all.

'He'll agree to help us all the same. His father is very ill, so he's still in the area, but in hiding. Bujang often goes hunting and knows the jungle – he understands its dangers. It's thanks to his local knowledge that Mohan is now a free man. He was the one who planned the escape route,' said Amar, speaking just as quietly as Ella.

'Where can I find him?' she asked.

'You'll have to be very careful. I don't know how much Compton's people know about us. Bujang worked on the Foster plantation for a time. They might have asked who Mohan knew there and put him under surveillance. They might even be watching you too,' said Amar.

'We have no other choice,' she replied.

'His house is around a mile to the north of Mohan's, and has a red front. He lives there with his parents. Tell them I sent you, otherwise they'll say he isn't there. You just need to keep following the road from Mohan's house, past a small waterfall.' Amar looked at her with concern. 'Promise me you'll be careful,' he demanded.

There was a knock at the door. Their time was up.

Wordlessly, Amar took her into his arms and Ella drew strength from the closeness of his embrace. It would be their last for two days.

◆ ◆ ◆

It was surely no coincidence that a carriage had lingered for an unusually long time on the road leading to Mohan's house the previous evening. She had seen the uniforms clearly, even from a distance, and only when she lit the paraffin lamps, bringing parts of the house's interior into view from the road, did the carriage depart. Compton was evidently checking whether she was still in the country. As she breakfasted on a few pieces of fruit, Ella wondered how she had managed to get any sleep at all the night before. She had jumped at every little sound, however harmless, only to lie wide awake once more. Strictly speaking, there was no reason for anybody to do her any harm – but who could tell what Compton was thinking, or how far he would go? Ella therefore decided not to risk any more sleepless nights here, but to pack her bags and make her way into town to seek refuge at Lee's. That would look more logical to Compton too, for he was presumably expecting Amar to be sentenced, and Ella to leave the country sooner or later. Lee and Otto would be at the boarding house too, and she trusted them both.

In solving one problem, however, she created another. Amar had described Bujang's house to her, and it stood outside town, just like Mohan's. In order to get there, she would have no choice but to cross the entire town without being spotted. Ideally, she would have discussed the problem with Otto, for she could always rely on his resourcefulness and ingenuity – but Lee informed her that he was out on business and wouldn't be back until the evening. That would be too late, for Ella felt it would be too risky to introduce herself to Bujang's parents in the middle of the night – assuming she could even find her way there in the dark.

She soon ran into further difficulties. One of Compton's officers had asked about her while she was busy settling into her room, and Lee had come up straight away to let her know.

Lee's agitation at the officer's visit was written all over her face. Ella owed her an explanation, but she didn't dare go into too much detail. It was true that Lee had reliably passed all Ella's letters and messages on to her, and that she had always offered Ella her help – but who would want to get into trouble with the governor?

'I'm being watched,' Ella admitted frankly.

It wasn't often that Lee lost her smile.

Ella sat on the bed and gestured for Lee to sit down beside her. She did as Ella asked.

'Amar has been arrested – the British think he was involved in rescuing a prisoner. The trial is scheduled for the day after tomorrow. They won't sentence him, as they don't have any watertight evidence, but he's a thorn in the side of the governor here. As am I, for that matter.' Ella hoped she wasn't about to lose Lee's goodwill.

Lee said nothing. Even these few fragments of information were probably more than a peace-loving innkeeper would ever want to know.

'They're going to keep enquiring about me and watching over the building,' Ella went on.

Lee nodded thoughtfully. She was probably trying to imagine what Ella might ask of her. After all, her guest would only be able to leave the boarding house for longer periods if Lee was willing to lie for her. But perhaps she would agree to do so if she understood what was at stake. Ella therefore decided to tell Lee the whole truth.

'Officer Puteri thinks we won't be safe here after Amar is acquitted. We'll have to leave the country, but I need to make preparations first. It would be best if they didn't notice me leaving the boarding house at all,' said Ella.

Lee nodded again, and her silence came to an end. 'I can always tell them that you're in your room, as far as I'm aware – and you could leave a light burning at night too,' she said. Ella was relieved to see Lee's smile return.

'Thank you, from the bottom of my heart,' she said.

Lee furrowed her brow and seemed to briefly mull something over. Ella decided not to interrupt. 'But how will you get out without being seen?' asked Lee, once her brow had smoothed itself out again.

'Well, they won't be able to keep a constant watch,' Ella replied, though she hadn't found an answer to that question herself yet.

'One of them is still sitting out there on the other side of the road,' remarked Lee somewhat uneasily.

Now it was Ella's turn to fall into pensive silence. If only she had stayed at Mohan's house! But who could say that she wouldn't be watched around the clock there too? Perhaps she should hide inside a coach and leave the boarding house unobserved that way. Or could she escape over the roof? Or just wait for the guard to answer a call of nature? Ella realised she had run out of ideas.

'The boarding house has a second exit – it leads into my brother's restaurant on the other side.'

She could hardly believe that Lee was willing to assist her like this.

'But the street is very busy, so even then, you might still be seen.' Lee made a valid point.

'Stand up,' Lee told her.

Ella did as she was told, though she had no idea what Lee was driving at.

Lee inspected her, examining first her waist and then her arm. She emitted a series of humming noises – now cheerful, now sceptical – much to Ella's bafflement.

'Your hair is long enough, but nobody in my homeland has the same colour skin as you,' Lee mused.

Ella began to realise what Lee was planning, and her mind boggled at how far the woman was prepared to go in order to help her.

'You want to leave here unnoticed, don't you?' the ingenious Lee now asked. 'I know a way to dye your hair, and one of my old robes might fit you. Do you know how to make a plait?'

Despite the seriousness of the situation, Ella couldn't suppress a smile. It seemed Lee had decided to make her Chinese for the day.

◆ ◆ ◆

Ella looked at her reflection in her bedroom mirror and laughed at what she saw. She didn't recognise herself. Lee had done a sterling job, and now Ella finally knew how it felt to wear a rice hat – and she also understood why they didn't constantly slip off the wearers' heads, for there was a ribbon tied under her chin. Lee had lent her the biggest one in her collection, which had the advantage of concealing most of her face, making it the perfect disguise. The robe covered most of her body, but that was fairly typical for this style of clothing. Her hair was dyed black and woven into a plait that hung down her back, and thanks to Lee's face powder, there was no longer any sign of the ruddy complexion she had acquired since arriving in the tropics. Ella marvelled at the transformation, and Lee seemed satisfied with her work too – her glance made that much clear when Ella appeared at the reception desk.

'We need to hurry. I've already told my brother. Come on!'

Lee headed off towards the kitchen and opened a door, revealing a darkened corridor behind it. Ella followed her for a few yards into another, much bigger kitchen. A portly Chinese man – presumably Lee's brother – beckoned them in and gestured for them to hurry. In just a few steps, they reached the restaurant area, which lay directly behind Lee's reception desk. There were no diners around at this time in the morning, and there was a cart waiting outside the door. It was much smaller than Mohan's, which Ella had left in a prominent position in the courtyard of the boarding house for all the world to see.

'Good luck,' whispered Lee, once Ella had mounted the cart and picked up the reins.

Everything had gone according to plan so far, but she now faced the riskiest part of her mission. The restaurant lay on a dead-end street, and the only way to leave it was via the main road. Just a few minutes earlier, she had taken one final look out of the window of her room and seen a young officer pacing back and forth in front of the boarding house. She had every faith in her disguise, but she still felt her heart pound faster as she turned onto the main street. Only after a full minute had passed did she venture to look back over her shoulder. There was nobody suspicious following her – only a wagon laden with fodder that had turned onto the road behind her, which fell further and further behind her smaller, faster cart.

After a few minutes, Ella turned off from the main road and drove on past Mohan's house, keeping her head lowered, although Compton's people would probably be under the impression that she was still in the boarding house. According to Amar's directions, she would come across a small waterfall before long – and sure enough, it appeared. Now all she had to do was drive along a row of houses until one with a conspicuous red façade came into view.

Bujang's parents' house looked like a wooden cabin of the sort one sometimes came across in rural areas in the far north of Europe. Unlike Mohan's family home, it had windows and a door that concealed what went on inside. There was a lay-by on the road directly in front of the house, and Ella stopped her cart there and dismounted. As she made her way up to the door, she noticed the curtain twitch – somebody was watching her from the window. Amar had already warned her that the occupants of the house would exercise the utmost caution, and so it proved. All the same, she walked up to the door and knocked. It opened a crack, and she could just make out a figure in the gloom.

'What do you want?' asked a female voice.

Ella's eyes had by now grown accustomed to the dark, and she saw it belonged to an elderly woman.

'Amar sent me. I'm here to see Bujang,' she stated.

For a moment there was silence. The woman remained at the door.

'Who are you? And why are you wearing Chinese clothes?' she asked suspiciously.

Ella was unsurprised at the question, for her European origins were obvious close-up.

'You should leave. They've been watching the house for days. Don't look towards the barn. Do you know the small lake nearby?' asked Bujang's mother.

Ella nodded.

'Bujang will meet you there in half an hour. Wait . . . I'll give you a couple of baskets to take with you. That way, it will look as though you were here to collect something,' she said.

Ella could almost feel a pair of eyes boring into her back, but she didn't dare turn round. Bujang's mother vanished into the house, then returned a few seconds later wearing an exaggeratedly friendly smile and handed her two empty baskets.

Ella took them from her and gave a small bow, mimicking the manner of giving thanks that she had seen among Chinese people elsewhere in Malacca. Then she carried the baskets back to the cart. As she climbed onto it, she couldn't resist glancing at the barn. There was a carriage parked behind it. Ella turned her cart around and made her way back down the road.

It was only a short distance from Bujang's house to the lake, which she had visited once before with Amar. Ella hoped nobody would follow her, and so it proved – however, she wasn't the only person there. A group of Malay children on the far shore were leaping excitedly into the water, while their mothers sat together on a raffia mat eating fruit. They scarcely took any notice of her.

She walked down to the edge of the lake and whiled away the time with recollections of her stop here with Amar. It had been such a wonderful moment. She prayed that they would manage to get away safely.

'Ella?' She soon heard a male voice calling to her. That had to be Bujang. Amar must have already told him about her several days ago – there was no other explanation for how he knew her name.

Ella turned and saw a man around Amar's height, who must be roughly the same age too. Beyond that, however, they had little in common. There was something wild and rugged about Bujang. His alert, watchful eyes nestled deep in their sockets beneath a pair of bushy eyebrows and a shaggy mane of hair, and a large knife strapped to his waist completed the picture. Yet his smile was warm and friendly.

'How is Amar?' he asked.

'He's in prison.'

'I know,' he said, squatting down beside her.

'His trial is tomorrow. He has a good lawyer, and we're hoping he'll be acquitted – but then we'll need to leave the country as soon as possible,' Ella explained.

'Do you mean to go to Siam, like Mohan?' he asked.

'No, we intend to travel to the east coast, to Mersing. But we'll need equipment for that – a carriage that can travel across rough terrain, and horses.'

'I can find you those. You'll need food and water too – you'll be on the road for at least two days,' he said.

'I'm aware of that,' said Ella, for she had already studied the map.

'The way is perilous.'

'I know. There are checkpoints,' she said.

'That's not what I mean. You'll need to go through the jungle. Amar doesn't understand the dangers.'

'We have no other choice,' she said.

'I'll come with you,' Bujang assured her.

Ella looked him in the eye. He was determined to help them.

'I'll arrange everything we need. Let's meet again here. I'll wait for you at eleven o'clock the day after tomorrow.'

'I don't know how to thank you.'

'Amar is my friend, and the Englishman our enemy,' he explained.

Ella knew that Bujang was referring to Compton.

It almost seemed as though Lee had decided to join the rebellion too – for why else would she have sprung so joyfully into Ella's arms when she finally arrived back in the boarding house's small kitchen? The mission couldn't have been more successful. Nobody on the street had taken any notice of her – and nor did the diners in the by now busy restaurant. Then again, who would pay any attention to a Chinese woman walking into a restaurant with two baskets?

'But how will I get the dye out of my hair?' Ella asked. She could hardly appear in public looking like this.

Lee merely laughed, and beckoned for Ella to follow her into the kitchen. There, a basin full of water and lye was waiting for her. Lee truly had thought of everything.

'The dye comes from plant roots. We need to wash your hair in this,' she explained.

Ella dipped her head into the lye, but before she could start washing it, Lee took over. Ella submitted to being scrubbed. It reminded her of her childhood when her mother had washed her hair like this too, although unlike Lee, she hadn't gone about it particularly gently.

The lye solution was now stained black with dye, and Lee rinsed the final traces from her hair with two jugs of water. She had also remembered to leave Ella's clothes out for her. Ella now understood why Lee was so firmly established as a businesswoman around here – she had a talent for organisation and she worked quickly.

'Otto is in his room,' Lee informed Ella, once she had changed back into her regular clothes. She had probably already told him that her guest wanted to speak to him. Ella really could depend on Lee for anything.

The same could be said for Otto. He was already fully informed, and he immediately sat down to review their escape route towards the east. During their conversation, Ella also filled him in on what he didn't know. He had noticed the near constant surveillance, and he suggested that they make a show of walking over to the main square, just to demonstrate to Compton's people that she was still here. Otto too seemed to take great pleasure in helping her. That she managed to walk right under the nose of one of the officers without even glancing in his direction was only possible thanks to Otto's presence at her side and his uninterrupted flow of conversation – which naturally revolved around the weather while they were within earshot of their guards.

'You shouldn't complain – there'll be nothing but grey skies waiting for you in Hamburg. Make the most of your last few days in this wonderful country,' he had said, speaking in clear and deliberate English for the benefit of Compton's thugs. Once he was sure they were out of hearing range, he changed the subject. From the corner of her eye, Ella could see that nobody was following them.

'Henry Jones implied that Mary Bridgewater is also one of his clients.' Ella decided to broach the subject with Otto, for he knew both Mary and Henry Jones. She hoped he would be able to make sense of the lawyer's mysterious behaviour.

'I don't think there's anybody here in the south who isn't represented by his firm,' answered Otto.

'He asked me for my date of birth,' Ella told him.

'For his records?' asked Otto in surprise.

'No. It must have something to do with Mary Bridgewater. She seems to be gathering information about me, or possibly about the Fosters. At least, that's what Jones implied.'

Otto furrowed his brow and walked on beside her in silence for a few steps.

'Mary knows your true identity. She's a very inquisitive lady. You could even call it an ingrained sense of curiosity. That's probably how she gains so much influence in the world – by unearthing information about one thing or another,' he said, lost in thought.

'When I spoke to her at the Hamiltons' party, I didn't tell her the real reason I came to Malacca. But we did talk about the Fosters. She told me that Marjory only rejoined society many years after Richard's death, and that Richard was known to be something of a libertine. But now that I think of it . . . Mary also mentioned that she had noticed the resemblance between me and Heather. She admitted it was far-fetched, but she thought that might be why I visited the Fosters,' Ella recalled.

'I suppose she wants to establish whether you are Richard's illegitimate child,' Otto conjectured.

'But what does she hope to get out of that?'

'To be quite honest, in this case I see no reason other than that she wants to help you.'

Ella had no choice but to be contented with that. If Otto couldn't explain it, then there was no point in racking her own brains over it any further.

'Let's go for dinner. I can't bring myself to so much as look at another curry, but I know I'll miss it again once I'm home,' said Otto.

'You leave tomorrow, don't you?'

'Unfortunately, I can't put off my trip to Siam any longer. Business is business. I only wish I could stay here to help you, one way or another,' he sighed.

'Do you like Chinese food? I think Lee's brother has earned himself a handsome tip,' said Ella.

'A splendid idea,' Otto declared, and gallantly gave her his arm to escort her across the road.

◆ ◆ ◆

Dinner with Otto proved an excellent choice, and not just in terms of the food. His countless stories about his adventures on his recent travels reminded Ella of the anecdotes he had told her on the long voyage from Germany. He always found ways to distract her with his agreeable manner.

'You wouldn't believe how many businesspeople manage to fall foul of the local customs. There are a handful of basic rules that help make a good impression as a foreigner. For example, you should never stand with your feet directly on the threshold – always take care to step over it instead.' Otto was in his element once more.

'Never point the soles of your feet at other people, and only ever use your right hand for greetings or to touch anything,' Ella continued.

'I see, I see. You've already learned a few things during your time here,' he laughed – but then his face grew serious. 'You must write to let me know how you get on,' he urged her.

'You can depend upon it,' Ella assured him, before gesturing for the bill. As she did so, Otto took out a business card and handed it to her.

She tucked the card away for safe keeping and realised how fond of him she had grown – just as she had when they had bid each other farewell after the crossing.

Their walk back to the boarding house was all too brief. Otto's presence not only gave Ella strength, but distracted her from the many challenges she faced too.

As they walked the last few yards, they passed another officer, who must have relieved his colleague from earlier, and they slipped into small talk once more – this time discussing not the local climate, but the delicious food, which Otto lavished with effusive praise. Although it was still early, Ella understood when Otto announced his intention to go back to his room.

'I haven't packed yet, and the ship leaves at six tomorrow morning,' he told her when they reached the courtyard of the boarding house.

'I expect we'll only see each other again when we're back on home ground,' he added.

'God willing. I truly hope so,' Ella replied.

'I wish you all the luck in the world.' He spoke with great sincerity, and Ella couldn't resist giving him a final warm hug. Then he went inside.

She briefly considered going to bed too, but there was little chance that she would get any sleep. Instead, she sat down on the edge of the fountain in the courtyard and listened to the soothing plash of the water for a while. She could see onto the street from here, and the officer was still pacing back and forth. Compton was keeping watch over her as if she was a dangerous criminal. Just two more nights, and then this nerve-jangling situation would hopefully be over.

'Ella,' came a sudden voice from inside. Lee was calling to her. Otto must have let her know they had returned.

She stood up and walked inside.

Lee had an envelope in her hand, which she gave to Ella. It could only be a message from Henry Jones. Who else would write to her?

'It was handed in about an hour ago.'

Ella examined the handwriting. It couldn't be a piece of official correspondence, for only her first name was written on the envelope. The lettering was fluid, as if drawn by a female hand.

'Who gave it to you?' she asked.

'A very tall man – I think he was Indian. He didn't introduce himself, and when I asked for his name, he told me you would know who he was. There was something else he wanted me to tell you too: if you feel you need to meet him once you've read the letter then he'll be waiting for you at midday tomorrow in the big Indian temple.'

Ella knew only one tall Indian. The message must have come from Raj. She stared at the envelope. It seemed to give off a threatening aura and her hands began to tremble in agitation.

Lee noticed her reaction and looked at her with concern.

'I'll open it in my room,' said Ella.

Lee gave her the key.

'If you need anything . . .' Lee volunteered.

She nodded gratefully and hurried up the stairs. Had Marjory written to her? It must be from either Marjory or Heather.

By now, Ella's hand was shaking so violently she could hardly get the key into the lock. When the door finally swung open, she flew over to her dressing table and grabbed a hair pin, which she used to open the envelope. Inside it were two or three sheets of folded paper covered in German writing. The pages were rough and coarse, and felt old. The edges were frayed too – almost as if somebody had ripped them out of a book. There was also a text in English enclosed, which had been written on a typewriter – it looked like a translation of the German manuscript. Ella hurried over to the window and unfurled the handwritten pages first. What she saw left her paralysed with shock. She knew that handwriting. There could be no doubt that she was holding entries from her father's diary in her hands.

CHAPTER 19

Singapore, 21 May 1877

My hands are still shaking. Even so, I will try to set down the key details. Although there are far more urgent matters to attend to, it is important to record how it all happened. Force of habit guides my pen. Who knows how long the child will sleep for? I must hurry.

Captain von Stetten upheld the good old tradition: shore leave for the whole crew the day before an ocean voyage. Most of the men ended up in the brothel. Chinese women are pliable and buyable – Johansson cracked jokes about that idiotic rhyme all morning. Decided to go for a haircut. The Indian barbers are skilful and know how to give a close shave too. The others started teasing me – said I was only smartening myself up for the whorehouse. I left the mob to it and went for a stroll through the market. Bought a present for Rosa. Indian silk. She loves red. Took a turn along the waterfront, as usual. I see a new building going up every time I visit. I'll never understand why so many people want to live here. The humidity is oppressive, and even during the day there's no getting away from the mosquitoes. The Chinese manage to avoid them, though. They burn incense. Smoke everything out. Gets rid of the pests. The Chinese will be running the place before long.

Took a short nap on the beach. Knut and Johansson found me. Wanted me to come into town. I have no objections to a glass of beer, but it went further than that. Turned into a regular booze-up. Long faces next morning. Carousing always comes at a price – but the price I paid was much higher. I fell asleep, and they forgot to wake me up. Just left me lying in the corner. Drunken louts. Only a few hours until we set sail. Not long before dawn. It was so quiet at the harbour, but then I heard the cries. Thought they must be coming from one of the piers behind the ship. The wailing of an infant. So loud, so desperate. What was happening? I walked across, saw a black carriage and then – him. Black cloak and hat. Like a fine gentleman. A basket in front of him. There had to be a screaming child inside it. He paid it no heed. 'What are you doing there?' I called. Why was nobody else around? No lights on the ship. Where was the mate who was supposed to keep watch? The man in black ignored me, made as if to leave. I reached the carriage. There really was an infant in the basket. More wailing. I grabbed his coat before he could shut the door and hauled him back out. Never have I seen such a malignant glare. He shoved me. I saw red. He wasn't going to get away. I threw my full weight on top of him and hit him, once, twice, three times. He lay dazed on the ground. I asked him why he was leaving the child here. No answer. So I searched his pockets for his wallet. He tried to defend himself, but he was too weak. No backbone. Delicate hands like a woman. I knew he would have some identification on him. Everybody is required to carry papers round here. I pinned his arms down with my knees. He whimpered in pain. An Englishman called Richard Foster, going by his passport. He wanted to give me money, everything he had. 'Whose child is that?' He didn't answer. An emergency, he claimed. He'd changed his mind – wanted to take it to the hospital or an orphanage. The infant cried and cried. I didn't believe a word he said. Glanced over. Such a bonny baby. It looked back at me and stopped crying. He told me he'd get me more money if I let him go. Said he was rich. Said the child belonged to a whore. She'd passed it off as his. Simply placed the basket in his carriage. I knew he was lying. He begged me. Said he'd give me as much money as I wanted. He had such

330

false, wicked eyes, but the child was looking at me too. A foundling. It wouldn't be the first brought home by a sailor. Should I make his lie my own? Rosa would be thrilled. I didn't need to think about it for long. Told him I'd look after it, but he'd have to pay for it. He agreed. Asked for his passport back. I said he'd get it once he paid. His hateful expression sickened me. I let him stand up. He asked for my name. Quickly! He noted it down with my address in Hamburg; said he'd go to the bank tomorrow. A numbered account – everything anonymous. He promised to send enough money for the child. I'll send him his passport through the post once the money arrives. I threatened to tell the world too. He had no choice, since that's what he's afraid of. Foster didn't even look back at the bundle of rags in the basket. He got into his carriage and drove off. The child was quiet. Stopped crying. Did it know it was in safe hands?

I need to speak to von Stetten. He'll help me. They'll make fun of me, say I must have paid a secret visit to the whorehouse during our last voyage nine months ago. I don't care. It'll make Rosa happy. Will he pay up? He has to. Nobody can make a child disappear without leaving a trail. The baby belongs to a whore who doesn't want it. And even if that was a lie – a mother who gives her own child away is no better than a whore. Admittedly, the baby doesn't look like it had a Chinese mother. Then again, there are English and Dutch prostitutes out here too. Fallen women who sell themselves for money. She must have been one of those.

There's goat milk on board. The child will be hungry. I . . .

◆ ◆ ◆

Ella was still staring at the pages from her father's diary. The pain she had felt as she read them through was still with her, and seemed to paralyse her soul. She panted shallowly. Her whole world had shrunk to just these few sheets of paper in her hand. Ella could almost smell the salty air of the harbour, mingled with the odour of fish. She could feel the hard basket pressing against her back – could see the starry sky above her, divided in two by a huge wall of wood. That terrible fear. She could feel it now. It was so strong, she was unable to move, to lift herself from the side of the bed. A whore. Her mother was a whore. That was certain now. To suspect it – to view it as a mere possibility – was far less painful than to look the truth in the face. Ella shivered, even though it was warm in her room. Tears welled up in her eyes and dropped onto the paper. Even after all these years, the ink still ran. She quickly put the pages to one side. Richard really was her father, then.

Ella dried her eyes. She finally had certainty – but then again, how certain could she really be? She understood now why Father had asked her for forgiveness, although there was nothing to forgive. She debated reading through the pages again, but she let them be. She needed to gather herself – try to think clearly once more.

She went to the washbasin and filled it from the jug. The water felt good. It seemed to wash the pain away, although a dull ache still remained. She tried to pull herself together, and went to the window to drink deeply of the fresh air.

The officer was still standing there, reminding her that she urgently needed to regain a clear head. The past couldn't be changed – better to look to the future! But that only raised new questions. Why had Raj brought her these papers? On whose behalf? Heather couldn't have sent him – at least, Ella saw no reason for her to do so. Had Raj himself found the diary, perhaps? Was she overthinking things? Did he want to help her? Maybe he did. After all, why else would he have suggested a meeting?

Ella's eyes went back to the extracts from her father's diary. The presence of an English translation confirmed Rudolf's sinister intentions. He had known the truth the whole time. Father must have hidden the missing diary with the von Stettens. After all, Captain von Stetten had helped her father pass her off as his natural daughter in order to procure the necessary documentation.

Wasn't it obvious that Father would store the diary with someone he trusted? In a secret place? Perhaps Rudolf had stumbled across it when his uncle died, and had seen an opportunity to make a lot of money after gambling his own fortune away – though it was also possible that he had only searched for it after Father's death, and that his discovery had been the real reason he had offered to accompany her to Malacca. His intended had suddenly become the potential heir to a plantation, which meant he could use her as leverage to blackmail people for money. The thought seemed so monstrous that she could still scarcely believe it, even though Otto had already suspected it. On top of all that, if Rudolf had been carrying this document with him when he visited the Fosters, that would seem to confirm her suspicions that he was murdered. But by whom? And above all, how?

Ella collapsed exhausted onto the bed. Her father's diary had suddenly lost all its terror. She picked up the pages and gently ran her hand over them. Perhaps he was looking down at her right now. If he was, he would surely be able to hear what she was thinking. 'There's nothing to forgive. If it weren't for you, I might not even be alive,' she said to herself, and as she spoke, she felt a certain lightness and consoling warmth that rose from her belly and spread throughout her whole body, leaving her at peace.

◆　◆　◆

The next day, Ella found two messages waiting for her: one from Puteri, and the other from Jones. The trial would begin the following morning at nine o'clock. Jones wanted to meet her half an hour beforehand, and had already been in touch with Puteri. These glad tidings caused all Ella's agitation from the night to melt away, and she even found herself feeling hungry.

As she sat in the courtyard of the boarding house and enjoyed a late breakfast, Ella debated whether she really ought to meet Raj on her own. Otto had already departed and Amar was sitting in jail. By now, Ella felt sure that Lee would be willing to leave the boarding house unattended for an hour to come with her, or would ask her brother for assistance, but in the end, she decided not to enlist her help. What could possibly go wrong? Nor was there any need for another disguise. After all, it was normal for travellers to visit the region's landmarks, and an Indian temple counted as a landmark.

It would only have driven her mad to wait in her room until the appointed time, so Ella thought it better to leave Mohan's cart at the boarding house and wander over on foot instead. She would take longer to reach the temple that way, for it lay at the other end of the town. It came as no surprise when the officer turned to look at her as she left her lodgings. Would he follow her? No, he stayed where he was. It seemed that Compton only wanted to make sure she was still in Johore. The officer would doubtless have reacted differently if she had taken the cart.

On her way through town, Ella realised that she now attracted fewer curious looks than when she had first arrived in Malacca – and for her own part, she too had grown accustomed to her surroundings, from the architecture and the food stands with their enticing aromas to the shoeshines squatting at the side of the road and the rickshaws trundling past her. It all felt so familiar. Could it be that she was projecting that same sense of familiarity onto the people around her? She seemed to have become a completely natural part of this world in the eyes of others. And now she was becoming acquainted with a whole new world, for this would be the first time she had set foot in an Indian temple.

From what she could recall, they looked more modest than the Chinese ones with their red, gilded roofs, and at first glance, the Great Temple was no exception, being surrounded by a plain white wall – and yet the entrance to the building proved extremely impressive. It took the form of a pyramid-shaped tower that was overflowing with colourful painted ornaments depicting people, horses, local plants and all kinds of mythical creatures. Ella walked inside and immediately met with yet another surprise. The places of worship she had visited in Germany and England were set out in an orderly fashion, but here, there were neither seats nor a central altar; instead, she saw a dozen small podiums with sculptures of Hindu gods standing on top of them. The worshippers decorated them with sweet-scented floral wreaths, giving the room a joyful atmosphere that was far removed from the oppressive, gloomy feel of churches back in Europe. The floor was tiled and the walls were decked in small, colourful mosaics, as were the columns that held up the roof – and as if that intoxicating riot of colours weren't enough, there were yet more paintings hanging on the walls, depicting figures who also had to be Hindu deities. Ella found one of them rather comical: a figure with the head of an elephant on top of a rather portly human body, which looked even bulkier thanks to the many garlands of flowers hanging from it. An Indian mother lifted her young son so that he could place a wreath on it too. Ella was in her way, and the woman asked her to move to one side: 'Sorry, would you mind?'

Ella took the opportunity to ask the deity's name.

'Ganesha. The god of wisdom and success,' the woman explained. Her offering of flowers was presumably intended to bestow those qualities on her son.

Ella turned round and wandered back along the row of deities, but she didn't get far before a tall figure emerged from the gloom to join her. She recognised him.

'Thank you for coming to meet me,' said Raj.

Just then, she was standing beneath a painting of a striking Indian woman, who was riding a lion and carrying a spear in her hand.

'She's beautiful,' said Ella. The painting fascinated her.

'Her name is Durga, the mother goddess. She vanquishes evil and protects the righteous,' explained Raj. 'Perhaps it was she who sent you,' he remarked mysteriously, without taking his eyes from the painting.

'Who gave you the envelope?' Ella demanded.

'It was Miss Foster,' he answered without hesitation.

Ella needed a moment to digest this news. Why in the world had her half-sister done this? Ella hoped Raj would continue to answer her questions instead of palming her off with vague hints, as usual.

'Do you know what was inside it?'

Raj merely nodded. How was he able to remain so calm, given what he knew?

'Miss Foster found those pages inside the house. Mrs Foster was keeping them in the safe, but Miss Foster knew where her mother hid the key,' explained Raj.

'So Rudolf really did blackmail her.' Ella still couldn't believe he had behaved so wickedly. To suspect it was one thing; to be certain of it, quite another.

'Evidently,' replied Raj curtly. He beckoned Ella to follow him towards the back of the temple, where there were fewer people. Their conversation was not for public consumption.

'There was a row. I could hear them shouting from outside. Miss Foster ran out of the house in tears and took me into her confidence. She wants to get away from here. She would like to leave the country with you and turn her back on her mother forever.'

'What? But why? Does she also believe that her mother murdered Rudolf?' Ella had a thousand questions, but this was the one that interested her most.

Raj didn't answer or change his expression.

'Does Marjory know that Heather was looking in her safe?' asked Ella uneasily.

'No – not yet, anyway. Miss Foster would get into a lot of trouble for that.'

'In that case, why did she open it in the first place?' Ella demanded.

It was plain to see that Raj was under enormous pressure, and that his silence was costing him a great deal of effort. All the same, he was giving answers to some of her questions, so Ella doggedly persisted.

'And why did she send me the pages from the diary?'

'Miss Foster wants you to know the truth,' said Raj.

'What truth? I already know that Richard was my real father,' she exclaimed hotly.

'The truth isn't always what it looks like at first glance,' he answered cryptically.

Ella felt her anger mounting. He was being evasive yet again.

'But you know what really happened. I think you know more than you're willing to tell me,' she accused him.

'It's not about what I'm willing to tell you, it's about what I'm allowed to tell you.' He tried to justify himself.

'Did Heather forbid you? Or is it because of the oath of loyalty people say you swore to Marjory?' she asked.

'It's not up to me. Miss Foster wants to explain everything to you herself.' Raj's lips were sealed again. 'When are you travelling back to Europe?' he asked her next.

'I can't go back. Amar is in jail, accused of high treason, rebellion and abetting the escape of a prisoner. The chances are good that he will be set free, but Compton won't leave us in peace. Amar's life is in danger. We have to leave the country.'

Raj nodded in understanding. 'What should I tell Miss Foster? Do you even want to see her?'

'Of course I do.' Ella still couldn't believe that Heather had plucked up the courage to break away from Marjory – but then again, she must be under the impression that her own mother was a murderer.

'How do you plan to escape?' asked Raj.

Could she really trust him? For a moment, Ella even considered the possibility that all this was just a trap – but that was unlikely, given that the pages from her father's diary incriminated Marjory.

'Via the east coast. A village called Mersing. German freighters sail from there to German New Guinea, and a ship will call there in two days' time.'

'How will you get there? Over land?'

'There's no other way. I'm being watched, and if I wait at the harbour for a ferry then Compton will soon hear about it.'

'But Miss Foster could take one of the steamers to the east coast. I know Mersing. There's only one boarding house. She could wait for you there,' Raj suggested.

'Couldn't she join us tomorrow?' asked Ella out of concern for her half-sister's safety – but also because that meant she would find out sooner why Heather had sent her the extract from her father's diary.

'I'm afraid she can't wait that long. Mrs Foster attends to her business every morning, and she'll open the safe when she does. Miss Foster will need to escape the house before then.'

Raj's concerns made sense to Ella.

'What time is the trial tomorrow?' he asked.

'Nine o'clock. Why do you ask?' she enquired.

'I expect I'll be in attendance too. If I know Mrs Foster, she won't want to miss it,' said Raj.

That was all Ella needed. She had hoped she would never have to see the woman again in her life.

The conversation seemed to be at an end, and Raj asked that they leave the temple separately. Ella would have suggested that herself, since she couldn't be sure who was watching her or if somebody had decided to follow her after all. Yet there was another reason she decided to stay behind. With its garish colours, the temple seemed the perfect physical counterpart to all the thoughts whirring through her mind like a lurid nightmare, and the figures she saw seemed to represent the people who surrounded her in real life. Even Marjory was here, as a sinister form with evil eyes and wrapped in snakes. A painting of a vulnerable young woman offering a sacrifice to a many-armed deity reminded her of Heather, while another depicting an army of sabre-wielding monkeys called the British to mind. Projecting her thoughts into these images and giving free rein to her imagination in this way helped Ella to relieve her inner tension, and created a sense of detachment in the midst of so much chaos.

Just as she was about to leave, she was stopped by an old Indian woman wrapped in blankets, whose face had been marked by the sun and was shrivelled like a raisin. The woman held a garland of flowers towards her, and there was a wooden box beside her containing many more. She was selling them to the worshippers. Ella bought one and wondered where she ought to hang it. Once again, it was Durga – the beautiful woman riding the lion – who caught her eye. Would she hear the prayers of a Christian? Ella laid the wreath below her statue and hoped fervently that the forces of evil wouldn't carry the day this time.

Now that the start of the trial was only one day away, Ella felt it necessary to pay a visit to Puteri – especially as he would have met with Jones by now. She was only too glad to pass on Puteri's – or rather, the lawyer's – good news to Amar. 'The mask has been accepted as evidence in court,' were the first words out of her mouth once he had released her from his close embrace. But that wasn't the only thing he needed to know. She recounted her meeting with Raj.

Amar sat down on his bunk, overwhelmed by the flood of new information from both her father's diary and her encounter in the temple. It was a lot to digest in just ten minutes, for once again, Puteri couldn't let them spend any longer together without being accused of giving them preferential treatment. And they still hadn't discussed everything that was weighing on Ella's mind.

Amar likewise had plenty to say.

'Have you told Puteri about your father's diary?' he asked her.

'No.' After careful thought, Ella had decided against it.

'Why not?' Amar was baffled. 'It would have incriminated Marjory.'

'Raj expects her to attend the trial in the morning. I've already told Puteri about my suspicions that Marjory might have something to do with Rudolf's death. If I also give him a concrete motive then she'll be placed under arrest tomorrow. There is nothing I would like better than that – but then I wouldn't have anything to use against her in court.'

Amar didn't look as though he quite followed her logic.

'I feel sure she was behind your arrest. She wants to harm me indirectly and force me to leave the country.'

Amar nodded thoughtfully.

'To do that, however, she needs Compton. I don't know what obstacles she will try to put in my path tomorrow, but it can't hurt to have an ace up my sleeve to play against her,' Ella explained.

'But why would Heather do this? What would drive a woman to incriminate her own mother?' Amar seemed just as puzzled by Heather's behaviour as Ella.

'She must believe that Marjory had a hand in Rudolf's death,' Ella answered.

Amar paused to reflect. He obviously wasn't entirely convinced. 'But Marjory is her mother . . .' he objected.

He had a valid point. She recalled how loving their relationship had been. Heather seemed to mean the world to Marjory.

'Something terrible must have happened. Something we don't know about yet,' he conjectured.

And then came the knock at the door. The visit was over. As she gave Amar a farewell embrace, she hoped this was the last time she would have to see him behind bars.

◆ ◆ ◆

The following morning, Ella found the wait before she had to leave for the courthouse unbearable, so she set out half an hour before she needed to, as she didn't know how else to occupy herself or what else she could possibly say to Lee. The innkeeper had joined her at breakfast and given her a few words of encouragement, but Ella's anxiety was such that she had no idea how to respond. Lee had also been a godsend the previous night, as it was only thanks to her knowledge of Chinese herbs that Ella had managed to get any sleep at all. Before Lee's intervention, she had stayed up late into the night, reading and rereading her father's diary entries, noticing as she did so that the pain they caused her was gradually giving way to a different emotion: anger towards Richard Foster. Her fingers had instinctively reached for Rudolf's document case – which she had obtained from Puteri – as though she could draw strength from it.

Now Ella found herself circling the courthouse, which shared a wall with the plain-looking police headquarters, for at least the second time. With no sign of Jones just yet, she went back to sit on her cart. There was no point in keeping a lookout for Amar. The police station and high court were interconnected, so she wouldn't see him until she entered the courthouse herself. Instead, she used the time to consider how the two of them could leave Johore and meet Bujang as quickly – and above all, as safely – as possible. The road in front of the courthouse was broad and bustling with people. Compton wouldn't be able to apprehend them here – but what would happen when they reached the edge of town? Puteri had intimated to her that the police couldn't stand up to the army. In other words, he wouldn't be able to help her. That worried Ella more than the outcome at the court, which Puteri had told her would be in the English tradition of a trial by jury.

Jones still hadn't appeared, but she spotted the familiar sight of the Fosters' carriage with Raj sitting on the coach box. He drove right up to the courthouse entrance before dismounting and helping Marjory down. Ella felt a cramp in her stomach and instinctively reached for the document case.

'Miss Kaltenbach. I knew I would be able to rely on German punctuality.' Jones had come on foot and appeared beside her cart as if from nowhere.

'I've already met with the Crown prosecutor. There will only be one witness – an officer named Bennett, who allegedly saw Amar at the scene. I'm already looking forward to cross-examining him in the witness box.' Jones seemed so confident of victory that Ella felt certain she would soon have one thing less to worry about.

Jones had made sure that Ella had a seat in the front row. Although the sight of Marjory made her feel ill, she wanted to be as close to Amar as possible. He was sitting in a wooden dock that looked a little like a theatre box, though it was far from luxurious.

The jurors sat down on some benches off to the right, while Jones and the prosecutor shared a long table directly in front of Ella.

As she took her seat, Ella sensed that Marjory was looking in her direction, and when she turned to face her, the other woman shot her a baleful glare before looking away again to concentrate on the opening address given by the judge – an elderly man in a white wig. Ella kept her head held high, since for once she knew more than the black-clad plantation owner did. Marjory probably had no idea that Heather had already made her way to the harbour in Singapore and abandoned her mother forever. Nor did she know what Ella had in her case. Ella was unsurprised to see Compton take the empty seat beside Marjory just before the judge began to speak.

The list of charges was read out – an endless succession of trumped-up nonsense. No wonder Jones was already rolling his eyes.

'Not guilty.' Jones's voice was so emphatic it made an impression not only on Ella but on the jurors too. Then the prosecutor rose to his feet and described the events of Mohan's rescue. Bennett was called to the stand. Ella thought he looked nervous, and he kept glancing across at Compton – clearly looking to him for encouragement. As he described the course of events, Bennett began to look calmer and more composed. That was hardly a surprise, for he was telling the truth. Amar had already told Ella what had happened, and Bennett's account roughly matched what she already knew. The crucial moment came at the end, however.

'Can you identify the man who lost his mask as he fled the scene?' asked the prosecutor – a gaunt figure, to whom Ella took an instant dislike.

Bennett nodded and pointed at Amar.

'No further questions, Your Honour.'

Ella didn't know what made her angrier – the prosecutor's smug smirk or the triumphant glint in Compton's eye.

Jones stood up and began by walking over to the jurors and surveying them closely. Then he turned to face the witness, but remained standing by the jury. He evidently wanted to give them the impression that he was on their side. Jones was certainly a very skilled lawyer.

'I believe you are an officer of the British Army?' he opened.

The officer calmly confirmed that he was.

'And do you have to follow orders from your superiors?' Jones went on.

'Yes, sir.'

'Objection,' the prosecutor. 'This question is irrelevant.'

The judge gave Jones a quizzical look.

'I will demonstrate to the court that it *is* relevant,' he said, before glancing over at Compton and Marjory, who looked unmoved.

Ella could see that the officer was growing nervous and beginning to sweat. That was no surprise, for Compton had instructed him to lie – an Achilles heel that Jones was plainly bearing down on.

'Did somebody order you to identify the defendant as one of the individuals involved in the crime?' asked Jones.

A murmur passed through the hall.

'This is outrageous!' Compton shouted over the tumult.

'Order, order!' The judge pounded his gavel on the wooden block in front of him.

'Of course not,' Bennett stuttered.

'I am glad to hear it,' said Jones, before casting another significant look at Compton, who seemingly still felt secure in his sense of complacency and godlike omnipotence. Only Marjory began to gnaw at her lip.

'Can you identify the mask that you claim the defendant was wearing?'

Bennett nodded.

Jones walked over to the table where the mask was lying. He picked it up and held it out to the officer.

'Is this it?'

The officer looked at it and nodded.

'Are you quite sure?'

'Positive,' he confirmed.

Still holding the mask, Jones walked over to the jury.

'Would you try this mask on for me please?' he asked one of the younger jurors.

'Objection. What is the point of this game?' the prosecutor spluttered.

'Overruled. I'm intrigued to see what Mr Jones is getting at,' said the judge.

The young man tried to put the mask on.

'I'm sorry, but I can't quite get it to fit,' he admitted, after trying in vain to place the grotesque-looking wooden mask over his face.

Jones took it back and walked over to Amar.

'Would you also try the mask on for me?'

Amar tried too – just as unsuccessfully.

'This mask is made of rigid wood. It needs to fit perfectly, as it's impossible to see through it otherwise. The eyeholes need to fit. The breathing holes need to fit.' He turned Amar's head to let the jurors see it in profile.

'As you can see' – Jones pointed to the contours of the mask – 'it doesn't fit.'

Another murmur passed through the courtroom.

'Do you stand by your statement that you saw this man? I trust you are aware of the consequences of lying under oath – and I am prepared to insist that you be sworn in as a witness. Moreover, you are an officer of the Crown. That status alone would make the consequences facing you even more severe.' Jones delivered his threat in a caustic tone.

By now, Bennett was drenched in sweat. The judge had noticed too. It was plain for all to see.

'Do you stand by your statement, or would you like to reconsider the matter? Take a good look at Amar. It is easy, in the confusion of an affray, to make a mistake. You said yourself that it all happened so quickly. Are you still entirely sure that you saw this man?' Jones demanded. He fixed his gaze on the jury as he spoke.

The lieutenant sought eye contact with Compton, and then thankfully lost his nerve. 'No. I can't be certain,' he confessed.

The jurors exchanged meaningful looks among themselves.

Jones laughed confidently – though not arrogantly – before looking at Compton. 'No further questions, Your Honour.'

Ella could see that Compton was incandescent with rage.

'Next, we will call the defendant to the stand,' announced the judge, once Bennett had shuffled back to his seat opposite the jury like a dog with its tail between its legs.

The prosecutor stepped forward and turned to Amar, who was now standing in the witness box beside the judge.

'Let us discuss the second charge – that of high treason. You stand accused of being the ringleader of a collection of agitators and rebels whose goal it is to disrupt the peaceful rule of law in this country.'

Jones rolled his eyes again and looked encouragingly at Ella.

'That isn't true,' said Amar – and because he didn't have to lie, he sounded credible. He wasn't the ringleader, because there was no ringleader, as Ella knew from Puteri.

'We have a statement from the former detainee, Mohan bin Bhatak, which he made personally to the governor,' the prosecutor declared.

Jones shot a baffled, quizzical look at Ella. He seemed to be worried now.

'That can't be true,' she whispered to him.

'So – do you stand by that claim and maintain your innocence?' asked the prosecutor.

'Yes, I do,' said Amar, his head held high.

'No further questions. I ask the high court to call the governor to the stand,' the prosecutor requested, while Amar made his way back to the dock.

'I knew nothing of this,' said Jones to Ella.

'Don't worry. It won't get that far,' she answered.

Ella now sought eye contact with Marjory, who gave her a triumphant smile. But Ella planned to wipe it off her face. She quickly pulled out the document case and held it so that the witch couldn't help but see it. With a certain satisfaction – but with trembling hands too – Ella pulled out the three pages from her father's diary. She didn't need to say anything – it was enough to simply wave the pages back and forth like a pendulum.

Marjory went deathly pale. Her eyes gaped as she stared at the document.

'Governor Compton. Would you please come to the stand?' The judge was growing impatient.

Compton was about to stand up when Marjory's hand clawed at his arm. She whispered something in his ear.

Now it was Compton's turn to stare at the three pages, which Ella held out towards them both – although she did so in such a way that it looked as if she were merely reviewing her notes. This time, she shot Compton a triumphant smile, and he too turned white with shock.

'Governor Compton?' asked the judge, by now somewhat confused.

Compton waved the prosecutor over and whispered to him.

When he had finished, the gaunt lawyer turned to face the judge. 'Governor Compton no longer wishes to testify before the court. He should not have interviewed the prisoner, so it would be against due process under English law. It would serve no purpose for him to take the stand,' explained the lawyer.

The judge scrutinised first Compton, then Jones, who gave him a knowing smile.

'In that case, there is nothing for the jurors to decide. The charges are dismissed.' Visibly irritated, he brought the trial to a close with a clap of his gavel.

Marjory stood up, staring blankly ahead, and hurried past Compton out of the courtroom.

Amar beamed. He looked as though he might leap from his seat at any moment and fall into Ella's arms. Ella felt exactly the same, but she knew that the most difficult part still lay ahead of them – and judging by the hateful glare that Compton had given her before he stormed out of the court in a fury, it would likely be hell on earth.

CHAPTER 20

The air above the courthouse almost seemed to crackle as if there were a storm coming, even though the trial had ended well and Ella had been able to leave the building unmolested together with Amar and Jones.

Jones was still laughing at Compton's loss of face. Everybody had noticed it, since the prosecutor's reason for why Compton declined to give evidence was patently just an excuse.

'What leverage did you have?' Jones eventually enquired as they reached the steps at the front of the building.

Ella saw no reason not to tell him. 'My father's diary.'

Jones was baffled, and gave her a quizzical look.

'An incriminating document. It was obvious to me that Marjory Foster egged Compton on to arrest Amar. The diary entries were found in her house, and the man who presumably used them to blackmail her over the fact that I am the illegitimate daughter of her late husband is now dead.'

Jones must have seen and heard many things throughout his career as a lawyer, but this still took him by surprise.

'Why didn't you tell me earlier? I could have called Mrs Foster to the witness box too.'

'I only came into possession of the papers yesterday, and to be honest, I never expected Compton to go so far as to commit perjury,' Ella explained.

'That was indeed an unusual course of action for a governor. I wonder what Marjory is holding over his head. After all, it was obvious that it was she who induced him not to speak,' he mused.

Ella was wondering the same thing, but she put those thoughts to one side. There were more pressing matters to attend to right now.

'Amar and I need to leave the country as soon as possible. I'm afraid it'll be a few days before I can pay you for your services.'

'There's no need. My fees have already been paid,' Jones answered.

Now it was Ella's turn to look baffled. 'I suppose your duty of confidentiality means you can't tell me by whom?'

'Not necessarily,' Jones replied.

'Was it Otto Ludwig?' she asked.

'I wouldn't put it past Otto, but in this instance, it wasn't him. Mary Bridgewater instructed me to send the bill to her.'

Ella was speechless.

Amar was every bit as astonished. 'Why would she do that?' he asked.

'I'm afraid that's connected to my other mandate, so . . .' He said nothing more.

'You aren't permitted to share that information with me, I presume?' Ella conjectured.

'Precisely.' Jones held out his hand. 'I wish you all the best. Do look after yourself,' he said, before extending his hand to Amar to bid him farewell too. Then he flagged down a rickshaw and climbed aboard.

'We mustn't lose any more time. Bujang will be waiting for us by the lake, and I still need to fetch my things from the boarding house,' said Ella.

Amar's eyes suddenly grew wide, and only when she followed his gaze did she understand why.

Compton was offering Marjory his hand to help her into her coach, and from what Ella could make out at this distance, Marjory swore at him and pushed his hand away. Where was Raj? That was normally his job. Ella scanned the forecourt, but he had vanished without trace.

Compton seemed to say something to Marjory, and then climbed up onto the coach box. Before he drove off, he looked at Ella. Even from afar, his vengeful glare sent an icy shiver down her back.

'If he's driving her home then that will give us more time,' Amar remarked.

Ella hoped he was right.

Back at the boarding house, Ella found it strange that Lee wasn't at the reception desk. Perhaps she was in one of the rooms. At any rate, leaving without saying goodbye was out of the question. She decided to fetch her other suitcase first, in the hope that Lee might reappear in the meantime. The key to Ella's room was hanging from one of the hooks behind the counter, so she took it and climbed the stairs.

Amar followed her – but then halted abruptly mid-step and gestured for her to stop too. Ella could also hear the creaking on the staircase. Although it was probably just Lee pottering around upstairs, she found the noise unnerving all the same. If there was somebody walking around on the top floor, their footsteps would be audible too – but there was only this creaking, as if somebody were trying to avoid being heard.

Amar listened intently, then moved forward again and reached the door to her room.

Ella followed him, but hesitated to unlock it. Her sense of unease lingered.

Amar gave her a meaningful look and nodded as if to say that she could go ahead.

Everything moved very quickly after that. A hooded figure shot out of her room and slammed his fist into Amar's stomach. He crumpled to the floor in pain. Before Ella could go to his aid, a second attacker rushed down the stairs and snatched Rudolf's document case from her hands, before dragging her into the bedroom and throwing her on the bed.

Only now did she realise that these weren't native men. Their heads were wrapped in cloth, but the skin around their eyes was white. They had to be Compton's thugs.

Ella heard the sounds of a struggle in the corridor. She tried to sit up so she could see what was happening, but the masked man threw himself on top of her, his hands seizing her throat like a vice. She desperately tried to defend herself, but the fingers around her neck gripped tighter and tighter. Straining to reach the lamp on the bedside table, she turned to shift her position. Managing to grasp it at last, she swung the heavy iron lantern against her assailant's head with all the strength she could muster. The man let go of her and rolled sideways. He lifted his fingers to the spot where she had hit him and grimaced in pain.

Ella leapt up from the bed, intending to hurry out to the corridor to help Amar, but the man recovered and launched himself at her once more.

She fell to the floor, but managed to free herself from his clutches, shaking him off and climbing to her feet. Then she felt a hand grasping at her ankle. The attacker was trying to drag her back down to the floor.

Ella gripped the doorframe and managed to keep her balance. By now, she could see Amar and the other masked attacker wrestling each other. Amar's hand was clamped around the wrist of his assailant, who was pointing a knife at his chest.

The attacker's second attempt at overpowering her proved successful. Thinking quickly, she rolled onto her back, and before the man could throw his full weight on top of her, she kicked at his torso with all her strength – but to no avail. He kneeled astride her. Ella scrabbled with her hands and feet to prevent him from pinning down her arms.

Just then, she heard more footsteps on the stairs. Somebody was rushing up to join the fray. More of Compton's men, presumably. From the corner of her eye, she saw only a dark shadow.

Her attacker likewise glanced at the corridor in confusion. Ella took advantage of the distraction and lashed out at him with all her might. Her fist landed squarely in his face. He tumbled backwards, colliding with the iron bedframe, and lay in a daze.

She heard bangs and crashes coming from the corridor, so she sat up and looked through the door.

Amar's attacker lay lifeless on the floor. A pair of dark hands were still wrapped around his head, which now sat on his shoulders at an unnatural angle. The hands belonged to Raj. He dropped the man and rushed into her bedroom.

Ella's attacker came to his senses and fumbled for the knife on his belt.

Raj stormed in, disarmed him and slammed his fist into his face. The masked man slumped motionless to the floor.

'We need to leave. Quickly,' Raj told them, and gave Ella his hand to help her to her feet.

She was unable to move. Only when Amar entered and she saw that he was unhurt did her paralysis wear off.

There was now a corpse lying in the corridor outside her room, and as soon as the other attacker regained consciousness, the manhunt for her and Amar would begin in earnest.

Ella and Amar hurried downstairs while Raj carried their bags down for them.

'Where's Lee?' asked Ella, terrified that the assailants might have harmed her. It had dawned on her that Compton's minions must have needed to get Lee out of the way, and she had to know if the boarding house owner was still alive before they left. Perhaps they had overpowered her and locked her in one of the bedrooms or in the kitchen. Ella checked the latter first. The door to the passageway leading to her brother's restaurant kitchen was unlocked.

Lee was behind it, lying bound and gagged on the floor.

Amar hurriedly grabbed a knife from a wooden chopping board and cut through her bonds, while Ella untied the gag and removed it.

Lee gasped for air and took a moment to compose herself.

'It happened so fast . . .' she stammered, before clambering to her feet and examining Ella from head to toe. 'You're unhurt,' she declared in relief.

'You need to go to the police and say you were attacked. Ask for Officer Puteri. Tell him that one of the men died in the struggle,' Ella instructed her.

'He fell and broke his neck,' Amar explained. Lee didn't need to know that Raj had killed him in the heat of the moment.

Lee nodded. Ella knew she could rely on her.

'I'm so sorry, Lee. I never thought they would try to ambush us here,' she said.

'It's all right,' Lee said valiantly. 'Good luck,' she added.

Although Amar was tugging impatiently at her hand to pull her outside, Ella refused to leave before she had given Lee one last farewell hug. She owed her so much.

Ella wasn't in the least surprised that Raj had asked to come with them. He had joined their cause, and was now driving their cart towards the meeting point by the lake. One of the attackers was still alive and would be able to describe Raj, which meant that he now faced arrest and the death penalty. Ella didn't need to ask him why he had rushed to their aid at Lee's boarding house, for he volunteered an explanation during the journey.

'I heard Compton talking to two of his men. He mentioned a document and ordered them to go to the boarding house to retrieve it. Whatever the cost,' he told them.

'Why are you helping me?' Ella demanded to know.

'Miss Foster has already left home. There's no reason for me to stay any longer. Mrs Foster will have to answer for what she has done, and when that happens, where will that leave me?' he answered.

'Heather is safely on her way to the east coast?' Ella asked.

'I took her to the harbour myself. You don't need to worry about her,' he said.

Ella wondered whether she ought to ask any further questions, but she lacked the strength just then. Besides, Raj's attention was focused on the road, the houses and the patches of impenetrable greenery they were driving past, which grew thicker the further they travelled and might conceal all kinds of dangers. He kept his knife close at hand.

Amar was also plainly afraid that they might encounter a checkpoint before they reached the lake. He sat tensely on the back of the cart.

No sooner had they turned onto the narrow path leading through the jungle than Amar's face visibly relaxed. Within five minutes, it was clear that they had successfully completed the first stage of their escape.

A robust-looking wagon was standing by the lake in the middle of the forest, laden with all kinds of food and supplies and harnessed with two horses. A third horse was also standing beside it, laden with saddlebags.

Bujang noticed them approaching and waved – but his smile froze when he saw they were accompanied by an unknown man.

'This is Raj. He saved our lives. He's coming with us,' Amar explained laconically.

At that, Bujang gave Raj his hand.

'You can leave your cart here. My mother will collect it tonight and tend to the horse,' Bujang announced.

Ella was impressed that he had thought of every last detail. That improved their odds of successfully escaping to the east coast.

To begin with they made rapid progress thanks to the flat paved road, which Ella hoped they would be able to stay on for as long as possible. However, she soon realised that the vegetation on either side was becoming more dense and the road was growing narrower. Suddenly, their way was blocked by a tree trunk that had been felled by a lightning strike. But Bujang had thought of that too, and had packed suitable equipment – an axe and a saw.

Bujang also knew exactly where the checkpoints were and was confident that he could safely bypass them. He rode ahead, for a wagon could be heard approaching from some distance away, whereas his horse could travel through the jungle alongside the road.

That didn't allay Ella's fears, however. After the incident in the boarding house, there was no way Compton could believe that she would be naïve enough to turn up at the harbour to collect her tickets for the steamer to Hamburg – let alone take Amar with her.

'What if Compton has warned the checkpoints?' she wondered aloud.

'The only way that could happen would be if British soldiers overtook us on the road.' Amar's point made sense to Ella.

'But he might have sent word to them anyway. Compton is a shrewd man. Perhaps he never expected you to board the steamer. And this route is the only way to reach the east coast,' remarked Raj.

'But how would he know where we were going?' Ella objected.

'By the same logic Otto used when he came up with the plan. German freighters call at Penang too, but it would take us far too long to get there. We should be very careful,' said Amar.

Bujang returned barely a minute later.

'Three soldiers. All armed,' was all he said.

Ella had been hoping that they wouldn't encounter the first checkpoint until much later. Here they were with a wagon that could travel over rough terrain, and yet they would have to leave it behind before they reached the most difficult part of the route, for there was no way they could drive it through the jungle. Unfortunately, Bujang hadn't known that there would be four of them. They had only three horses, so they had no choice but for two of them to ride together.

Raj's bulk meant he needed a horse to himself, so Amar and Ella were forced to share.

Food, blankets and the essentials for their overnight camp now had to be divided between the three horses – but the saddlebags were big enough to store everything inside.

It took them another half hour to drag the wagon into the forest, since they couldn't just leave it in the middle of the road. Between them, the three men managed to haul it around thirty feet before its wheels stuck fast in the mire. Bujang and Raj covered it with ferns and leaves to prevent any passers-by from noticing it, while Amar used some branches to sweep over the tracks left by the wheels on the road. Then he mounted one of the horses and helped Ella up onto it.

Bujang rode ahead, as before. Ella and Amar followed and Raj brought up the rear.

Rapid progress was now out of the question, even without their wagon. The ground was heavily rutted and criss-crossed with thick tree roots, while ferns proliferated over everything and made it difficult to judge the terrain. There was no road – not even a dirt path – and their route led steeply uphill. They had no option but to rely on Bujang's instincts and those of their horses in order to avoid stumbling. He assured them that before long they would cross a hunting trail used by locals looking for quarry, and that this would lead them to the summit of the hill. He soon found it, but it proved even more challenging than the rest of the route so far. It led ever more steeply upwards, while the vegetation grew thicker around them. They forced their way through an endless tangle of branches and scrub. Spiderwebs hung from twigs and creepers. With every step, Ella heard the voices of the rainforest grow louder – a surreal cacophony of bird calls and howling monkeys.

Although they had passed the checkpoint by now, there was no way to get back to the road without heading even more steeply downhill, and the horses wouldn't be able to cope with the descent. It would be another half hour before they reached the summit.

An acrid stench rose to Ella's nostrils. It grew more and more insistent until they reached a stream that lay around thirty feet below them. The plants on its banks had been trampled.

Bujang raised his hand and signalled for them to halt, then listened intently.

Ella could just make out a deep, guttural growl; then she saw the blood in the water. The hindquarters of a dead animal protruded from behind a bush. Ella had heard that there were tigers in Malacca, and there was evidently one nearby.

Raj instantly drew his machete and scanned the forest for signs of the animal, while Bujang calmly dismounted and reached into his saddlebag. He pulled out something that resembled a bamboo stalk, though it seemed to be hollow.

The predator's intimidating growl rang through the jungle again, more clearly this time. The tiger must have drawn nearer. Everything around them fell silent. A flock of parrots fluttered from the treetops and disappeared into the sky.

Bujang held his blowpipe in one hand and carefully pushed a dart inside it.

The horses grew increasingly nervous, beginning to stamp their feet.

'It's trying to reach its prey,' Bujang whispered to them.

If he was right and the tiger was approaching from the other side of the stream then it might not see them through the scrub.

The vegetation on the other side of the creek rustled, and it wasn't long before Ella saw the tiger's stripy back. Her heart pounded in her throat. She clung onto Amar.

'We're upwind. It can't smell us,' he whispered to her.

Bujang clambered adroitly into a tree. One of its thick branches extended almost all the way down to the stream, where the cat was advancing with smooth, sleek movements. It walked straight up to the dead animal and dragged it out from behind the bush. At first glance, it looked like a wild boar, with black flanks and a white belly. Its neck gaped with a bloody wound. The creature had a small trunk on its face, and Ella recalled the travel books she had read during the crossing – the carcass had to be that of a tapir.

The tiger ripped another chunk from its prey's body – but then it suddenly froze and seemed to listen for a moment. Its huge skull pivoted to face them directly, and its muscles tensed, ready to pounce – but before it could do so, an object struck the tiger in the throat, and it roared and bared its teeth. A second projectile followed, and only then did Ella realise there were two darts protruding from the animal's neck. The tiger scrabbled at them with its paws. It seemed to know where its attacker was, and with a single bound it reached the tree Bujang was sitting in. Then it tried to climb the trunk.

Bujang yelled at the tiger, presumably to goad it into climbing higher so that it would tire more quickly.

The tiger roared and made one final attempt to reach the upper branches. Its claws clutched at the trunk, but then it slipped down once more. Suddenly it seemed to lose all its strength and, unable to make a second attempt, the animal began to totter to one side. Its left hind leg gave way.

'The poison in the darts works slowly,' said Amar.

The tiger looked up and seemed to notice them. It staggered to its feet and lumbered in their direction. Bujang's horse bucked and whinnied in fear while Amar and Raj struggled to keep their own horses calm.

Raj gripped his machete firmly, ready to strike.

Ella could already smell the tiger's breath – but it was too weak to cover the remaining distance. Both its hind legs collapsed, and the animal began to slide down the slope, its limp body tumbling back to the stream.

Bujang climbed down from his tree. 'It can't hurt us now,' he said.

'Will it die?' asked Ella.

'Probably not. It would take more poison to kill an animal of that size. Three or four darts . . .' explained Bujang.

Ella now understood why they didn't have any guns with them. Since Mohan's arrest, she knew that the resistance had access to firearms – but shots could be heard from miles away, whereas blow-pipes were silent.

She felt certain that the horses wouldn't be able to cope with the descent once they reached the top of the hill, for thick rainforest lay before them as far as the eye could see. It was only thanks to Bujang's local knowledge that they managed to safely find their way back to the road. He continued to ride ahead to keep a lookout for further checkpoints, although there weren't normally any guards stationed on this section of the route.

With the onset of dusk, it made no sense to go on any further. Ella wouldn't have been able to do so, anyway. The exertions of the day's ride had taken their toll and she ached all over. The constant strain of keeping her balance on her horse as it moved over the uneven ground had placed demands on every muscle in her body. Her companions evidently felt the same, for none of them said a word beyond what was absolutely necessary as they prepared their dinner, handed out their tin plates and set up camp.

Bujang had selected a small clearing for them to sleep in. There was no question of lighting a fire, since that would be seen from afar. All the same, their meal of bread, dried fish and fruit was almost lavish under the circumstances – though they were forced to share it with a horde of ants.

Ella felt sure she wouldn't be able to sleep. Not only did the ants refuse to leave her alone –though there couldn't be a single crumb of food left on her clothes or her blanket by now – but the mosquitoes had evidently decided to eat her alive too. Yet once again, Bujang had come prepared. He planted incense sticks in the ground, just like the ones Ella had seen inside the Chinese temples in town. Four on each side of her rattan mat and another two at her feet produced a thick cloud of smoke, as well as a sickly-sweet fragrance that made it hard to breathe. But it worked, and the insects withdrew.

Amar had already fallen asleep at her side, but not before reassuring her that they would make it to the east coast unharmed. His confidence and his close embrace made her feel safe, and her eyes gradually grew heavy. The sickly scent of the incense that turned their encampment into a Chinese temple dulled her senses. The last thing Ella noticed was Bujang's outline, silhouetted against the moon. He was fetching water for the horses. Did the man never tire?

◆ ◆ ◆

The following morning, it had proven much easier to sneak past the second regular checkpoint than the first. The ground here had levelled off, and all they needed to do to bypass the two soldiers was to move around a hundred yards off the road into the protection of the forest, where they encountered easily navigable terrain. Half a mile later, they found their way back onto the road, and fifteen minutes after that, Ella realised they must be getting close to the village when they passed two Malayan farmers. Their water buffalo were drawing heavy wagons laden with large barrels, and they turned onto a path leading into a palm plantation. Evidently, palm oil was produced around these parts. The farmers hadn't paid them any notice.

From the top of the next hill, they could already glimpse the sea in the distance. Ella hoped they would reach Mersing without any further difficulties, and so it proved. The tropical jungle began to thin, giving way to palms and shrubs that extended into the village and right down to the shore. A settlement came into view with around one hundred small wooden huts, most of which were built directly onto the beach.

'We did it,' exclaimed Amar proudly. Ella shared his joy, but her thoughts had already turned to Heather. Had she managed to get this far too? What would she say to her? Ella's uncertainty even dampened her delight at seeing a German freighter already moored at one of the two large landing stages in the small harbour to their right, ready to whisk them beyond the clutches of the British. A second smaller sailboat lay opposite the steamer, with just a single Malay on board wearing a captain's hat. Perhaps that was the boat from Singapore that docked here every day, Ella thought. There didn't seem to be a dedicated area for fishing boats here. The local sailors moored their boats to poles that protruded from the water all across the bay, or tied them directly to the jetties belonging to the handful of stilt houses along the shore.

'The boarding house is on the edge of the village,' Raj announced once they had reached the outskirts of Mersing. They had only a few hundred yards left to go, and until they found Heather, there was no point in going to the harbour to book tickets to German New Guinea.

Just three blocks lined with houses, grocery stores and fishing supply shops lay between them and their goal. The boarding house stood at the end of the muddy street, and wasn't much taller than the rest of the buildings in the village. It had a veranda, and resembled a row of interconnected bungalows. Ella guessed that there were seven rooms, assuming that the first part of the building was the reception. Three of them seemed to be occupied. Washing hung from a line in front of one of the rooms, while the door to another was ajar, and the table outside the third was laden with crockery.

'It's nice here . . . right by the sea,' she said to Amar, concealing her mounting unease with small talk.

'It isn't luxurious, but it's perfect for traders travelling through the area,' explained Raj, who had heard her remark.

Ella wondered why Heather wasn't sitting on one of the small verandas and impatiently awaiting their arrival. Perhaps she felt it was unsafe and preferred not to be seen.

Bujang slowed his horse to a walk and looked around. Without saying a word, he turned left onto a narrow lane that led towards the rest of the houses in the village. Ella felt sure that was purely a precautionary measure. He had been just as careful throughout the whole of their journey here.

Raj was the first to dismount, and he took hold of the bridle of Amar's horse.

Ella wondered in which of the rooms Heather would be waiting for them. Why didn't she come out? Was it impossible to hear when somebody was approaching? Perhaps, for the surf was loud enough to drown out all other noises.

Raj entered the first building, which seemed to be where the reception was.

Ella didn't have long to wait, for Raj re-emerged barely a minute later. He was smiling – something he rarely did – and she took that as a good sign.

'Heather is in the room at the far end. Number six,' he said.

A weight instantly fell from Ella's heart.

'Do you want to go on your own?' Amar asked.

By way of an answer, Ella reached for his hand. She could feel her knees growing weak. Heather and she had parted ways in anger, and she could still vividly remember their last encounter – the desperate screams of a woman who feared she would never see her sister again.

Why couldn't Heather hear the footsteps outside her door? She must have fallen asleep. Ella tried to peer inside the room, but a thin curtain blocked her view.

She knocked at the door.

'I'll wait here,' said Raj.

Then she heard Heather's voice.

'Ella,' she called from inside.

Why didn't she come to the door? Ella glanced at Raj and Amar. They both seemed to share her uneasiness.

Amar finally opened the door.

Heather was sitting at a table in the centre of the room and rose to her feet when she saw Ella standing in the doorway. She gave no sign of pleasure. Not a smile. Not a word.

'Heather, is everything all right?' asked Ella, who was so shocked by Heather's silence and listlessness that she didn't dare enter the room.

But Amar did – and although Raj had said he would wait outside, he too barged past Ella and threw himself against the door with all his might. It flew backwards, but didn't strike the wall – rather, it bounced back, followed by a dull cry. Lieutenant Bennett staggered out of his hiding place, and Raj instantly grabbed him by the collar and pushed him against the wall.

Bennett tried to reach for the gun in his holster, but Raj was too quick for him. He smashed Bennett's hand against the edge of the doorpost and struck him down with his fist. The revolver clattered to the floor.

Heather stood as if paralysed. She was trembling with fear. Before Amar could reach for the weapon, Compton emerged from the darkness of the bathroom, aiming his revolver directly at Heather.

Ella's breath caught.

'Stay calm and nothing will happen to you,' he said. 'Give me the gun. Kick it to me,' he ordered Amar, who hesitated but then complied.

Compton squatted down, picked up Bennett's revolver and tucked it into the holster on his belt.

'The diary,' he demanded.

'It's in one of the saddlebags,' answered Ella truthfully.

'Raj can go and get it,' Compton ordered.

Raj refused to move until Ella nodded at him.

'You don't appear to have a very high opinion of the British Army, Miss Kaltenbach. Did you really think I was so stupid? It borders on insult.' He gave an unbearably self-satisfied grin. 'I don't know anybody who would only reserve tickets for a voyage to Hamburg. One either sails or one doesn't sail. And then our dear Heather . . .' Compton ran his hand through her hair. Heather flinched at his touch and began to tremble like a leaf. 'That's the trouble when one travels as an unaccompanied woman – especially a white one. I merely had to ask at the harbour to find out whether she bought a ticket,' he continued.

Ella felt her rage mounting. It began to outweigh her fear.

'Why are you doing this? How is my father's diary any of your concern?' she hissed.

'I don't think you're in a position to ask questions,' Compton replied arrogantly.

Raj reappeared. He had retrieved the case and approached the governor slowly and carefully out of respect for the gun that was still aimed at Heather. But then he leapt forward with lightning speed, hurling the case at the revolver. The gun fired but missed its mark. Raj took advantage of the surprise and leapt onto Compton. Before he could fire again, Raj knocked the gun from his hand, and Compton fell to the floor.

Ella was gripped with the same paralysis as Heather, who was still unable to move.

Amar tried to reach the gun from the other side of the table.

Raj and Compton grappled with each other. Compton briefly managed to free himself from Raj's grasp, and he grabbed the revolver just before Amar. Then a shot rang out.

Raj sank lifeless to the floor.

Compton instantly aimed the gun at Amar, who froze and raised his hands.

'I should shoot the both of you,' Compton spat at them as he rose to his feet. The revolver veered indecisively back and forth between Ella and Amar. In the end, he opted for Amar. Yet just as his finger was squeezing the trigger, he suddenly gave a start. His left hand fumbled at his neck. A dart protruded from his skin, quickly followed by a second. It pierced his carotid artery, and a fine ribbon of blood trickled from the wound. He began to sway back and forth.

Only then did Ella see the blowpipe poking through the back window. A third dart whistled into Compton's neck. He had no strength left to hold up his gun, and sank to his knees, turning to face Ella as he did. His eyes bulging, Compton gasped for breath and reached out a hand to steady himself against the edge of the table, but to no avail. He slumped to the floor and his body began to convulse. It wasn't long before he drew his final breath.

Heather seemed to want to make sure he was really dead. She awoke from her trance and bent down over his lifeless body. Then her eyes filled with tears.

Ella walked over to her and took her hand.

'I never did anything to him,' Heather sobbed.

Ella took the still trembling woman into her arms. 'It's over, sister,' she whispered in her ear.

She had hoped that her embrace would soothe her. She could feel Heather's heart pounding – could feel her entire body trembling too. Why wouldn't she calm down? The tears continued to flow as she let go of Ella and looked her in the eye. Heather looked distraught.

'I'm not your sister,' she finally said.

Now it was Ella's turn to freeze. She glanced at Amar. Like her, he looked as though his world had turned upside down.

CHAPTER 21

The boarding house owner informed Ella that he had already sent his son to tell the checkpoints outside Mersing about the recent events at his establishment. That was dangerous, for Compton might have instructed his soldiers to keep a lookout for Ella and her companions, ready to arrest them. To her relief, however, the governor had travelled directly to Mersing by boat. Ironically, that meant they could have spared themselves the arduous journey through the jungle after all. And because there was no police station in Mersing, they had no option but to report Compton's death to the only public officials in the area.

Amar had tied up Lieutenant Bennett and locked him in one of the boarding house's sheds, for it would take at least two hours for the soldiers to arrive. Now it would be Bennett's turn to sit in the dock – but that was the least of Ella's concerns right now. Everything she had hitherto believed had collapsed around her like a house of cards. The same was true for Heather, though she seemed to recover a little with every word she uttered as they walked from the harbour towards the beach at the end of the bay. Ella realised that Heather was finally unburdening herself of secrets that had tormented her for many years. At first, Heather hadn't known where to start, but she decided to relate everything in chronological order, since her troubles had all begun with Jack.

'You were right, and that was why I couldn't stand to be near you any longer,' Heather admitted at the start of the conversation.

'So Jack *was* the love of your life?' Ella sought confirmation.

Heather nodded. A bitter smile flitted across her lips, but it no longer seemed to cause her pain to talk about him, for she continued speaking of her own volition.

'We met at the harbour. He was a dapper officer — somewhat older than me, but I fell head over heels in love with him all the same, and he with me. My God, I'd only just turned seventeen . . . We had to keep our love secret. Only Mother knew about it. Mothers can tell these things. We had to hide it from Father. Everything went well for a few weeks. I was so happy, though we couldn't meet all that often. You've seen our little love nest.'

'The oleander house?' Ella asked.

'It was the whole world to me. Mother knew all about it and let us do as we pleased. I dreamed of marrying him, of going with him to England — but then, suddenly, it was all over.' Heather gave a bitter laugh.

'I fell pregnant with you . . . and from then on, he began to behave strangely . . . Wasn't he happy? I asked him. "Of course I'm happy," he said — he was just surprised . . . and then he was redeployed to India. We had no time to discuss our future . . .'

Ella felt Heather's hand tighten on her own. She could see that the memories pained her still.

'Jack promised me he would talk to the governor, and that he wanted to return to Malacca, but he never came back.' Heather had to pause for a few breaths before she could go on.

'What happened?' Ella asked.

'His ship — it was caught in a storm . . .' Heather continued.

They walked on in silence for a while. Heather's words had whipped Ella's emotions into turmoil. It was incredible — at long last, she knew her real mother, and she understood why she had always felt so comfortable around her. Heather's emotional outburst when Ella had spoken to her about her former love now made sense too. Ella could almost physically feel the pain that Heather must have gone through back then.

'Father wanted me to go to a Chinese doctor as he didn't want me to carry you to term, but Mother was against that plan. Women often die from such procedures. Then he made us promise we would send you to an orphanage. Father thought he would be ruined if it came out that I was carrying an illegitimate child. People would have asked questions. They would have said that I had seduced Jack, a high-ranking officer. Father was afraid of being shunned, and as for me – I was still practically a child. I was forbidden from leaving the house. Nobody was allowed to see me,' Heather continued.

'You were locked up for nine months?' asked Ella incredulously.

Heather nodded, with a heavy heart.

'A Chinese midwife brought you into the world. It was the happiest moment of my life. Mother pleaded and pleaded with Father, and eventually he relented. She wanted to make it look as though they had adopted a sailor's child, for charitable reasons. You can't imagine how relieved I felt,' Heather went on.

'But then why did your father leave me in a basket at the harbour?' Ella asked in a tremulous voice.

'I knew nothing about it at the time. I only found out about it from your adoptive father's diary. You simply vanished one night. The glass on the veranda door had been shattered. Father called the police, and they told me that somebody had abducted you. They blamed the midwife. She also assisted with births in brothels, and there is a trade in such children around these parts. They had me believe that you were stolen from me.'

Heather could no longer repress her tears, but she rallied herself and wiped them from her face.

Ella threw her arm around her and tried to keep herself from weeping too.

'When you arrived at our house, I instantly felt a connection with you, but I couldn't explain why. You made me so afraid with all your questions . . . but then at the harbour, when you argued with Mother . . . after that, I couldn't stop wondering why you thought Richard was your father and had sent you money . . . Then, one evening, I saw Mother sitting in the drawing room. The safe was open, and she was holding the pages from your father's diary in her hands. She was sitting like a statue staring at them. That was when I remembered that you had spoken of that German man, and how you thought he had blackmailed Mother. I waited until she fell asleep. She had no idea that I knew where she hid the key to the safe. I read the English translation of the diary, and that's when I realised you were my daughter.'

'Do you think Marjory was aware that your father abandoned me at the harbour?' Ella asked.

'I don't know for sure, but I expect she did know – because of the monthly payments, if nothing else. Why else would she be so afraid of the truth coming to light?'

'Perhaps she wanted to spare you any pain,' Ella conjectured, although she didn't mean to defend Marjory in any way.

'I just don't know,' Heather repeated. She stared out to sea as she spoke, as though she could find the answer out there.

'Mary might be able to help us uncover the whole truth,' said Ella.

Heather looked at her in surprise.

'She hired a lawyer to investigate me, and probably your family too. I want to know the truth – every last detail,' said Ella.

'And then? Will you go back to Hamburg?' asked Heather, looking Ella straight in the eye.

'No, you'll stay here. But not just for my sake.' Heather answered her own question, and as she spoke, she cast a meaningful look back at the small fishing village. In the distance, they could see Amar standing by the horses and waiting for the arrival of the British soldiers.

'I'd stay for your sake alone,' Ella declared.

The sight of Heather smiling once more told her that was the right thing to say.

◆ ◆ ◆

As arduous as the overland journey to Mersing had been, the voyage back by boat around the southern tip of the peninsula proved brief and straightforward – though this time, they were accompanied by two British soldiers, whom they had managed to convince with their account of the incident and Compton's demise. It had been a matter of life and death after all. The sailboat they had seen moored in the harbour beside the freighter belonged to the British navy. It had brought Compton and Bennett to Mersing, and if the wind remained favourable, the very same boat would get all of them back to Johore by dusk. The presence of a naval vessel anchored in the port had made Ella, Amar and Heather's version of events seem more credible to the soldiers, but even so, it had taken another two hours for their statements to be officially recorded. Bujang had nothing to fear, but he still needed to come with them to Johore so that the local police could conclude their inquiries.

On board with them were two linen bags containing the mortal remains of Compton and Raj, and one prisoner in the ship's hold, who was already getting used to his future existence inside a dark cell. The tragedy of Raj's death and his selfless sacrifice to save their lives had only fully sunk in for Ella after she had managed to digest her conversation with Heather. Raj had always seemed to believe in the power of fate – that everything was predestined. He may not have seen it as his duty to bring the truth about the Fosters to light, but he had contributed to it indirectly all the same.

Two hours into their voyage back to Johore, and Amar was still clearly shaken by Heather's revelations. He was tactful enough to withdraw from them. It almost seemed to Ella as though he no longer dared to come near her when she was in Heather's presence – but Heather sought out Ella's company in his stead. She had grown from a friend into a sister, who in truth was her real mother, and yet that seemingly did nothing to change the friendship they had felt towards each other from their very first meeting. Ella was sure that the word 'mother' would never cross her lips, even though the emotional ties between her and Heather felt stronger than ever before, and she couldn't tell whether they were speaking as mother and daughter, or as two friends, when their thoughts turned to Amar. He seemed to realise that they were talking about him, for he gave them a warm smile from the back of the boat.

'It won't be easy,' said Heather.

'I'm not British. The Brits dislike Germans anyway, and the local population won't care who I marry.'

'You must promise me that you'll live with me one day. I won't take no for an answer.' Heather's voice carried a tone of almost maternal admonishment.

'But don't they always say that it's better for children not to live with their parents? That's how it works in Germany, anyway,' Ella said slyly.

'Don't argue with your mother!'

Ella laughed, and so did Heather. But then her face grew serious once more.

'I hope Mother will go back to England,' said Heather softly.

'She'll have to stand trial first. Compton wasn't acting alone,' Ella answered.

Heather nodded, but looked almost relieved.

'Do you think she had something to do with Rudolf's death too?' Ella asked.

'I'm trying not to think about it,' Heather replied.

'What about Amar? I'm afraid I've grown rather used to having him around. Where will he live?'

'With us, of course. Amar can run the plantation – assuming that he wants to – and we . . .' Heather sighed. 'So many lost years.'

'I want to show you my homeland. I know yours already . . . fairly well, anyway,' Ella replied.

'Then let's go travelling. Hamburg, London, and if we're in Europe anyway then I'd love to see the Eiffel Tower in Paris.'

Heather was looking to the future once more and making plans – yet Ella felt sure it would take her a while to leave the shadow of her past behind.

It wasn't long before Heather's face grew gloomy once more – and not because the weary travellers had now passed Singapore and were following the narrow strait leading into the port of Johore by the last rays of the evening sun. Heather would soon have to face her mother. Ella could vividly imagine what a burden that must be – not least because of the possibility that Marjory had committed murder.

Ella's thoughts revolved around her own impending obligations, which included a visit to Mary Bridgewater.

'Do you think Raj guessed you were my mother?' Ella enquired.

'What makes you ask that?' Heather replied.

'He gave me certain hints that I couldn't make sense of, about you and Jack . . .'

'He must have realised what was going on. Jack had to cross the plantation to see me, and Raj would surely have wondered why I never left the house. Who knows, perhaps he even saw my belly . . .'

'And do you think he knew about my abduction?' asked Ella.

'I'm quite certain of it.'

'He always said that the truth would find a way. All in good time – that was how he put it,' Ella recalled.

'Whatever he knew, he'll take it to his grave – or rather, into the flames,' said Heather as they reached the dock. The two officers moored the boat.

'Flames?' asked Ella in confusion.

'Hindus prefer to be ritually cremated. Ashes to ashes . . . I wish I could get rid of a span of my own life in the same way,' Heather sighed.

'But it's part of you, and if it weren't for you and Jack then I wouldn't exist,' Ella pointed out.

Heather nodded. She seemed to take comfort from the thought, for she gave Ella a hopeful smile.

◆ ◆ ◆

On the way to Mary Bridgewater's house early the next morning, Ella reflected that there couldn't be many things that would ruffle that tough woman's composure, but an unannounced visit at an ungodly hour would surely be one of them. They still had another half hour to go, travelling on Mohan's cart, which Bujang's mother had dropped off at Lee's boarding house, as promised. Lee had also told them that Officer Puteri had taken a statement from her about the attack on her establishment, and he had privately mentioned to her that he hoped Ella would manage to leave the country unscathed. By now, Lee would be on her way to tell him that Ella was planning to visit him that afternoon, together with Heather. The reason for their visit ought to be obvious enough to him, given that he would have already heard the soldiers' report and received Lieutenant Bennett into custody by the time Lee got there. Strictly speaking, Amar could have visited Officer Puteri on their behalf, but he needed to organise Raj's cremation. That was also the reason Ella and Heather were now on their way to see Mary Bridgewater without him. It wasn't just curiosity that had prompted her and Heather to disturb Mary so early in the morning, but also the need for Marjory to assume that Compton was in possession of her father's diary. It would be for the best if she believed her position to be secure.

Mary Bridgewater's house was already in view. An Indian servant came out to meet them. He knew Heather, and remembered Ella from her attendance at Mary's garden party. That was enough grounds to request an audience with the *grande dame*.

'Please, take a seat on the veranda,' he said, before hurrying into the house.

Ella wasn't in the least surprised to see Mary appear barely two minutes later, looking completely flabbergasted when she found them. A speechless Mary Bridgewater in her dressing gown – that sight alone made the journey worthwhile.

'Before anything else, I think I need a strong cup of tea. Would anybody else like one?' she asked, once she had recovered from her shock.

Heather and Ella both nodded.

'I only learned of Amar's arrest and trial three days ago,' said Mary.

'From Jones?' Ella asked.

She nodded. 'I drove to Johore on the day of the trial to speak with you, but when I called at that Chinese boarding house, I discovered you were no longer there. Where in the world were you?' she asked anxiously.

Ella had planned to get straight to the point and ask her what Jones had found out – but what use would that be if Mary didn't have all the facts? Whatever he had told her, she would only be able to make sense of it if she knew what had happened over the last two days, so Ella began to tell her. Given the nature of her account, Ella was unsurprised when Mary immediately poured herself a second cup of black tea – and then washed it down with two glasses of sherry.

For a long while, Mary sat in silence. Ella could tell she was still trying to digest everything she'd heard. Ella had been expecting that – but there was one small detail that caught her attention: Mary hadn't seemed particularly surprised to hear that Heather was Ella's mother rather than her sister.

'I went to see Jones – I assume you know that already,' she then began.

Ella nodded.

'I asked him to do some digging into the past. I simply couldn't stop thinking about it. I wanted to know if Richard was Ella's real father,' she explained to them both.

Ella stared at her every bit as intently as Heather.

'My goodness, the things he managed to find out,' declared Mary – more to herself – as she poured another sherry.

'Jones looked through the newspaper archive and asked around among his clients. It was the similarity between you and Heather that struck me most, and when I stopped to consider Richard's penchant for minor infidelities . . . Richard simply had to be your real father – or at least, that's what I thought at first. But Jones went to a good deal of trouble. It seems Richard and Marjory wanted to adopt a child at one point. Applications of that kind are noted in official registers. And then there was the report to the police saying that a child had been abducted, allegedly by the Chinese. It seems that the case was closed at the Fosters' request, since such

377

kidnappings aren't unusual around these parts and the investigations generally lead nowhere. I can well imagine that nobody
would have asked any questions about that – not even on a purely
human level, as it's easy to think that the parents wouldn't be able
to develop an emotional bond with an adopted infant in such a
short time. That was when I managed to put two and two together.
And then there was Jack. Although you tried to keep it secret, my
dear Heather, men are stupid. They like to brag about their love
affairs . . .' said Mary.

'Jack did that?' Heather plainly found that hard to believe.

'He was just a man. A British officer at that, and one of the
most contemptible kind, if you'll permit me to say so.'

'Contemptible?' Heather was so bewildered that she couldn't
speak in full sentences.

'Did he ever formally agree to marry you? You must have been
seventeen years old, am I right?'

Heather exchanged glances with Ella.

'I thought so,' Mary went on.

There was no need for Heather to say anything more.

'You see, Jack was already married – to a woman named Isabel,
who I'm sure had no idea about his escapades,' Mary continued.

'What?' Heather was open-mouthed with astonishment.

'Now, just imagine the scandal. Isabel has blue blood in her
veins, and Jack's family is one of the most distinguished in England,'
Mary added.

Heather clung to Ella's hand.

'Fortunately, there appears to be such a thing as poetic justice,
for Jack's life came to a tragic end.'

'I know. He drowned. Somewhere in the Strait of Malacca,'
Heather interjected.

Now it was Mary's turn to look astonished. 'He did nothing of
the sort, my dear. In point of fact, he contracted a venereal disease,

which he expired from a year after his return to England. Hopefully in agony,' she added indignantly.

'But Father told me . . .' Heather objected.

'What else could he have told you? The truth? You might have decided to get on the next boat to England and hold him to account.' Mary's logic seemed unimpeachable to Ella.

'My parents lied to me the whole time. Even Mother . . . She must have known about all this . . .' Heather seemed to slowly grasp the true dimensions of the lie.

'So I assume,' said Mary, taking another sip of her sherry. 'Yet there is another interesting aspect to this affair that I'm sure you will find no less astonishing.'

She seemed to be enjoying her role as a bringer of light into darkness.

'Haven't you ever wondered why Compton was such a close friend of the Fosters? Marjory only needed to snap her fingers for him to come running,' Mary went on.

'You mean the accusations against Amar had nothing to do with Compton's jealousy or the fact that I rejected him?' Ella asked.

'That might have played a role – but I can see another more pressing motive. Jack Jenkins was Edward's youngest cousin.'

For a moment, Ella was completely thunderstruck.

'Sherry?' asked Mary.

Heather and Ella nodded simultaneously, and a slug of Mary's famous pick-me-up soon restored Ella's faculty of speech. Suddenly, everything made sense. All the same, she felt the need to sum up the situation to make sure that she had understood it all correctly.

'So . . . just one word from Marjory would have been enough to bring shame upon Compton's family. Isabel – Jack's wife – would have found out that her husband had impregnated a young Englishwoman, and that the woman's child was still alive. Marjory knew where I lived because of the monthly payments. And that could have been dangerous for Isabel's family, because my existence would mean they could be open to blackmail, which would probably leave them with no choice but to use their influence to posthumously ruin Jack's reputation, which in turn would have caused the Comptons to be socially ostracised.'

'That's about the long and the short of it, my dear,' Mary congratulated her.

'So did the idea to get rid of Ella come from my father? Mother had insisted on adopting her after all,' Heather recalled.

'I imagine so. Perhaps he came under pressure from the governor and his family. Subtle pressure, of course, but he probably felt he had no other choice. . . People do say that Richard was always very worried about his personal reputation,' Mary added.

'Perhaps there really is such a thing as poetic justice, then,' said Ella quietly to herself.

Heather and Mary both looked at her quizzically.

'After all, he died soon afterwards,' she added.

'His heart. It was his heart,' Heather interjected.

Mary stared at her. 'Was it really, now? Didn't Rudolf von Stetten also die of heart failure?' Her question carried a note of alarm.

'What do you mean by that?' asked Heather.

Mary thought for a moment before she replied. 'Come with me. I want to show you something in the garden.'

Heather shot Ella a puzzled look, but they both rose to their feet and followed Mary.

'Ella, didn't I once tell you that Marjory and I share a passion?' asked Mary as they walked around the side of the house.

'You mean the oleander?' Ella recalled.

'You must have seen the two of us in the garden often enough,' Mary said to Heather, who nodded.

'Rudolf von Stetten was found close to the Foster plantation. Of course, he might have been poisoned by the local flora or fauna, but when I learned about the circumstances of Richard's death – Jones really did sterling work there! – I felt that was a coincidence too far. It seems that he died in the same manner as Rudolf von Stetten.'

'You think Marjory murdered Rudolf *and* her husband?' asked Ella in astonishment.

Mary stopped by the first hedgerow, knelt down and plucked one of the green stems, whose tip was covered in fresh buds.

'Every part of the plant – from the branches and leaves to the stems and the flowers – is highly toxic, but the milk of the oleander is the most poisonous of all. Even diluted, it's deadly – regardless of how it is administered. The poison works by gradually slowing the victim's pulse, and it also causes shortness of breath. Eventually, the heart stops beating altogether. To all intents and purposes, the victim appears to have died of heart failure. Not many people know that, admittedly,' Mary explained.

'Did my mother know?' Heather asked.

'Yes. She warned me once that I should always wash my hands thoroughly after working in the garden, or wear gloves while pruning the hedge. It's so easy to absent-mindedly rub one's eyes,' Mary explained.

'But why would she murder her own husband?' Ella could make no sense of it.

'That, my dear, can only be answered by Marjory herself.' Ella could see that Heather was just as desperate to find out the reason as she was.

It was no shock to Ella that Heather was torn about confronting Marjory. On their return to Johore, Heather had even seriously considered remaining at the boarding house – and not just because of Mary's revelations and conjectures. Before her journey to the east coast, Heather had already inwardly bid farewell to her mother. After all, Marjory had lied to her and deprived her of her only child. Yet Ella felt certain that Heather was also afraid of seeing Marjory again – and with good reason, for she was Heather's mother, and by Heather's own admission had always loved her and cared for her.

Ella had already climbed onto the cart ready to drive to the police station when Heather finally plucked up her courage and decided to go with her.

'I simply have to know the truth.' That was all Heather needed to say, and no further words passed her lips. She maintained a tense silence until they arrived at Puteri's office.

Amar was already waiting for them. He had had to make a statement about the attack on Lee's boarding house and Compton's death.

'Will Bujang go free?' was the first thing Ella asked.

'Compton clearly exceeded the bounds of his authority and acted out of self-interest. He was prompted by base motives to murder Raj. I don't think there will be any further consequences, not even when the new governor arrives,' Puteri assured them.

'Should I come with you?' Amar asked.

Heather seemed to consider the offer, but then shook her head. The road to Calvary was Heather's alone, but Ella agreed with her that it would be better if only the two of them accompanied Officer Puteri.

'I'll wait for you at Lee's,' said Amar, and embraced Ella. Then he put his hand on Heather's shoulder for a moment – a consoling and encouraging gesture, which Heather accepted with a grateful smile.

'I have no choice but to place Mrs Foster under arrest,' said Puteri before they reached the police carriage. He seemed to want to check that Heather was ready for what lay ahead of her.

She merely gave an apathetic nod and climbed aboard.

Ella could all too vividly imagine what was going through her mind.

◆ ◆ ◆

The journey to the Fosters' house was now familiar to Ella, and life on the plantation seemed untouched by all that had happened. Raj's absence was unnoticeable; the workers were still carrying their shoulder poles, their buckets filled with the white blood of the earth, as he had called it. As they passed the spot where Ella had met Raj for the first time, accompanied by Rudolf, she thought about how badly she had misjudged him back then.

She could see that Heather was growing more tense the closer they got to her home, her hands gripping the iron frame of their padded seat. She wondered where they would find Marjory. Most likely she would deny everything in her imperious tone of voice. After all, it was impossible to prove that she had poisoned both Rudolf and her husband. That she had conspired with Compton and incited him to commit murder was beyond dispute, however, and for that alone she would land in jail – or so Officer Puteri had assured them.

There was no need for Puteri to drive the carriage all the way up to the main building, for Marjory was sitting on the veranda of the oleander house. She must have seen them coming, but she didn't stir. It looked as though she had sat down to rest in the shade after a hard day's work. On the table in front of her stood a jug and a glass of cordial. She was staring into the distance, and she didn't move even when Heather got down from the carriage. She seemed to be looking straight through everything.

Officer Puteri approached her, presumably intending to tell her that she was under arrest, but he didn't get the chance.

'Compton failed, then. I thought he would,' declared Marjory coldly. The last thing Ella had expected was for her to confess like this. 'What's keeping him? He should have been here this morning,' Marjory went on.

'The governor is dead,' said Puteri.

Marjory merely gave a contemptuous smile.

Puteri exchanged astonished glances with Ella and Heather, but recovered more quickly than they did. 'I must ask you to come with me, Mrs Foster. You stand accused of incitement to murder and blackmailing a Crown official. You are also suspected of having murdered Rudolf von Stetten.'

Marjory cackled like a madwoman. Then she gave a deep sigh and reached for the glass in front of her, which she emptied in one draught.

'Mother!' Heather burst out. She instantly realised what Marjory had planned.

'It isn't worth arresting me now. I won't live longer than an hour. A sweet death. The cordial masks the bitter taste,' said Marjory.

'Mother? Why are you doing this?' Heather cried desperately. How awful must it be for Heather to watch her mother take her own life?

Marjory's iron expression softened slightly. 'I can't live with this guilt any more,' she said dully.

'Did you poison Father too?' asked Heather. She didn't dare to approach her mother.

Marjory gave a bitter laugh. 'Have you forgotten how badly you suffered? And who caused you all that pain? *He* did!' Her voice told Ella of the hatred she nurtured for her husband. 'Every day, I would look at his face in the drawing room so I could tell myself I'd done the right thing. I hope he burns in hell,' Marjory went on. Then she turned to look at Ella.

384

'Poor Ella . . . We didn't want to give you away, Heather and I. But he felt otherwise, because he was afraid of losing his power and his reputation. He wouldn't listen to me.' Marjory's voice broke. It grew soft, almost sentimental. 'I begged him. "She's just a child. Nobody will ask any questions. Nobody. Do you hear?"'

'Did you know that the kidnapping was a lie?' Heather asked.

Marjory nodded, with a heavy heart. Ella could see that she was already struggling to hold herself upright.

'How did you find out?' Marjory gasped, her voice weakening.

Heather was so distraught that she couldn't utter a word.

'Mary Bridgewater,' said Ella.

'Mary . . .' Marjory emitted a noise that sounded almost amused. 'Mary gets wind of everything . . .' she coughed. Then she looked at the oleander. 'Isn't it beautiful? I've always hoped I would be able to sit down here one day and just peacefully fall asleep,' she breathed. Her voice was barely audible. A convulsion passed through her body. She lifted her hand to her chest and wheezed.

Heather now walked over to Marjory.

Ella could see how helpless Heather felt – how uncertain about what she should do. But then she took her mother's hand, and Marjory turned to face her.

'I did it for you . . . Heather. Please believe me. I didn't want you to suffer any more . . .' Once again, Marjory gasped for breath. 'I couldn't forgive Richard . . . and then that German, after all these years . . . I couldn't let him hurt Heather,' she said, looking at Ella and Officer Puteri.

She turned back to her daughter. 'Please sit down with me, my child . . . It won't take much longer . . .'

Heather couldn't refuse, and she sat down on the chair beside her mother. Her eyes filled with tears.

'Forgive me, child. Please forgive me . . .' she whispered, before clutching at her heart once more. Her breath began to rattle in her chest. Marjory no longer had the strength to hold her head up, and it sank on her daughter's breast. She looked like a child seeking comfort from her mother, although the opposite was the case.

'We should leave them alone,' said Ella to Puteri, and he nodded sympathetically.

Heather shot her a grateful look.

Ella turned round and walked with Puteri back to the carriage, but they didn't linger there.

'The property has an extraordinarily beautiful garden,' said Ella.

'I would be glad if you would show it to me,' Puteri answered.

Ella sensed that she was doing the right thing. At least Heather could now make peace with her past. Although she still couldn't believe that Marjory had murdered two people in cold blood, her deeds were mitigated by her motives: after all, she had been acting out of love for her daughter.

EPILOGUE

Wasn't it said that time heals all wounds? There had been a time of funerals. Raj had found his peace in the flames. He didn't seem to have any friends or family, and only Amar, Bujang, Heather and Lee had accompanied Ella to his cremation – though on arrival, they had all been surprised to find Officer Puteri there too. He had paid his respects, just like the rest of the mourners. The second ceremony had taken place two days later at the local cemetery. A stonemason had engraved Marjory's name alongside that of Richard Foster's. Ella had welcomed Heather's decision that only the two of them should go to bid her farewell. Yet a few days later, a handful of new wreaths had appeared alongside theirs. The loveliest of these was from Mary Bridgewater. An arrangement of oleander was unusual for a funeral, but in this case, Mary's choice couldn't have been more appropriate, macabre as it was. Mary had also done much to ensure that the days following Marjory's death brought some positive news. Ella had casually mentioned to her that she missed her work, and that Doctor Bagus had offered her the opportunity to put her expertise to good use by giving lectures on naturopathic medicine at the local hospital. Two days later, Henry Jones himself had appeared at the door of the Fosters' house to present her with a work permit – and Ella intended to use it.

She had finally set all these events down in a letter to her adoptive mother too. Although Ella knew that many weeks would pass before she received a reply from Hamburg, she felt sure that her reasons for wanting to stay in Malacca would meet with understanding. Would her mother accept the invitation to join Ella here once she learned the truth about her daughter's origins?

Inside the house itself, very little had changed; only the painting of Heather's parents had been cut in two and reframed, at Heather's own insistence, leaving only her mother's portrait on the wall. Ella had thus found herself attending a second cremation, although Richard was no Hindu. Heather had burned his likeness on a ceremonial bonfire as if she were executing a traitor.

Certain changes to the household had proven inevitable, however. Although Ella wouldn't have minded staying at Lee's, Heather had insisted that she move in with her instead. Ella had been unsure whether Heather would agree to Amar joining them; after all, she still hadn't quite overcome her aversion to men, and on top of that, she was unused to a male presence at home. But to Ella's surprise, she had welcomed him with open arms. Amusingly, Jaya had initially thought that Amar was now employed in the house – until she saw him walking arm-in-arm with Ella, that is.

'Why should I care what people think?' Heather was already beginning to sound like Mary Bridgewater, who came to visit them at least every third day, with a different excuse each time. Ella was unsurprised to find that she had already been researching mixed marriages and their legal status.

Amar spent his days on the plantation, doing the same work he had always done. The men respected him because he had already been one of the two foremen before the tragic events had unfolded. At any rate, there would be no more whippings on the Foster plantation from now on.

Over the last few days, Ella and Heather had taken to sitting together by the oleander house to escape the midday heat. The shady terrace was the perfect place for that. Today, Heather took the opportunity to tell Ella about Jack. It seemed as though she almost had to force herself to think only of the beautiful moments she had spent by his side, in order to gloss over his betrayal.

'Who knows – perhaps he really did love you, and was just too cowardly to stand by that love,' Ella ventured to say.

'He truly did,' Heather answered. She rose to her feet. 'Come, I want to show you something.' Heather gave Ella her hand and beckoned for her to follow.

Ella couldn't imagine what she was getting at. 'Do you mean the heart on the tree?' she conjectured.

She allowed Heather to lead her to the spot, but when she arrived, she saw something on the tree that she hadn't expected. A second heart had appeared alongside the first. Ella took a closer look. The letters 'A' and 'E' were engraved on it.

Ella laughed. 'Did you carve that?' she asked.

'With Amar's help.' Heather gave a rather wistful sigh. 'He loves you very much,' she added, but then she retreated into her own thoughts for a moment. 'Even when you're married, you'll always think of him as your lover,' Heather declared.

'Well, that's exactly what he is,' Ella answered with a smile.

'Yes – and as for me, I'll probably end up a lonely old woman who spends her days looking after her grandchildren,' said Heather.

'For now, you're just my mother. I'd rather wait a while before I make you a grandmother,' said Ella frankly. 'Besides, you've spent far too long hiding from the world! We should go out together. Singapore isn't far from here,' she hinted. She hoped that Heather would one day be receptive to male company once more.

Heather understood exactly what Ella was getting at.

'At times, I have suffered greatly from my loneliness – but whenever I found a man I liked, I couldn't get close to him. I was so afraid of being hurt again. But you're right. Perhaps one day . . .' she said, casting her gaze out over the plantation.

Ella could scarcely believe what she had just heard Heather say. The mere fact that she could raise the subject so openly with her was a sign that Heather's wounded heart was beginning to recover.

What was it Raj had said? 'The white blood of the earth. They say that it heals afflicted souls.' Yet the trees of this plantation had taken a long time to go about their restorative work, Ella reflected silently. She followed Heather's gaze over the endless lines of the rubber trees and said a silent prayer for her adoptive father, whose dying words had sent her on a voyage that had ultimately led to her real mother.

ABOUT THE AUTHOR

Tara Haigh has many years of experience writing hit television shows, as well as women's fiction with plenty of heart and humour under the name Tessa Hennig. All of her books have been bestsellers, and many have already been adapted for film and TV too. Her carefully researched historical novels tell thrilling love stories in exotic locales and address aspects of world history that are comparatively little known or only rarely depicted in literature. For full information about Tessa's work, visit: www.tessa-hennig.de; for news, discussions, reader events and competitions, or to get in touch, follow Tessa on Twitter – @tessa_hennig – or on Facebook: www.facebook.com/Hennig.Tessa.

ABOUT THE TRANSLATOR

Photo © 2014 Jozef van der Voort

Jozef van der Voort is a literary translator working from Dutch, German and French into English. A Dutch–British dual national, he grew up in south-east England and studied literature and languages in Durham and Sheffield. He is an alumnus of the Emerging Translators Programme run by New Books in German and was also named runner-up in the 2014 Harvill Secker Young Translators' Prize. His previous translations include *Mother Dear* by bestselling Dutch author Nova Lee Maier.